FOR GG

ANOTHER SOUTHSIDE
DEL STAECKER
APRIL 2024 ~ FIRST EDITION

FOR INFORMATION REGARDING PERMISSION, EMAIL LIONHEART GROUP PUBLISHING: PERMISSIONS@LIONHEARTGROUPPUBLISHING.COM

COVER BY SANDRA MILLER

PAPERBACK ISBN: 978-1-938505-65-2
HARDBACK ISBN: 978-1-938505-66-9
LIBRARY OF CONGRESS CONTROL NUMBER: 2024935961

10 9 8 7 6 5 4 3 2 1

PUBLISHED BY LIONHEART GROUP PUBLISHING, LANDER, WYOMING, USA

PUBLISHED IN THE USA ~ ALL RIGHTS RESERVED.

VISIT US ON THE WEB AT WWW.LIONHEARTGROUPPUBLISHING.COM

LIONHEART GROUP PUBLISHING IS AN IMPRINT OF
LIONHEART GUILD, INC; A NON-PROFIT

ANOTHER SOUTHSIDE

TABLE OF CONTENTS

TABLE OF CONTENTS CONTINUED

Table of Contents Continued

TABLE OF CONTENTS CONTINUED

BLIND ONE-LEGGED JOHNNY

GREETINGS. I'M JAKE THOMPSON, A worn-out has-been cop who is tired of chasing phantoms and hoping for miracles. And although the situation I'm involved in could resurrect my career and redeem my reputation, right now it does not hold my attention.

At this moment, my butt rests in a comfortable rattan chair overlooking the beautiful blue Caribbean. But, I'm not interested in the water. I'm eyeballing a stack of cash—a hundred thousand dollars to be exact. It and a lot more could be mine. Or not.

They say today is yesterday's tomorrow. *They* don't know crap.

Maybe I should explain from the beginning. My name really isn't Jake Thompson. It's Jan Tomaszewski. Jano to my family and the close friends of my youth.

My father changed our name to Thompson a year or so after I was born. That was when we moved from the old Polish neighborhood on Chicago's Southside to the new Polish neighborhood just a bit south of the city. Urban blight's creep pushed, and the suburb's allure pulled—so, many of the Poles, Italians, and the Irish moved to the city's edge. Still Chicago, but on the Southside's rim.

As much as my father's generation wanted to get away from the city, I was attracted to it. That's why when I finished college, and after a stint in the military police, I became a Chicago cop. To be honest, I didn't do it out of any great love of law and order. Nor did I really want to help people. I simply craved a life with some real action and no routine.

My dad hoped I'd become something a bit more upscale and somewhat more sedate. Maybe a teacher, or—well, it doesn't matter. Especially now.

All I can remember about my decision is him asking me, "Jake, is this a decision you can live with?"

Truth be told—carrying a gun and busting some deserving heads was more on my mind than escaping life in the new Polish neighborhood. I know—I know. Some folks believe cops are supposed to be the first line of service in the community. Social workers with badges, right? But get real. Do you think we all join up only to protect and serve?

My Army time as an MP clearly taught me that even amongst America's best citizens there are creeps requiring someone to ride their asses. The Chicago PD and I were a perfect match.

I encourage you to ask around. I was a good cop.

Six years on a solo-motorized beat in some of the city's worst neighborhoods, a string of righteous busts, and a dirt ball's lead in my leg were my merit badges. Good time on the streets and my rep was solid enough stuff to get me into plainclothes.

A few years later, I moved up—made detective, due to being at the right spot at the right time. Although I wasn't to be one of the glamour boys in Homicide, I was okay with duty I drew on the robbery squad.

Like I said, ask around—I had a good reputation.

Had is the operative word. One not-so-fine day, an undercover case went screwy—my life was forever changed—and LIFE PLAN NUMBER ONE was seen no more.

Here's my sorry-assed tale:

Our assignment was based at the *Hilton* hotel in the Loop. Hundreds of thousands of dollars of supplies—towels, sheets, liquor, even several small furniture items—walked out the back door of the city's finer hotels each month.

Don't let appearance fool you. It was a big case—not very sexy, but important, nonetheless. As I said, there was a lot of money involved, and to break it open, someone was going to go undercover for a long time. Me and my partner, Gino Cavellini, were that *someone*.

So, after months of mopping floors and cleaning johns we were ready to seal the deal and bring down the bad guys. Or, in that instance, the bad girls. We had learned the brains behind the operation were some really nasty ladies from Guatemala.

Their scam was simple and brilliant—an inch deep and a mile wide.

Did you know that if you steal a penny a second it takes less than two weeks to walk away with a million dollars? A little here, a little there—it adds up.

Hardworking maids, mostly under threat and coercion, were responsible for creating a steady flow of small portable items that were leaked from the downtown establishment. The items went into a system of repackaging and were sold over a multistate area. A lot of second- and third-tier hotels and motels looking for cheap stuff were the unquestioning customers. The deals were *that* good. And as said, the money was big.

Gino and I had to work the case from the bottom up. So, we paid our dues and did the grunt work that allowed us to blend in with the low-level workers' subculture that every city has but hates to admit it needs.

Our work was menial, low paying, and boring. I acquired an appreciation for the path immigrants take in making it in our culture.

Me being Polish and Gino as an Italian made it possible for us to assimilate with the lowest rung of the working class. We were judged as failures by the Latinos who made up the bulk of the hotels' staff and therefore not seen as threats. Without much effort, we blended in.

It wasn't a complicated investigation. Gino and I easily figured out who was snatching the goods and how they took each item, one at a time, out of the hotels—hidden in a purse or under a dress or jacket. The reason we stayed under so long was to unravel the entire operation. Catching a few terrified low-level thieves was not our goal. We wanted the ringleaders.

Our break came after a union-sponsored Christmas party. One of the maids confided in Gino how things were structured and, most importantly, who was in charge. An extra bottle of wine and some smooth talk got her to open up—above and below the waist.

To erase any trail back to the volunteer, we sat on the lead for a couple of weeks. Then, in a bold move, we tempted the chain of command to expose themselves by offering to join with them.

Our plan was direct. We let it be known we could provide the operation with enough supplies to open a new product line. All it took was a quick delivery of a sample load of goods (pilfered mini bottles of booze) and more of Gino's easygoing charm.

Soon, we were losers no more. And before we could blink, we found ourselves in direct contact with the top of the organizational chart—three hard-as-nails women and one cute little babe, Maria, who took a shine to Gino.

Things moved fast from that point on. We didn't sleep. We worked our undercover jobs, hustled supplies, and wore wires 24/7 in order to gather enough evidence for a bust. We totally focused on nabbing the leaders amid their ill-gotten loot.

It all came together on a brutally cold night in late January when Gino and I found ourselves inside a warehouse on Touhey Avenue near O'Hare airport with plenty of backup outside ready to pounce when we made the call.

The plan was simple. We pull the plug on the entire operation and make a name for ourselves. Too bad the bust soured.

Here's how things played out.

Gino and I entered the warehouse for a meeting with the lady bosses. We confirmed the latest deal, took our cut, and called in the cavalry—just as planned. Reinforcements arrived, and that should have been that. But little Maria saw it otherwise.

Who would have thought she was the most dangerous one in the bunch?

I blew it when it came to cuffing her. That was my mistake. Maria's diminutive frame and overgrown affection for Gino was my excuse for hesitating.

I should have known better. Before I could react, she grabbed a pair of scissors and wailed on Gino.

Maria plunged the needle-sharp points of her improvised weapon into my partner with the rapidity of a *Singer* sewing machine set on overdrive. She paid particular interest to his face.

My reaction was to grab my piece from my ankle holster. In a flash—one that I see over and over—always in slow-mo—I emptied my piece and Maria stopped jabbing my pal.

In my memory, the next hours are a blur. The subsequent days aren't much better.

Gino lived, but he was seriously injured. Because I goofed, his career was over. Gino pretty much lost the use of his left arm and the sight in one eye. His face wasn't easy to gaze upon. It took a lot of plastic surgery to make him passable as human.

No matter how righteous the bust, it's a failure when your partner pays for your mistake.

My fellow officers politely avoided me. Sure, they said all the right things, especially throughout the board of inquiry for the shooting. But my fellow boys in blue made it clear I was tainted. Gino's life was forever changed. My error could not be overlooked.

From that point on, finding someone willing to be my new partner proved to be difficult. Following my reaction after the board's report, it was impossible.

No, I wasn't held accountable for the shooting. Considering the circumstances, the outcome was a slam dunk. My troubles escalated when I shot myself—by opening my big mouth.

As I left headquarters, I was ambushed by one of those phony self-promoting socially aware reporters. Truth and detail be damned, in the reporter's eyes, I was just another trigger-happy white male who cold-heartedly gunned down an *unfortunate* slip of a waif—a brown female one at that.

When asked about the shooting from that left-of-center perspective most cops hate, I exploded with the callous remark, "The skanky little *Guat* maimed my partner. She had it coming."

At the time, given the situation, my words should have been seen as what they were—a thoughtless rant. There isn't a racist cell in my body. As a Southside Pollock, I give and take friendly slurs as part of being. Plus, size, gender, and national origin of a violent perp are irrelevant in some situations. Ask Gino. But, add it all together and you have one total mess.

I truly wish I could take back those words.

I pray as my mantra, "Dear World, I'm so sorry."

Still today, I think I should have been given a pass. But that's not how my comment was viewed by the media. And, you are right in assuming that my outburst graced the airwaves. It played for days.

Looking back, I'm not surprised the name I made for myself was a complete one-eighty from anything Gino and I had dreamed about. The media whores who delighted in shaming me and the internet quickly shared my quote with the world—over and over and over.

In no time, I became *persona non grata* for more than just the department. I filled the role for an entire city, and then some. My soundbite bit me—it chomped clean down to the bone—and then, it began to gnarl.

If my fifteen minutes of fame had lasted a second longer, I'd have slit my wrists.

That was years ago.

My politically correct penance has been long. Although my ill-chosen words have faded from the public's memory, I live in a professional exile worthy of the old Soviet gulag.

My work life is spent as a slug in an office mis-named the Administrative Investigations Unit, where a group of misfits like me chase down a never-ending pile of petty cases.

Each day is the same. Lost wallets and misplaced umbrellas—crap assignments—are my life. I'm still a cop, but in name only. I hung on only because I could not imagine what else to do. For me, no decision was a choice. My life has been ground down to the mini-mums.

My routine is simple, boring, and unalterable. I schlep to work, muddle through the day, eat at *Jimmie's Diner*, and go home. That's where I sip bourbon and read to escape the gnawing fact that my treadmill has at least four more years to go—when I can retire early and do what I want. Whatever that is. In a previous life I dreamed of being a writer, but my dreams are as dead as that girl.

So, you ask, "What does all this have to do with me gazing at the deep blue sea?"

Everything and maybe nothing at all. I'm not much of a philosopher. I'm just an ostracized, never married, less-than-good-looking burn-out facing middle age. I have few real friends, limited prospects, and a sense of lost optimism bordering on faithlessness. On a good day, I look up to it being average. On a bad day, I'm a depressed failure—and I have many bad days.

Did I mention that I eat at *Jimmie's*?

I'm in there at least once a day. I'm not a morning person, so it's never at breakfast. Most days it's lunchtime, or later.

Occasionally, I come in really late and hold off the end of day by sitting in my favorite booth making small talk with Earline, the waitress.

I count her as one of my friends, but I never see her outside the diner. I sense she'd like more, but I'm not the one to provide whatever *more* is for her—or anyone.

* * *

It was the end of the first week in March and Earline wasn't letting me off easy. She had asked for a favor a couple days earlier and I had balked. Now, she laid on the heat—as only Earline could.

"Jake," she almost shouted, "I'm serious. Johnny is missing—and, I *know* something ain't right."

"Earline, he's old. It's been a hard winter—maybe it was just his time."

"Maybe. But I want to be sure. And, I'm not the only one. That's why I asked you to look into it."

"Okay—okay. I'll do something. First thing tomorrow, I'll—"

She cut me off. *"Damn right* you will." She reached below the table. "Here."

She thrust a completed MISSING PERSON REPORT at me. I looked at it and winced.

"I see you filed it this morning," I said. "And, it's already been assigned." My eyes stalled on the part of the form which bore my name.

"I made a special request."

"Thanks."

"And?"

"I'll do my best," I offered, as I folded the form and placed it inside my breast pocket.

"You better." Earline leaned over and stared straight into my burnt-out core. "Jake, I want you to succeed. Find out what happened to Johnny." She tapped hard on my chest and the form.

"I'll get on it."

"When?" Her voice had that edge—the one that slices through comfortable sloth.

"Like I said... Tomorrow."

She asked again, but with more edge. "When?"

"*Okay*. Now."

"That's better." She smiled. She had won.

I reached inside my jacket, extracted the paper with my name on it and a pen. On the flip-side of the form, I wrote as I asked Earline questions about Johnny.

"Is Blind Johnny the *only* name you can come up with?"

"Yes. I've never known him by anything else."

"Jeez—that's a wonderful start."

Earline slapped my head, more than playfully. "Jake, stop being such a jerk—a man is missing."

"*Believed* missing." My voice dripped with disbelief.

"No, Jake. I got a feeling—he's missing."

"How can you be so sure?"

"Jake, follow along with me on this." She pointed to the diner's large front window. "Every workday, almost ten months a year, for more than thirty years, the man parked himself out there in front of the diner.

"Blind Johnny was a neighborhood fixture— from the first week of March through the Christmas season—on the sidewalk accepting handouts. Johnny was as dependable as time itself. And, this year—he didn't show up."

"Like I said, maybe it simply was his time."

"If that's true, I want to know it." Her voice was clear, strong, and full of the sort of concern that made me long for a world full of people like Earline.

"Earline, I said I'd do my best."

"I know—I know," she purred and smiled as she pointed to the door. "Johnny didn't show up this Monday—so the trail is five days cold. Get to work, *detective*."

I did as I was told. I got up and left the diner. For the first time in many years, I actually felt like working. Maybe I *could* find him.

* * *

Out on the sidewalk, I stood where Johnny normally set up shop—if you could call it that. My senses recalled all I knew of him, and like a hound savoring a scent, I closed my eyes and sniffed the brisk March air.

I was more alive than I had been in more than a decade. My skin tingled. My ears hummed. With an overwhelming sense of purpose, I knew exactly how and where to start searching for the mysterious blind beggar with one leg and no real name.

As a cop, I knew Paper-man Billy had a reliable set of eyes. On more than one occasion, he had provided me with useful information. So, I began my quest at the corner newsstand. My plan was simple. I'd pretend I was Johnny and just follow his path home. All I needed was a start. Billy would give me that.

"Sure, Jake. I know where Johnny headed at the end of each day," Billy assured me as he made change for an impatient customer ready to bolt for the nearby bus stop. "Follow her," Billy instructed. "Johnny took the bus at the end of each day. He'd shuffle down to the stop and hop on the Blue Line."

He referred again to the departing customer, pointed, and said, "If you hurry, you can make that one."

I sprinted to the stop and made it on board after pounding on the door. The friendly looking driver was even friendlier when I flashed my badge and asked her about Johnny.

"Sure, I can tell you about him," she answered. "He rode my route often."

"Where'd he get off?"

"Edge of Old Town—people say he lives some-where on Sedgwick."

"Ever see anyone giving him trouble? You know—trying to get at his daily take?"

"Naw," she told me. "Nobody ever fooled with Johnny—too much trouble."

"How so?" I asked.

"Well, first of all, his collection pot is welded onto his walker—you'd have to take the whole rig if you were after his money. And second, his pot is like one of those Salvation Army-type kettles—the money went into a slot and wasn't easy to get at—it was locked.

"Finally, Johnny must have kept the key at home. He never opened it in public. I never saw him pay for a bus fare with his collection pot's money. He always paid with coins from his pocket."

I thanked her for the information and rode the Blue Line to where she said Johnny always got off, and I did the same. Back on the street, I walked toward Old Town and looked around for any locals who might know Johnny. After not finding any, I headed for the nearest convenience store.

Inside, the Pakistani owner easily pegged me as a cop and told me what I needed to know.

"Yes, yes—I know Mister Johnny. He passed by here often, but he seldom came in. He went home... Down there," he answered and pointed.

I bought a candy bar and followed his direction.

As I walked along and munched on chocolate, I suddenly became aware I felt more than good. My investigation was less than an hour old, and I had made progress. In fact, I felt really great—better than I had in a long time—and it wasn't due to chocolate. I was even a bit glad Johnny was missing.

Up the street, I decided to make a stop at the neighborhood tavern. How far could a blind guy with one-leg shuffle? He had to live close by. I presumed the local barkeep would know something—they always do.

I slid onto an open stool at the nearly empty bar's end and ordered a draft. When it arrived, I flipped my badge so fast that only a seasoned hand would know who I was and why I needed some answers.

Bartender Ed leaned on the bar. He asked, "You looking for someone in particular, detective?"

"Yes," I said, as I slid a twenty his way. "Blind Johnny, the beggar—he ever come in here?"

"Once in a blue moon," answered Ed as he palmed the note.

"Last one was when?"

"Long time ago."

"Any ideas where he might be?"

"Try seventeen-twenty-eight North Sedgwick— used to be a bird shop. A painter lives there now. The blind guy rented a room from him."

"Thanks," I said.

Ed eased back down the bar where a profession- ally dressed woman sat drinking what looked to be a martini.

I should have recognized her, but my mind was elsewhere. I finished my beer and made toward the door.

On my way out, I heard a familiar voice. It pierced me deeper than Maria's scissors.

"Hey, Thompson. Shot any little girls lately?" It was the voice of that friggin' reporter.

All the good I had recently felt escaped in an instant and years of painful loneliness encircled me.

I froze.

I must have been a pathetic sight. I know I felt like one. I wasn't prepared for what came next.

The woman I had known in my nightmares as "the evil one" walked toward me with the uneven gait of a well-practiced drunk. As she neared me, I saw that her professional look was frayed and worn. She looked to be one martini this side of terrible.

"I'd stop to give you a hard time," she quipped as she passed by, "but, I need to pee."

She drifted toward the ladies' john—half tight and looking like ten long years of hard-worn cynicism in heels and a suit. I took a deep breath and forced myself to go for the door.

"Pay her no mind," Ed called out. "She's been soaking in booze ever since she realized she'd never get another story like you."

I didn't respond. Revenge wasn't called for. The woman had flayed me on an unforgiving spit called journalism—and I lived. It was her problem that all she got was a hitch-hiked ride on my fifteen minutes of pain.

Our paths had crossed again, but there was nothing to bind us. An unburdened feeling engulfed me. I was free of the bitch and the nightmares would come no more.

I stepped into the night air and headed for the address Bartender Ed had given me.

As I walked, all I could think was, *I'm on a case.* And that good feeling grew with every step I took away from that barroom.

At the Sedgwick address, I hit a wall. The place looked abandoned. Notices from all sorts of city departments and agencies papered the door. There were no signs of recent habitation. Whoever had been there must have left months ago.

I pondered my options.

"You looking for Jeremy?" was the question that came from a window of the building next door.

"Jeremy?" I answered the phantom. "No—not Jeremy. I'm looking for a disabled guy. John... Johnny... I don't know his last name."

"He didn't have one," said the voice.

"What?" I strained to see the voice's owner.

"I mean he never used one—at least I never heard it mentioned. Johnny is all we called him—Blind One-Legged Johnny."

A dim light appeared, and with it, a barely visible face. An attractive mid-thirties woman waved to me. "I'm Miriam—neighbor and friend of Jeremy's."

"Jeremy? Who's he?"

"Painter—lived in the building. Left a couple of months ago. Why are you interested? You the police?"

"Sure am." I flashed my badge.

"Okay—just checking. Jeremy rented an apartment with Johnny. Took care of him, too. Both of them were on the recluse side. Never saw Jeremy outside during the daytime. He must have done his painting then."

"What's Jeremy's last name?"

"Westlawn—Jeremy Westlawn."

"W-E-S-T-L-A-W-N?"

"Yes, he's got a web page. Check him out. His paintings are good—very sale-able." She looked over her shoulder. "Sorry. I've got to go."

That was it. She turned off the light and disappeared.

I would have knocked on her door and asked more questions, but I had the distinct feeling I had learned all I would for the moment.

My cop instincts were back one hundred percent. With a name and all those notices, I knew, as solidly as I had ever known anything, that Jeremy Westlawn was my key to finding Johnny.

I felt good enough to treat myself to a nice dinner. For the first time in ages, I ate away from *Jimmie's*. I made my way to *The Italian Village*.

* * *

Later at home, I sipped, rather than drank, my cheap bourbon. I checked out Jeremy Westlawn's watercolors on the internet and jotted down his agent's details.

My sleep that night was totally peaceful for the first time in years.

The next morning was a shocker at *Jimmie's*—I came in very early for breakfast.

"You are impressive," beamed Earline. "One night on a real case and you're like a new man."

"Don't get all sappy on me, Earline," was my embarrassed reply. I snuck a peek at my reflection coming off the polished stainless steel coffee pot. "Does my small amount of success show *that* much?"

"Yes, it does." She poured me a cup of joe and ignored three non-regulars in the corner booth. "Fill me in, Jake. What did you find?"

"Seems like Johnny had an address, but no last name. Some painter may have been his nursemaid. The painter is Jeremy Westlawn. Ever heard of him?"

"Nope. The only painters I know wear white coveralls and work with ladders."

"That's funny—real funny. I'm on your case and you joke about it."

"My case?" She donned her serious face. "Jake, this is *your* case—the one you've been wanting."

"Wanting? Me?"

"Yes, Jake. Maybe you can find your way back with this one. Don't blow it." She poured a second cup, tossed me a bear claw, and said, "Get moving. You won't find Johnny here."

* * *

Westlawn's agent was helpful. But I learned fast that if I was going to solve the case, some travel was in my future.

"I'm sorry," the agent told me. "He's out of the country—in the islands, painting. He cleared out a few months ago and retired. Anyway, I barely know anything about Jeremy Westlawn. We seldom met. And, it was always at night only to hand off his paintings. As to whether or not he was a friend or caretaker for this blind guy you're after... I don't know anything that might help you."

"I'm not after anyone," I explained. "I'm just checking out a missing person report."

"For a guy with no last name?"

"Yes, I know it sounds irregular. But Jeremy Westlawn is the only person who has, or had, what appears to be a relationship with the man I'm looking for."

"I'm sorry, detective. If you want any more answers, you'll need to pack sunscreen and to talk to Mr. Westlawn yourself."

I agreed.

And since I had more leave time than I could ever use, I booked a flight south on my own dime. No one at the Administrative Investigations Unit made so much as a peep when I phoned in to announce my upcoming absence.

That afternoon, I grabbed my passport, packed some duds, and headed to O'Hare's International Terminal.

From my examination of Jeremy Westlawn's work, it was clear he knew well the numerous islands of the Caribbean. Each of his paintings was a passionate rendition of real sites he visited and loved. The man could paint. I looked forward to meeting him and envied his ability to totally transport me through his work.

Deciding to track him down was easy. Doing it was easier. Jeremy Westlawn's paintings told me where to find him.

That was yesterday.

And this morning I got his call.

I was sitting on a balcony overlooking the most beautiful harbor I had ever seen—or imagined—when he called. When I had left my message, I had mentioned only one name: Blind One-Legged Johnny.

I knew I was on to something—he made the call himself—and, I had not said I was a cop.

"Detective Thompson?"

"Yes."

"I believe we should meet."

"I was hoping we could."

"Fine. I'll have my driver pick you up at one. We can have lunch at my hotel. See you then."

That was all. Well, not really *all*.

I did attempt to find out more about Mr. Jeremy Westlawn, but I was politely deflected—if not outright ignored—by everyone I queried.

It seemed Mr. Westlawn was one of the island's most respected and influential residents.

When his driver arrived, I learned that lunch at his hotel meant at *his* hotel. Among other things, Jeremy Westlawn owned one of the most luxurious commercial properties on the waterfront.

When I entered the hotel, I was escorted to a waterfront suite suitable for the wealthiest vacationer. A beautiful lunch was laid out for my arrival. I was surprised and impressed.

My expression must have showed it. When he entered, he told me so—in a nice way.

"A little better than the fare at *Jimmie's*, right?"

The comment came from my host—a late middle-aged man, expensively dressed, immaculately groomed, and extremely confident. He strode into the room with a strong but irregular gait and made his way across the room to shake my hand.

My cop instincts immediately went into overdrive. Although Jeremy Westlawn was the sort of man you'd never see near a grease pit like *Jimmie's*, to my street-trained eyes it was oh, so clear. My search was over.

"Yeah," I grinned, as I shook his hand. "The chow here is much nicer, *Johnny*."

"Excellent work, detective. I am curious—how did you know?"

"Your limp sealed it. I was certain when I saw you walk. You're taller than I recall, but then, I always saw you with only one leg and leaning on your walker."

I looked at him some more.

Decked out in immaculate resort clothes, it was certain no one from Chicago would have recognized him. His gray hair was perfectly groomed—not at all like the matted mass that usually crept out from beneath the soiled cap that was part of his trademark look.

But it was his eyes that intrigued me most. Both were blue. One was definitely made of glass.

"Shall we have a drink first?" he asked, attempting to break my gaze.

"Sure—I think I need one."

He poured for me a brand I never could afford.

"It's bourbon, right? I always smelled a trace of bourbon on you in the mornings, Jake."

"Damn, so it is true."

"Of course—I thought we already settled I am who you are looking for."

"No—no. I know *that*. I meant your sense of smell. A heightened sense of smell is supposed to be true only for the blind—and, you... You are not blind." I took the drink he handed to me and sat down.

"Maybe I should explain," he offered.

I took a big swig.

It was his turn to grin, and he did with obvious pleasure. Then he poured himself a glass of what appeared to be iced tea. I finished my drink, signaled for more, closed my eyes, and said, "Please—I'm all ears."

"I expected someone to show up—eventually. But to be quite frank, I'm very surprised it is you—and so *soon*."

"Sorry," I said with a smirk. "I'm surprised I'm here, too."

He laughed, and I laughed back. Then he continued.

"I'm curious—did you track me with a particular set of criminal charges in mind?"

"What did you expect?"

"Charges such as fraud—tax evasion?"

"No—no, it's nothing like that. You are a missing person."

"Really?"

"Until now—legal wise—I wasn't thinking of anything else."

"Maybe I shouldn't give you any ideas."

"Too late."

"Really?"

I stifled another laugh and said, "Look, Johnny—Jeremy, or whoever you choose to be. Like it or not—as a missing person, you are sort of a celebrity."

"Celebrity? Me? Impossible."

"Well, maybe you are a small celebrity. You were missed—more than one concerned citizen wants to know what happened to the guy who was a fixture on one of Chicago sidewalks."

"*That*, I never expected."

"Played right, you could become an urban legend."

"Oh, no. No, thanks. I've had more than enough city life—thirty-two years' worth."

"Let's go there. You were about to explain your heightened sense of smell. You have sight in one eye—we all thought you were blind."

He poured me another and told me his story— how he became Blind One-Legged Johnny.

"I was injured in an industrial accident at the old *International Harvester* plant—back in the early seventies. A load of iron pipe rolled off a truck as it wheeled through the parking lot. I was unlucky. I lost an eye, and my leg was crushed—no way to save it. They took it off in less than an hour after I got to the hospital."

"Damn," was all I could say.

"Yeah—it gets worse." He deeply sighed. "Normally, an accident like that is a cash-laden meal ticket, but not for me. The company, their insurance carrier, and some heartless lawyers, squashed my dreams of a secure financially recovery." He sighed deeper. "It was my misfortune to have had a beer at lunch—that's what screwed me."

"One beer?" I asked. "C'mon. I'm a cop, and I can't tell you how many times I've heard that. One beer? Truly?"

"Yes. It's true. A single beer—just one lousy beer. In the eyes of the company, I was under the influence of alcohol and the accident was therefore my fault."

"No way."

"Trust me—it happened. The fact that I was crippled meant nothing. I was tossed out on my ear. All I received was few dollars a month in the form of a government disability check."

"Made you bitter, right?" I thought of my own feelings after the case that ruined my career.

"Yes—bitter, and self-destructive. It didn't take long for me to spiral down and become the street persona you were looking for. I was addicted to pain killers and booze. I couldn't work, had no family to speak of—it was a quick, hard drop.

"One morning, I woke up on Michigan Avenue—across the street from the Art Institute. I found eight bucks and change someone had placed in my baseball cap. It was too early to drink, so I went inside the museum. I looked at the paintings and decided to turn things around. That money was a godsend."

"So, you lucked into begging as a way to support yourself?" He visibly flinched at my use of the 'B' word.

"Begged!? No. I never begged—never even asked. I only accepted what was freely given. I sunk pretty low after the accident, but I *never* begged—check it out."

"I believe you."

He drummed the table with his fingers. I wanted to get him back to his story, so I asked, "You lost an eye. How'd you get known as being totally blind when you weren't."

"Simple. I didn't want to run the risk of being found out, so I wore a patch over my good eye and, in effect, became blind. Out on the street, in front of the diner, I wasn't a fraud. If someone tested me—poked at my face—I wouldn't have known it and flinched. In every way I was what people saw—a one-legged blind man with a tin cup."

"Some cup," I quipped as I surveyed the room. "All this came from... From..."

"Don't say begging," he said with a slight laugh. "I made—no, correction—I was *given* a fair amount over the years."

"Care to say how much?"

"In the beginning—at least a hundred thousand a year."

"Say what!?"

"That was long ago. In recent years, after I became the fixture *you* said I am, people have been very generous."

"And naturally, all cash."

"Naturally—and that's why I came to the islands. The cash became quite a problem."

"Cash? A problem?"

"Yes—I had plenty of money and no way to launder it. Remember, I had a minuscule legal monthly income. Although I obtained the money out on the streets, I wasn't a criminal—and I didn't want to get involved with any criminals."

"And that led you here?"

"Yes. During a particularly brutal January cold snap, I decided to find a warm spot to thaw out and try my hand at painting. I studied how to move money offshore. Each year I came to invest and paint."

"How'd you get cash out of the country?"

"Who would look inside a prosthetic limb?"

"It makes sense—makes perfect sense."

"It worked well for years. You know, the place I sat each day was perfect. It was a safe spot with the ideal mix of regular customers from the diner, daily commuters, and tourists. I sat there each day minding my own business, my good eye closed—painting."

"Painting? What are you talking about?"

"To spend the hours wisely, I meticulously planned and then made every brush stroke of my paintings in my mind's eye. I completed the actual works at night, on weekends, and, of course, here in January and February."

"That's amazing. Your art is actually quite good."

"Thank you."

"Who would have guessed that such beautiful art came from the sidewalk in front of *Jimmie's*."

"No one—that's the beauty of it."

"So, why quit?"

"My sixtieth birthday," he said, as he pointed around the room and then at the sea. "And as you can see—I have enough. Also, at some point, everyone retires—even blind one-legged cripples." He smiled.

"So, Chicago has definitely seen the last of Blind One-Legged Johnny?"

"Yes. In fact, there is no Johnny—never was. On one of my first days on the street someone called me Johnny and it stuck. For years, I hid the fact that by day I was Johnny and at night I was Jeremy, the Painter. The deception is over. My life is here now."

There was a long silence. I knew the next move was mine.

The non-cop part of me finally asked, "So, Mr. Jeremy Westlawn, what comes next?"

He reached over to the table where our lunch was laid out and picked up a brown-paper-wrapped package. "That is entirely up to you." He tore at the package's paper.

When he finished, I was staring at a stack of bills.

"Jake, I'm a wealthy man. I invested wisely and have more than enough to fight extradition, the IRS, and with anyone else you care to share my identity." He gestured to the money. "On the other hand—I'd prefer to spend my time painting. I'd like you to do whatever it takes to cover the trail that leads here to me."

He pointed to the money and said, "So, there's this. It's in cash."

"Meaning?"

"Meaning, you can have it. Use it however you wish. Stay a while and enjoy the sun. Come back each winter for your vacation. Chicago's winters are brutal indeed." He patted the cash. "There will be a similar amount each time you visit."

"My money. Just like that?"

"Yes. Just like that. Maybe you'll find something, or someone, to change your life. Maybe you'll just fall in love with this place like I did."

"Sounds easy. Maybe too much so."

"Look, I don't presume to *really* know you, Jake. But I do now some things about you."

"Like what?"

"Standing in front of *Jimmie's* is a great place to learn things—things that add up. My knowledge of you is based on always smelling bourbon on a slow walking, late arriving, unhappy man."

"It was that obvious?"

"Even a blind man could see your pain." The joke made him smile.

"Funny one."

"Jake, everyone in life makes mistakes, has tragedies befall them, and runs into bad luck. How we deal with it—that's what makes us who we are."

"I'm confused," I almost whispered. "Who are you? What are you saying?"

"I'm not Blind One-Legged Johnny—the guy who collects coins in front of *Jimmie's*. I'm Jeremy Westlawn—the artist. The question today is: '*Who are you?*'"

I took a good look at the man whose disappearance brought me there, and then I looked at the money.

He told me the truth. "You were looking for the wrong man, Jake."

My head was spinning. I heard voices. I stared at the blue sea, and they kept it up.

Whose voice am I hearing? His? The drunk reporter's? Paper-man Billy's? Earline's? Gino's? Maria's? Bartender Ed's? Miriam, the neighbor's, my dad's?

Maybe... Jan Tomaszewki's.

Time stopped. I continued to stare at the money. I ignored all the voices I have ever heard, and I asked myself the only question that mattered.

Jake, is this a decision you can live with?

A Girl Gone Missing

O N THE SOUTHSIDE, WHEN YOU are orphaned by luck, it is said, "You can't win for losing." I agree, and staying on the right side of the law was my choice because it is a good side to be on when you lose.

Truth be told, AIU isn't so bad—except when it's freezing cold and all you can dream of is the warmth of the Caribbean Isle you turned your back on. There is no such thing as easy money. Cold and safe beats warm on the *wrong* side.

It is March and still cold.

March in Chicago can be nasty. I know it all too well—I could live nowhere else. I've spent my entire life experiencing the third month's unpredictability in this city. Mean and spiteful, yet interesting, with hints of winter's end, March is the perfect example of the topsy-turvy weather that makes me love hating this place.

Now, here's the deal about March in Chicago. Just when spring is within reach, the last cold air of winter hugs the lake shore like a frozen barnacle and just won't let go. Everyone is driven indoors, cabin fever is rampant, and the city's frosted air bursts with yearning for a warm opening day at Wrigley Field. It is amazing how a simple need can overwhelm all else.

This March is one of those cruel ones when a late arriving arctic mass creeps south to extend the cold season beyond its normal end. On this seventeenth day of the month of March to honor St. Patrick, Chicago is one huge chunk of frozen blarney.

The public relations spin-masters collecting bloated salaries from city hall can dye the Chicago River green, but the city's party spirit has the flu. Our beloved St. Paddy is wheezing, coughing, and tossing back blue *NyQuil* shooters. This frigid March, the Siren of the Shamrocks is more cold-hearted bitch than flirtatious tart, and the goddess of green beer is acting like an ex-wife with attitude and a sleazy lawyer.

But—not to worry. I've got a fool-proof plan to whip the flu—just hunker down in my favorite booth at *Jimmie's Diner* and guzzle some fortified coffee. I'm not joking about the *NyQuil*—it lends itself well to the caffeine-flavored oil Earline, my favorite waitress, sloshes into cups at *Jimmie's*. A couple of jolts of my special medicinal brew, and all is well.

Before I know it, I'm back again to being a slug cop, nearing retirement, and wasting my days assigned to the bottom-rung of the Chicago PD. We in the Administrative Investigation Unit are a mixed bag of casts-offs and politically incorrect screw-ups muddling through a mountain of cases no one wants. Our motto, "We're slow, but we do poor work," is not a joke.

For more than a decade, I've been dreaming of my release from this professional purgatory, but even a perfect landing on the front pages of both the *Trib* and the *Sun-Times* with me finding out what happened to a street icon named Blind One-Legged Johnny got me bupkis. I did the right thing—turned the money down and turned *him* in.

What a story. Get this—Jeremy Westlawn becomes a cult hero for screwing the system. Billy the Kid with a paintbrush, as I call him, gets bail, jumps it, scurries back to his island hideout, and along the way sells more paintings. Now that he has even more money, extradition is nigh impossible.

Me? I'm portrayed as the blind pig who randomly found a truffle—the loud-mouthed loser cop who got lucky. **THE BLIND FINDING THE BLIND** was one news' story's jokey headline.

I've learned a sad truth: In the Chicago PD they mean it when they say, "Once AIU, forever AIU." The fickle gods did their thing. Westlawn gets the Caribbean's warmth and I get Chicago's cold shoulder.

As you might imagine, AIU's offices match our reputation as the lepers of police department. In winter, my cubicle is bone-numbing cold. So, I camp out at *Jimmie's Diner* to do my paperwork. That's where I'm parked and plan to stay 'til the city thaws or Jimmie tells me he needs the booth for a real customer.

And just when I'm ready for a *NyQuil* nap, I hear my name being taken in vain at the main entrance.

"Hey. Anybody see that Polish wetback, Jake Thompson? I heard the Immigration boys are after him. They found out his real name is Tomaszewski and that he washed ashore as Lake Michigan's first boat person."

I am not offended. The jab is good natured. It comes from my old high school pal, Dwight "Dewey" Eisenhauer. I wave him over to my booth and motion for Earline to bring a second cup of *Jimmie's* poisoned java.

"Hey, General," I say, as he slides into my booth. "Are you here to even up on the five dollars you owe me?"

Without a word, Dewey yanks out his wallet and produces a ten, which he slides across the table. I put the offered bill in my shirt pocket and grin.

Dewey grins back and says, "Now *you* owe *me* five bucks."

"Yep—a good reason to stay in touch, *General*."

The exchange ritual was a running joke between us—our way to stay connected. We'd been doing it since our days playing football at the Southside's Brother Rice High School. That's when I began calling him, *The General*, and he started ribbing me about my original Polish surname.

Dewey hated his nickname and wanted everyone to know why. The General had two standard objections to being associated with the real five-star general who became President of the United States.

Dewey would bend the ear of anyone in range with, first, "My name is *Eisenhauer*, not Eisenhower," and second, "I'm named Dwight after Dwight H. Green, a distinguished Illinois Governor, not the President."

It really pissed The General off that no one really cared. It's funny what kinda stuff riles a guy.

In his prime, Dewey was one helluva football player—a speedy bone-crushing linebacker like Dick Butkus. Dewey would have been in the NFL had not a nasty clip by a sore loser bent his leg into the shape of a pretzel.

Although the incident relegated him to a life of 'what ifs' and 'could have beens', Dewey Eisenhauer was not a bitter man. In fact, he was an oasis of good-will in an otherwise crap-laden world. Seeing him always made me feel better.

"So, what brings you to the Loop, General?"

Dewey lives about a dozen miles south, in Blue Island. He tends bar at a place on Western Avenue, one of those neighborhood joints where the pizzas and sandwiches are passed through a window from the restaurant next door.

If I remember correctly, Dewey is sleeping with the owner's daughter, along with half the female customers.

Like I said, Dewey is a one-man delegation of joy. Women cling to him as if they are fabric and he's covered in Velcro. Dewey calls it 'the Lint Effect'.

At this moment, he is uncharacteristically lint free—with a funny look on his face.

"I need help with a woman," he explains.

I grin. "That's a first. But I guess at our age, it does happen. Tried *Viagra*?" I grin some more.

I grin a lot when Dewey is around.

"It's not what you think. I need *your kind* of help." He looks serious. It is not a pleasant sight, and it causes me to stop grinning.

"You mean—professionally? Like police help?" I point to my piece strapped under my jacket.

"Yeah." He stays with the serious look and reaches into his pocket. He produces a folded piece of paper. "Here—take a look."

It's one of those flyers. You know, the type desperate family members distribute when someone is missing? It's the adult version of the picture on a milk carton. Surprisingly they do work—proves long shots come in.

I give it a good look and ask, "Family or friend?"

"Neither."

I raise an eyebrow.

"Co-worker," he answers. "Rose Capell."

"One of your lady friends?"

"No—part-timer at the bar. I didn't know her that well. Most of the time she was just a pain in the ass."

"Was?"

"She's been gone two years."

"Two years?"

"That's right—last time anyone saw Rose was a little over two years ago."

"Let me get this straight. Two years after a pain-in-the-ass part-time barkeep goes missing you decide to pass out flyers. Did you change your mind about sleeping with her?"

"Jake, that was lame. I should take my money back."

"Oops, so sorry." I give him my best buddy smile. "Just trying to figure it out. What's changed in two years?"

"Elmo."

"You are too old for *Sesame Street*." I smile.

He smiles back. "Wrong Elmo."

"Sorry. What other Elmo is there?"

"Elmo Warren."

"Should I know him?"

"Not unless you collect Elmos."

"Always dreamed of it." I grin a big one. "Gotta love it—who names their kid Elmo?"

Dewey eases more than a bit. "His parents must have had some sense of humor."

"I'm all ears. Tell me about poor Elmo."

"He's a slurp."

"A what?" I'd heard all the slang used in Chicago—or so I thought. This is a new one.

"A slurp—comes in the bar everyday—slurps beers, hangs out, and takes up space. Also, they never tip."

"Got it. Go on." I make a mental note. *Lingual creativity is not dead on the Southside.*

"Elmo lives on a small disability check—never a bother to anyone. He usually keeps to himself. Watches TV and slurps himself into an all-day buzz. When it's closing time, he's out the door at the very last minute."

"Afraid to go home to the wife?"

"No wife. Lives with his sister and her husband, Joey Pascal. The sister is a fox. Joey is world-class slime."

"You got a thing for the sister?"

Dewey doesn't answer. It wasn't like him to clam up about any woman he'd rate that high. Something troubles him and he remains silent. So, I try a different approach.

"What's Elmo's connection to Rose?"

Dewey comes to life and taps the flyer lying on the table before us.

"Yesterday—out of the blue—he gives me this."

"This is an old flyer?"

"Yeah. Like everyone else, I had pretty much forgotten about Rose. At the time—two years back—her family distributed them after there was a piece about her on *WGN News*. The thought at the time was that she lit out for some exotic locale—she was always yakking about leaving the Southside for someplace like Vegas or Hollywood."

I look closer at the picture before me. "She looks okay, but no movie star. Any leads come out of the flyer effort?"

"Nope. Rose was low priority for the cops, and even for her family. Her boyfriend at the time was none other than Joey Pascal—local n'er-do-well. Joey claimed she cleaned out his wallet, packed a bag, and bailed on all things local. The mom and dad circulated the posters only after Rose failed to call home for weeks. I think they did it to ease their consciences over being so-so parents."

"So, that brings us back to Elmo."

"Right."

"And?"

"Like I said, yesterday—last night, at closing, Elmo's buzzed way more than usual... And he hands me this flyer."

"Let me guess. He had a tale to tell. One good enough to get you to come here."

"Jake, you ever think about being a detective?"

"Now, you're being *real* funny. Tell me Elmo's story."

"It's simple. Elmo shoves the flyer my way and sez straight out that he knows what *really* happened to Rose. He blurts out that she's dead, then catches himself and goes all mysterious on me—tries to be evasive when he realizes he's drunk and said too much."

"And you came to me because..."

"Because you are the *only* cop I trust."

"General, you blew it. You were supposed to say I'm the *best* cop you know."

"Oops. So sorry." He smiles and shoots me the kind of look only a smart-assed life-long friend gets away with.

"Save the charm. It won't work. Besides, I'm a *Chicago* cop. Blue Island is outside my jurisdiction."

Dewey points at the flyer. "Check the address. Rose last lived at one-seventeenth and Western. Last time I checked a map, that's still Chicago."

"Okay, okay, but come on. Do the brown-nose thing. Tell me I'm the best again."

"Cut the crap, Jake. Elmo knows something. He was about to spill his guts but he hesitated. All you have to do is lean on him. The guy will cave, easy."

"If he's so ready, why don't you do it? You're bigger than me—meaner, *and* uglier. Just rough him up a little. He'll talk."

"Jake, you're a cop. You can do something about it once you find out what happened."

"Okay. For you, I'll look into it, but not because you seem so certain that old Elmo wasn't just buzzed and blowin' smoke. I'll do it only because you're a pal."

"*And*, you're the *best detective* I know."

We both laugh as I tell him, "For some strange reason, General, I believe you."

We nurse another mug of *Jimmie's* darkest brew, catch up on the gossip, and eventually drive south to Blue Island.

* * *

I wanted to check out Elmo firsthand, and truthfully, I did not want to drive. Driving had become such a pain that I hitched rides whenever I could. Besides, Dewey's car was warmer than mine. Cleaner, too.

We headed south and found Elmo without a problem. He was in the bar, taking up space in his usual spot. I wasn't expecting much from a guy described as a slurp. There was no surprise in what I find.

Elmo was average sized but appeared smaller. There was a sucked-in quality about him.

You see it on guys who are afraid and timid. Life is too much for them, so they withdraw into themselves. At some point they just disappear.

When I first laid eyes on him, Elmo was camped in a booth slurping his way into a buzz of nothingness.

I nodded to Dewey, indicating I'd make my move alone. He nodded back and took a seat on a barstool with the best view of the booth. With my back covered, I slid into the booth, blocking Elmo's exit route.

"Hey, Elmo." I showed him my badge and placed the flyer before him. "Got a minute?"

Elmo froze in mid slurp.

I didn't say anything else. I didn't need to. I just smiled and kept eye contact.

Elmo gave me that sick queasy look—the one a guy gets when he's been made. Elmo wiggled back into the corner of the booth. I'd bet if he could, he would have burrowed a hole.

I have to admit, I love the way a guy squirms when you blindside him. And... then... make... him... wait. Waiting drives the Elmos of this world crazy.

This Elmo was no exception.

He peeked over my shoulder for help and got none. Dewey sat stone faced at the bar and eyed Elmo with his best linebacker stare.

I smoothed the flyer and pushed it closer. Elmo squirmed like a worm on a hook, and sighed.

In a quivering voice he said, "Okay, okay. I know what's up. I should have kept my mouth shut, but—"

"But, you didn't..." I interrupted. "So, cut any crap you might be thinking. What do you know about Rose Capell disappearing?" I had him and I knew it.

Elmo knew it, too.

For emphasis, I leaned close and tapped the flyer with my finger.

Elmo tried the "I'm a little guy" sympathy game. He retreated further into his burrow and whimpered just above a whisper, "Wait... I'm... I-I—"

With a slap and grab, I jerked him by the collar and pulled his face to within an inch of Rose's image.

"I said *cut the crap*, Elmo. Come clean about Rose."

I hate the sympathy game and Elmo was not a good player.

"It ain't me. *No way*. It was *Joey—Joey's* the guy."

"Joey, who? You know the drill. Say his full name."

"Pascal—Joey Pascal. He did her. *Joey did*. I know it. Trust me. I didn't do anything. It's Joey. I'm tellin' the *truth*."

"I don't even trust myself, Elmo." Easing my grip, I pushed him against the back of the booth. "You gotta do better, Elmo."

I gave him my best pissed-off cop stare. "Elmo, what's the temperature today?"

"What? What? I-I—" He was stalling.

I slapped him hard and hissed, "I get cranky when it's cold, and I didn't come *all the way out here* to listen to any weak-assed BS. Start making sense— *fast*."

Elmo started talking like a toddler. "Sure— Sure— Like I told, Dewey. I know what happened. Joey. He did it. I know he did. He's married now—to Callie, my sister, but he was with Rose when she went missing. He got looked at good by you guys back then, but there was no evidence. Rose just vanished. So, nothing was done. He got a pass. Joey killed her and got away with it."

"You say you *know*. How? *Spit it out, Elmo*."

"Joey got drunk a couple nights ago. He gets ugly when he drinks. He roughed up Callie and threatened her after she was riding him about something. Joey said he'd kill her for starting a fight. He said he'd hide her so good nobody could find her—just like Rose. I heard it all. Callie was so freaked she lit out."

"You sure she's okay?"

"Yeah, I guess so. She goes south—heads down-state—whenever she's upset."

"Why south?"

"Our grandparents have a farm... About thirty miles east of Springfield."

"You said you 'heard it all'. What else do you know?"

"After Callie booked, Joey wanted to keep on drinking. I joined in."

"You weren't afraid like Callie?"

"Sure. But, by staying with Joey I was keeping him from going after her. Sometimes he'd rather drink than do anything else. 'Sides, everybody knows I like to drink."

In my years as a cop, I've found that people talk for a lot of reasons. The stupid ones just blab. Squealers are getting even. Braggers are attempting to cover flaws. The scared ones are seeking safety from a threatening world.

Joey sounded like a bully trying to scare little Elmo. It worked. Elmo was as scared as he could be.

"I take it that Joey was talkative. Did he say more?"

"Yeah... Yeah, he told me *a lot*. Joey said he hid Rose 'right out in the open' but where nobody would think to look. He was bragging, saying 'like fish in a barrel'. He kept repeating, 'fish in a barrel'. Also, he made it clear that he'd do the same to my sister—me, too—if I squealed out anything about it."

"Elmo... You *are* talking about it. *Why?*"

"I'm scared. Can't sleep. Haven't been home in two days. Joey isn't the type a guy to let me walk around knowing what I know. Callie did the right thing by leaving." He peeked over my shoulder again and offered a weak wave toward Dewey. "I should have run, too. But Callie always said Dewey was a good guy, so I felt maybe Dewey could help—maybe I did right to see him 'cause you're here."

Elmo shot me a smile that was probably supposed to make me feel like I just bought a new puppy. I'm not a dog person. But I did bark.

"*GIVE ME SOMETHING REAL,*" I shouted.

A couple of guys at the bar looked over. Dewey waved them off and they immediately continued their arguing about how lights screwed up Wrigley Field more than thirty years ago.

I look to where Dewey sat, gave him a shrug, and said, "All I got so far is hot air, Dewey."

Dewey came over to the booth. I slapped at Elmo again, and told Dewey, "He's your pal—talk to him."

Was it time to play good cop, bad cop? No way. I prefer bad cop, and worse cop.

Dewey took my cue. He leaned in, and in a God-like voice told Elmo, "Time to let it all out, you little weasel. I asked my good friend to help you, and all he gets from you is your dribble? If you embarrass me any more, I'll call Joey myself and tell him you are squealing. Give up all you know or hit the streets—try your chances alone."

Elmo squirmed, sweat, squirmed some more, and finally whined, "Sure, Dewey, sure. Just let me have a smoke. You know, clear my head."

Elmo shyly motioned for me to let him out of the booth. I eased out, turned to head for the can, and told him over my shoulder, "It's a filthy habit, Elmo."

"Spoken like a reformed smoker," Elmo countered. He tried the doggy look again. I softened.

"I miss 'em like hell," I told him. "A day doesn't go by that I don't crave a smoke. But I've wised up—so should you."

I needed to pee, so I walked to the rear of the barroom. The men's is always in the rear of joints popular with slurpers.

"Yeah—yeah," Elmo chirped as left him. "I'm meaning to quit."

"Now would be a good time," Dewey told him. "Do it while he's gone."

"Just one. That's all. Then, I'll be right back," Elmo promised. "Just a couple puffs." He nodded toward the front door. "I need a puff bad."

"I'll keep an eye on him," Dewey told me as I kept walking.

I waved over my shoulder without looking and said, "Fine by me."

It was my best attempt to air out the ambivalence I was feeling. I knew I could get Elmo to talk, but I was not dead certain he really had anything for me to investigate. *Unimpressive* was Elmo's middle name.

I was in Blue Island to squeeze Elmo for Dewey. He asked, so I said I'd give it a try. My plan? Take a leak, let Elmo kipper his brain, and come back for another round. One, two, three—I find what he knows. And, for the record, I really didn't care. I should have, but I was tired of the cold, tired of being a cop, and... Just plain tired of being.

The men's room had that bar-toilet smell created from mixing urine, sweat, and stale booze. A monsoon of disinfectant would never cover its stench. But as bad as the smell was, for some reason I wanted to linger. I was beyond tired.

In the cracked mirror, I saw an old, fleshy, washed-out version of the Jake Thompson who smashed heads on the gridiron with Dewey. Seeing myself gave me the creeps. Lingering was no longer an option.

I peed, washed my hands, and pushed open the door with my knee. I made a mental note to launder my trousers when I got home.

Show time, I told myself. *Time to finish with Elmo.*

With one quick step, I was back in the barroom... But it was too late to play 'tickle me Elmo'.

In the hallway leading back to the bar, my cop sense went into overdrive. I smelled violence. The barroom's air was thick with tension spawned by fear. Half of the customers were on the floor and the other half were frozen in place.

I called out, "*Dewey*," and sprinted through the barroom to where I had last seen my friend.

"I'm okay," Dewey replied, as I hurdled a prone patron.

Through a forest of terrified mannequins, Dewey's linebacker form was visible, leaning forward, inspecting Elmo's lifeless form crumpled in the doorway.

"What happened, Dewey?" I shouted as I approached.

"Cigarettes."

"What do you mean, *cigarettes*?" I halted at his side.

"Bad habit—they sure can kill a guy." He pointed to Elmo's bloody head. "As soon as he opened the door to step out for a smoke—*Bam*! It was that fast. Whoever did it must have been waiting."

"You see anything?"

"Nah. Door was in the way," Dewey explained. "Didn't hear anything, either. Must have been a small-caliber rifle. Distance, street noise, jukebox..."

I stepped forward and took a closer look. Elmo had caught one in the chest and one in the mouth.

"They made a statement." I observed. "Clear warning... The face shot was extra—the penalty for squealing."

People started moving. Someone stepped behind us, and my ambivalence fled. My cop nature was natural again.

"Stand *back*. I'm a police officer." I called out. Obedience and murmurs answered me. "Anyone call nine-one-one?" I asked.

Dewey's colleague answered from behind the bar, "We got a panic button—I hit it right away."

A patron tried to ease around me, looking like he wanted to leave *really bad*. Maybe he wasn't supposed to be at the bar and wanted to get home before his wife found out. Maybe he was a spotter.

He looked more nervous than scared and much too interested in leaving.

"Hold it. Nobody leaves," I commanded.

Mr. Nervous eased back toward the bar and tried to blend in with other patrons. Before I could follow up on why he seemed so antsy, the hometown police arrived in response to the panic call.

I lost track of the anxious patron while helping Dewey cope with questions and doing my 'brother-cop' thing with the locals.

When the smoke cleared, Mr. Nervous was gone. Later, I asked the locals if he was questioned, and they drew a blank.

"Some folks snuck out the back," was the word shared by Dewey's bartender pal.

Dewey looked more than disappointed—bordering on shocked. His goodhearted effort to find Rose had spun out of control.

Elmo was dead. And the local rats were jumping ship.

"It's to be expected," I explained. "Cops pour in the front and witnesses scamper out the back—happens all the time—people avoiding involvement. One, in particular, looked like he had a good reason to make himself gone."

I described Mr. Nervous. Dewey's friend said he didn't know him.

"Do we try to find him?" Dewey asked.

"No. Let the hometown boys do their work. It's their case. We filled them in on why we were talking to Elmo. They'll track down Joey. It will probably end there, as far as they are concerned."

"End?"

"If I'm any judge of character, Joey will have an airtight and squeaky-clean alibi."

"Is that it? He walks? Twice?"

"Yes and no."

"Explain *that* to me."

"Yes. As in, the locals said Joey was clean two years ago. With a strong alibi, where do they go now? I'm guessing Elmo's death is not going to be viewed as a great loss to the community. So, what is going to push the local boys in blue to dig deeper? The National Slurper Appreciation Society?"

After a reluctant chuckle Dewey said, "Tell me about the 'no'."

"The 'no' is you and me."

"I hoped so. I *knew* you'd never let me down."

"Yeah. I'm Mister Reliable."

"How do you want to handle moving forward?"

"Simple. I buy the beer. You, the steaks. We cook. I rack out at your place. And tomorrow we visit Mister Joey Pascal."

After picking up supplies, we spent the rest of the day and night revisiting the old days. Braving the cold, we grilled meat outdoors, sipped beers in the kitchen, and talked incessantly of football, the Cubs, girls we dated, and those we wanted to but didn't.

We wallowed in the bittersweet longing of lost youth that middle-aged ex-jocks exude in place of sweat. Our talk avoided Elmo's death, Joey's guilt, and Rose's disappearance knowing we would be waist deep in their swampy intrigue all too soon.

I had shared my cell number with the local lead detective and the next morning he called. In doing his cop thing, he filled me in on Joey's alibi and the overall 'going nowhere' nature of the investigation.

"Looks like I was right on both counts," I told Dewey. "Three people claim Joey was at his office when Elmo got clipped. *And,* the locals have been given higher priority cases to occupy their attention."

"Jake, I must admit I had some doubts when you called it that way."

"I wish I'd been wrong, but nobody cares about nobodies like Elmo."

"And Rose," he added with a touch of genuine sadness. "Two years passed, and I did nothing. If

Elmo hadn't opened up to me, Joey would have gotten away with killing Rose. Now, he gets another pass?"

"Maybe not. I don't like free passes—and two is way more than Joey's got coming." I tossed Dewey the keys sitting on the table. "Drive time, General. Get us to Joey's place of business. I want to eyeball the creep up close and see if Elmo was right."

"What have you got in mind?"

"I have no idea—but I'm sure I'll think of something."

Dewey drove while I tried to think.

It was hard. My cop nature was hammering to get out. It just wanted to give Joey the finger and goad him into doing something stupid.

I shared my thoughts with Dewey about a ballsy course of action.

"It's not much of a plan," he told me. "We just go in and piss him off?"

"It's the best I can do. I guess I'm just a follow-your-gut kind of cop. You know, if Elmo was right about Joey, we may get hurt."

Dewey pressed down on the accelerator. "So, we give him the finger."

"Glad you see it my way. The best defense is a good offense. Let's go see Joey and be really offensive."

We angled off Vincennes Avenue and crossed the train tracks into a semi-derelict industrial zone that had seen much better days.

Tucked in a back corner, Joey's combo garage and wrecking yard was well hidden from observation behind a screened chain-link fence. From its appearance, I figured Joey ran a chop shop instead of a legitimate auto business.

Also, I'd bet my scrawny pension his backroom had seen a drug deal or two—maybe more.

Before Dewey could park us in front of the building, two frowning goons in work clothes and a pit bull with a million teeth materialized from behind a row of oil barrels near the building's entrance.

"Nice welcoming committee," Dewey observed.

"Yeah, we certainly aren't in Mister Rogers' Neighborhood." I rolled down my window a couple of inches and flashed my badge.

Both goons and the mutt instantly disappeared behind the barrels and into the building.

Dewey eyed the newly vacated area outside the car and asked, "Think it's safe?"

I checked my piece, opened the door, and told him as I got out, "I'll go first."

I walked in front of the car and headed straight for the building. Dewey followed—at a safe distance.

We were greeted outside the building's main entrance by a new goon wearing an expensive suit and a big smile.

Slick and greasy. It has to be Joey.

"Can I help you?" Joey asked. He expanded the smile and cocked his head.

I'm sure you've seen the move—teeth flashing, head at an angle. It oozes smart-ass.

I let it pass, but I felt Dewey bristle behind me. I knew if I did not jump in quick, the General was going to deck Joey.

I opened with a verbal groin kick. "I'm Detective Jake Thompson, and I'm looking for a *suspect* by the name of Joey Pascal."

Joey's smile vanished. "*Suspect!?* Suspect?" he shouted more than asked. "That's *crazy*. I told the other cops I was here *all* of yesterday—got witnesses to prove it. Come on. They're inside." He waved for us to follow, turned, and quickly entered the building.

We followed.

The inside of the building was a total disconnect with its exterior—much cleaner and neater than I expected. The place only had the appearance of a garage. Joey had made an effort to look like he ran a real business, but to the trained eye it was clear—the junked-up outside was a sham. If the local detectives had interviewed him inside, their cop radar should have been humming. If any real auto work was accomplished inside, I'd pay for it.

Joey had scurried through the *faux* work area and into the office where he wailed through his intercom, "Tito— Lou— Paulie— Get in here."

Like I said, we followed.

By the time we entered the office, Joey had situated himself into a large leather chair and lifted his feet onto his desk. The office was spacious and decorated in what I'd call 'American Safari'.

Joey was a hunter. Stuffed animal heads and hunting rifles lined the walls.

In less than a minute, Joey's minions answered his summons by entering the office through a rear door.

I was not surprised that two of them were the goons we had seen earlier. I also was not surprised that Mr. Nervous was the third.

"Tell them," Joey said. "Tell them how I was *here* all day."

Before they could comply, I glared at Joey and said, "I'm not interested in yesterday."

Joey glared back. The goons, preparing to pounce, looked to Joey and then to Mr. Nervous for directions.

Dewey, still bristling, took position at my side. To defuse the tension, I held my hands up and displayed my best, 'Gee, can't we all get along,' smile, saying, "Let's all try to keep it friendly."

Then, I waited.

After a long silent moment, Joey said, "Okay. But you better explain why you're flashing a worthless Chicago badge and taking up my time."

He waved off his boys and all three quietly, but reluctantly, disappeared through the door they had entered.

"Like I said," Joey mouthed from his kingly seat. "The local cops know where I've been. I'm sorry about Elmo, but I'm clean when it comes to him getting clipped."

He shot me and Dewey that same smart-assed grin from the cocked-head position.

It was my turn. I was just as pissed as Dewey.

"Like I said," I repeated. "I'm not interested in yesterday. I'm here to talk about an old friend of yours... Rose Capell."

For an instant, Joey's face dropped its smirk. He recovered fast, but I saw the slip. I had caught him off guard.

"Rose?" Joey asked. He stood. "Rose is ancient history. She's long gone—over two years ago. The locals grilled me about her, too. They sniffed around here and never found a thing. She lit out—always talking about Vegas, or L.A."

"That's not what Elmo said," I countered.

"Yeah," Dewey chimed in. "Elmo fingered *you.*"

"Elmo said a lot of things. What else would you expect from a drunk?"

Joey protested a bit too much. He next pointed at me and said, "You said you weren't interested in what happened yesterday."

"I lied. I'm interested in everything. You still need to tell me about Rose."

Joey turned a deep shade of red and waved for us to leave. "I told you—she's ancient history. Elmo, too. So cuff me or *get out of here.*"

He tried to give us that smile again, but it just wasn't possible. Joey was shook. I knew that with one more push, Joey would crack and show me what I wanted.

I looked to Dewey and said, "Come on, General, time to leave. We got what we came for."

Joey exploded with, "What!? What have you got? You got *nothing*. You hear me? *Nothing*. You got nothing."

I headed for the door and motioned for Dewey to follow. We quickly walked through the shop and out the main entrance with Joey in tow.

"Nothing—you GOT NOTHING," he yelled at our backs.

As we walked, I think, *Come on, Joey, make a stupid move.*

Every con has a "tell" and I was looking for Joey's. I prayed that my tactics had worked, and Joey would expose his.

In the parking lot, we slowed our pace as I eyed Joey.

Come on, Joey. You're not as smart as you think you are. Make your dumb-assed move.

He did.

As Dewey and I approached the car, Joey took up a position in front of the oil drums lining the front wall of the building. His eyes nervously darted back and forth—drums to us, us to the drums.

He yelled, "Get outta here and don't come back without a warrant."

Pulling out the gated drive, Dewey asked me, "You getting a warrant?"

"No," I explained. "I've got nothing solid. Even a newbie Assistant DA would laugh me off."

"So... Why are you smiling?"

"Because... I got *something*."

"What have you got?"

"I've got a hunch *and* a plan. Care to drive me on a couple errands?"

"What sort of errands?"

"Get me to a toy store and a paint shop. I need some supplies."

* * *

They say, "If you don't like the weather in Chicago, wait a minute. It'll change."

That night, a warm front eased up from the Gulf of Mexico and it was almost balmy when Dewey drove us back to Joey's with my supplies.

"Care to explain what we are doing with a gazillion balloons filled with iridescent paint, maple syrup, fish oil, and God knows what?" Dewey asked.

"Simple. We toss 'em."

"That's it? We mixed up this stinking mess just to toss 'em... Like kids?"

"Yep. We simply toss 'em... And make a phone call."

"To whom?"

"The Feds."

"Feds? How are they going to help?"

"Dewey, we are going *Green*. I can't get a warrant, but I can get the EPA to find out what Joey is hiding in those barrels. He was guarding them like a hen sitting on eggs. This stuff will glow like it's radioactive and smell so bad it'll guarantee the EPA inspects everything in sight."

"Brilliant!"

"Yep. I'm the best detective you know. Remember?"

* * *

We pull up to the outer fence at Joey's place and pitch the balloons at the stack of barrels. All but one hits the target. The errant balloon is an overshot and lands on the roof.

"Perfect!" I exclaim. "Next, we make some calls, and then we wait."

"So, that's our total plan?" asks Dewey. "Waiting on a bunch of bureaucrats is all we got?"

"General, thinking outside the box and operating within the law is sometimes the best anyone can do. Don't sell the EPA short—especially when the AIU is poking their lazy butts. I'm calling in all my markers."

Within thirty minutes, the EPA's switchboard is jammed with calls complaining about the "radioactive goo" dripping from Joey's storage barrels. I top off the groundswell of calls with my own to a friend, Larry Peters—an EPA investigator who owes me a favor.

His line is jammed, so I leave an urgent colleague-to-colleague message.

"Larry," I say. "This is Jake Thompson. You better get on that Blue Island radioactive thing, pronto. I suspect you'll find some really interesting stuff in those barrels. Matter of fact, I'm so certain that I'm tagging you for a steak dinner at Morton's over this one."

After the call, I tell Dewey to drive me back to the Loop.

"We'll just have to sit back and wait," I tell him. "There is no way Joey can clean up all that mess. Eventually, the EPA boys will show up. Let's hope they are inquisitive."

That was it. Not much of a caper. No daring do. No shoot out. Just a really large smelly mess that glowed in the dark.

What more do you want from a burnout like me? Remember—once AIU, always AIU.

* * *

Okay. So, I admit I wasn't surprised when Dewey came into *Jimmie's Diner* two days later all smiles and good cheer to eke out a favor.

"Heard the news?" he asks.

"'bout what?"

"Don't play dumb."

"Ain't playin'."

"Joey's on the run."

"From?"

"Everyone. It was just like you figured."

"I take it the EPA cracked open a barrel and found Rose."

"Yes—and Callie, too."

"Callie, too? Well—I'm not really surprised. Joey was so damned full of himself—it was all about him. The arrogant bastard."

"Yeah, the gun used to kill Elmo was right there in the open, hanging on a rack in his office. You read him like a book. Jano Tomaszewski, You are *brilliant*."

I grin, and it is a big one.

Did I tell you Dewey has that effect on me?

"You should get a helluva promotion over this one."

I laugh so hard, some of *Jimmie's* coffee spews out my nose. I'm glad it was not laced with *NyQuil*.

"What's so funny?" Dewey demands.

"Dewey, my name will never be mentioned in any report related to Joey."

"What!? No way."

"Sorry, but that's the *way* it is." I shrug and leak out a weary grin. "Not my jurisdiction—not my case. I'm more than glad for the Feds to take the credit."

"Damn." He looks seriously sad. "Is that any way for the system to treat the best detective I know?"

I beam from ear to ear. "Your praise is enough for me."

Dewey remains a little glum, so I motion for Earline to bring over a second cup of *Jimmie's* oil-based coffee, reach into my wallet, pull out a ten, and slide the bill toward him.

"Here's that five I owe you."

Dewey pockets the money and warmly smiles. I smile, too.

For me, Chicago's winter was definitely over.

DUCT MAN

MY BUTT IS REALLY SORE. I've been riding the "L" at least twelve hours a day, seven days a week, for three weeks looking for signs of Duct Man, Chicago's phantom vigilante. So far, my efforts have been a bust. All I've got to show for my work is a set of raging 'roids and an encyclopedic knowledge of all eight Chicago Transit Authority's commuter lines.

Oh yeah, and I've acquired something else— new friends. Like security guard Eddie Moocha. He's number one in the running to be the CTA's poster boy for 'How to blow a cop's undercover identity'. I've learned not to even blink in Eddie's direction or he'll blurt out something monumentally stupid like, "Good morning, Officer Thompson," or, "Hi, Jake. Any sign of the Duct Man?"

Whoever assigned him to assist me ought to be fired. Maybe they caved to Eddie's request to serve with me. The kid seems to be up on all the high points of my career. Fan or not, he is getting on my nerves.

So... What else have I learned?

A lot—like how the city I love is losing its flavor, being watered down—you know, going modern. Take my favorite example of bureaucratic groupthink—the Pink Line. Jeez—what sort of name is that?

At one time the "L" had authentic character. What was wrong with names like Ravenswood Line, Evanston Shuttle, and Skokie Swift? I go mad thinking some soulless idiot actually got paid to transform the Douglas Branch and the Paulina Connector into the Pink Line. Watered down? No—*dumbed* down is a better explanation.

Chicago sure ain't what it used to be. Any day now some talentless new-millennium wannabe will defile Carl Sandburg's memory with a poem entitled *Chicago: City of Padded Shoulders*.

Studs Terkel has to be spinning in his grave.

Me? I need to relax. I'm ranting. My blood pressure is up, and my 'roids are screaming like an operatic chorus. I get surly when I'm on an assignment that is more dead-end than usual. I'm a ticking bomb with a zero-tolerance trigger level.

I really need to put things in perspective.

Like any sizable city, Chicago has its ration of loonies and whack-jobs—Duct Man is this summer's goofball *du jour*. A couple of months ago, Duct Man materialized out of nowhere to intervene in a series of purse snatchings and muggings.

I've got to admit his MO is unique. What makes Duct Man stand out from the other weirdos is his proficiency in an unorthodox martial-arts technique—the use of duct tape to restrain the perps he encounters.

The eerie fact that despite a city-wide web of cameras, his work has not been recorded. Duct Man is a ghost.

Chicago PD's higher ups finally figured out that applying old fashion cop work is the only way to catch Duct Man. So, my unit has been assigned to find him. It was a win-win solution for the bosses. They could claim they had a special unit of cops on the job—AIU, and they also had the perfect patsies should their special effort fail. In any other life, we at AIU would never get close to a case with this much visibility.

Although it is officially known as the Administrative Investigations Unit, AIU is routinely tagged with a lot of impolite names—mainly, because we deserve them. AIU is where careers are buried and getting low percentage cases is standard. Everyone in the unit has screwed up their career in some way, especially me.

I'm within spitting distance of retirement—so why am I so out of joint over Duct Man? If I nab him, I could be a hero. But if I did, my batting average would still be below the Mendoza line.

Maybe I just need some rest. No—I know I need sack time. The attempt to snare Duct Man has required some strange hours.

Today, I'm getting off duty just as the morning commuter rush tails off. On the way off my last ride, I hoped I could dodge Eddie, but no such luck.

"See ya tomorrow, Detective Thompson—Jake?" Eddie asks.

My intent is to keep walking, but for some reason I stop. "No—no, Eddie. I'm bushed. I'm taking a day off—even if they fire me. I plan to sleep without setting an alarm."

"Sounds right, Jake—you look beat. See ya in a couple days, *partner.* Right?"

I look to the departing Red Line "L." Eddie waves and flashes a quick smile just as the doors close. My crust cracks and the professionally based animosity I held for the young man melts. The kid has soul.

I definitely need a rest.

And rest I did. I put the world on hold. Duct Man and AIU did not exist to this early-middle-aged burnout. I stumbled home, turned off the phone, passed on my usual glass of bourbon, and spent the next twenty-two hours in the rack. Without as much as a twitch, I slept as only the truly exhausted can.

The following morning, after a shower and a shave, I head to *Jimmie's Diner* for some breakfast. As I slide into my usual booth, Earline, my favorite waitress, pours a mug of the oily liquid Jimmie calls coffee, and slides me the *Tribune.*

"You boys missed him."

"Duct Man?" I reach into my jacket for my cheaters.

"Yep—he taped some scumbag pervert to a utility pole."

As I scan the article, Earline shares one of her pithy truths. "If you cops catch him, there'll be hell to pay. Duct Man is just catching bad guys. The public pays you cops to do what he's doing for free."

After weeks of no activity, Duct Man has appeared again. The *Trib's* headline lays it out:

COPS IN A BIND, CAN'T FIND DUCT MAN.

The front page above-the-fold article describes Duct Man's latest act of daring-do.

The synopsis: Duct Man, as always, appears out of nowhere. He is seen by several eyewitnesses, all giving the same description of the mysterious man who interrupts criminals in the act, disarms them, and apprehends them with liberal amounts of duct tape.

In this instance, an exhibitionist was in front of the Art Institute at dusk flashing his wiener. Not only did Duct Man detain the perp by securely fastening him to a pole, he cleaned up the criminal's X-rated image with a strategically applied portion of tape.

"Ouch!" I remark. "Adhesives and pubic hair. Earline, did you read this?"

"Yeah—and, if you ask me, the pervert got what was coming to him," Earline offers. "I'd love to be there when they yank the tape off his dork. I hope it was stuck to his pubes like *Super Glue*."

"There's probably a hundred whacko-liberal lawyers lined up to defend the guy. Lousy bottom feeders. They'll contort the law like a pretzel—protecting the poor baby's rights. You know how it goes. They'll claim his momma didn't breastfeed him long enough, or maybe she did it too long. Either way, I bet he's already hiding behind a bunch of lame-assed excuses."

"I don't get it. If that's so, why go after Duct Man? At least he did something. Duct Man got the creep off the streets, didn't he?"

"Earline, if I didn't know better, I'd swear you're a Duct Man fan."

"Damn right, I am. And if you weren't trying to find him, you'd be one, too. Jake, you're on the wrong side on this one."

I've long considered Earline to be an excellent thermometer of populist opinion. Day in, day out, she encountered people from varied walks of life and read them quicker and better than anyone I knew. My comeback to her position was weak and I knew it.

"Earline, it's my job. I've got to do what I'm told."

"Flimsy excuse, Jake. Didn't work at Nuremberg. Doesn't work here."

With that, Earline leaves me alone with the paper—and my thoughts.

What kind of man am I chasing? What motivates him? Can't be the fame—he's remained unidentified. How does he do that, I wonder? The city is teeming with video feeds, not to mention that almost everyone alive has a cell phone with a camera, yet no one has taken a clean pic of the guy.

Just thinking about Duct Man tires me out.

So, I decided to let one side of my brain rest and turn my attention to the sports news. I've learned that wallowing in the never-ending misery of being a Cubs' fan is therapeutic. After slapping the paper in disgust at least a half dozen times, I chuckle my way through the comics, and finally land on the crossword puzzle.

Earline takes it as her cue to return under the ruse of filling my coffee cup.

"I'm serious, Jake."

"Huh?" I say in that absent-minded manner men unconsciously use.

"Don't ignore me, Jake." She purposely spills some brew on my paper.

"Whoa!" I flinch. "What's this?"

"You *were* ignoring me."

"No—I wasn't."

"Yes, you were."

"Earline, I was doing the crossword. My thoughts were on a seven-letter word for sea siren."

She taps my soggy paper and says, "Try mermaid."

Before I can pencil in a letter, she lifts my chin with a coffee-laced finger and adds, "But don't try bullshitting this woman, Jake. You were ignoring me."

I know when I'm beat.

"This is about Duct Man, right?"

"Bingo! Jake, I always knew you were smart." She puts down the coffee pot and slides into the seat on the other side of the booth.

I hunker down. When Earline sits, you are in for a lecture. I drop the pencil and push my wet puzzle aside.

"Listen to me. The world needs heroes. Look around you, Jake." She waves about at the patrons in the diner. "Regular people like me and them. We shuffle to and fro, inside the boundaries of life—day in and day out. We hate our ordinary existence, and, all the while we're dreaming about busting loose. And, that's where the Duct Man comes in. Do you know why we love Duct Man?"

"No, but I believe I'm about to be told."

She launches a playful swipe across the booth. "I said you were smart, *not a smart-ass*."

"Sorry."

"You're that, too, but it's a topic for a different talk." She swipes again. "Now, listen up. I'm not going over this twice."

"I'm all ears."

She gets serious. "Jake, not only does Duct Man get rid of some of the creeps dirtying up the streets. *He gives us hope*."

"You gotta be kidding."

"Jake, it's simple. If Duct Man can do it, anyone can. That's the hope. He's our Robin Hood. And we all want to be just like him. Every one of us *little people* want to *do something* about the insanity going on around us. We want to act like Duct Man. But we can't."

"So... You want him to go free?"

"What's so wrong with that?"

"Never happen. The Powers That Be demand structure. They can't have independent agents roaming about screwing things up."

"Good will prevail—always does."

"Not in my world."

"Jake, you're wrong, and I think in your heart of hearts you agree with me."

I'm about to say something witty when my cell phone comes alive. I know it is work. No one else calls me.

"Sorry, Earline—I gotta take this." I flip open my phone. "Thompson here."

It is Dennis Gilbert, my supervisor—a three-pack-a-day smoker and a class-A boozer.

His raspy voice croaks, "Jake, I hope you love overtime. HQ is crazy over that idiot's last act. Get your butt in here. *Asap*!"

"On my way," I answer. To Earline I add, "Looks like Robin Hood is today's most wanted."

As I fumble with my wallet to pay my bill, Earline gives me a final shot.

"I'm serious—don't mess up the Duct Man. He's got the right stuff."

* * *

At AIU, Dennis gives me the bad news as he puffs on one cigarette and lights another.

"Duct Man is making the entire department look foolish. It's double shifts 'til he's caught. Jake, you're back on the rails. Start at Monroe Station."

"Why us—why *me*?" I whine. Whining doesn't work, but you know that.

"It's simple. AIU is officially ground zero, and we are expendable," he says between puffs.

"Great," I whine some more. "That explains why I feel like a media target wearing a day-glow bulls-eye."

"You got it—*when* Duct Man is caught, HQ gets the credit. If he skates, we take the heat. It won't be on the judicial system or, God forbid, any politician—it's on us."

"Yep, this case is way beyond us, Denny. By the way, you have two smokes going."

"Damn!" He stubs them out, and without thinking immediately starts a new one. "I've got more detectives to brief and assign. The brass have dumped every loose cop in the city into my lap. Now *scram.* Go catch a train. Better yet, go catch that pervert of justice."

"Whatever you say, fearless leader." I flip him a 'friendly' bird as I aim myself toward the CTA station nearest the site of Duct Man's latest offense.

With an attitude as low as my physical condition, every step on the way to 26 S. State is an effort. My 'roids are in full rebellion. And to make matters worse, when I get to the station, Eddie is waiting for me, lugging an all-purpose leather satchel I call a purse, but he insists is a man-bag. Add to that, he is all elbows and knees with oversized glasses and an ill-fitting CTA uniform—Eddie does not project an image that instills confidence.

I heavily frown at his presence. It reminds me of every boring wasted moment of my three weeks on the "L."

"Jake, you look terrible," Eddie informs me. "Worse even than the last time I saw you."

My attitude bottoms. With a pound of sarcasm, I lash out. "Thanks, Eddie. I *really* needed to hear that. Got any poison I can guzzle?"

I immediately regret my words. Eddie looks truthfully hurt. I suddenly realize that after Eddie had dutifully covered my back for three weeks, I had shared little with him. In fact, I had treated him quite badly. I can be tough, but I'm not heartless.

"I'm sorry, Eddie." I offer, "I guess this case is just getting to be too much for me."

"Gee, Jake, too much. How?" He has that little-whipped-puppy look.

So, I soften up—I lie. "Eddie... I may not show it, but I like you."

The kid beams. I keep it going. I'm a sucker for a beaming kid. Especially one who thinks I know what's what.

"You've been a real help these past weeks, and maybe I've not treated you as well as I could have. Let me explain—you know, let you in on things." He looks so happy I believe I could have sold him Navy Pier.

"I'm tired. With a good breeze behind me, I can spit and hit my retirement date. Soon, AIU will just be a bad memory and my lousy career will be over. I just wasn't ready for a nut-job like Duct Man to drag me down at the end."

Eddie looks puzzled. "Do you really think Duct Man's a nut-job?"

"What else could he be, Eddie?" I don't wait for an answer. "He's running around *playing* cop."

"He's helping—isn't he?"

"No way. He's a danger to himself *and* a bad example for the people he thinks he's helping."

"But someone has to act."

"Eddie, Duct Man is taking the law into his own hands. This isn't the Wild West—vigilantes are a thing of the past."

"But, he's catching bad guys." His puzzled look remains.

"Sure, he's caught some perps. But, look at them—all small timers. Not a one of them is a *real* bad guy."

"But—"

I interrupt. "Duct Man has caught a flasher here and a purse snatcher there. But what would happen if he—or anyone trying to be like him—came up against a thug packing an automatic or a psycho hacking away with a machete?"

"I don't know. I just don't—"

I interrupt him again.

"Right. You don't. Maybe that's why you weren't issued a piece." I place my hand on his shoulder and give him the best 'big brother' look I can muster. "Eddie, I've stared down the barrel of a gun. It isn't anything like in the movies."

My mind involuntarily races through the times I pulled my gun in the line of duty. It stuck on the one that ruined my career and exiled me to AIU.

"Violence—even just its threat—can be terribly ugly."

"But—"

"There are no buts. The streets are no place for an amateur."

"So, we leave it to the pros—like you?"

"Yes. And even they—we—have trouble handling it."

"Sounds like you know."

"I do, and I wish I didn't. I can't shake the image in my head. It's my maimed partner and a dead civilian, a female. Even though she had it coming, I will never get past the guilt in taking a life. And, the worst can come later, Eddie. I *know* all too well." My big-brother demeanor dissolves.

"I'm sure it wasn't your fault, Jake."

"Thanks, kid. Thanks."

The balance between us shifts. Eddie's expression holds me motionless. It is a mix of empathy, shared regret, caring, and much more. I feel there is a lot more to Eddie Moocha. I'm ashamed to have treated him so badly.

Turning away, I take a couple long strides, and mumble, "We should get moving."

By moving, my line of sight was all wrong. I did not see the gang of robbers rushing out of the bank's doorway and onto the sidewalk. One of the creeps bowls me over.

My head hits the concrete like a melon falling off a fruit cart. The other two trample my body. The last guy to step on me spots my holster, looks me over fast, figures out my profession, and yells, "Cop!" as I attempt to stand up.

Between the clanging of bells in my head and swearing, I hear Eddie's warning, "Jake! He's gonna shoot."

I lose track of Eddie. Is he behind me? Also, I don't know where the shooter is located. My head terribly aches. I'm disoriented. With great effort, I will myself up from the pavement.

I'm lucky—their first shot misses. Then, I am unlucky—a piece of it ricochets and finds me. My leg burns.

I ignore the pain in both my head and leg. I whirl about, hoping to spot the shooter. I reach for my piece.

Again, I was lucky—the shooter had turned to escape. He was not an immediate threat. Then, I got unlucky for a second time—his accomplices had unwittingly blocked his escape. The shooter drew strength from his companions and they from him. All were armed and in no mood to talk.

The trio faces me. I aim.

They do, too.

Out of nowhere, Eddie seemingly appears—limbs flailing, and yelling, "Jake, look out."

Shots are fired. My head explodes with pain.

With unfocused eyes, I blindly fall to the sidewalk again. Someone grabs the backup piece from my ankle holster—a *Seecamp* .25 cal. More shots are fired. My head fills with images of my last injured partner and a life of shamed exile in AIU.

Mercifully, I blacked out.

* * *

When I wake up, I smell Denny Gilbert before I see him. Stale tobacco and spilled scotch permeate the air of my hospital room. My boss is so proud that he wanted to be the first to congratulate me.

Denny looks like he has slept in his clothes longer than usual. My eyes are barely open when I learn everyone assumed I had taken down all three of the robbers. Before I could speak, Denny thrusts the newspaper at me to show the headlines.

"Look at this," he says as soon as he detects I am awake.

UNDERCOVER COP NAILS THREE IN FOILED ROBBERY

"Some piece of work, Jake," he beams like a new dad. "You're one helluva sharpshooter. Two guns— three perps. *Wow!*"

I give him a blank stare. He continues as if we are chatting over a cup of coffee at *Jimmie's Diner*.

"There's no chance you'll ever get transferred out of AIU, but you really did take the heat off the rest of us."

I make an attempt to focus on the front-page photo. Three chalk outlines of bodies are shown near the spot where I lost consciousness. My mind tries to process the information.

I hear my voice ask, "What happened to Eddie?"

"Eddie? Eddie who?" Denny asks.

"Eddie. The CTA guy you gave me."

"What are you talking about? You work alone. I didn't assign anyone to you."

For a second my head goes blank, and I'm sure it shows on my face. But I figure it out. Denny lives in an alcohol fog. He just didn't remember.

"You've been through a lot, Jake." He buzzes. "You need to rest—take as much time off as you want. Anything for an AIU hero."

Before I can ask another question, he rushes toward the door. The aroma of a thousand cigarettes and a gallon of booze trails behind him.

As he exits the room, Denny says, "We still can't find Duct Man, but who cares? I'm glad he's gone missing. Life's back to normal at AIU. We're back to chasing down lost school kids and purse snatchers. Damn! Life is good."

With the paper as my guide, I try my best to catch up on what I'd missed.

You can bet that a story, even as good as this one, will fade from the public's attention within a week. A shootout with three thieves leaving all of them dead has legs for a day—maybe two. My coma had lasted for almost eight days, so I missed the media buzz that placed me on the front page for the third time in my career.

The first time was for shooting my mouth off about shooting someone. For my politically incorrect views, I was painted as the world's most insensitive lout and exiled to AIU.

The second time, I located a missing urban legend known as Blind One-Legged Johnnie and unmasked his decades-long scam on the public. For that effort, I was pretty much ignored. The quirky lost-then-found street-person/artist became wildly popular. I stayed in AIU.

This time is different—I'm a hero.

But they got it all wrong and I did not deserve that bit of fleeting fame. It died as it should, and I did not care. Eddie was the hero.

As I lay in bed, I figure out what *really* happened. The first spill with me landing on the concrete produced a subdural hematoma and my week-long nap. It put my lights out, but I clearly remember firing my primary piece only twice while falling forward— right before losing consciousness.

The story, as I read it in the papers, gave me all the credit. But I knew Eddie had to have done most of the shooting—the effective part. He must have been the one who grabbed my ankle piece.

My leg twitches. The stray bullet that found me stung like hell when it happened, but it is no big deal. The twitch is me healing. Then it hits me. Me. *Me?* Everything in the account is about me. What the hell happened to *Eddie?* With the speed of light, my left brain begins talking to the right, and pieces of the puzzle fall into place. The clues are all there. All I had to do was see them.

In a couple days, when I was given a clean bill of health and the okay to head home, I pretty much had it figured out. When I put on my clothes and gathered the items from the closet in my room, I had the definite proof in my hand in the form of Eddie's man bag. One peek inside the satchel was all I needed.

Finding Eddie wasn't going to be difficult. I couldn't wait to hit the streets.

Let me explain. Duct Man first appeared late in June. It took a couple weeks for both the media and the public to latch on to him. By the way, Earline was dead-on with her call. Regular folks saw him as a modern Robin Hood. News hounds viewed him as a loose cannon vigilante but a great story, nonetheless.

By the time AIU was put on his trail, I clocked almost a month on my keister, got winged, knocked silly and released, we had burned through most of Chicago's summer.

So, what does all this mean? Not much—unless you have Denny's comments to chew on. When finished, I spit out a plan of action.

My first stop is the CTA's Security Office and, as I expect, there are no records of an Edward, Eddie, or Ed Moocha. I ask around, describing my *faux* partner, draw a lot of blank stares, but keep pushing my face in front of people.

I finally catch a break when an old timer agrees to my suggestion that I scan the parking lot's video system.

"Good thinking. If anyone like you described was around here, he had to get a hold of a badge, ID, and a uniform somehow. Maybe one of the surveillance cameras picked up something," the grizzled veteran tells me.

It isn't much, but it's a lead.

* * *

My butt is sore again. But that's to be expected after two days parked in front of a video screen, eye-balling the comings and goings of a parking lot. I'm not complaining. If this was supposed to be easy, someone other than me would be on it.

So far what I've learned is, the world of Big Brother is not as airtight as imagined.

Like any other system relying on humans to maintain and manage it, the CTA security system is merely adequate in design and borderline effective in performance.

The camera angles are less than optimal, due to improper installation. The recorded quality is poor from using lowest-bidder equipment. Storage/retrieval of tapes is problematic because of bureaucratic inattention and mismanagement.

But, all-in-all, my effort was a success because I'm an old fashion cop who grinds and grinds on a case and never quits. I was about forty-eight hours into my effort when the image I looked for appeared.

There he was. Skinny as a rail, all elbows and knees, getting out of a tiny foreign model hatchback and heading into the building. He's in uniform, but not the CTA getup I had known as his.

"Damn!" I say as I catch sight of a familiar decal on the windshield of his car. "I should have guessed that a guy latching on to me like he did would come from my home turf."

Before I can see more of his activities—like how he purloined a badge and the other security goodies—the video screen turned into flitting snow and static. All efforts to fix or explain the glitch fail. For some reason, the cameras quit working. I wish I knew more but believe I have enough.

"Looks like I'm in for a visit to my high school alma mater," I tell myself as I leave the CTA head-quarters behind and head to the Southside campus of Brother Rice high school where I had played football, learned to box, and drove a bus wearing the same uni-form I saw on the video.

"Eddie the bus driver has a load of explaining to do," I mutter to myself.

Eddie looks ready to come clean when he greets me after parking his bus in the school's lot.

"You look pretty healthy, Jake." He shakes my hand and eyes what I'm carrying. He looks relieved. "Sorry I didn't visit you in the hospital."

"No problem, kid." I give his satchel back to him, "It's a little light. I disabled that cute little jamming device by removing a part or two. It was a brilliant way to disable surveillance cameras."

"Thanks," he briefly flashes a tiny mischievous smile. "If found, I guess it could be seen as incriminating evidence."

"Yeah, but not as much as this." I toss a roll of duct tape his way. Eddie catches it and immediately places it in the satchel. There is not a trace of even the slightest of smiles on his face.

Instead, Eddie Moocha, bus driver, and the wannabe vigilante known as Duct Man, projects a well-pronounced aura of grim seriousness.

"It's all behind me, Jake."

"I know."

"Damn, Jake," he blurts out while trying to hold back tears. "I'm all tied up inside. I-I-I—"

"Killing three men—*even to protect your partner* will do that."

"So... You're here to arrest me?"

"No. I'm here just to say thanks... And to see if you are alright."

"Really?"

"And also, to tell you to ditch the purse."

"Say what?"

"Yeah, Duct Man—sporting a purse doesn't look very hero-like."

CHEESE CAKE

JIMMIE'S DINER HAS A FEEL all its own. The worn wood and patched pseudo-leather of the booths catch and hold smells in a manner all their own; just as the counter tops, windows, and walls bounce and echo sound like no other space occupied by humans. Toss in Jimmie's clientele, and you have an urban martini mixed by God in his favorite dented shaker.

I know what you're thinking, "Jake, every joint is special to its regulars."

That may be true. But what does truth have to do with the atmosphere at *Jimmie's*? Everything, I suppose. Nobody comes to *Jimmie's* for the food.

It was noon on a Tuesday in June. I was finishing breakfast and just about to ease into my day. I was deep into the *Trib*'s daily whine on why the Cubs perpetually fail (winning a series was a one-off) when the atmosphere in Jimmie's changed.

The temperature rose, yokes broke on an over-easy order, Earline dropped a cup of joe—and I caught a whiff of her.

In an instant, I was a couple of decades into my past.

"Same perfume," I whisper. Peeking over the top of my paper. I add, "Long time no see," just as she slides into the opposite side of my booth.

"Yes," she purrs. "It has been a long time—too long, Jano." She flips back her hair and wiggles away from a fur jacket that cost more than I could drink in a decade.

Dropping the *Trib*, I shoot her way my best 'I'm doing fine' look, and say, "A bit warm for that rig."

She ignores the bait, and smiling ever so slightly, replies with that look—the one that melted me back in the days we were 'a thing'.

I ask, "Did your limo break down somewhere nearby?"

She drops the look and mimics a hurt little girl frown. "Fair enough," she sighs. "It was worth a try. Right, Jano?"

"Depends on the intent," I say, noting her second use of the familiar form of my other name. It was a bit of a joke with my intimates, to use the diminutive of my dad's handle. I was Jake to the world and Jano only to them.

And now, after years of forgetting her, she is in my space again. I inspected her and enjoyed the effort. The light in *Jimmie's* would not flatter even a saint. But in this instance, flattery is not required.

She knows I am studying her. She does not mind. She enjoys it. Probably expected it, too.

Ashley Morant is accustomed to being watched. Attention is the companion of the rich and beautiful. It comes with being one of the blessed who have won the gene-pool lottery.

More than two decades had passed since we last shared space. And the years had been good to her— the years, success, and a whole lot of money. She had escaped my planet and was now an alien. Hers was a world of red carpets, spas, and personal trainers. She lived "the good life" in a place full of wonderful things—the kind of things a cop like me knows about but can't afford.

Yes, she was an alien from a different universe— one without a Southside.

We sit in silent awkwardness until, Earline, my favorite waitress, stops hovering and thank- fully breaches the edge of Ashley Morant's celebrity awe-bubble. With a fresh cup and a pot of Jimmie's oil-based coffee Earline asks, "Can I get you some- thing, Ms. Morant?"

Without making eye contact, my companion con- sents to being served. Only royalty and residents of the awe-bubble have that ability.

"You're my favorite you know—you really are," Earline offers, along with the cup of joe, cream, and the hint of a bow.

A simple "Thank you," is the reply. The Queen has spoken.

With reverence, Earline half-says, half-whis- pers, "You really are—your female adventurer in *Night of the Ghost* was so much better than any of *Super Woman*, or the others. And, you were so *real* as

Madame Clarice in *The Countess Returns*. You should have won the Oscar. It was a shame. I cried, you know? I just.... Just..." She drifts into that space between the demi-gods and fans—where worship takes place.

"I am retired from all that," says Her Highness to the pleb.

"Oh, no," gushes Earline, "*No!*"

The woman I knew in my youth as JoAnn Parello is gracious. After scanning Earline's name tag, she quickly produces a pad from her clutch purse, pens a note, and signs it. She gives it to Earline with a smile.

Earline is impressed into silence. And clutching the note as if it were a precious gem, she floats toward the wait station, where her equally awe-struck plebeian peers huddle and gawk. Faint murmurs of, "Ah" and "Oh, my" drift into the ether.

I say to my booth mate, "You're not the usual type they see in here."

"I know."

"And you are most certainly the last person they'd expect to visit *me*."

She smiles and returns to her alien-silent world.

I take the initiative. "So—what's the occasion? You aren't here for the menu selection."

"Jake, it's good to know you haven't changed. Always did cut straight to the point."

I notice she had stopped calling me Jano. Simultaneously, I feel good and bad.

She sniffs the coffee. "Is this good?"

"No—it's terrible," I warn.

She takes a sip and frowns.

"Told you."

"But you drink it."

"Only with some of this." I produce a small flask and doctor her cup with a liberal amount of Old Jimmy Jack, my signature mixture of the three bourbons.

She sips again, grimaces, and pushes the cup to the center of the table.

"It's still ghastly."

"Like I said—you didn't come here for the refreshments."

The buzz at the wait-station grows, so I push her to explain her presence among the lowly. "Get to the point, or prepare for a lengthy autograph session."

She nods understanding and points toward the door. "My car is right outside."

I quip in my best smart-ass voice, "So, it *did* break down."

She frowns and means it. "Jake—Please. I need your help."

In a single exaggerated motion, I exit the booth, sweep her upward, grab her fur, toss a ten on the table, and move us toward the exit. The diner erupts, and we make it outside just as the throng of fans disguised as wait staff jam into the doorway behind us.

"There's my car," she says, pointing to the only limo in sight.

"Can't be mine," I say.

She waves to the driver. I toss her the jacket, and more than gently, guide her away from *Jimmie's*. We jump into the rear seats of her ride and are out of sight in seconds.

Within the limo's confines, our knees touch and her perfume once again ignites memories long suppressed. I am catapulted into the past and, for a few moments, I am Jano once again.

* * *

We had met the summer after high school, and for a short time were inseparable. Everyone assumed we would marry. We did, too, but we never really spoke about the specifics. Looking back, I clearly see it was never meant to happen.

People assume too much.

We wanted different lives. It was as simple as that.

I am jerked back to the present by the ring of the limo's intercom. She answers the call.

"Where to?" She looks to me.

I shrug. "It's your limo."

"Take us to Grant Park," she instructs the driver. "We'll find a place to stop." She looks to me again. "We can take a walk... If you like."

"Okay," I say.

"You will help me—won't you?"

"Why—after all these years. Why did you look me up?"

"Oh, Jake. I need help—*your* help."

"Go on. Tell me about it."

"Again, straight to the point. That's good—that's the Jake I knew. You *really* haven't changed. I was counting on that. I was told otherwise... That you'd... Well... That..." She pauses in that place where the speaker wants you to fill in and tell all—to do their dirty work.

I say nothing.

In the second awkward silence of our reunion, I look her over again—this time with my cop's eye. Her good looks—the clothes, jewelry, the image— they hide the obvious. She is tired and at the edge of her limits.

Whatever drove her back into my life had to be nasty.

At Grant Park we get out to walk.

A few steps from the car I ask, "The trouble you are in—is it really so bad that you need my help?"

"Yes," she says without hesitation. "It's the kind of thing that needs a man like you."

"Like me?"

"Yes."

"What kind is that?"

"Direct... Street wise... And—"

"And?"

"And... Well... Discreet."

"I see."

"I knew you would."

"I take it that you don't want your current husband—whatever number he is—to know."

"Oh no—Jake, you've got it wrong. Wayne—Wayne Carter, my husband—he knows all about this. In fact, it was his suggestion that I talk to you. Wayne has friends and resources, but not the right sort."

"He sent you to me? Wayne? Number... What is it?"

"Three—he's my third husband."

"Just three? I could have sworn that it was more—like five or maybe... Six. Are you sure he's just number three?"

"Jake, stop it. I'm not in the mood for your brand of humor."

"But... You want my brand of help?"

"Yes."

"Well, it comes with the humor—it's part of my brand."

That began our third period of awkward silence. We walk some way before she speaks again.

When she does, it is to explain the photos of the girl. "Here," she says. Handing me three shots of an attractive, well-groomed, expensively dressed teenager—a miniature Ashley Morant. "Jake, this is Whitney, my daughter—she's missing."

I look at the pictures. "Your daughter? Not an ours? I mean you and Number Three's?"

"Yes—mine, not mine and Wayne's. But Wayne has adopted Whitney. Her biological father is... Was Jacque Roushard, the artist. He's... He's no longer in the picture. Jacque is not a part of either of our lives."

"Dead?"

"As good as."

"Meaning?"

"He's on permanent retreat... In Southeast Asia. He became a Buddhist monk."

"I can understand that. You have that effect on men."

She looks at me knowing more would come. I give it to her. "After you—I thought about becoming a monk. But I turned to drink instead."

"Jake—*please*!"

I grin and say, "I told you—the humor is part of the package."

Instead of beginning our fourth silent stretch, my grin gets her to open up.

It must have been a sight—even better than her waltzing into *Jimmie's* and sitting at my booth. For half an hour, we strolled back and forth—the burnt-out cop and the movie star. When it was over, she was less tense, drawn back from her ledge, and I had learned all I needed to know about the disappearance of her daughter.

"Jake, I am counting on you."

"I'll do my best."

"Please, Jake, find my Whitney. Kids today—they're not like we were. The drugs—pressures... Everything—it's so much. She's been gone two days. And it is killing me to think what she may be doing."

"I'll do what I can."

"They said you could find her."

"*They?*"

"Wayne has contacts—I told you. They said you were the best. Wayne's friends said that even though you were banished, or something like that—they said you had an excellent reputation for getting things done. You know, with the real police—the guys on the street—not the politicians and the phonies."

"That's nice to know."

"Jake, is it true? Have you been placed in some type of exile?"

"Yes. But, it's a long story—one I am not about to share."

We are back at her car and she makes all the signs necessary for me know it is time to part. I ask for a number where I can reach her. Again, I give her more assurances I will do everything possible to find her daughter.

"I'll drop you wherever you want," she offers.

"No—I need to walk," I tell her. "Besides, leaving the diner in a limo was a necessity, but coming back in one is... Just... Well... It's not me."

She fully understands. I am sad that she does, but I rally. "Sorry, but you're really not my type," I quip.

"Jake, you really haven't changed."

"I can't."

For her exit, she leans close to land a perfume-laden peck on my cheek. I wave goodbye and head back to *Jimmie's*, taking the long route.

I had work to do. I made my calls to friends on the force, some others, and I stopped along the way at spots that reminded me of better days—and her.

* * *

Back at the diner, I am received with an unexpected coldness. I was to learn I had let people down.

"I can't believe you, Jake," accuses Earline. "All this time you've known Ashley Morant and you never let on—even to me?" Her hurt is deep and real.

"The subject never came up."

"Never came up? Jake, are you crazy? How many times haven't I told you about me watching all of her movies—or seeing her picture in a magazine? Why, it was not that long ago I told you about her moving to Chicago—when she starred in that play at

Steppenwolf—remember? I'm her biggest fan. When she walked in here, I almost fainted. And then... I lost it when she went straight for you. You *know* I am her biggest fan. Really. Jake, how could *you*!?" She stomps back to her usual spot at the end of the main counter.

I do not respond. What can you say to the star-struck?

Earline stays at her spot and refuses to look in my direction. After waiting for what seemed an eternity, I get up to fetch my own coffee. When I reach the wait station, she relents and comes over to speak to me.

"If Jimmie sees you doing that, he'll scream."

"Let him scream. I'll explain. I'll fill him in how I ruined your life."

Earline replies with an elbow to my ribs. "You have to tell me, Jake. How do you know her? How do you know somebody like Ashley Morant?"

I draw in a deep breath, hold it, and then exhale. "It's no big deal—we were together a while... As a couple."

Earline clutches my arm and cries out, "No *way*."

Everyone in the diner stares at us. I try to peel her off me.

"Easy, Earline. You are getting scary."

"Jake—*you*? And *her*?"

"Yes—but it was long ago."

"I don't believe it."

"What's to believe?"

"Jake, Ashley Morant is the last person I'd ever expect to walk in to see you."

I laugh as I say, "That's what I told JoAnn."

"Who?"

"Ashley Morant."

"Huh?"

"I knew her before she became Ashley. Her real name is JoAnn Parello."

"Impossible. She's a genuine California girl. I know all about her and—"

"Earline, you've got to stop believing what you read in those magazines."

Thankfully, my phone ends our chat.

An old friend is calling, and if I am lucky, I will soon have something to hang my case upon.

* * *

Larry Wesselhoff and me go back a long way— junior high, high school, and Babe Ruth League baseball. Larry was an in-the-zone lefty with a mean curve and an absolutely filthy change up. But catching for him was an up-and-down affair. When his control was on, he was unhittable. If not, he was a nightmare of walks, wild pitches, and hit batters.

We dreamed of being the opening day battery at Wrigley but lost touch for some years after finishing high school. We renewed our friendship as rookies at the police academy and kept close on the force while still bleeding for our beloved Cubs. What did you expect from two Southside traitors who turned their backs on the White Sox?

Like me, Larry did some solo patrol work and earned his way into plainclothes. Later, he split his career between the vice squad and narcotics. Larry knew more about Chicago's dark side than anyone I could imagine. When he returned my call, I soaked in very word he said.

"Jake, your lost little lamb ain't lost and she didn't stray far from home. I ran what you gave me against my database and got an instant hit. That high-priced prep school of hers has been on the watch list for some time. I know where she is and what she's doing."

"Fill me in."

"Shoreline Prep serves the upscale types living on and near the Miracle Mile."

"Pricey neighborhood—full of rich and powerful families."

"Yeah. And their kids have to spend the daytime hours somewhere. Shoreline is not much more than a high-price daycare—and doing a pretty poor job, I might add. In our day it was alcohol, now its drugs—a lot of them are hardcore. The school and its clientele see a good amount of action."

"Hence the watch list."

"Right. Over-sized allowances and too much free time."

"Larboy, I'm a little surprised that you'd be on it. Are preppies an endangered species?"

"Things have heated up, Jake. There's a new drug of choice in town and the spoiled brats from that part of town have latched on to it in a big way. Cheese is a real problem."

"Cheese?"

"Yes, Cheese—a potentially lethal mix of heroin and crushed *Tylenol PM*—snorted, not shot. The acetaminophen tones 'em down after the heroin does its thing."

"What will they think of next?"

"You name it—they're smoking bath salts in Dallas."

"*What!?*"

"You heard me—and flavored weed is on the horizon—genetically engineered. Pretty soon you'll be able to pick a flavor and scent as you mellow out."

"Makes those beer parties we had look tame."

"Sure does. In the meantime, Cheese is keeping us busy. Plenty of kids have overdosed—several cashed in. That's why it's on my list of to-dos."

"You said my lost lamb was on your radar."

"Yes. I'm two hundred percent certain Whitney Morant is in one of the surveillance pics we have on file for the dirt-bag running junk in her circle. We tag 'em by the nicknames they sling while playing at being tough street kids. I've got a Momma Whit Mo' who fits the description you shared. I'll send it to you for verification—also one of the charming guys she's been seen with."

"Momma Whit Mo'?" I laugh. "That handle certainly makes Whitney Morant sound upper crust."

He sends the pics to my phone, and I confirm it is Whitney. "That's her alright."

"Her folks have reason to worry." Larry replies. "She's in over her head—running with Dirt Dawg DuWayne."

"Dirt Dog what?" I look at the second picture.

"It's Dawg, Jake. Spelled D-A-W-G. He's the nutcase peddling the Cheese. Thinks he's a gangsta rapper. When he is performing—if that's what you call it—his name is supposed to be cut down to simply Three-D."

"Catchy handle." I study the second photo Larry had sent. "Ugliest sucker I've seen in a long time."

"He does have a following." His tone tells me there's more.

"And?"

"He harvests girls from the preppy crowd he sells Cheese to—likes to have a stable of them around at all times."

"And Momma Whit Mo is one of them?"

"Bet my paycheck on it—yours, too." The tone is still there.

"And?"

"Pimps them after their allowance money runs out."

"I suspect that if she is with him, she's in deep—and headed deeper. Anything else I should know?"

"Yep—but I can't it say on this line," he almost whispers.

"Fine. I know what to do—give me a minute."

I make my way to one of the last decent pay phones in Chicago. There aren't many left like the one Jimmie stubbornly holds on to. It was my need for a phone in an enclosed booth that brought me to his diner years ago. Maybe that's why I like the place so much.

I call Larry's private cell phone. He answers and starts without a greeting.

"This is strictly between you and me. I'm hanging my ass out by telling you this, but since you never muffed a ball I tossed your way..." He pauses, then remarks, "I should have recognized Momma Whit Mo' right away. Remember, I knew her mother before she was famous, too. *Damn*! I must be getting old."

"We both are—but from what I saw today, one of our old gang has found the fountain of youth."

"Did it bring back any of the old feelings?"

"Nope."

"Liar."

"Larboy, you are getting old, and your memory isn't worth squat—you were going to share some state secrets, remember? Don't you trust me anymore?"

"I know I can trust you, Jake. Growing up together has its benefits."

"Go ahead—I'll keep mum."

"Okay—Three-D is untouchable."

"What? How?"

"DEA has put a hold on any actions against him."

"DEA? What's their interest?"

"Word is, he's negotiating a deal. The feds think he'll name his upstream suppliers."

"So... He's free to stay in business?"

"Basically, yes."

"Damn! You mean—"

"Yep. His deals are watched but not stopped."

"And... The..."

"The pimping? Yes. It still goes on."

"*Mother of God*. You mean to tell me he's selling lethal heroin and peddling under-aged girls with government approval?"

"Exactly... And the worst of it is his suppliers are already known. There's nothing new coming to us if we wait for him to conclude a deal. We don't need his info."

"So why not bust him?"

"We can't."

"*Can't*? There isn't any *can't* in police work."

"It's a turf war. You know the politics, Jake."

"Screw the politics."

"I figured you'd say that." He has that tone again.

"What are you telling me?" I have a good idea where he is headed, but I want him to say so.

"Jake, you never were any good at coloring inside the lines."

"You know as well as anyone that I've sent signals for a bean ball or two—what of it?"

"Call it for what you like—I can't pitch anything to Three-D."

I was right. I knew exactly what he meant. His hands were tied, but...

"You can't, but I can."

He laughs. "Jake, we never had this conversation—and I never heard you say what I know you are about to tell me." His laughter becomes uncontrollable. I wait as long as I possibly can.

Cops like Larry seldom get to let it go in the way he was experiencing that moment. I wanted my friend to enjoy the situation as much as possible.

Finally, I say, "Of course, this is all speculation, Larboy. You would be forced to sit back and allow events to transpire... Should say... Some rogue cop... On an unrelated investigation... Waltz in on Three-D... And execute a clean bust for... Let's say... Something like... Harboring a missing teen?"

"Oh-oh-oh-*Jano*!"

It was good—and a sign—that I heard my old name again in one day.

"Yes?" I say in my best sneaky childish voice.

"Oh, my. It would be a tragedy for the DEA and their plans. But, yes. It would be beyond my control."

"Oops," I snicker. "Jano has been resurrected."

"God, *how I love you, man.*" He snorts more laughter and almost convulses.

"Just do me one favor, Larboy."

"Sure—anything."

"Make certain the surveillance equipment malfunctions this evening. I definitely foresee a visitor in Mister Three-D's future."

Between his gasps for air, I hear my old friend's continued pleasure. "Oh-oh-oh, *Jake.* You are my hero. Jeez, how I miss having you around. It's such a shame the department stuck you in that useless backwater."

"Thanks, Larboy," I say. "Just watch my back—and don't record anything. I may be sentenced to spend the rest of my career on worthless cases in AIU, but I am not crazy about answering to internal affairs for every move I make."

He closes our conversation with assurance. "Jake, don't worry about a thing."

Despite what Larry said, I did worry. Things go wrong—they always do.

My career and life had been derailed by past events when I was naïve and assumed too much. I was exiled to the Administrative Investigation Unit in an act of open-ended punishment to teach me a lesson and serve as an example.

That is why I contacted Eddie Moocha, to borrow the rig he had used to neutralize Chicago's complex surveillance system when he captivated the city as Duct Man.

Eddie, the self-appointed people's vigilante, owed me a favor and it was time to collect.

* * *

"It's all set, Jake," Eddie tells me. "Just flip the switch and you'll be as good as invisible."

I adjust the cinch of the fanny-pack to fit my waist and shake his hand. "Thanks, Eddie. I appreciate the help."

"You sure you want to do this alone?"

"This is my deal."

"I'm more than willing to go along." He grins and winks. "I brought a roll of duct tape—just in case."

I laugh. "I don't think the city is ready for you to come out of retirement, Eddie. Matter of fact, I doubt if any spot in the world is ready. You better stay below the radar."

"It was worth a shot." He flashes his empty hands. "I was just funning. Good luck."

I wave goodbye and drive to Lakeview Condos where I know I'll find what I'm looking for.

* * *

The intel provided by Larry was spot on. 3-D was in his lair and in the company of Momma Whit Mo' and an array of prep-school druggies—that was easy to confirm.

After strolling through the lobby, I step before the building's security desk.

"Hey, Kenny," I say. "Long time, no see."

"Jake!" comes from the man behind the desk. He points to a small TV monitor. "I thought it was you—but the picture went fuzzy. See?"

I peer over the counter. Eddie's contraption is working perfectly. I had switched it on before I entered the building. The monitor's screen jumped with static.

"How you been, Kenny?"

In my early days on patrol duty in uniform, I knew Kenny Evans as a highly respected senior patrolman. He was old school and a great role model. Kenny carried the nicks and dings of thirty years in uniform—along with a pile of commendations. I was both pleased and surprised to see him.

"Is this your retirement gig?"

"Yes and no," he replies. I know an explanation is coming, so I wait.

Kenny bangs the monitor a couple of times, curses it, and then fills me in on why and how he came to be there.

"Wesselhoff looked me up a couple of weeks ago—said the Feds were monkeying with his case on the scumbag in One-C. I naturally said 'yes' when he asked me to help out. I fit the bill for the sort of guy this place would hire for the desk—retired ex-cop—you know."

"And, you were probably itching to get back into harness—right?"

He laughs. "Was I ever. Couldn't get into gardening or yard work, can't stand golf, too old and poor for chasing skirts—retirement sucks."

"So, you took Larry's offer to get back in the game."

"Damn right. I may be slower than in my prime, but I've got good eyes. Been keeping a tab on the doin's around here." He shows me a surveillance notebook. "If the Feds ever let go, this and the videos will send some folks away for close to forever."

I points at his notes. "Is the object of your affection in?"

"Yep. And he's got the usual herd of snot-nosed punks with him."

I show him Whitney's pic and ask, "She in the bunch?"

"Yep. Front and center."

"Just point me to One-C."

He points down the hall. "Last unit—you can't miss it. Playin' that crap music of his all the time.

"Lovely. A sound track."

"I take it that you're going in?"

"Right."

"Wesselhoff know about it?"

"Yes... And under oath, no." I grin.

"I see." He smiles broadly, tosses the notebook in a drawer and says, "I'm stepping outside for a smoke. With the cameras on the fritz and me being outside—I can swear I never saw you come in."

"Thanks, Kenny. This shouldn't take long."

"Going to snatch the girl and blow the case wide open?"

"Something like that."

"Figures. I'll give you five minutes—then I'm in here as backup. Say the word and I'm at the door with this." He pulls back his jacket to reveal he is carrying. "If I see anything or hear gun play, I'm in sooner."

"Fine, Kenny," I say. "It means a lot."

We share one of those awkward moments—the kind tough guys never admit having.

"Sure, kid," he says. "I always said you had grit." He makes for the door. "Clock's running, Jake. Good luck."

* * *

The music, or more correctly, the noise, gets louder as I approach the door to 1-C. I knock *loud*.

Getting no response—I bang on the door with my fist until I hear shuffling inside.

"Who's there?" comes weakly from a female throat.

"Pizza," I reply.

"Oh... Okay..."

There is some inaudible mumbling, more shuffling, and the sound of the lock being moved.

I tense up a bit.

When the sounds tell me the door is unlocked, I say to myself, *Here goes,* and shove hard. The door swings all the way open, pushing a girl of maybe fifteen against the wall.

"Wha... Wha... Wha... What da?" she mumbles.

I check her out as she slides to the floor. The girl is incapable of responding. Her eyes roll back. I check her vitals. She is in serious trouble.

"This mouse has had too much Cheese," I say.

I pull her into the hallway and leave her there. I know Kenny will see her and send for help. My focus is back on what's inside the condo.

"How many more?" I ask myself.

The answer comes quick. I make my way inside the condo to the hallway's end and enter a single great room full of drugged-up bodies. Strewn about sofas, stuffed chairs, and the floor are a dozen or more kids—mostly girls. Like the one I already encountered, they all appear to be on the downside of the drug's effects.

In the center of the room, a glass-topped coffee table serves as their altar of pleasure. It is littered with opened packets of Cheese.

I scan the group but do not recognize Whitney as one of them.

"Partying's over," I say in a loud voice. No one stirs.

I know Kenny will arrive soon, so I push on. The noise that impersonates music comes from a second hallway off the backside of the great room and my instincts tell me I will find 3-D and Whitney there.

The hall has one door at its end, obviously leading to a master suite. That's where I head.

"Knock, knock!" I shout, bursting through the door.

3-D is caught totally off guard and literally with his pants down.

"Wha' da—?!" he yells, jumping from the bed.

Whitney Morant remains prone with her schoolgirl skirt flipped up to her waist. She is almost unconscious.

"Sorry to interrupt, but you're under arrest."

"Who da' fugg are you?" he screams. "You can't touch me. I got 'munity."

"Not from me."

He pulls up his pants and comes toward me, still screaming. "You can't—you can't."

Although 3-D was somewhere in his mid-twenties, and should have had the edge on me, he must have been a nerd or wimp as a kid. He looked more *Sesame Street* than gangsta rapper.

The punch he tossed was third rate and off mark. I dropped him with one quick counter jab. As soon as he hit the floor, I attended to Whitney.

Her breathing was shallow, and her eyes were rolled back. She was drugged heavier than the girl at the door. I adjusted her skirt for modesty and was about to lift her off the bed when 3-D came to.

"Damn," I mutter. "Should have cuffed you right away."

3-D makes an attempt to stand. "I told you, man—I got 'munity. No cop's supposed to touch me. I made a deal."

"And I told you—I don't care." I grab his scrawny neck and shove him toward a dresser. "You know the drill—hands down flat and spread your feet."

He starts to comply when I hear a moan from behind.

Whitney had tried to get off the bed but failed. The moan was her hitting the floor. I should not have cared, and I should not have looked.

3-D uses the distraction as his chance to move on me. Instead of placing his hands on the dresser's counter, he goes for an automatic in the top drawer. My back is turned. I am the perfect target.

In quick succession, he fires two rounds.

Gunfire in a confined space can be deafening— but I'll take the noise over bullets smashing into an electronic device strapped to my ass any day. Sparks, battery acid, and bits and pieces of the jamming device flew in every direction.

I wail in pain and swear, *"Damn it!"*

3-D had used the fanny pack as the center point of his targeting. Eddie Moocha's gizmo saved my bacon—literally. 3-D was as confused as I was mad. He was also startled enough to halt firing.

That was his mistake and my opportunity.

I quickly regain the initiative.

I am pissed—as much for my error in not securing a collar as I was with him shooting me. I ignore the pain, spin around, knock the gun away, and land a vicious punch to his face.

3-D folds like a lawn chair at a church picnic. Going down, his head tips my way and I put a second fist in his path. It wasn't necessary, but it makes me feel good. The third and fourth blows make me feel even better.

My ass is aflame with all sorts of debris, so I feel justified in completing my arrest in an aggressive fashion.

To avoid another surprise, I cuff him wrist to ankle, and make certain the cuffs are tight—very tight.

"I hope your circulation is cut off," I say to the unconscious form at my feet. "Serves you right for assaulting a cop." I yell while landing a slightly more than playful kick in his midsection.

Like I said—I was mad.

"Whoa, *Jake*! Oh-oh-oh! Where... Are you?" It is my backup, puffing and breathing hard. "Whooow! I-I-I-" Kenny fights to catch his breath and finally asks, "Jake, are you, okay?"

"Easy, Kenny. Fun's over. I'm fine—just dinged a little."

"Damn, Jake. You know how to get an old man moving. When I saw the body in the hallway, I came running—sprinted through the mess outside when I heard the shots." He bends over to inspect 3-D. "I see you nailed him good."

"Had to—the little son-of-a-bitch shot me."

Kenny spins around my side to take a look. "How bad is it?"

"Can't tell for sure, but I know I'm lucky. He hit this thing I'm wearing—splattered pieces of it into my flesh—stings like hell."

Kenny peels back the remains of the fanny pack, inspects my back and side, and grimaces. "Looks messy. But you're lucky, Jake. One round grazed you and another never made it through whatever you had strapped in there—looks like junk. What is it?"

"A jamming device."

"A what?"

"Friend of mine's rig—guaranteed to block out surveillance cameras. It's the source of your static."

"Damn, Jake. You think of everything."

"Not hardly. If I *had* thought of everything, I wouldn't have been shot."

Whitney moans again and Kenny stoops to check her out. I begin to feel faint and tenderly sit on the edge of the bed.

"She's in need of help. We better get—" Kenny halts for a moment at the sound of reinforcements arriving in the condo. "I called Wesselhoff—must be him. Let's get you and this girl medical attention."

I vaguely remember telling him to look after Whitney.

"Kenny, she's why I came—give her special handling," I mumbled. Then, I passed out.

The second bullet had more than grazed me.

In the heat of the moment, I was unaware of how much blood was tricking down my side. My wailing on 3-D had aggravated the flow, and for me the lights went out.

Luckily, I missed all the hoopla associated with the bust.

* * *

The Feds raised hell. To them I was an "off-the-reservation rogue gunslinger". Their mixed metaphor using an Indian-cowboy description made me laugh when I heard it in the hospital a couple of days later.

"You are definitely *persona non grata* in the federal building, Jake." Larry Wesselhoff chuckles. "They hate it when their plans are blown. Shame on you."

"*Screw them*," I offer from my hospital bed. "You were there. That condo was a hell hole. And they *let it* exist. I'm more than happy to muck up their case."

"The media agrees with you. Jake, you are a hero in their eyes. The *Trib* actually did a real nice piece on you."

"Screw them, too. If it had gone down bad, I'd be their goat. Remember, the media whores got me exiled to AIU."

"Yes—and speaking about the department..." There is that tone again in his voice.

"Why do I feel there's more?"

"Because there always is." The tone remains.

I stay silent.

It bugs him and he pleads, "Just listen, Jake."

I make him sweat. Finally, I say, "Go on—give me the bad news."

"Well, Jake... Even though you rescued the daughter of a newly appointed federal judge—"

"What? You mean to tell me a federal judge's kid was in that pile of doped-up kids?"

"I thought you knew—thought you were up on whom married who."

"Explain what that means. I must still be under the influence of the pain killers. Whose kid did I rescue?"

"JoAnn's of course—Ashley Morant's and Wayne Carter's little girl. Wayne Carter is the judge."

"So that's bad news?"

"No—let me finish. Even though you saved the judge's kid, and a bunch of similarly spoiled brats, the surveillance cameras came back on just as you were abusing your prisoner."

"Shit," I scream. "There were cameras in that bastard's bedroom?"

"Of course. I told you he cut a deal."

"You mean the Feds—"

"Yes. They were totally aware of Three-D's harem antics. The pervs got their jollies watching."

"Makes screwing up their case a pleasure. So, what's the downside to me being seen roughing up their stool pigeon?"

"They are applying full-court pressure on the department to discipline you."

"They can't. You said it—I'm a hero."

"There was no missing person report on the kid."

"So?"

"They want to get you for interfering with a federal investigation, torturing a suspect, and a long list of other piddling crap. No report for the missing kid means you were one hundred percent rogue."

"Their precious suspect was dealing dope—to minors. Selling said minors for sex... *And* sexually assaulting the judge's little girl. That's in addition to shooting me. The charge list on him has to be a mile long."

"It is—and that's what will save you. The department is pushing back for a deal."

"Deal? I should get a medal not a deal."

"I know. I know. But will you settle for quietly going back to AIU?"

"Sure. I've never expected to get out of that pit anyway."

* * *

I spent a couple days longer in the hospital at the department's urging. It allowed them time to seal a deal with the Feds. Also, it gave the media enough time to get tired of waiting to see me. Soon other stories captivated their interest. Before long, I was just another slug cop grinding out life for a paycheck, dreaming of retirement, and living my routine.

The only regret I had was not seeing the Morant-Carter family reunion. I bet it wasn't an episode of *Little House on the Prairie*.

Instead, I got a nice thank-you note telling me I was still the same guy of days gone by. It smelled of her perfume and carried a couple of news items: Whitney went to rehab, Wayne was *sooooo* happy on the bench, and there was talk of a Hollywood comeback. It was addressed to Jano and signed by JoAnn.

I read the note and then put it in the trash. It was not a keepsake. If I have learned anything about women, it's that they can break your heart if you let them—so, don't let them.

"You look full of yourself," Earline tells me as she sloshes more coffee into my mug.

"Really?"

"Yes. You have a happy look today. What's your secret?" She gives me her own look—the one that says she'll wait forever to hear the answer.

I flip open the *Trib*, search for the crossword, and say, "Nothing special, Earline—just comes with helping friends."

Some Guys Can Change

BEFORE I CAN GET FRUSTRATED with my crossword, I hear the sound of two fannies sliding into the opposite side of my booth. I smell cop and am not surprised to find two of the Fed-type ruining my "me" time.

They flash FBI credentials and try to stare me down.

I am not impressed, and I let them know.

With a smirk, I say, "It was a tough loss for you boys. I suppose you're here to give me *Lecture One-oh-one* on meddling?"

Their appearance is peculiar. Special Agents Young and Smith look like a mismatched set of book-ends.

Never have I seen two guys look so similar without being twins. Except for their heights, they were identical—blonde, blue eyed, square jawed. Yet, there was at least a head difference between them, causing the mismatch. Even sitting on their butts couldn't hide the height difference. Otherwise, they were clones.

Tall One speaks first. "We are not here to lecture."

Shorty chimes in, "No. In fact, we admire your display of initiative in the unfortunate situation concerning the judge's daughter—a characteristic that will be useful for the assignment we have for you."

"For me?" I hiss. "Last I checked, I still work for the Chicago PD. Granted, it's in a poop pit, but it's a city poop pit—not the Fed's."

"Doesn't matter. You've been drafted," Tall One informs me.

"I waive my draft rights—so, *take a hike*. Nothing sez I gotta associate with Feds. Especially after what I've learned about your methods. Nothing you do, or say, could get me to ride in your clown car."

Shorty whispers, "John Roland."

"Johnny? What about him?"

"He needs your help," comes from Tall One.

"The kind and level of help he needs is out of my league."

"Our records say that at one time you were in the same league," Shorty says. He goes on with, "You worked with him, was a close friend, even introduced him to his wife."

"You dated her at one time, right?" adds Tall One.

I am pissed. These assholes probed my past, invaded my booth, and desecrated my password ritual—*the nerve*. I toss them some well-deserved venom.

"Ancient history. And your shitty records missed some points—like, Johnny went bad, and he would have been jailed if not for some caring souls in the Blue Brotherhood. Even with help, he lives in a black hole—one so deep even you jerks couldn't find him."

"That may have been true," Shorty says. "But, he found us."

"Now, why would a has-been like Johnny Roland seek out you?"

"Your former friend has information—*vital information*—and he won't share it without you. Like it or not, *Detective* Thompson—*you* are the key to the most important case the City of Chicago has *ever* seen."

* * *

There are times when there is no time. In a flash, all I knew and remembered about John Roland presented itself and propelled my mind to a long-ago place.

Being a member of a loose gang was a big part of my youth. Guys from my high school, players on ball teams, pals, cousins, Boy Scouts, garage band members—they came and went in the years I wandered along the border of Chicago's far Southside. From 111th to parts of Blue Island, Alsip and Cal Park, my teen years were peppered with personalities. Johnny was one of them.

He had movie-star looks and a devastating smile, leavened by average intellect, and vague morals. The girls loved him. And secretly, all the guys envied his easy-glide path through every type of situation.

Johnny was blessed—never pressured by life. Johnny simply cruised, avoiding being serious about anything, always one step from the edge, smiling his way out of predicaments and into the arms of adoring babes.

The bookends were misinformed. I did not introduce him to his wife. Butt-hurt, I lost track of them after he snaked Katy Schwab away from me at a graduation party. They quickly became a thing and married.

It was love-hate for Katy. Johnny strayed more often than a tomcat on *Viagra*, but he always smiled his way home. Their story was one of splits and reunions followed by splits and reunions. Their make-up sex was reportedly epic. Johnny was Johnny. Katy was a saint. She suffered much for her two kids and put up with God knows what.

Johnny re-entered my life when I was a patrol cop on the Southside. Specifically, it was when I was part of a joint Chicago PD-suburban cop task force aimed at nabbing smash-and-grab artists who skipped back and forth across the city's limits into areas around Blue Island. Johnny was my BI partner. At first, it was old-home week. But I was soon up to speed on the new Johnny, and things did not go well.

As a member of the Blue Island force, Johnny had kept up his habit of cruising through life with low standards. He lived on the edge of legality, took small bribes from bar owners, extorted drivers at traffic stops, and generally was known to be "on the take".

He was not *dirty* dirty, but always close to that narrowest of edges one can never return from after going over.

Johnny also had trouble with his dick—couldn't keep it from escaping his uniform.

Good looks and a smile can be a curse, not a blessing.

On the task force, we were not happy partners. Johnny kept straying from the mission to chase pussy, nab petty payoffs and low-level bribes—free booze, food on the cuff, stuff like that. I tried to talk sense into him, but he was as deaf to my voice as he was to the others before me.

As soon as the perps we nailed got put away, the unit was disbanded, and we went our separate ways.

Years tumbled by, and through the rumor mill, I learned of Johnny's fall. If there was any surprise to it, it came in the form of its cruelty.

Six months before hitting the magic twenty-year retirement mark, Johnny—still handsome, smiling, and dancing along the edge—finally slipped over the line. What happened was more than ugly.

One of Johnny's pet moves was driver extortion. During routine traffic stops, he'd size up the driver for their potential to fork over some cash, or an item of value, to avoid a ticket.

One night, Johnny's overactive "little Johnny" coupled up with his oft-used scam of terrorizing a driver, and things went way over the edge.

The stopped driver was an under-aged girl, out for a spin in the family vehicle. She was sixteen, attractive, a little tipsy, and very frightened when pulled over for zipping through a stop sign.

Johnny, ever on the make, instructed her to park in a secluded spot where he made it clear what he wanted. She did as she was told and gave up her treasured virginity.

Afterward, as soon as Johnny left, the shaken and terrified girl bolted for home and confessed all to her father—who was not a man to be crossed.

Daddy was no wimp. He quickly assessed the potential ruin of his little princess's reputation, considered the possibility of a drawn-out legal situation, and decided to take immediate action of the vigilante sort. In minutes, he assembled like-minded accomplices and went on the hunt.

Johnny never saw it coming.

As he was leaving his favorite coffee stop, Johnny was approached by the pissed-off father and his backup crew. When confronted, Johnny made a serious mistake by flashing his well-known smile. He was beaten senseless and marred.

The final act of the vigilantes focused on his smile. It was an act of Biblical retribution. Every tooth, upper and lower, was removed by way of brute force and industrial pliers, with the extraction being so brutal his jaw bones were monstrously fractured.

When found, the EMTs were shocked beyond belief, remarking that only a miracle prevented Johnny from drowning in his own blood.

Normally, such an assault on a cop would have seriously rallied the Blue Brotherhood. But the facts, when learned, dampened their ardor. The father was defiantly upfront about his actions.

Upon reflection, Johnny's colleagues saw their predicament. Public sympathy would be split between the girl as one side of the victim equation and the brutality meted out as the other. Everyone—the cops, the girl, her father, and Johnny—were going to come out ruined in some way. So, the investigation came to a compromised solution—a lie.

Local media, co-opted, but still happy to have a *great* story, pushed the tale of a diligent cop getting injured during a high-speed chase. There was no mention of the father and his helpers. The girl was sent to boarding school, Johnny was induced to take an early medical retirement, and a lid was placed on any mention of the vigilantes. Soon, the next "big story" appeared, and the whole thing slid off into the ether of forgetfulness.

When I heard the public tale versus cop rumors, I was ambivalent and cataloged it away. I moved on thinking, *What Johnny got was bad, but it was a lucky pass.* There was no sympathy because he brought it on himself.

* * *

Shorty brings me back to *Jimmie's*, and all memories disappeared to that place where they go inside your head.

"As said," he explains. "We believe Roland has vital information for the success of our case."

I am back, and still feisty. "Hard of hearing? I'm not interested."

Tall One pushes. "To be clear, we are not after him. He sought us out and we *need* him."

"Sounds like a personal problem to me." I feign interest in my puzzle.

"Yes, it is personal. He made it personal—for *you.*"

That gets my attention. "You two dopes better have a great explanation for that. I haven't seen or heard from Johnny in ages. What does your case and his info got to do with me?"

"He trusts you," Shorty says. "He'll only cooperate if you are involved."

"*Involved* is very vague."

Tall One explains, "He's gone rabbit—we have no idea where to. But we do know he won't come in unless you are the one to escort him."

"Who's he hiding from?"

"We can't say."

"What's he got?"

"We can't say."

"What's your case?"

"We can't say."

"Even for Feds, you don't have many cards to play. Is that all you got? Or, can't you say?"

Shorty coughs. He glances at Tall One, and then drops his trump card. "He wants witness protection... For himself *and his wife*... Eh, ex-wife. We... Ah, we... Thought you might help us... For her."

Good play. It makes me think.

After a pause, I say, "Looks like I've got some investigating to do."

Tall One beams. "You're in? Fantastic."

"No."

"Ah-ah-ah-" Tall One sputters. "But you—"

"I said, 'I'd investigate'. Meaning, I'm going to get a read on you—who could be just a couple bozos. Also, I aim to do a bit of snooping into Johnny's activities since I last saw him."

I return to my puzzle.

The Twins sit in silence.

After a while, I whisper, "Boys, you should know that if you piss in the dark, sometimes you miss the bowl." I pause to let that sink in.

Their silence continues.

Finally, I point to the door. "That's the way out."

Hitting the door, they look back.

I wave and say, "I'll be in touch."

* * *

I'm not big on long-ago times rattling my brain with memories of the good old days. But, at one time, I did like Katy. I felt I owed her for not putting up more resistance when Johnny invaded her life. A few calls would not hurt me. Besides, the puzzle had lost its appeal, and my morning was ruined.

The first call I make is to Dewey, my best source for all things Blue Island. It's before sundown, and I know he won't answer. My call goes straight to voice mail.

All I say is, "Call me."

As expected, the next one quickly produces results. Larry Wesselhoff picks up on the second ring.

"What's shakin', Jake?" Larry likes to get to the point.

"What's the word on two odd-sized lookalike Feds named Young and Smith?"

"Jeez, Jake. I hope you're not on their radar."

"Why so?"

"We call them the Mormon Twins. They have real clout—only work on the highest of high levels. Washington gives them a ton of support, including cash, sets them loose, and they deliver."

"You said, 'Mormon'. What's with that?" I am stumped.

"Squeaky clean church boys. Rumored to be the great-great grands of their belief's founding fathers. They may look peculiar, but they are the real deal—this generation's *Untouchables*."

"Any idea why they are in town?"

"Everything about that is tight lipped."

"Meaning?"

"If I tell you, you never mention my name."

"Larry... You know me."

"Sure—sure. But this has to be on the super *super* QT."

"Check."

"One name... Tony Mollenari."

"Shit. I'm impressed. I'm *very* impressed."

"Yeah." He sighs big time, then adds. "If you have *anything* to do with what they are nosing into, be very, very careful. You don't want to end up as collateral damage."

"Thanks, Larry."

"Be safe, Jake. And remember—I said zip on the subject."

"What subject?"

* * *

It was clear why Johnny had gone rabbit. If it was even thought he had information useful to the Twins in their chase after Mollenari, Johnny would have a price on his head and a day-glow target on his back.

It was hot—so hot. Just having the Twins drop by to interrupt my morning gave me an uncomfortably warm sensation. Crossing Tony Mollenari was akin to putting nitro in a paint shaker.

Johnny was in deep trouble, and if he requested witness protection for Katy, she was in serious danger, too. I had to help.

The Twins had given me their contact number, so I 'got in touch' as promised.

After asking to speak to either Smith or Young, a curt underling informed me, "Both *special agents* are unavailable."

When I pressed, all I got was pushback bordering on the snippy. I was in no mood to argue. I had an ex-cop to find and a friend to protect.

"Just tell them, 'Thompson is *in*'."

* * *

My next move is easy to figure—talk to Katy.

I phone for a *Lyft*, and on my way, Dewey calls. He is awake—sort of.

"What's up, Dude?" a groggy voice asks.

"I need some intel on our old pal—Johnny Roland."

"Gums?"

"What'd you say?"

"Gums Roland—he's got a new hook. That beating he took left him unable to even wear cheap dentures."

"Sounds bad," I comment.

"Worse than bad." Dewey fills me in. "I walked right past him the last time I saw him. He's unrecognizable. Plus, I was avoiding the smell."

"Smell?"

"Yeah. Johnny scrambles for a living doing any and all sorts of dirty jobs—swabbing toilets at the bars he once pressed for payoffs, cleaning out sewers, scrubbing septic tanks, and scraping roadkill are on his list."

"He's fallen a long way down."

"Yeah—and that ain't all. He smells like the stuff he cleans. His condition is sad, Jake, but maybe it's fitting. In a lot of folk's eyes, Johnny got what he deserved."

I let the thought sink in. Then ask, "Any thoughts on where I can find him?"

"Nada. He sleeps in his van—sorta like his all-in-one mobile home and storage site for his mops and buckets. Haven't seen it in a while. I can ask around, but I doubt if anyone knows or cares where Johnny is—he's sunk that low. Why the sudden interest?"

"Can't say."

"By that, I assume it's work related."

"Sort of."

"That's a load of bull. What's up?"

"Nothin'. *Really.*"

Disappointed, not believing me, Dewey replies, "More bull. But if that's your line, I'm cool. Boy, I need to piss and get a beer."

"Sounds like a plan. I'll be in touch."

"Dude. Say 'hello' to Katy for me." The phone goes dead.

Dewey could always read me. I hated keeping him in the dark about why I was looking for Johnny. But until I learned more, I had to avoid sharing details about Mollenari and the Feds.

It's easy to create collateral damage. Especially when nitro's in the paint can.

* * *

The *Lyft* drops me at the corner of 119th and Western, the site of the old *O'Brien's* drugstore. *Katy's Kards & Krafts* takes up half of the spot where I bought candy bars and comic books as a kid. The other portion of the building is the home of one of those ubiquitous Asian nail salons that dot America.

Inside the gift shop, I find my old girlfriend. I sense she was expecting me.

"Hello, Jake," comes from a beleaguered Katy. The years have been good to her, but she appears tired and nervous. "Johnny said you'd be around."

I get straight to the point. As I said, strolling down Memory Lane was not the reason I got involved.

"Katy, are you in touch with him?" I ask.

"Yes—but he calls me. And before you ask, I have no idea where he is." Her tired look deepens. "I know he's into something terrible. Two federal cops have been here—several times—asking me a lot of questions. And all I know is that Johnny has warned me to be careful and not to share anything with anybody but you. Jake, I'm scared. He's disappeared because he is scared to death."

"You said he calls. What's his number?"

"I don't know. He must be using cheap throw-away phones."

"Smart—I'll bet he's also moving to different cell towers so no one can back trace his location by zeroing in on your phone."

She gives me a look full of both desperation and sincerity. "Jake, you have to help him." Before I can reply, she adds. "He's gone through a lot. I know—I know. He was a pisser—always charming his way along. He was a soiled cop and a smiley creep most of the time, but he always tried to make up for it. After what happened... Have you seen him?"

I shake my head.

"He's a mess. Teeth gone. Hardly can eat. Has no money."

"I thought he got a medical pension."

"He never took a dime for himself—set up a trust and signed it over to me. By doing disgusting work, he ekes out just enough to live. He even gives part of the pittance he makes to me and the kids. They made it through college because Johnny cleaned up shit and slept in a van. Jake, you have to help him. Johnny's not the man he was. He's changed."

What Katy shared was not what I had expected to hear. A lot of ex-wives spit venom. But this one shows respect—even love—for a guy who everyone would have expected to be a deadbeat dad.

I only joined up with the Twins out of concern for Katy, but here she is, wanting me to act on behalf of Johnny, not herself.

"When does he call?"

"There's no rhyme or reason to it—he just does. The last one was two days ago. That was when he said I should expect you. Jake, he trusts you. Will you help him?"

I tell her, "Yes." Then, I scribble out a number on my notepad, hand it to her, and say, "Give him this."

She takes the number, emits a huge sigh, and gives me a desperation-filled hug.

I hug her back and leave.

There was nothing more to say or do. All I could do was wait.

* * *

Two days crept by. I punched in at AIU, ate at *Jimmie's*, diddled some crosswords, and waited.

On the third morning, while I sipped Jimmie's oily brew and stared at the *Trib*, a no-ID call hit my phone.

"Hey, pal," Johnny says.

"Hey," is all I can say. It is his call—his play.

"I'm in a fix."

"I've heard."

"There's a way out, but I don't trust nobody but you."

"I'm flattered. Is this where I get all weepy and dream about us swapping spit?"

Johnny laughs. "Jake, you always had a sick sense of humor."

"Cut the crap, Johnny. I'm only doing this for Katy. For some sad reason she's still on your side. I don't know why, but she thinks you're salvageable."

He is smart and says nothing.

I continue, "The Feds have talked to me. Bottom line is they think you can be useful to them. And if I know you, you're in a deep pile of shit only a dope like you could find."

"It ain't that way, Jake—*honest*. I stumbled on to what I know. It's just who I know it about that makes it dangerous."

"Save it. Just tell me how you want to play this. You want to come in? Or, you gonna try to make a deal first?"

"No deal—not yet. I'll bargain with the Feds when you get me in to them. What they want—what I got is *so* hot, I'll be lucky to live that long. That's why I need you, Jake."

"Are you really *that* scared?"

"More than scared—I'm a dead man walking. As soon as I learned what I learned, I broke for the hills. Jake, I need to be in protective custody—bad. I'm radioactive. You gotta come get me... And escort me all the way into their arms. Jake, help me. *Please*."

"Okay—okay. Let's get this over with. Just give me the details on where you are."

Agitated, he blurts out, "I been on this phone too long. I'll text my location from another burner."

The call goes dead. Again, all I can do is wait.

Based on his shaky voice and the reference about 'the hills', I assume Johnny is not to be found anywhere within what is lovingly called Greater Chicagoland.

I tell myself, "I'll need an invisible set of wheels." So, I cash in a favor and drive off the city's impound lot in a nondescript and untraceable car suitable to secretly pick up my "package" ...wherever he may be.

As I clear the lot's exit, I get Johnny's cryptic text. It just says, *STEINKE*.

I whisper a comment to the dashboard, "At least he knows where to hide."

It is then that a giant wave of Johnny's anxiety hits me.

"Can I really trust the Twins?" I ask myself. After some thought, I gas up the car, call in sick, and stop at *Jimmie's*.

"Here—hold my phone," I tell him.

From his perch at the door, Jimmie takes it, and asks, "Afraid of being tracked?"

"Yeah," I mumble. "Something like that."

After a minute, I am headed for Michigan.

* * *

Johnny had picked the right spot to hide. Steinke's is a private campground resort hidden along the shore of a small lake just north of the Indiana/Michigan border. Access is through a working farm but the actual entrance to the campground is disguised by a stand of woodland. It was the perfect place for Johnny to disappear, especially in the off-season when the entire resort is buttoned up. No lights, no water—nobody there.

Upon arrival, three hours later, I park near the boat dock where I am easy to see. I beep the car horn just once and get out of the car. I wait.

After ten minutes, I beep again.

"Okay, *okay*," I hear whispered. "Keep it down."

Johnny appears from nowhere.

He is almost unrecognizable. Thin, matted hair, spindly limbs, bulging belly, and a mouth that would make a cartoonist proud hides the man I once knew.

And then there is the smell.

Johnny's aroma is unusually strong and very distinctive. Think urinal, rotten eggs, and puke—with a dash of diaper. Even in the open, it lingered.

My first thought is, *No way am I driving three hours with this*. But here I am, on a mission of mercy. So, I push the thought away and greet him... Sort of.

"Hey. You certainly look like shit."

"Good to see you too, Jake."

Talk about awkward. The scene is funny, sad, and desperate.

Johnny's scared eyes dart about. "You certain you weren't tailed?" Before I can answer, he adds, "Tried to call you on another burner—got not answer." His eyes search about.

"I ditched my phone—didn't want to be tracked..."

"Smart—*smart*." Eyes still searching.

"And, my car is from the impound."

Twitching joins his darting eyes. "*Real* smart. Yeah, Jake, you're smart. That's why I trust you."

His vibe is unnerving, and contagious. "Let's get out of here," I insist.

He does not move.

Pointing to the car, I shout, "I mean—like *now*." I quickly make for the car door.

Johnny moves, but not as I expect. He sprints to a nearby tree, reaches around it to retrieve a soiled knapsack, and darts back to my car.

I've never seen a human move so fast. Before I can close my door, Johnny and his aroma are inside. My anxiety is replaced by a gagging revulsion.

"Jeez, man. You *stink*. Roll down your window."

All I get out of my passenger is a weak, "Sorry" which prompts me to drive as fast as possible out of Steinke's, through the farm, and toward the nearest store.

Fifteen minutes later, I hit the Three Rivers *WalMart* and buy two spray cans of room deodorizer. Then, I soak a very silent and embarrassed Johnny.

* * *

It was the only stop I made on our three-hour drive to the FBI's Chicago office. On the way, I queried Johnny about the how and why we were in a non-traceable vehicle, headed for a witness hand off, and scared to be found out while doing so.

Here's how he explained it: "It ain't no secret that I make a living mopping up after sick drunks and the like. Most of the joints I work for pay me no mind. I just come and go in the very late hours of the night or early in the mornings. I got keys—they trust me. Sometimes I get tired and sleep in one of them for a couple hours or so. You know, my van is cramped—not much of a place to live in. Plus, no heat in the winter. No A/C in summer.

"One night about a month ago, I'm sleepin' in the back of *Hanrahan's*. You know, they got that big room they used to let out for parties and such? Well, I'm curled up in the corner, trying to keep warm under a pile of old bar towels and cast off/lost clothes and such. Nobody knows I'm there. Nobody sees me.

"About three o'clock, I wake up and I'm not alone. There's more than a dozen guys standin' around. A bunch of them are Mollenari's bodyguards, and he's right in the middle of 'em. The rest of the guys are a mix of Blacks and Latinos—leaders from Southside gangs I figure, by the small talk they're makin'. You know, bullshit stuff—they wanted to sound impressive. I recognized a few of them from my days on the force. It was like all the crime leaders for the worst half of the city was in one spot.

"Pretty soon, Mollenari sez a few words, and out of nowhere—*pfft-pfft*. Two guys drop dead from silencer shots—and Mollenari's guys got pieces aimed at the survivors. I coulda pissed myself.

"Mollenari sez a few more words—stuff about how it's gonna be—lays out the law. The guys left standing all agree, and then Mollenari's guys make the survivors wrap up the two stiffs in plastic and carry 'em out. It's all over in a jiffy—and get this, I got it all on my phone. I must have left it on—maybe butt dialed it in my sleep—but I got it all. That's why I vanished. I figure soon—real soon—somebody's gonna remember my van parked outside and I'm dead meat.

"I went straight into hiding. Took me a while to get to the Feds without being tracked. At night, I'd drive as far away as Detroit, Lansing, Grand Rapids, and even down into Indiana to get burners and hit cell towers at random. I told the Feds what I had and to get to you. Jake, I got the goods on Mollenari. And I figure it's my way out of the shit life I'm in. I can fix everything—for Katy, too. I just gotta get into the program—and you gotta get me there."

* * *

It was quite a tale. And it brought my anxiety back in spades. The bright spot of the situation was that I had no phone to trace—no paper trail to the car we were using. My only thought was to get Johnny into custody as soon as possible. No. Sooner.

"How clean is that burner of yours?" I ask.

Johnny rummages in his knapsack, hands the phone over, and says, "Here—only used it for the text and that unanswered call."

"Someone may ID this phone through your contact with mine, but we're mobile—so it's safe to make one call. It's all we've got."

I use the burner to alert the Twins, telling them when we'd arrive, and agreeing that the hand off would be in the parking garage serving their office.

"I want to see some heavy security at the entrance—armed perimeter and real muscle," I demand. "It better not look soft in any way—else we disappear."

"Got it," confirms Tall One. "We want what he has. There'll be no mistakes."

* * *

A couple hours later, as the canned scent wears off, I sight the entry to the parking garage. It looks like an armed camp. At least a dozen SWAT-clad figures line the entrance.

The Twins, in identical suits and shades, stand almost at attention with their armed assistants circled around them.

"They certainly do understand muscle," I say to Johnny. "You ready?"

His caved-in mouth forms a grin, "Yeah—let's do it."

I aim straight for the entrance. We are immediately surrounded, and, in a blink of an eye, Johnny is lovingly grabbed and whisked away.

The last trace I saw of him was through a phalanx of movement that looked like a Ninja convention being tailed by two Mormon missionaries.

I drop the car at the impound lot. The smell guarantees I have forever drained my favor-reservoir at that location. I don't mind. Helping Katy, and Johnny, is worth it.

Also, I do not mind the Twins left without saying, "Thanks."

At my core, I'm a cop. I was just doing my job.

A week or so later, I ask Dewey to nose around and fill me in on Katy's status. What he reports back tells me that all is well.

"I dropped in at her shop," he says. "Katy's gone—quickly sold out—no forwarding address. Plus, buzz on the streets is that a lot of low-life higher ups are scrambling for cover. Indictments and arrests galore is the cause."

My mission was accomplished.

* * *

Time moved on. I sunk back into the AIU routine of cleaning up scrap cases, and I ate at *Jimmie's*. During one of my customary noon-time breakfasts, with my face in the *Trib*, I sensed the slide of two familiar butts move along the other side of my booth. It was the Twins.

"Hello, Detective Thompson," they chime in unison.

I ignore them just long enough to make them twitch. I break the silence right when Shorty is about to speak.

"If you want something, the answer is, 'No'," I inform them.

Shorty quickly replies, "No—no—no. We've only come to say, 'Thanks'."

I put down my paper.

Tall One jumps in, saying, "Here." He hands me a photo.

I look at it and smile.

It was one of those type of pictures people include with Christmas cards and the like. It was an outdoor scene—low mountains, blue sky with cirrus clouds. A beautiful backdrop for a couple embracing and smiling like, "Life is perfect". It was Katy and the "new" Johnny—with teeth.

"Looks like Utah to me," I quip.

The Twins smile.

"Yeah. We wanted them to be safe," Tall One says.

"Nice—real nice." I tell them, as I return to my puzzle.

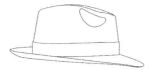

Mustard, Relish, and Larceny

E VERY COP SPACE IS THE same. At first glance they may look different, but trust me, they are all alike. Police stations, jails, sheriff departments, parole offices—they all have that identical gray-brown patina. You know what I mean.

Even if they are in brand-new buildings, all cop spaces have the same grimy glaze of angst which forms from the constant slow seeping of despair and frustration into a confined unhappy place. If you don't know what I mean, lucky you.

Oh—did I mention the aroma? It's peculiar to cop places, too. The smell comes from sweat, urine, dried puke, spilled coffee, and cigarette smoke slowly circulating through poorly maintained government air conditioning systems. Dysfunctional air flow is the standard for law enforcement offices.

"Cigarette smoke?" you ask.

Yes, I know it may come as a shock, but cops do break the rules. We sneak smokes like anyone else. We do other stuff, too.

AIU, the Administrative Investigations Unit of Chicago's PD where I work could be the model cop space. That's why I seldom go to the office. It's the kind of place that makes you want to take a shower as soon as possible.

Great work environment, right? Like I said, I'm a member of AIU, Chicago PD's dumping ground and least admired police unit. You can safely bet any case sent to AIU is a low-priority loser. Our workload stinks as much as our office space.

The AIU office, being what it is, is not where you will find me. This afternoon, I'm working out of my booth at *Jimmie's Diner.*

Jimmie's is where I eat, read the *Trib,* chat-up Earline—my favorite waitress, and do my paperwork. I get away with hanging out at the diner because I've solved a few noteworthy cases, and I don't really care if my colleagues, or even the boss, do not like my 'cubicle' at *Jimmie's.*

I'm the one with the problem—mine is all about accepting the fact AIU is what I have become. Even though I have a decent reputation within AIU, I know I'm stuck there forever. As far as the Chicago PD is concerned, if you screw up bad enough to get assigned to AIU, you never leave.

"Once AIU, forever AIU." It's really not worth the effort to think about any other assignment.

Me at AIU is me in cop purgatory.

* * *

I am halfway through my daily crossword when Earline slides me a freebie slice of cheesecake.

"Here ya go, Jake. You'll need this," she quips.

I look up. Before she could embellish the jibe, I get a good whiff of a bad smell—stale cigarettes and cheap booze. It puts me off my freebie treat.

"Hello, Jake." The greeting comes from Denny Gilbert, my boss. He looks stressed as he takes the seat across from me. Correction. He looks like himself—like crap.

Jimmie enforces the city's no smoking law like a southern preacher rallying against demon rum. So, Denny, in just minutes, is experiencing withdrawal. He also looks strangely alien without a cigarette dangling from his lips.

I simply greet him with, "Hi."

He fidgets and replies. "Jake, we gotta stop meeting like this." Denny punctuates the comment with a weak grin that exposes nicotine-stained teeth that make you ill to look at. His grin, aroma, and the lame attempt at humor sends Earline back to her favorite spot behind the counter—after she pours him a coffee and fans the air.

Earline's move is not lost on me. I figure Denny's craving is too intense for him to notice. Maybe he does notice, but doesn't care. Addicts are all alike—only the drug is different.

"Really, Jake, I can't leave the office every time I need to talk to you."

"Ya know, I got a phone."

"No. No. I mean in person—to make an assignment. I can't give you evidence files over the phone."

"Assignment? Did some city hall VIP lose their briefcase—leave an umbrella in a cab?"

"Cut it out, Jake."

"Why? Everybody knows we only handle the crappiest of cases. That's why AIU exists."

"No, Jake. It's not like that—not this time. I have a real one for us to handle." He pulls a folder from under his arm and places it before me. "This case comes from me, not the higher ups. Take a look."

I point at the folder and ask, "How'd you find it?"

"I didn't find it—my neighbor brought it to me."

"Your neighbor?"

"Yeah. He's an association exec, and— "

"Whoa!" I push the folder away. "I don't do white-collar stuff. A business investigation gone bad landed me in AIU. Remember?"

"It's not like that at all. Best I can tell, it's a conspiracy." He shifts in his seat.

"Conspiracy?" I watch his fidgeting. "Are you Jonesin' for more than a smoke?"

"I'm good." He continues to squirm.

"You need a drink?"

"I *said* I'm *good*." His fidgets line up, converge, and become the shakes.

I get up and head for the door. Over my shoulder I bark, "Come on. We'll finish this outside where you can have a smoke and sneak a drink." I know he always carries a flask.

"Sure." Denny grabs the folder, springs from the booth, and beats me to the door.

By the time he hits the sidewalk, a cigarette and lighter appear. When I catch up to him, he's on his third drag and a whole lot calmer after a couple deep swigs from his flask.

He hands me the folder, explaining, "Howard Dewar, my neighbor, is one of the head guys with the Greater Chicago Area Food Distributors Association.'

"Lucky him." I accept the folder, but do not open it. "Let's just say my enthusiasm is restrained."

"Yesterday he came to my Bar-B-Q and..."

I laugh and interrupt him with, "He's even luckier than I imagined—you cooking for him? That's *real* sweet."

"Stop it, Jake. This is nothing to joke about."

Denny is really pissed. He seldom gets angry— even when he drinks. I've known him to down a gallon of Old Jimmy Jack, my homemade bourbon concoction of *Old Grand Dad*, *Jim Beam*, and *Jack Daniels*, without skipping a beat.

He goes on a rant and I let him. This time, I deserve what I get. I stay silent.

"Trouble with you, Jake, is that you can't keep that sarcastic mouth of yours shut long enough for a guy like me—a friend—to explain the whats and whys and wherefores of a situation. *No*, you have to wise-ass it. A couple of good collars is all that keeps you from being flushed all the way out the system." He points at the folder. "Here—I give you our Golden Ticket to get out of AIU, and all you can do is give me that lip of yours. Jeez, you act like you want to stay in AIU."

Nobody escapes being sent to AIU, I could argue but stay silent. Like I said, I had it coming.

"Listen, Jake. Howard's trade group makes the right donations and is in tight with the powers that be. By that, I mean the guys downtown—the mayor, and about a dozen alderman, syndicate bosses and the like—the people who run this city. So, hear me out."

I hold my hands up to signal compliance.

"Howie brought this to me and asked that I look into it *as a favor*. Somebody is screwing with his members. Someone has to find out who—and fix it. If I—no—if you and me can do that, we get out of AIU."

I have to say something. "You gotta be kidding. NO ONE LEAVES AIU!"

"No. This is for real—believe me. If I get out, you come, too. I'll request a transfer for you."

"Where?"

"Hell—I don't know. Are we in any position to be picky? Anyplace but AIU is fine with me." He points to the folder again. "Just read that—give it your best shot."

I hold up the folder. "You said something about a conspiracy."

"I may have exaggerated... A little." He lights another cigarette.

I open the folder. "Let me have a look."

I am not impressed with the contents.

"This is just a bunch of incident reports." I thumb through the papers. "Denny, what gives? These are from all over—Chicago precincts, the county—and half a dozen suburban communities."

"Yeah, I know." He fires up another cigarette.

"You know... *What*?"

"What do you mean by '*what*'?"

"*Stop it*, Denny."

"What?"

"*That*. That's *what*. You're doing it again."

Denny has a habit of subconsciously sinking into his own version of the *Who's on First* routines.

"Sorry." He lights yet another smoke, realizes he has one going, and shuffles them between hand and lips in an attempt to look put together. "See?" He displays his smokes. "This has me all upset."

"What?" I cannot help myself. Anyone this lame deserves a shot.

"Now, don't *you* start that."

I tap the folder. "Look, Denny, this is a lot of crap to go through standing outside a diner. Why don't you get to the meat of it and tell me what is *really* going on?"

"Okay—okay."

"Spit it out." My patience is dying.

He goes to light yet another smoke. I slap his paw and tell him, "Cut the fidget crap—*or I walk.*"

"Here is what I know—"

"*Finally.*"

"The file describes a real mess. Lots of stuff is missing from a long list of food wholesalers—break-ins, hijackings, theft of all kinds—crosses all the jurisdictions in a hundred-mile radius."

"Meaning?"

"I don't know. That's what you have to figure out."

"Why me? Can't your neighbor just ask his pals downtown?"

"No, he can't. He's afraid."

"Of what?"

"He thinks that maybe the whole thing is being orchestrated by someone with bigger connections—more clout—than him."

"What led him to that?"

"He's tried to get it looked at through the usual channels—been blocked, or pushed off, at every turn. So, he came to me—"

"Out of desperation," I finish the thought. I love stating the obvious, so I interrupt. "It makes perfect sense now that I know he's tried the usual route—no one would end up on AIU's doorstep unless they were desperate. But, why give this to me?" I hand back the folder.

Denny steps back and waves both hands down across himself. "Jake, get real. Take a look... Do I appear capable? I get the shakes by nine A.M. I smoke more cigarettes than the entire unit combined. I'm a wreck—the chief screwup leading a unit full of screw ups."

"I won't argue that."

He steps on two butts and continues without acknowledging my jab. "AIU is a joke. The whole damn unit is full of misfits waiting to get canned— except you. Jake, you've got undeniable talent. Hell, if it weren't for that unfortunate shooting, you'd be a detective lieutenant... Or captain running a top-flight bunch of good cops."

"Thanks for reminding me. My partner is a cripple because of my screwing up."

"I'm not much better than you in the eyes of the department. Forget them, Jake, Take this—and run with it."

He pushes the folder at me again.

* * *

That all happened the day before I found myself camped out at Charlotte Rhodes' high-rise apartment on the 93rd floor of the John Hancock Building.

Charlotte is a highly regarded and even higher-priced CPA with an office on the fourteenth floor with a super residence up above. Her commute is a forty-second elevator ride.

Sometimes I hang out at her place. Charlotte likes me.

The view of Lake Michigan from the condo is tremendous, but that's not what has my attention. I'm wallowing in the reports from the folder and do not notice her in the doorway.

"You look good in pink." She is dressed for work. I am wearing one of her bathrobes. Charlotte *really* likes me. Enough said?

I look up and lamely offer, "Oops... Sorry."

She gives me that, 'It isn't enough' look, and adds, "You going to say goodbye?"

I wrap her robe tightly around me as I stand, and, in my sexiest cop walk, approach her. I place my hand on her hip and smooch her on the cheek.

"Better—but I'm still jealous," she hisses.

"Of what?"

"That pile of papers." She gives me that *other* look—the one she can use like a whip *because* she likes me.

"I said I'm sorry." Lame, I know. But it's all I can muster on short notice.

Her look downgrades to the one that says she puts up with me. She points at my mess and asks, "Jake, why did you come here?"

I freeze. My interpersonal skills with women are minimal, at best. I stall for time to think, *What's the desired "right" answer?*

Charlotte is too quick for me.

She moves her hands at the apartment interior like Vanna White in front of a bank of brightly lit letters on a sound stage.

"You could have it all, Jake. Quit the force, do like I ask—become a private investigator. Living here, being with me. It could be good. But, *no*."

She abandons Vanna for the Wicked Witch of the East, and leads me over to my pile of reports. "You want something that's in these papers. So, what is it? It sure isn't me."

I give her my best blank look. Not because it is that good, but because it really is all I have. Truth is, I did want what was in those papers. It's a case—maybe *the case*—the one that gets me out of AIU.

At least that's what Denny thinks.

Charlotte scans the pile and sneers, "Not even accounting. You could have at least brought something vaguely related to what I understand. This crap is all about restaurant menus."

BINGO!

It hits me like a splash of cold water on a torrid day. I scoop up the papers, blow Charlotte a kiss, and head for the door.

I stop in mid-stride and head back to her bedroom to change out of her robe and into more sensible and suitable clothing for a cop.

* * *

"Easy as pie," Jimmie says as he returns the reports to me. "Hot dogs—it's hot dogs, Jake. Chicago Dogs to be exact."

"Wha...?" My face certainly amuses him as I stare at the folder.

Jimmie chuckles, gives me a quick wink, and explains. "I stopped selling 'em years ago. Too much bother in a place like mine. I need quick turnover and they take time to make if you're gonna do it right— and you gotta make 'em right. People are finicky about Chicago Dogs."

I keep my mouth shut. You do that when Jimmie speaks his beyond-Yoda wisdom.

"It's all there—see?" He points at the folder, motioning for me to open it. "Look at the stolen items—all the ingredients you need to make Chicago Dogs. You got tomatoes, yellow mustard, poppy-seed buns, white onions, pickle spears, atomic relish, the sport peppers—all the stuff."

"Hot dogs," I muse aloud, "*Hot dogs*?"

"No—not the dogs. They're not listed. The items in the reports are just condiments. The only thing missing is the actual dog—a kosher beef wiener. And it better be kosher beef—in a natural skin. Vienna brand is best. Like I said, people are finicky 'bout their Chicago Dogs."

* * *

I soon had a plan. Explaining to Denny what had to be done was easy. Getting him to give me the manpower to do it was impossible.

"Jake, what you came up with makes sense, but I assigned this case to *you.*" He has two smokes going in his ashtray and reaches for another.

"Yeah... And *now* I need some help."

"What part of 'this is your case' don't you understand?" He lights number three.

"I thought this was the 'miracle case' that was going to spring us from this dump?" I reach over and stub out both of his orphans.

"It *is.* I just can't assign anyone to help you. AIU has been tasked to beef up security at city hall. Everyone—including me and you—is supposed to be there until election day. Letting you slide off the detail is the best I can do."

"Okay—I'll go solo. If I can't stake out the meat suppliers to catch the thieves, I'll have to infiltrate the fast-food restaurant community."

"It shouldn't be *that* hard to find out who is planning something big in the world of hot dogs." He lights another cigarette.

"Damn," I say, and reach into my pocket to pull out a box of nicotine patches. "Here, Denny. Slap on a couple of these." I toss him the box.

"Thanks, Jake..." He looks at the gift. "But I've tried 'em. They don't work—just get me more wired." He flashes his best taxicab yellow smile and heads for the can.

Over his shoulder he says, "Stay away from city hall, keep me in the loop, and don't cuff anybody without me being there. I can't give you help, but I did give you this case—it's a sure-fire ticket out of here, and I'm taking it, too."

* * *

Denny was right. Finding out who was planning a big move in the world of Chicago Dogs was easy. Jimmie was the key. As a matter of fact—he did my job.

"Jake, there has to be over a thousand joints making 'em," he explains. "But there's only a couple of chains making any real dough on Chicago Dogs as their main item."

"Any idea as to which one I should start on?" I ask.

"Relax, Jake—I got something better. I asked around after you showed me those papers. I nosed about to see who was set to be making money from hoarding the stuff. Like they say, 'Follow the mustard'."

I am slumped in a corner of my regular booth, slurping on *Jimmie's* famous oily coffee.

"You're so right, Jimmie. Call it mustard, cheese, or bread—it's always the money. So, what do you have?"

"Mikey White. Junior."

"As in Mikey White, the big-time alderman, connected to everywhere, and owed by everyone?"

"Yep. His kid, Junior, has plans—big plans—to open a chain called...*tad dah!* Guess what?"

I hold my head in a poor imitation of a psychic. "Hot dogs—I sense the presence of hot dogs... Wait... Wait..."

"Dirty Dawgs," he blurts.

"Dirty Dawgs?"

"Yep. New city-wide venture—been in the works for some time. Word is that he's planning to launch a chain with at least a dozen locations just to start out. Everything fits—through his old man he got the investigation into what happened to all the fixings quashed. All he needs now are wieners, and he's the new king of Chicago Dogs. I'd stake out the two or three largest suppliers handling kosher meats—that's where the next robbery has to take place."

"Jimmie, you saved me a mountain of work. You are wonderful—a *saint.*"

As Yoda, he says, "Nothing it was—around, I just asked."

* * *

It was as easy as that.

Well... Almost.

Based on Jimmie's information, I found Mikey Jr and became his shadow's shadow. In less than a day, I made him, the gang of thugs he used for the heists, located the condiment cache, and then nabbed him mid-heist with a load of wieners.

With surveillance photos and arrest reports in hand, I aimed myself for city hall and dreamed of a future without AIU.

Yeah—it was as easy to nab Mikey Junior. But dealing with the backlash was a nightmare. As you can imagine, Mikey Senior was not thrilled his name-sake was caught with his hands in the mustard jar, so to speak.

The senior Mr. White rallied his considerable list of downtown pals, and, being much less than perfect, AIU was an easy spot to lean on.

Politicos meddling with Chicago's Finest is a highly refined art form in the Windy City.

They leaned heavy on AIU.

I was pleasantly surprised, however, that Denny held up under the pressure. The collar stuck. But the wheels fell off Denny's plan, and my dream of being free of AIU died when we got the news of our reward for being such damn good cops.

"I'm really sorry, Jake—man, am I sorry," Denny whines. He continues cleaning up his desk and loading boxes. "I had no idea... No idea..."

"It's okay, Denny," I tell him. "You tried. Thanks. You put me in for the transfer—just like you prom-ised."

"Unintended consequences—that's what it is. Unintended consequences."

"Nah—it's AIU, Denny. It's just AIU. Nobody gets away from it. Well, now—except you. I told you so. I should have listened to myself and not expected anything else."

He keeps apologizing as he smokes and packs. "Jake, I can't tell you how bad I feel. I tried to get them to change their minds, but—no luck." He sets a half-full bottle of bourbon on top of a box of ashtrays. "Let's have one—for old times. Okay?"

"Sure, Denny, why not?"

Denny pours two big ones in a couple of semi-clean coffee mugs and lights up another smoke.

"Here's to us."

I clink his mug and say, "To the new Director of the Chicago PD's Employee Health Task Force."

He laughs, clinks back, and toasts, "To Jake Thompson, the Interim Director of AIU."

Like I said, cop spaces are all alike. My office stinks as much as my job. That's why I choose to run AIU from my favorite booth at *Jimmie's*. I figure with any luck, in six weeks—two months, tops—I'll be demoted.

THE SHERIFF OF WEST KOWLOON

HAS THIS EVER HAPPENED TO you? All of a sudden out of nowhere—*Pow*! A name you haven't thought of in a very long time pops into your head.

It happened to me the morning James McIlveen arrived in Chicago and asked for my help.

The Administrative Investigations Unit is the department's wastebasket. It's where the Chicago PD sends embarrassments to toil away their time. Mine is running out, but I still dream of being back in a legit unit.

Chances are slim and getting slimmer ever since I was named interim head of AIU. My previous boss had a fool-proof scheme to get us both transferred. Of course, it failed, and I'm patiently waiting out the last days of my career at AIU.

As a cop I had professional idols, and Jimmy McIlveen is at the top of my list. Jimmy originally hails from Aberdeen, Scotland, but his accent is not what you'd expect to hear in the office he directs on a daily basis.

Jimmy is the currently sheriff of West Kowloon, Hong Kong.

I'll bet you're wondering—how does that happen?

Here's the story: Jimmy was immediately recruited after law school by Her Majesty's government to be a police officer in the colony of Hong Kong. That was in the day that Empire still held on to the idea it was still an empire—in the early eighties. Ancient history, I know.

After a two-month cram course in Cantonese, Jimmy hit the streets as a foot-patrol officer. He was a good one, and his remaining on the force after the Brits gave up the colony is a testament to his professionalism. Jimmy is one tough customer, and a smart one, too. Jimmy's specialty is gangs—triads, to be precise.

Founded centuries ago as a rebel movement to drive out the Manchurian's of the Manchu Dynasty, the triads have evolved into a combination of mafia, street gangs, and corporations. Jimmy's reputation was built on his bringing several key triad members to justice for their roles in some highly visible kidnappings.

His expertise is in high demand since the triads have gone global. Jimmy lectures and trains cops worldwide on how to deal with the threat of foreign-based infiltration into local crime markets.

I met Jimmy after he caught wind of my early success in busting a Guatemalan ring of thieves filching assets from swank hotels in The Loop. How he found out about that case, I'll never know, but he liked it enough to share the undercover technique we used as an example of "good police work". A compliment like that from an expert such as him is as good as it gets.

Jimmy took a shine to me, and we exchanged ideas about cop work and Chinese cuisine—keeping in touch for several years.

I lost the connection when I drifted out of sight into the dull routine of AIU. Thinking of him lifted my spirits.

Did I mention when that *Pow!* hit me?

I'm not a morning person. *My* mornings start at noon, when I hit my favorite diner for breakfast. That's where I caught the sheriff of West Kowloon making sweet moves on Earline, my favorite waitress.

Earline is a sucker for any utterances other than my Southside accent. Sometimes, I swear, I'd give my left nut for a brogue like Jimmy's.

The best I can do is interrupt Jimmy's romantic banter with the weak remark, "Chicago is a long way from China, Jimmy."

"Hey, Jake. How are you, me lad?" Jimmy shakes my hand, gives me a guy hug, and goes right back to hitting on Earline.

"Now, me darling, as I was telling you—I'm here to see me old friend, Detective Thompson. I hope you'll pardon me leaving your company by honoring my request for you to accompany me to your favorite restaurant one evening."

Earline blushes the tiniest bit, whips out her receipt book, scribbles her number, and says, "Why... Of course. Here. Call anytime." Then, she addresses me, "Jake, shame on you for not telling me about this darling man. Where did you get a friend like him? He's definitely a step up for you."

It is her way of letting me know she is glad Denny Gilbert, my chain smoking, half-drunk ex-boss, is no longer coming to the diner.

"No argument there," I say, as I motion for some coffee and usher Jimmy into my favorite booth.

Since my elevation in the hierarchy, I've been spending even more time at the diner. I absolutely despise everything about AIU, especially its physical setting. A booth in the diner is where I conduct most of my work.

"They said I would find you here," Jimmy remarks. "You don't go to the office?"

"Not if I can help it."

"You *actually* run things from here?"

"AIU practically runs itself, Jimmy. It's got a vibe all its own. Junk cases and busy work is all we do—unless the downtown boys want a scapegoat. Then we do that, too."

"It sounds depressingly terrible."

"On a good day it is. But, I forget when I saw the last good day. Most times it's worse. I can't wait to retire."

"Why not put in for a transfer? Jake, you are a natural policeman—one of the best I have ever known. If I were you, I wou—"

I cut him off.

"But—you *aren't* me, Jimmy. I made one mistake, and it seems the department isn't ever going to forgive me."

"In my department, we would certainly overlook a mistake, or even two, for a fine policeman like you."

"Jimmy, this is Chicago—not Hong Kong."

Earline arrives with my coffee and a fresh one for Jimmy. I use it to change the subject.

"I see you have you tried the oil they serve as coffee," I joke.

My joke flops. Earline frowns. Jimmy shrugs.

"So, what brings you to Chicago?" I ask.

"Escorting a prisoner home."

"Must be a doozy for you to be involved."

"Yes, a triad leader by the name of Sonic Kwan."

"Doozy of a name, too."

"The younger generations in Hong Kong have stretched the custom of taking a Western first name to new limits. The Mister Kwan I came here to bring home for justice is only twenty-two. He grew up playing video games and took his name from one of his favorites."

"Crazy kids."

"Yes—and this one is the craziest. Also, the meanest and most cruel triad member I have ever encountered—that's why I came for him personally. But things are not progressing as planned. And, that's why I am here to see you."

"Let me guess—you want me to tag along on the ride back to Hong Kong?"

"Yes—after we catch him."

"Catch him?"

"He escaped from your Cook County jail just before I arrived."

"How convenient for him. Were friends of his involved?"

"Yes, I would suspect that. He is a member of the Fourteen-K Triad. They have local assets here."

"So, why come to me, Jimmy? There are plenty of good cops doing gang work in Chicago."

"I agree. But, *good* will not suffice in apprehending Sonic Kwan. As I said, you are an excellent cop. I need excellence. Plus, I know you."

"Jimmy, I am touched. But AIU is not the sort of place that nurtures excellence—I'm rusty. And besides—I'm only the *Interim* Director."

"Were."

"Say what?"

In his brogue he replies, "I have used me considerable influence to have you reassigned as me liaison."

I went limp. *Me—out of AIU?* My mind fried its wiring. I went blank.

Jimmy's voice nudges me back to reality. "Jake, I asked for your help because I know how good ye can be. Forget AIU. Just be the policeman who impressed me so much when I first learned about ye."

"Sure, Jimmy," is all I can say.

My mind clicks into a long-gone gear.

I'm not in AIU. It's a chance I thought would never come. *But, how do I find a crazy and vicious Chinese triad member in Chicago?*

The rust fell off my unused gears and my brains ground out an old song. Me at work—*real* cop work.

* * *

We hit into it right away—or, *straight* away as Jimmy says it.

On the street outside the diner, I muse aloud, "If I were Sonic, I would lay low for a couple of days—give the impression that I had already skipped town."

"So, your police senses believe that Kwan is still in Chicago?" Jimmy knew how to oil my old machinery.

"His description is out there. It's not all that distinctive for a big city. But remember, Chicago sits in the heart of the Midwest. If he strays too far—he'll be noticed. He can't make a dash for the airport, bus, or train—at least, not right away. Yep—he's here. Tell me more about him."

"He's very smart and brash. At sixteen he left the best private school in Hong Kong to join the Fourteen-K Triad. It is the second largest—twenty thousand members. Kwan convinced them to take him in based on his ideas of selling drugs to wee kids."

"An ambitious little devil."

"He is—and has no concern for the havoc he sets in motion. Overnight, we had a youth drug problem beyond any past experience. Kwan is a master at making and marketing to kids—part of the new culture. He is part techno-freak, part Kung Fu master, and total sociopath."

"So... How did he end up in custody here?"

"After a series of brutal beatings and one murder, we were on to him in Hong Kong and putting a great deal of pressure on his triad to give him up."

"Wait—you always taught that gangs lived on three principles: violence, *esprit d'corps*, and never ratting on a mate. Why would the triad ever consider giving up Sonic?"

"Believe or not, the triads are taming down. After the extreme violence of the 90s, when gun-happy mainland members came to Hong Kong, the triads realized the opportunities associated with the economic boom are far more lucrative—and safer. Now, they are focusing more on smuggling than the older methods. Drugs are too visible—and messy compared to sneaking cigarettes past customs."

"So, our boy Sonic went traveling to find new markets?"

"Right."

"How fortunate for us."

"Not only Chicago—London, New York, and Paris in the west—Sydney, Mumbai, and Bangkok in the east. He's been setting up operations in them all. It was amazing that your narcotics crew snatched him up in a raid. He was caught in a routine effort aimed at locals."

"Sometimes, we cops just get lucky."

"And it was unfortunate that luck was overturned by his escape."

"You said his triad has a presence here. Enough to spring Sonic from county lock-up?"

"I would certainly say so. Kwan's escape was fast, clean, and easy. He had help."

"Then he is definitely here—in Chinatown. He has friends and can blend in. There's more than sixty thousand Chinese to provide cover."

"Isn't that too obvious? Hiding right where we would look first?"

"Exactly. And that's what a brash punk named Sonic would do. You said he was a sociopath. Plus, as you always told us during your lectures, the best place to get Cantonese food is on the road."

Jimmy laughs. "I was only joking."

"So am I—but let's go check it out."

* * *

We take the Red Line on the 'L' and get off at the Cermack-Chinatown station. We are headed to the heart of Chicago's Chinatown, but not looking for food, even though Mark Soo's *Asian Palace* restaurant is our destination.

"Is the menu authentic?" Jimmy asks as we go inside.

"Best chili prawns in town. But, don't order any of them—let the owner suggest them as a specialty."

"Why?"

"It'll give him a reason to fawn over you—and provide enough cover time for checking you out."

"Check me out?"

"Yes. Mark Soo is Hip Sing. In Chicago they are known as "The Crew". The Hip Sing gang has been here forever—longer than the United Bamboo or the Four Seasons gangs. Jimmy, if you taught me anything it's that a rival gang is our best weapon. I'm going in straight on this—I aim to tell Mark everything."

Jimmy grins ear to ear. "See? I told ye, Jake. I knew ye'd be just the asset I'd need to catch Kwan."

"Easy, Jimmy. This is just where we start, because it's all I can think of. I don't want to disappoint you, but beyond Mark Soo, I've got nothing."

"It's enough, Jake. Good police work just needs a start."

More oil for my gears. It brought back memories.

A couple of months into my solo patrol career (back in the dawn of time) Mark Soo was about to be dismantled by a rival gang when I wheeled my police cruiser up a dark alley. I broke up the party,

ANOTHER SOUTHSIDE

and ever since Mark has been a reliable resource—if not a friend.

While posing as the *maître d'* of the *Asian Palace*, Mark operates a number of businesses out of his father's restaurant—some legal, some not so. All of them lucrative.

We slip in, find a quiet table, and wait for Mark to join us.

"Good to see you, Jake—been a while," comments Mark. "It is always good to see you."

"Likewise, Mister Soo, likewise."

Mark smiles, gives a knowing look, and nods toward Jimmy. "I see you have brought a distinguished guest with you." He bows to Jimmy and greets him. "Welcome to the *Asian Palace*, Sheriff McIlveen."

"You don't miss much—do you?" I say to Mark.

"We learned of the sheriff's visit even before he left China. The capture of Sonic Kwan traveled quickly in our community, as did the news of his extradition. Kwan's presence has been... How shall I say... Problematic."

"So, ye would not be distressed if we caught him again?" Jimmy asks.

Mark chuckles. "What I was told about you is true. Indeed, you are very direct. To answer your question, our community would be relieved if Sonic Kwan was back in China. His brand of business is not appreciated by many of us here in Chicago."

"Including some members of Fourteen-K?" I ask.

"I cannot speak for them directly but, yes, I believe they are tired of the old ways."

"Old ways? Meaning?" My gears keep grinding.

"The excessive violence," answers Mark. "It is the twenty-first century. We need to move on—adapt. China and the Chinese today are interested more in high finance, less in Kung Fu and Mao's tactics." He smiles.

Jimmy nods. "Jake, they'd rather buy America than fight it."

"Based on what I know, they have the cash to do it," I offer. "But, I'm just a slug cop. For me, it's good guys and bad guys. So, I ask, 'What the hell does the march of world history have to do with us catching Sonic Kwan?'"

My companions smile and knowingly nod to each other.

"So, what gives?" I ask.

Jimmy gestures to Mark, who replies. "In the orient we have a saying: 'An honest man, even in ignorance, can slay a dragon.'"

"Screw the dragon," I say with a grin. "Just show me a punk named Sonic."

* * *

Mark Soo was known for two things: being a tough customer and a great host. He was insistent we enjoy the hospitality of his establishment.

Only after a sumptuous meal and suitable amounts of alcohol did we discuss our plan to capture Sonic Kwan.

"Now, let me get this correct," Jimmy says. "We are going fishing?"

"Only in a manner of speaking," Mark answers.

"But I heard you say we will need Chicago River bait." Jimmy looks toward me for clarification.

It is my turn to be on an inside joke. "In Chicago, we also have a saying, 'If you plan to fish in the Chicago River, use a lot of bait.'" I deliver the line stone-faced.

Jimmy says, "But ye told me, there are no fish in the Chicago River."

"That's correct." I let a smile seep out.

Jimmy sips from his glass of Old Jimmy Jack and grins back. "It's a metaphor. So, what we are doing is fishing for Kwan. Right?"

"Right." Mark accepts a note handed to him by one of his staff. Mark reads the note, gives me the high sign, and announces, "It's all arranged."

I nod. "There's nothing like Chicago River bait."

"Tell me—what exactly is Chicago River bait?" Jimmy asks.

I lightly tap his chest and pour him a stiff one.

"Me?"

"Yes," I say. "Chicago River bait is always human in nature."

Jimmy downs the contents of his glass. "Jake, I had a thought ye brought me here for more than the food."

"And we're staying a while longer."

"Yes. I definitely *do* feel like bait."

"Me, too," I tell him. "I'm in this with you—all the way."

Mark pours another round for the three of us and further informs us about the contents of the note, "Word has been circulated. It is only a matter of time before Kwan appears. He knows you are in China-town to find him."

"Find him?" I say, "What we are doing is more like deer hunting wearing brown."

* * *

I've got to hand it to Jimmy. Being a target really had no effect on him. Pros accept the risks that come with tracking down serious bad guys. Jimmy just let the worries roll off.

Mark excuses himself. He has a business to run.

I knew he'd be keeping an ear to the ground as to any of Sonic Kwan's movements. Jimmy and I killed a couple hours chit-chatting, playing cards, and shar-ing yarns.

At closing time, Mark appears again. This time to escort us to the main entrance.

"He's sent word," Mark tells Jimmy. "Kwan told my men he'd be waiting for you outside."

"Not very subtle," I quip. "He doesn't seem concerned at all about making a scene."

"He needs this to be public," Jimmy says. "If he takes me out in plain sight and in the middle of his new home, he reclaims all his lost face."

"And he makes a statement in Chinatown he's a serious new force to be reckoned with," adds Mark.

"Whatever he's got planned, I don't like it," I say. "Waiting? In the street? Why?"

"He wants it to be *very* personal," Jimmy explains. "He knows I'm a practitioner of Kung Fu. I suspect he wants to have a go at it."

"A *go at it*?" I blurt out. "You're way more than *twice* his age."

"It has to be done," Jimmy says as he steps out the door.

"Whoa—this is *crazy*." I shout.

I am right behind him, and we are both out on the street in seconds. The night air washes over us, bringing with it the smell of Chicago pavement and the taunt of Sonic Kwan.

Hey, old man." The fugitive stands on the opposite curb. "You came a long way to die, *Guiz*."

Jimmy ignores the insult and walks as normal as can be to the center of the street.

There, facing a riled youth approximately one-third his age, Jimmy calmly speaks.

"Laddie, ye should be more respectful. Chinese culture is built on heeding the wisdom of elders."

Before the startled youth can reply, Jimmy continues, "And, no, I have not come this great distance to meet me maker. I have come to take ye home. You will stand before a judge in Hong Kong and account for ye'r deeds."

That was it—as far as Jimmy was concerned.

Kwan was dumbfounded. For what seemed like an eternity he did not move or speak.

Finally, he whispers, "No," and steps forward assuming a menacing Kung Fu stance.

"Have it ye'r way," Jimmy replies as he also assumes a stance that suited a man his age.

I am aware of Jimmy's ability in martial arts, but in this instance, he is hopelessly mismatched. A lifetime of police work's wear and tear has reduced his skills.

"This isn't going to be good," I mutter, as Kwan makes his opening move.

In the time it took for me to reach my piece, Kwan deftly landed a kick that spun Jimmy around like a top. Jimmy's attempt to avoid the move's full impact was only partially successful. I surmised a second blow would be the last.

So did Kwan. He moved fast, but I was faster.

My piece is a five-shot snub-nosed thirty-eight. Its effective range is squat. I, therefore, only use it up close.

Before Kwan can send off another kick, I jump into the street to get a good angle and let loose some lead in his direction.

In my opinion, the results were more than just okay—I hit him three times below the waist. Three out of five ain't bad in my book.

Kwan lay crumpled and moaning. One round had shattered a knee, while two others found home in the other leg's thigh and a calf. The two rounds that missed completely had harmlessly ricocheted off the pavement. Thankfully, no bystanders had been hit. I quickly checked to see that Kwan was not armed.

When I was certain he was clean and not going to bleed to death, I look at Jimmy.

"You okay, pal?"

"Yes, and thank ye, Jake," Jimmy says with a slight grin. "But I was preparing to take charge of the situation."

"Sorry for stepping in."

A patrol unit cleared the corner and came to a stop a few feet away.

"This is my town, Jimmy, and I play by Chicago rules. We can't have guest cops roughed-up by punks like him. What do you say we let the reinforcements handle the medical and escort duties while we figure how we are going to handle the media?"

"Handle the media? We caught an extremely dangerous fugitive."

"They have a habit of getting weird whenever there is gun-play—especially when I'm involved. My banishment to AIU all began with me shooting the wrong minority crook."

"Rubbish, I can't imagine anyone criticizing ye'r actions."

"I hope you're right. Only time will tell."

* * *

Time passed, and we got a pass from the media.

Sonic Kwan proved to be the perfect bad guy to catch, and Jimmy's on-screen image was even better. After a week of recuperation, Kwan was ready to travel, and Jimmy was tired of Earline. I begged off escort duty, and early one morning in a real show of friendship, I saw Jimmy off.

"I'm not good at farewells," I tell him. "Especially before noon."

"I appreciate the gesture, Jake. I'll repay it and all ye'r other kindnesses when ye come to Hong Kong for a visit."

"Sure, Jimmy. Maybe when I retire."

"I suspect it may be sooner," he says with a sly grin.

"What have you cooked up?"

"Nothing much—just that ye may be called to testify."

"Testify? For what?"

"I play by Hong Kong rules. We frown on striking police officers—and Kwan did land a blow. And ye are a witness."

I cannot contain a huge laugh. "Jimmy, you are something—really something."

"That, I am."

* * *

Later that day, I was back in my usual booth at the diner. A grumpy Earline filled my cup with oily java, I confronted the *Trib*'s crossword, and ordered the daily special. When the puzzle was finished and the special consumed, I finally called the office.

The capture of Sonic Kwan had been milked by the department for all it was worth. The case quickly became "old news" and was just as quickly closed.

The department would move on. But, as a one last act of international cooperation, I was informed by Pinkie, our receptionist, that I had been demoted.

"Jimmy, I love you." I said, after I ended the call. He had strongly suggested that I be sent back to the ranks in AIU where I belonged.

Things were back to normal—thanks to my friend, the Sheriff of West Kowloon.

BABYSITTING UNCLE VINNIE

MANY YEARS AGO, THE AREA around Oakley and 26th was one of Chicago's most vibrant Italian conclaves. To locate another sizable concentration of Italians on the Southside, you had to cross the city limits to Blue Island. There, you'd find railroad workers and their descendants, predominately from Rippacandida in the southern Italian province of Basilicata.

Only a few of the old Pisanos still frequent the two-block strip of restaurants that remain along the neighborhood's main street. You'd have to comb the suburbs to find pockets of the ex-pat Chicago-Italians who once called Oakley home.

Today the neighborhood is mostly populated by Mexican immigrants. I have no problem with the new residents, and only brought it up to spotlight the changes in the city. And, to prepare you for what I am going to share.

I bet you're wondering, "How does a slug of a cop with a name like Tomaszewski know so much about Chicagoland's Italian history?"

Of course, the answer is Gino Cavellini—my ex-partner and non-stop jaw-wagger.

All Gino ever talks about is himself and his family. He is one-hundred-and-ten-percent Italian. For him, family means more than it does to most folks. That's just the way it is.

Even though he was disfigured and partially crippled because of me, Gino calls and keeps in touch. You see, I'm family to Gino. And, no matter what goes down, family comes first.

That's why he asked me to keep an eye on Uncle Vinnie.

* * *

In the annals of Chicago crime, Vincent Cavellini is a footnote, not a chapter. As he was known during his working days, Vinnie Muscle was a much-sought-after enforcer for Chicago's *Syndicate*—the city's home-brewed version of organized crime.

With a wide smile, quick temper, and quicker fists, Vinnie made his living by intimidating foes and collecting money for the *real* bad guys who controlled every bit of vice, most of the crime, and all the politicians in the Windy City. In his prime, Vinnie was definitely not the guy you wanted looking for you. Visits from Vinnie were brief and unpleasant.

But, that was long ago, before Vinnie wailed a bit too hard on a slow-paying gambler and earned a twenty-five-year vacation, compliments of the State of Illinois.

Today, Vinnie Muscle is just Uncle Vinnie—an old ex-con making his living as a handy man. He is, thanks to Gino, also my responsibility.

Uncle Vinnie returned to civilian life a few years ago.

As I explained, the Chicago he knew no longer exists. He has done his best to fit in, but there have been some bumps in the road—enough for Gino to ask me to watch over his relative by blood, and mine by adoption.

I know babysitting an aging ex-enforcer with a record is not the usual duty for a cop. However, I owe Gino and I pay my debts. I am considered family and that means I do as asked. Like I said, no matter what goes down, family comes first.

Also, I am enough of a realist to know that at heart, cops and criminals have a lot in common, since they often rise from the same source.

Vinnie is "old school" and, having grown up on the Southside, I have an immense respect for some of the long-gone ways of the old neighborhoods.

Case in point being the following vignette from Vinnie's past:

Oldsters in the neighborhood remembered Vinnie had a twin named Paulie. They also recalled no one outside the immediate family could tell the two apart. Their alikeness was a boon to the twins and a constant irritant to the straight-laced law-abiding folks who suffered their antics.

One day, Paulie pulled a prank that lead to an outcome which forever caused them to be discernible.

During the twin's formative years, their neighborhood was overseen by a syndicate man named Dominick DiSanto. He was the guy everyone listened to. I mean *everyone*. Aldermen, business owners, working stiffs, hoods, and cops—they all respected Dom Dee. Bicycles were never stolen, doors were left unlocked, trash was dropped in cans, and no one had sticky fingers in the neighborhood shops.

It was Dom Dee's job to know what was happening in his territory. What he did not see and hear was told to him by a thousand sources that either owed or feared him, or both. It was commonly believed that nothing could sidestep Dom Dee's scrutiny.

Paulie thought otherwise. He tried to prove it by snatching and escaping with a charity coin canister from a local store's counter when the proprietor was in the stockroom, but he failed. The store had some awesome mirrors, and the owner was certain a Cavellini boy—one of the twins—was the culprit.

But, which one?

When word reached Dom Dee one of the twins had stolen from his greater Oakley family, he issued a summons. Carmine Cavellini, the community's mortician and the boys' father, immediately answered the call. As head of that particular family unit, it was Carmine's duty to hear directly from Dom Dee what was required to rectify the situation. And the situation was a mess.

Dom Dee had both of the boys in his care. Paulie, the perpetrator, would not confess and Vinnie, the loyalist, would not snitch. Normally, punishment would have been swift, but the boys' silence complicated its administration. Carmine's presence was not only required, it was a necessity, because the boys remained mum, even before Dom Dee and his associates. After being briefed on the scene, Carmine and Dom Dee conferred.

"I was gonna make an example outta the little thief," explained Dom Dee. "But, I'm not sure which one of your boys did it."

"Dom, I'm with you all the way. It was stupid of them to take the canister." Carmine had known Dom Dee since they were kids and held the same views on keeping the neighborhood safe and secure.

"Them?" asked Dom Dee. "I was told only one of your boys was involved. I just nabbed them both so you could sort it out."

"Dom, I know. But if they won't talk, they are in this together. I'm as pissed off about this as you are. Let me handle it."

"How?"

"Give me a minute," Carmine said. "I'll be right back." He left, and as promised, returned carrying a Louisville Slugger.

"Nice bat," observed Dom Dee.

"Not for them," answered Carmine. He pointed to the boys and ordered, "Come here." When they stood before him, he said, "You think you know it all. One last time... Who took the money?"

Silence. Neither of them moved.

"Okay, have it your way," their father said, as he motioned for them to follow him. "Outside—you have an apology to make."

The trio of father and his two sons stepped on to the sidewalk. They were soon joined by Dom Dee, his minions, and a small crowd of locals who had gathered as word spread that an event was developing.

They were all shocked when Carmine assaulted his own flesh and blood. With swings deserving a Comiskey Park audience, Carmine broke Paulie's right arm and then Vinnie's left. The crunch of the impacts could be clearly heard by all.

Twice the assembled crowd groaned at hearing the excruciating sounds and amazed at how both boys accepted the brutal punishment in absolute silence.

After the punishment was administered, Dom Dee shook Carmine's hand and said, "That took balls."

Then, at the sight of Carmine and Dom Dee patting the boys on their shoulders in recognition of the "stand up" manner in which they took their punishment, the crowd applauded and cheered.

"Let this be a warning for anyone thinking about messing with this neighborhood," shouted Dom Dee. "And nobody—and I mean nobody—can ever mention this. These boys are clean and new as far as I'm concerned."

That is how myths and legends are born.

Everyone in Oakley knew of the event, but no one openly spoke about the day that changed the course of the boys' lives. The twins became local celebrities—in life and death.

Paulie reflected upon his "criminal" act. And to repay society, he joined the Marines. He left home for Parris Island the day after he turned eighteen. He paid dearly. His homecoming from Vietnam was a community event—a closed-casket funeral attended by over four-hundred mourners.

Vinnie took it hard and would never mention his brother again.

Having impressed Dom Dee with his closed-mouth loyalty, Vinnie went to work for the neighborhood lord as a runner. Time and weightlifting filled him out and soon after his brother's funeral, Vinnie began his collection duties, becoming known by his nick-name.

Like I said, that was long ago.

Now, the neighborhood and its memories are all but gone and I'm babysitting Uncle Vinnie, formerly known by a dwindling few as Vinnie Muscle.

* * *

"Hey, Jake." Vinnie yelled from the back of the restaurant. "Take a seat, I'll be right there."

I did as told and grabbed a seat near the windows. There wasn't much to look at on Oakley, but I was there for the food and a visit, not the view.

Vinnie was in the back showcasing his humorous wisdom with a couple of locals about his age.

"When I was a kid, I asked God for a bike," he told his audience, "But I know God doesn't work that way, so I stole a bike and asked for forgiveness."

Laughter and back slaps were followed by a toast of red wine before Vinnie headed my way. He held two glasses in one hand and a bottle in the other.

He sat across from me. "Want some old-fashioned Dago Red?"

"No. Can't—on duty," I replied.

"So, this a work call?"

"No—no!" I protested.

"Then, here," he said. "Try some. It builds the blood."

He poured, I drank, and he poured again.

"Good stuff," I said.

He grinned and looked straight at me. "I take it that Gino called, again. This is the third time you've dropped in to check up on me."

"I'm not checking up on you." I protested.

"Don't bullshit me, Jake."

I was going to protest some more, but he cut me off. "Ah-ha! Let *me* talk."

I nodded, and he poured more wine.

"Jake, I may have been in stir for a long stretch, but I didn't lose my street sense. I know you have zero cop business to perform around here. And— please excuse my honesty—ever since that dame reporter sliced you up, you've been nursemaid to a drawer full of bottom-feeder cases. My son, you've been assigned to a third-rate desk job until they pension you out.

"Besides, in this neighborhood they only see a cop when there is a murder, armed robbery, or a break-in. You're here because Gino called."

My face must have said it all. With no witty response on the tip of my tongue, I gulped down the wine. "I'm still a cop," I almost whined.

"Don't take it personal, Jake." He poured again.

I gulped once and left some for sipping. "How else should I take it?"

"With grace," he answered. "With grace."

"Grace?"

"Or, something like it."

I sipped my wine and said, "That begs an explanation."

"Fate can't be explained."

"Fate? I thought you said it was grace."

"Let me explain."

"Please do."

"I can't tell you how many times I thought about the incident that put me away. I hit plenty of guys harder. But *that* guy died. I would have gone nuts thinking about it—unless I accepted it as my fate.

"You gotta have the grace to accept your fate. I found mine when I realized his fate—the guy I hit, was much worse than mine. And his was caused by me."

"That's deep, Vinnie. Very deep."

"And you, my young friend, have to accept your fate with equal grace."

"That's a tall order."

"Cop. Criminal. Makes no difference. Accept it all with grace and it'll set you free—trust me. Gino's wounds and your exile to that crap job will then make sense."

"Vinnie, you sound very Zen-like."

"Twenty-five years in a secular monastery can do that," he said.

"Now *that* is deep."

I sipped some more. Vinnie did, too.

We ordered food and talked about everything and nothing. Finally, Vinnie came back to why he was seeing so much of me.

"What did Gino say when he called?"

I ceased protesting that I had no mission. "He's worried about you."

"About me? *Sheeez.* He's turning into such an old lady."

"It seems you have been hard to locate—especially at night."

"So?"

"Wanna tell me about it?"

"No."

"Really?"

"Yeah. Really."

"Come on," I chided. "Accept your fate."

He laughed. I laughed. And we sipped some more wine.

"Okay," Vinnie said, "You are family—or why else would I be sharing what I'm about to share *with a cop*?" He tossed enough cash on the table to cover dinner and a sizable tip and said, "Come on. Follow me."

Outside, he headed for his work truck. It was a nondescript ten-year-old white van. It had no markings, logo, or lettering and could go past you ten times in the same day, and you'd never remember seeing it.

Vinnie opened the rear doors, and we hopped inside.

"Not what you imagined—right?" asked Vinnie when he saw the surprised look on my face. The interior was set up for performing surveillance rather than home repairs.

"Vinnie, you're not... Not—"

"Relax. It's legit."

"For real?"

"I'm strictly volunteer."

"*This* you've *got* to explain." I was flabbergasted. "I thought you were working as a handyman. This is... Is... *Wow!*"

Vinnie loved it. And after chuckling up a storm, he launched into his explanation of why his supposed work truck was the clone of a CIA snoop vehicle.

"Jake, when I got out of the joint I had more than enough dough stashed or owed to me to comfortably get by. But there was something missing. Guess what?"

"I haven't a clue."

"Purpose. Meaning. I had money, but I lacked a purpose. What was I supposed to do with myself?"

"What did you dream about in jail?"

"Getting out."

We laughed at the simplicity and truthfulness of his remark.

"So, tell me Vinnie. What's all this?" I asked, motioning about the van. "What on earth are you doing with all this equipment?"

He had night-vision goggles, binoculars, motion sensors, cameras, and stuff whose purpose I had no idea.

"It's my purpose—my passion."

"Surveillance? Snooping?" Another thought crossed my mind. "Dear God... Not *stalking*?"

"Relax, Jake. Don't blow a fuse. I said I was legit, and I meant it. Let me explain."

I nodded, and he told me how and why he became a one-man spy ring.

"When I was in the joint, I did a lot of thinking. And it was about more than letting my hair down once I got out. Sure, I fantasized about women, booze, and then more about women. But you can only do that for so long. After a while I focused on me—how I got there and why."

"You accepted your fate."

"With grace."

"I see."

"And, *so did I*. And what I saw is all that had passed me by. It changed me. I had no idea just how much." He paused.

I encouraged him to continue, "Go on."

"Outwardly I didn't change much. I'm still a talker, a joker—opinionated—stubborn as ever.

"But on the inside?"

"I'm a staunch law-abiding citizen, with the soul of a vigilante."

I flinched.

Vinnie immediately caught my being ill at ease and assured me, "I know all about your geeky side-kick. But don't worry. I won't squeal on you."

"You know about Duct Man... *And* me? How?"

"Jake, I got street smarts and all this." He pointed to his equipment overflowing the van. "It's my passion. I'm sort of an investigative reporter—anonymous, of course. Nobody will hire an ex-con who's out from a murder rap. Like I told you, I'm set. So I've been giving my information away for free."

"To whom?"

"Anyone who uses it."

"Anyone I'd recognize?"

"Maybe? Some of the mainstream media guys with sense have used my stuff. Most of what I produce is raw. By the time it's edited, even I have trouble recognizing it. A good deal of my work is used by bloggers and freelancers. I'm known as a 'reliable street source'."

"Alright, I understand why you have been hard to find at night. But I still don't get the spy set up."

"It grew out of what I call, *The Big Final Project*."

"Sounds ominous."

"It would be for the average street source."

"So, who are you watching?"

"Gangs."

"Street gangs?"

"Yeah—all over Chicago—suburbs, too."

"Nice hobby—somebody could get hurt." He was no longer Vinnie Muscle, and the thought of him mixing it up with toughs a third his age or less gave me goose bumps.

"I told you, I'm a changed man."

"Vinnie, today's gangs can be vicious. I was thinking that maybe you could be the one who would get hurt."

"Not likely. This van is invisible—it practically blends in with the pavement."

From the tone of his voice, I knew he did not want to hear any more along my line of thinking, so I changed gears.

"You said this was your final project. What did you mean by that?"

"I met a sweet lady who has her heart set on warmer weather."

"You're leaving Chicago?"

"Yeah—everything I knew is gone or going. For me this neighborhood is a ghost town. As soon as I finish, we're getting hitched and moving south."

"How long before that happens?"

He pushed a file box toward me with his foot and said, "Here—take a look. I've got dossiers on a number of them. You tell me how close I am."

I peeked inside the box and was amazed. My fingers landed on the files under the letter 'L'. I thumbed the files on LA RAZA, LATIN ANGELS, LATIN BROTHERS, LATIN COUNTS, LATIN DRAGONS, LATIN EAGLES, LATIN JIVERS, LATIN KINGS, and the LATIN LOVERS.

"You got a thing for Hispanics?" I asked.

He looked at where my hand was in the box. "I'm not particularly focused on the Latins. Those guys are just unimaginative when it comes to names." He pointed to the other files.

"There are more *not* starting with 'L'. We got Spanish Lords, Spanish Cobras, and the Maniac Latin Disciples—not to be confused with the Spanish Gangster Disciples, or the plain old non-Latin Gangster Disciples.

"Personally, my favorite is the Familia Stones. Then, of course, there are all the Black, White, and Asian outfits.

"I've stayed away from Chinatown, so I'm light on Asian gangs. They are in a league of their own. So are the wackos in the MP-Thirteen gang. They're organized crime and not gangs."

I scanned the alphabet and saw folders in the ABCs for the ASHLAND VIKINGS, BISHOPS, BLACK DISCIPLES, BLACK GANGSTERS, BLACK P STONES, BLACK SOULS, and CITY KNIGHTS.

The mid alphabet had them for GANGSTER DISCIPLES, HARRISON GENTS, INSANE DRAGONS, INSANE UNKNOWNS, and the KRAZY GET DOWN BOYS.

The Latin groups already seen were followed by the MICKEY COBRAS, PARTY PEOPLE, SAINTS, SATAN'S DISCIPLES, SIMON CITY ROYALS, TWO TWO BOYS, and finally, the VICE LORDS.

"Quite a pile of bad boys," I said.

"Girls, too," Vinnie added. "I got them in a separate file. Most have names spun from the guys they run with—like Lady Insane Dragons, Lady Bishops and such."

"Are they cheerleaders or real gangs?"

"Some of the stand-alone female gangs—like the One-Two-Three Girls are tougher than anything the guys can muster. I classify them differently." He laughed and said, "Knowledge like that is akin to knowing a tomato is a fruit and having the wisdom to not put it in a fruit salad."

"Vinnie—I swear you have turned into a Zen-monk crime fighter."

"Maybe I have. So as a cop, what do you think?"

I looked at the folders again, that time deeper and at length. They included names of members, descriptions, photos, maps and diagrams with hideouts, drug distribution points, gun caches, and much more.

After some minutes of reading, I asked him about the electronic gadgets he had scattered about the van.

"Have you used the devices much?"

"Every gang has been photographed and recorded. I've even got bugs planted. Since I'm a civilian—I evade the need for warrants."

I was amazed and told him so.

"These files—all this—it's really something, Vinnie. From what I see, you have compiled the most detailed examination ever on Chicago gangs. Someone could write one helluva series based on this stuff."

"How about arrests?"

"You mean if you hand all this over to some of my colleagues?"

"If they are the right ones—the real cops."

"Real ones?"

"Working in a police station doesn't make you a cop any more than standing in a garage makes you a car."

"More Zen?"

"Kinda."

"Let's say I know some *real* cops in the gang unit."

"So, you'd vouch for my stuff with them?"

"Am I enough of a *real* cop for you to trust my judgment?"

"Sure, Jake. Standing in the kitchen doesn't make you a chef any more than working at AIU makes you a failure." He smiled and winked. I couldn't help but smile back.

"Yes, Zen Master." I bowed as deeply as my seated position allowed. "What do you say? Would you hand over the information to my friends?"

"Only if they use it to go after these thugs."

"Of course—I understand."

"Great. Set it up after we finish tonight."

"What are you talking about?" I'd been recruited on the sly before, by partners, bosses, and even Earline, but never by an ex-con and never so smoothly. Vinnie knew I was beholden to Gino, and he had maneuvered me into place like a pro. I knew I was stuck.

"Okay, but I have only one demand."

"Name it."

"You've had enough wine. I'm driving."

"Done."

* * *

The strip of Cicero Avenue alongside Midway Airport is much nicer since the expansion of the terminal has been completed. A decade or so ago, it was much seedier.

Vinnie told me to cruise up and down Cicero a little under the speed limit while he scanned the sidewalks.

"Who are we looking for?" I asked, as we passed the parking deck for the third time.

"A couple of hookers."

"Business or personal?" I joked.

"Telling a lame joke does not make you a comedian any more than driving around makes you a cabbie."

"Vinnie, you need to write a book," I suggested. "The world yearns for wisdom like yours."

"I'll think about that when I'm— *Wait*! Turn in over there." He pointed to an alleyway between two stores.

I wheeled the van to through the opening and behind the stores where we found two under-aged streetwalkers nervously huddled together.

"Jesus!" I exclaimed. "They look like kids."

"They are," Vinnie replied. "I've been working with them to bring down the Mean Street Boyz."

"Mean Street Boyz? They weren't in the files," I said, as I parked the van.

Vinnie opened his door. The baby hookers had not moved. It was obvious they knew Vinnie.

"Yeah, the Mean Street Boyz are the last target. The scumbags' income stream is from pimpin' real young ones—girls and boys alike." Before he closed the door he said, "Stay put. It won't take long to collect the micro bug I planted on Sugar Buns."

"Sugar Buns?" I muttered as Vinnie walked toward the hookers.

I cracked the window and was about to ease back into my seat when my cop radar went active. In the corner of my eye, I saw movement.

"Hey, *Gramps*." A sarcastic voice called out to Vinnie. "Hold on, old man."

Two punks strutted into view. Headed toward and focused on Vinnie, they were oblivious of me seated in the van.

Vinnie turned to face them.

"You looking for this?" One of the punks held something in his hand, waving it above his head.

It was much too small to identify.

Vinnie turned to face them, the girls froze in place, and the punks closed in. Vinnie held his ground.

"You found your butt plug?" Vinnie taunted.

The punk and his companion were enraged by the insult and their ire allowed me to slip unnoticed out of the van.

"Real funny, old man. We'll teach you," the one closest said. "You don't mess with our street meat."

He unraveled a chain while his partner whipped out a long blade.

Vinnie was not impressed. "Bring it on, you little pussies," he challenged.

I was behind the pair and in Vinnie's field of vision, and certain his intent was to keep their attention on him and away from my approach.

Vinnie moved two steps back and they split up to attack. Everything was over in seconds. A chain arced through the air, the knife slashed, and I shot in the air.

Prison life had not slowed Vinnie down very much. He was still agile for his age. He allowed the chain to wrap around his arm and, in one motion, spun with its momentum. Simultaneously avoiding the knife, he pulled the chain-man forward and off balance.

My warning shot coming from their rear startled both thugs and, combined with Vinnie's acrobatics, they were completely caught off guard. The only thing that gang-cake needed was a little whipped cream.

That came from Vinnie when he stepped forward and dropped them both with a couple lightning quick punches worthy of a contender going after a championship belt.

"Nice work, Vinnie." I slipped my set of cuffs through the catch-rail of a garbage dumpster. Together, we dragged the unconscious punks to the cuffs and secured one arm each. "We'll wake them when the cavalry arrives."

I called for a back-up unit while Vinnie retrieved his bug.

"This is it, Jake," he said. "I planted this on more than one girl—Sugar Buns was the last."

Not seeing the girls, I asked, "Did the girls safely bug out?"

"As soon as our friends arrived."

"Word will spread quickly about this."

"Good." Vinnie held up the miniature device. "I'm hoping this has enough on it to put a big dent in the Mean Street Boyz' business."

* * *

It did—and then some.

Before I passed Vinnie's data to my pals in the department, I gave his information to my techno-wizard friend, Vick. Vick scanned, scrubbed, and massaged everything. When the Gang Unit received Vinnie's meticulously gathered information, it was quickly downloaded to street investigators.

It's true—gang life did not go away. But many gang members did. Thanks to Vinnie, the neighborhoods of Chicago were cleaner, nicer, and safer—and that's what he wanted. I learned that the day he left for Florida.

"Vinnie, why and how on earth did you decide on gangs?" I asked.

"It was nostalgia."

"Nostalgia?"

"Yeah... When I got out and saw how bad things had become in the old neighborhood, I wanted to push back time and have it like it was." He chuckled. "I know, I know. It can't happen. But who says a man has to accept everything the way it comes to him? You joke about me and Zen. Well, I am real un-Zen when it comes to the neighborhood. These punks, today's gangs, are nothing but trash. In my day we had rules, and the first one was 'do not disrespect your home— the neighborhood'."

"I'd say that it's *uber* Zen. Imagine. A criminal ethics system. You did all that work—almost two years of police work—because of ethics. Vinnie, I am in awe."

"Why? Cops and guys like me aren't so different."

"You have made your point, Vinnie. You have made your point."

Uncle Vinnie left Chicago for good, but not before he taught me there is more to the world than what I can see in my own field of vision.

THE SMELL OF PETRICHOR

I'M STUMPED. I DON'T KNOW what the name is for the smell that always appears right before it rains. I might be tempted to *Google* it, but I don't have one of those fancy phones. AIU only provides out-of-date models. So, that's that.

Besides, in my book, using *Google* while working on a crossword is flat-out cheating.

I bet such self-imposed rules take up a whole semester in some curriculum. Right now, a roomful of aspiring psychologists could be gnawing on an exam about them. I wonder if they are covering contradictory rules and cheating. Both the contrarian and the cop in me want to know.

"You need some help?" asked Earline.

"Yeah—what's the word for that smell right before it rains?" Asking for help from friends was allowed by the rules in my world.

"P-E- ...something," answered Earline.

"It's a start." I scribbled in the letters.

"I tried doing the crossword earlier," she added. "That one got me. Sorry."

Earline headed for the kitchen, and I plowed back into the puzzle. I skirted around the pesky word, hoping to solve the mystery by solving others. When I stalled again, I grabbed my phone and punched in the number for Neville Price at the *Chicago Insider*.

He wrote *Straight Shot*, my favorite column.

The Master, as he was known, answered after one ring. "Crossword problems, Jake?"

"Yeah—a serious one."

"Try me."

"The smell that appears right before it rains."

"Petrichor—P-E-T-R-I-C-H-O-R. It occurs when rain falls windward."

"Damn! Got it. Thanks for the assist."

"Any time, Jake." He quickly hung up.

He did that. We seldom chit chatted.

I've never laid eyes on Neville. Sometimes, after I'd been well laced with bourbon, I swore he didn't exist. Once I dreamed that Ned, his top-notch assistant, had him locked in a cage. Maybe Ned is really him. The mystery of that situation is delicious, but off limits. For all things difficult, Neville is my Deep Throat and he more than meets the billing as "the world's most intelligent" human being.

I completed the crossword and swilled down my coffee. Earline eased back to my booth with a fresh pot. "You want another?"

"No. Breakfast is over for me. I need to hit the streets. Gotta find a good reason not to show up at the office."

"If you really need one, Renee could use some help. She's been asking about you—has some kind of problem. Won't say anything to anyone. I think you should pop into the kitchen and check it out."

"Will do. By the way—it's petrichor."

"What?"

"I know. They dug deep for that one."

"How'd you get it?"

"Deep Throat."

"Huh?"

I left a tip, paid my bill, and jawed a bit with Jimmie before I made my way to the kitchen. It was a good time to peek in on Renee. Since I eat breakfast at noon, or later, and do my crossword slowly, it was well past the diner's midday rush.

I stepped behind the counter and pushed through the double doors into the kitchen. Renee saw me and spoke first.

"Jake, can we talk?" she asked.

"Anything for the lady who feeds me so well," I said. "What's on your mind?"

"Plenty. But, it will take more time than I can have right now. Could we meet later?"

"Just say when and where."

"Is tonight okay? I hate to ask a favor and then push you off, Jake. But I read to kids at the library. I've got them hooked on a book and I have to be there for the finale."

Renee's words reminded me how little I knew about the people closest to me in the "Wonderful World of *Jimmie's Diner*".

Renee was another mystery right before my eyes. She had been preparing my meals for years but beyond a wave and "hello", I drew a blank.

She jotted down an address and handed it to me.

"Is nine too late?"

"No. I'm a night person."

"That's good. If you believe what I tell you, you may be up late."

"Renee, you have me intrigued."

"I'll explain it all at nine."

"Fine with me. I'll be there."

"Oh, by the way. There are two entrances to my building. Don't use the smaller resident's door. Take the scenic route by the shops and through the lobby— it stays open until nine-thirty."

My blank expression prompted her to add, "It's part of why I need to talk with you."

"Sure—no problem," I stuck the address in my pocket. "See you at nine."

Without a reason to avoid AIU, I headed to the bleak offices that were quickly filling up with rejects from Chicago's PD. A block from the office I spotted a colleague's parked car and fought the urge to have it towed. I was desperate for a reason not to show up.

Goodness prevailed and I soon found myself where I did not want to be.

Something is brewing, I told myself as I entered. A deaf, blind, sleeping idiot could figure out money woes pushed the growth and transformation of my personal hell into an elephant's graveyard for cops. Crap equipment, no cars, slumps like me doubled and sometimes even tripled-up in an office.

The city is almost as broke as the State of Illinois. A couple more years and I'm out. Only a couple more years.

"Foister is looking for you," Pinkie, the receptionist, said before I took two steps inside.

"What? No hugs? No kiss?" I spread my arms way out in a *faux* hug.

"Fat chance, Jake. I can smell your cologne way over here. Bourbon again?"

"I take it that our engagement is off?"

"You better get moving. Like I said, Foister is looking for you."

"First, I have one question."

"Okay—shoot."

"Who is Foister?"

"Jake, *really*. You're kidding—right?"

"I'm serious as a heart attack."

"Foister is Mildred Foister—as in *Captain* Mildred Foister."

Ever since Denny Gilbert left, there has been a constant flow of new bosses in my life. Keeping up with them is not my top priority.

"Let me guess—she's my boss?"

"Good boy," she said, oozing with sarcasm. "Captain Foister said that as soon as—"

"Yeah... Yada, yada, yada." I headed to my worksite, "She'll find me... Eventually."

My office was a mess, and my desk was worse. From the look of things, two or three other detectives shared the space with me. I had avoided being in the office so much that I was uncertain who was assigned to be there.

I grabbed a note pad, pulled a chair to the window, and sat down.

On days when I complete the crossword, I dabble at writing Haiku. I'm not very good at the art form but therein lay the charm. I try.

Before I could settle in, Captain Mildred Foister found me.

"Thompson?" she asked from the doorway.

"None other."

"Here," she handed me a bunch of papers. "Get yourself over to accounting and sort these out."

"What are they?"

"Expense vouchers from your file."

I scanned the papers and said, "You gotta be *kidding*. These are ancient."

She frowned and ordered, "I don't care. Get going—and don't come back until they are all resolved."

I was happy. She obviously did not know what she was saying. "Don't come back until..." was a combined open-ended pass, get-out-of-jail-free card, and passport to infinity. Accounting's pace for resolving anything would make a glacier's advance look speedy.

"Sure, Captain—I'm on it."

"Good. Let's start out right. Handle it just like I said, and all will be good between us."

"Definitely, Captain. I understand." I was ecstatic.

I made my way to Accounting as instructed, waited as further instructed, and finally got to speak with a clerk who told me I'd have to wait my turn in order to talk to an auditor.

I turned my papers over to the clerk, gave him my cell number, and left.

Based upon my instructions, I figured that I'd get back to AIU sometime after Foister transferred, retired, or disappeared.

Freed from work, I went home and napped. I wanted to be fresh and able to follow up on anything Renee tossed at me.

I awoke at eight. I got dressed and headed to my meeting with Renee.

When Renee had given me her address, I correctly figured it was one of the newer mid-rise condos
popping up on the South Loop. When I got to the
fourteen-hundred block of South Michigan, I saw I
was correct and was impressed—the building was
beautiful.

At street level were shops and restaurants.
Offices and a spa took up space on the second floor. I
passed through the main entrance, as instructed, and
found a high-ceilinged and spacious lobby.

I wandered across the lobby. On the far side, I
found access to the residential floors above. Renee
lived on the third floor.

It was a short elevator ride.

At her door, Renee greeted me. "Hello, Jake.
Come on in."

I returned her greeting and stepped inside. She
guided me to a seat in her combination living room
and library. Without asking, she provided a drink—
three fingers of top-shelf bourbon.

"It isn't that strange mix you prefer, but I hope
it will do," she told me with a grin. She made herself
what looked to be a gin and tonic and took the seat
across from me.

"Cheers!" I toasted. She matched my move and
then we talked.

"Thanks for coming, Jake. I really appreciate it."

"No problem." I motioned to her vast book collection and added, "I see that your reading extends
beyond doing it for the kids."

"Oh, yes. I'm a big reader. Place a book any-where near me and I'm on it like glue. Thinking about what books I am reading is how I pass my time while cooking. After a while, cooking gets mechanical—I can do it in the dark and asleep."

I patted my waistline and said, "And, you're good at it—*too* good."

She raised her glass. "Thanks. And you're good at what you do, Jake. You are very good."

"Come on. I only—"

"Tuh-tuh-tuh," she silenced me. "Don't try to be modest. Just because you work in a den of losers, you can't fool me.

"Everyone at *Jimmie's* treats you like royalty—and for good reason. You keep solving important cases even though you are *persona non grata* with those numbskulls running the police force. Because your professional feelings hurt you, you sometimes act like an idiot instead of the genius you really are. In spite of that, I am counting on you."

"Wow! That's an earful of praise."

"Had to get it off my chest if I was going to get you involved in what's going on."

"What exactly *is* going on?"

"I can't say for one hundred percent certainty, but I think it's devil worship."

"Devil worship? Come on. You gotta be kidding."

"No. I'm not kidding. I truly wish I was."

Her face revealed she was serious and that I needed to listen. I gulped my drink and encouraged her to explain why she believed what she had said.

"You better fill me in—completely."

"Fine. You tell me if I'm being too detailed."

I nodded.

"My buying into this building was a bit of a fluke. You can imagine those snooty realtors. They tried to guide me away from it, but I kept pushing to be here. They just could not imagine that a cook from a diner could afford one of these condos. But, I've worked hard all my life. I often had two jobs—sometimes more.

"As you noticed I'm a reader. I've been one all my life." She sipped her G&T then continued. "As a young woman, after my fiancé abruptly left me hanging, I focused—maybe I even obsessed—on work and books. I was happy, saved a great deal of money, and always wanted a nice place to call my own—with a library just like this." She waved proudly at her books.

"Anyway—as is obvious—I prevailed." She giggled. "I guess they were afraid I might sue over access and the like. In the end, I got this unit. It's the one that shares a back wall with the lobby. You came through it. This unit was therefore supposed to be less desirable. *Hah*! They found out too late that as a reader, I knew a thing or two about condominium space and real estate law.

"I keep telling those kids at the library that it pays to read." She got up and motioned to me. "Come on—follow me. I want to show you something."

Renee led me through the master bedroom and into the john.

Inside, she pointed to the wall. "There," she said. "See that lightwell? I am the only one in this building who has one."

I looked and smiled. "Really?" My face told her I was puzzled.

"It's designed to bring in light, but it also funnels sound."

"You're hearing noises from the lobby?"

"I'll say." She held up her glass and motioned for a return to the library.

I sat down, she fixed a second round, and soon we were talking again.

"Jake, sometimes at night I tune in to talk radio and leave the station on. I'm a big fan of Rollye James. She has the absolute *best* voice in radio. Anyway, I use the radio as background noise to fall asleep."

"I've done that, too."

"Well, everything was fine until I installed the lightwell. Within a week, I was hearing things—really strange things."

"What kind of things?"

"Chants—I hear chants."

"Can you describe them?"

"The words are not always clear, but I know that what I hear are definitely chants."

"Have they ever been clear enough for you to make out any words?"

"Sure. That's the scary part. I've heard, 'Baphomet.' They have been chanting, 'Baphomet, Lord Baphomet. We call upon you to appear.' That phrase comes through loud and clear. The other stuff sounds garbled."

"Who is 'they'? Who do you think is doing the chanting?"

"I don't know, *exactly*."

"Which means you have an idea, right?"

"Maybe." She offered to fix me another, but I declined. She indicated she had had enough, too.

"Jake," she continued, "I'm not the type to see gremlins and spooks under every leaf and twig, but I have noticed a lot of borderline-Goth types near this building. I think they are the chanters and they are clustered here. I see them working in the shops, walking through the lobby, and on the streets nearby."

"Could you point one out to me if you had to?"

"Sure, there are two working at the newsstand right off the lobby. Speaking of which, I had you come that way so you would know the space I am referring to. The lobby is closed from nine-thirty until six in the morning."

"A perfect site for something *satanic*?"

"You said it, not me."

"I guess it could be possible."

"More than possible. I have something else to show you." She reached for a legal pad resting near one of her many books and said, "Here—take a look at this."

I took the pad and looked it over. In neat rows, Renee had listed the major and minor feast days associated with saints of the church. Across from the feast days she indicated the appearance of the chanting and whether or not she heard the signature phrase she had shared with me. Every incident occurred on the night before a feast day. The call for Baphomet always came on the nights of the major feasts.

I scrutinized the information and asked, "Are you certain about this?"

"Yes," she calmly said.

"Could I have another drink?"

"You sure you want another one?"

"Today is the twenty-seventh... The day before the feast day of Saint Simon and Saint Jude, right?"

"It is."

"Then, pour me another. I'm staying to hear if they chant tonight."

"I *knew* I could count on you."

I checked the clock and mistakenly figured I had ample time to relax and enjoy Renee's good bourbon. However, she had another, much more disturbing, surprise for me.

"Jake, you remember that I volunteer at the library, right?"

"Yeah, of course I remember."

"Well, I've encountered something that I think is related to both the library and what I suspect may be going on in this building."

"Why do I feel that this is the clincher?"

"Jake, don't make fun of me."

"I'm not. It's just that... That... *Damn!* I'm... I'm—" I took a gulp of my drink. "I don't know what I am, or *what is going on.*" I drained my glass, and in a moment calmed down. "Sorry, this is *a lot.* Renee, until today you just cooked my food, not my brain."

The lame joke made us both laugh.

"Okay... I think I'm ready for it. What do else do you have?"

"At the library, there was this homeless guy. Old Bill is what everyone called him. He was always around. And then, *poof!* He disappears."

"Happens all the time."

"But this is different. After a couple of days, he shows up. *Here.*"

"Here? Where?"

"Sitting in the lobby. But I barely recognized him. He was cleaned up and dressed in new clothes. Clothes that were... Weird."

"What do you mean by 'weird'?"

"Black. All black. With silver borders on the cuffs and collar."

"A new fashion statement for the homeless?"

"Jake, this is serious."

"I know—I know. Sorry. Go on."

"He's in the lobby and then, *poof*! He disappears again."

She paused in a way that telegraphed something big was coming. When I heard it, I was really sorry to have made light of Old Bill.

"And then... Then... Last night on channel nine's news, there's a report about a body found without any identification other than black clothes with silver borders."

"Wait a minute. Are you certain?"

"Certain enough to stay up all night, fret all morning, and tell you."

"Why not just call channel nine?"

"I did. They told me to contact the police."

"Did you?"

"*Jake, you are the police.*"

"But—"

"Don't 'but' me. You *know* me, and you aren't totally convinced—and won't be until you hear the chanting for yourself. What do you think someone *who doesn't even know me* would think?"

"I must say, you have a point."

"You bet I do."

Even though I had rested most of the afternoon, I was drained. The bourbon had not helped much. Rene saw I was fading and suggested I lean back and catch a wink.

I did.

At eleven forty-five she woke me.

"I think it's time we get in place," she said, gently shaking my arm.

We retraced our steps to the bathroom and sat within a few feet of the lightwell. Just before mid-night, we heard an eerie humming sound.

"What's that?" I asked.

"They're warming up. In a few seconds they'll sound like I described."

She was correct. A few minutes later, I clearly heard chanting. However, I could not distinguish the words. They were either mumbled or in a language not familiar to me.

They increased and decreased in volume and, in approximately five minutes, they stopped.

"That's it," announced Renee.

"How can you be sure?" I asked.

"Remember my chart? Tomorrow is nothing com-pared to the next one—All Saint's Day."

"Of course—the night before that is Halloween."

"The number one day for all things evil."

I headed for the door.

"Renee, I gotta go. If they are done, I need to follow some of them, or at least get some sort of identification."

Renee grabbed my arm. "Don't waste your time, Jake."

"What do you mean?"

"I've tried. It only takes seconds for them to disappear. The only trace of them I have ever seen was a split-second view of a caped and hooded black figure disappearing down the street. In a flash, they're gone."

"Crap!" I bolted for the door and took the stairs instead of the elevator.

When I got to the door leading into the lobby, I found it locked. Beyond the door, I briefly heard light shuffling then nothing. *Poof*—they *were* gone. I was left with no clues, no trail—just a lot of questions.

At home, I sipped Old Jimmy Jack and thought things over. Either Renee was part of a grand hoax, or I was on to something frightful. I saw absolutely no sign of subterfuge in Renee and that truth sent a chill up my spine. I needed help—serious help.

He picked up on the first ring. "Awfully late for being stuck on a crossword."

"Neville, don't you ever sleep?" I asked the world's most intelligent insomniac.

"Sleep interferes with my thought process. What's troubling you at this hour?"

"People who go bump in the night."

"Real or imaginary?"

"Very real ones."

"I don't take you for the *séance* type, Jake. That leaves burglars, peeping Toms, wanna be Goth-teens, and the others."

"By 'others' do you mean people who chant at midnight gatherings?"

"Have you crossed over to the Dark Side, young Luke Skywalker?"

I laughed. "No—but I eavesdropped on some folks who may have."

My conversations with Neville have usually been lighthearted. On the rare occasion when I was able to share my expertise with him, his tone was straight professional. I never experienced the serious Neville until he sternly asked, "What exactly have you been doing?"

That same eerie chill raced along my spine. When it finished tap dancing on my psyche, I filled Neville in on my night at Renee's. I finished by asking, "Are there *real* devil worshipers?"

After a silence that seemed forever, he said, "Jake, you need to be very careful."

"Because Halloween is a few days away?"

"That, too."

"That, *too*? What did I miss?"

"The call for Baphomet. It may be a serious attempt and not a hoax. Have you seen any overt signs—like a demon trap?"

"Demon trap?"

"A circle with a nine-foot radius and a hexagram inside. It's where Baphomet appears—or so some believe."

"Neville, you have me spooked. We have never had a conversation this long. It makes me think you might really be *serious*."

"I am serious—dead serious."

"Jesus. Don't say that."

"You may indeed need *his* help, Jake. Halloween, the Feast of the Dead, will be here soon. Be careful. Be *very* careful."

"I will. I will." The call ended on that happy note.

As soon as the Medical Examiner's office opened, I called to find out the details about the John Doe clad in a silver-trimmed black ensemble. No one was much help until I connected with Dr. Lois Chang, the Assistant ME in charge of the case.

I told her what I knew about Old Bill.

She insisted I come in to talk. Dr. Chang sounded edgy. She said she wanted to show me something.

For a cop, visiting the morgue was no big deal. I said I'd be there as soon as possible.

* * *

"Sooner or later, we see just about everything," Dr. Chang explained, as she pulled the body out of the cold storage compartment. She lifted the portion of sheet covering Old Bill's feet.

"I never thought I'd actually see this." She pointed. "See the peeled-back skin on the soles?"

I looked. "Yes. What do you make of it?"

"Ritualistic mutilation."

"As in devil worship?"

"Or as in occultism, satanism, the black arts... Call it what you will. Homicide is homicide."

"What was the cause of death?"

"Multiple blunt-force trauma, following mutilation, possibly torture. Some very sick people put him here, Detective Thompson. If you get anywhere near them, be very careful. Use extreme caution."

That chill danced on me again. "Sure, Doc—I'll be careful."

With warnings from two experts in such a short time, I oozed caution from every pore.

As I approached Renee's building, I assessed my case. I had a stiff in the morgue, a chart from a cook who read a lot, and my own bourbon-fueled memory of chants from a mystery choir.

I needed more. I had to unearth a clue, discover a trail, find... Something.

I started in their church.

* * *

In the daytime, the lobby of Renee's building was bright and cheery. *Sunlight, ferns, and marble— not at all what one would see as the potential site of satanic rituals*, I told myself as I looked for signs of the black arts. After a few minutes, I found half a clue.

On the floor where the rays coming through the skylights converged, I found a nine-foot circle. But it was empty—no pentagram, no hexagram. It was just a circle.

I checked out the newsstand adjoining the lobby. That was a bust, too. The little redheaded girl at the counter looked too scrubbed and wholesome to be a part of anything violent like homicide or as sinister as summoning the devil. She belonged in a road production of *Annie* not *The Exorcist*.

The kid in the back room appeared even more harmless. I bought a pack of gum, a paper, and a soda, and returned to the lobby.

Perched on the bench in the lobby, I sat back and studied every inch of the place. When I found what I needed, I headed to *Jimmie's*.

It was later than my usual arrival time. Earline was already gone. I slid into a booth and was soon joined by Renee.

"Have you found anything, Jake?" Her face was full of expectation.

"Yeah... Yeah..." I stalled. Renee would have none of it.

"Come on. *Out with it*," she demanded. "I have a right to know. It's my building—my home."

She was right. It was really her case. And, it was not the typical call-your-local-police situation. Renee was not only my friend, she was my client. I was obligated to fill her in—to report.

"It looks like the real thing."

"Oh, my God." Her expectation was replaced by astonishment. And something else—fear. It was not a run-for-the-hills-and-hide fear, but it was real. I knew it would grow if I did not say something reassuring.

"Don't worry, Renee. I'm on this thing."

"What are you going to do?"

"I've got an idea."

"Well? What is it? Come on, *tell me*."

"I think I'm going to attend their next meeting."

"What!? How?"

"I don't have it completely worked out."

"Jake, this is dangerous. Maybe you should get help."

"I can't... Just can't. For the same reasons you couldn't tell "the regular" police. Who would believe me if I asked them to accompany me to a 'let's sacrifice someone and summon the devil' meeting?"

"Can I help?"

"No. This I do myself."

"Why?"

"You said it before, Renee. *I am the police.*"

* * *

I had two days. I initially spent that time looking for information that could help me devise a plan. I needed to know as much as possible about the building and its inhabitants. But there wasn't much information available.

Everything about the building, its shops, and their owners was corporate gobbledygook. One entity owned another, and the individuals' names were hidden. Holding companies were owned by other holding companies who shared ownership with investment groups, and on and on and on. The ownership of many of the residential condo units was shielded in a similar manner.

At the end of my searching, all I knew for certain was that someone was hiding something.

I am a detective. I naturally dislike secrets, and I am impatient. I was not happy with what I had found, or not found, and I wanted to do something. I was certain the combination of my displeasure and impatience influenced my actions.

My plan was simple. I *would* crash their next party.

For those two days, I read about satanism in all its forms, slept, completed crosswords without calling Neville, failed to complete another Haiku, and checked in with the auditor.

I was sure Captain Foister did not intend to enable a freelance investigation into the occult, but I wasn't going to tell her.

When the evening of Halloween arrived, I was well informed about my opponents, rested, and ready.

Was my approach *simple brilliance*, or was it just *too simple?*

The plan had two anchors: Renee's lone sighting—which gave me an idea of what to wear, and from my bench-sitting session, an idea on how to slip into the festivities.

I headed for the lobby of Renee's building with confidence, a cheap Halloween costume, burglar's tools, and one of those little canvas seats made for campers. I was ready, and it was too late to back out.

I entered the lobby at nine-fifteen. All the shops on the first level were closed. Even the newsstand was buttoned up. No one saw me head for the blind spot near the doorway that led from the backside of the newsstand. The security cameras did not concern me as they were only recorders and were not manned.

Everything went as planned.

In the corner blind spot, I easily jimmied the lock on the door to the maintenance closet.

All I could think was, *Thank God some architect placed this closet out of view.*

I slipped into the closet, put on the costume, unfolded the camp seat, and began my wait.

At nine-thirty, I heard footsteps approach the closet door. *A security guard?* I prayed that I had remembered to lock the door when I closed it behind me. I waited. Sweat beaded my brow.

The steps drew nearer. I held my breath.

The steps stopped at the door.

Oh crap! I trembled.

The doorknob jiggled back and forth.

It held. *I remembered.*

I heard the rattle of keys.

My heart stopped.

I heard a mumble. Whoever it was blew their nose and mumbled again.

Then, I heard footsteps fade away.

My wait continued.

In the dark, I had plenty of time to think about my situation. If Renee's chart was wrong, I was spending a long evening in a closet for nothing. If the gatherings were just a sham group of wannabe druids, I was going to be terribly embarrassed.

I'd experienced worse shame, but never masked and dressed up in a black-hooded cape for Halloween.

At eleven-forty-five, I heard voices coming from the area near the doorway to the newsstand. The tone and volume indicated a group of people was in the mulling-around-assembling mode that occurs at ceremonies, behind stage, and in church vestibules.

When the voices sounded their loudest and most confused, I decided to make my move.

It's now or never, I told myself. *What's the worst they can do? Have me arrested?*

I slowly opened the door and stepped into the dark. The edge of the group was only a few yards away and I fully expected to immediately be exposed as an interloper. Instead, my timing had been perfect. I was ignored.

Just as I'd made my move, a shrill female voice called out, "Followers of the Most High Baphomet... *PREPARE.*"

I did not recognize the voice, but I did get a quick look at the caller's face. It was that of the sweet young thing from the newsstand.

Some detective you are, Jake. I chided myself. *When this is over you have to ask Renee how she was able to spot Annie as one of "them".*

The worshipers responded to the command by bowing their heads and folding their hands waist high. I followed suit—kind of.

The natural pose for Baphomet's followers included head-forward, eyes-down. I cheated in an attempt to get a peek at my companions, but hoods and bowed heads prevented me from getting a good look at any of them. Dressed as they were, they were indistinguishable, and I congratulated myself on fitting in so well. My two days of reading had paid off.

After what I assume was intended to be a moment of reflection, Annie ordered, "Come, brothers and sisters. *FOLLOW.*"

She turned and led the group to the center of the lobby.

The group again did as they were told. In single file, they followed. I fell in at the end of the line. We slowly made our way to the lobby's candle-lit main area.

Soon, we all stood around the circle I had examined earlier. It was no longer empty. It was completed with the design as Neville had described.

Next to the circle was a man seated in an ornate chair. He was definitely part of the ceremonies, but not a leader or even a follower. He was dressed in black clothes trimmed in silver, appearing listless—almost asleep. He was obviously drugged.

My cop-o-meter kicked in. It asked, *Jake, do you have enough for a solid bust?*

I quickly tallied the score. *Did I have them on trespassing? Maybe, maybe not—they could have rented the place. How about kidnapping? The dude could be a volunteer or an actor. What about bad taste in clothes? Yes, but if that was a crime the county lockup would be overflowing. For being creepy? Most definitely, but that's also not grounds to get arrested.*

I needed an overt criminal act, or at least a threat to call a halt to the kinky party. If I brought the weirdos in, I wanted charges that would stick long enough to keep them locked up and scared. Under pressure, one or more of them would give up Old Bill's killers. I had to wait.

A team comprised of Annie and two others made their way around the circle.

When they arrived in front of each worshiper, a thimble-sized cup containing a yellow-brown liquid was offered and consumed.

"Take. Drink. Prepare the way for Baphomet," Annie said to each recipient.

"Willingly, I partake," was the reply each time the small cup was returned.

As the trio made its way to me, I considered what to do. There appeared to be only two choices. I could participate... Or blow my cover. Drinking the bug juice did not appear to be optional. When Annie and her pals arrived, I withdrew inside my hood as far as possible, tucked in my chin, and lowered my head.

"Take. Drink. Prepare the way for Baphomet," Annie instructed.

I took the offered liquid, placed it just beneath my lips and poured it down my chin. I hoped it would drip into the gap I had created by the contortions I had made inside my hood.

A small amount had landed on my lower lip. It was sweet and numbing.

I remembered that I needed to reply.

"Willingly, I partake," I said, and handed back the tiny container.

Annie took it without comment. My deception had not been seen.

Two tests—two passing grades. I congratulated myself.

Annie made her way to a spot directly behind the man in the circle and her assistants took positions on either side.

"*Now* is the time," she announced.

She displayed a large knife. It did not look cer-emonial.

"The servants of Baphomet are prepared," came from all—except me.

"Summon our Master," she ordered.

"With devotion we obey," said all, as they swayed in unison to the left and right. I caught on and bobbed along.

Soon the assembly softly chanted, "Ba-pho-met, Ba-pho-met, Ba-pho-met." Over and over and over, the drugged assembly chanted in a one, two, three count. They continued chanting as they swayed, and the volume of their chants slowly increased.

"BA-PHO-MET! BA-PHO-MET! BA-PHO-MET!"

Annie held the knife aloft.

The chanting continued and grew to a shout.

"BA-PHO-MET!! BA-PHO-MET!!! BA-PHO-MET!!!!" They hovered on the brink of madness.

At the height of the group's frenzy, Annie's two assistants grabbed the black-clad man from his seat and placed him on his knees just inside the circle. He had no comprehension of his surroundings. The assistants remained on either side of him as Annie approached with the knife.

The chant's volume reached its peak.

"BA-PHO-MET!!! BA-PHO-MET!!!! BA-PHO-MET!!!!!"

Madness soaked the air. Abruptly, the chant stopped.

In the eeriest voice imaginable, Annie calmly said, "Come, Lord Baphomet. Witness our devotion, witness our sacrifice." She reached toward the dazed man before her.

I yelled inside my head. *This ain't gonna happen, Jake. Time to move.*

In a frenzy of action, I threw back my cape, grabbed my piece, and screamed, "Police! Everyone FREEZE," and lunged forward to stop Annie.

What happened then will forever haunt and puzzle me.

There are events where everything compresses, and time passes ever so slowly. An action that normally takes a second or less extends in our memory, and it becomes something longer and fuller. We remember such events in slow motion. They are the movies in our mind.

That one was a tragedy.

I got to Annie a split second too late. Her knife found its target. Blood spurted, and three people screamed—Annie, me, and the poor soul I failed to save.

The two assistants joined the melee a micro-second behind me and all five bodies tumbled into the circle.

Somewhere in the middle, with my vision blurred by flailing arms and legs, I saw what appeared to be a large figure towering above us.

Baphomet?

My mind struggled to comprehend the incomprehensible.

Did I see him? Impossible!

In an instant, what I saw—or imagined—disappeared. Time returned to its normal pace and crap rained down upon me.

Actually, it was not crap. It was fists.

The entire assembly had swarmed like rabid locusts on a green twig. Screaming and yelling, they relentlessly pummeled me.

My overloaded brain had room for only one thought, *If I don't act fast, I'm going to die.*

Without taking aim, I fired into the crowd. It was a good thing my attackers panicked. My back-up piece was a *Seecamp* and held a total of six rounds. Reloading it under the circumstances would have been impossible.

Who did I hit? I have no clue. Before I could find out, someone put my lights out with a solid thud to my head.

When I woke, it was to an EMT wafting smelling salts under my beak and applying ice to my head. I was still in the lobby but had been moved to a stretcher close to the main doors.

"Are you okay, Jake?" Renee asked. She stood behind the EMT.

Renee had ignored my instructions, manned the listening post, and called for help.

"Sure—never better," I answered. "What happened?"

"I heard the gunshots," she explained. "Hurried down the stairs, and pounded like hell on the doors. They were shouting and yelling. None of it made sense—then they scurried—faster than usual. *Poof*! Gone."

"They got away?"

"Yes."

"All of them?"

"All of them."

"What about the bodies? The guy—the guy—who—" I felt defeated.

"Jake, there's nothing here. Everything was gone by the time my nine-one-one was answered. *See*!?" She pointed at the emptiness of the lobby.

She was right. There were no bodies, no design in the circle, and zero signs of what I had experienced. All that remained was the movie in my head.

The rest of the night was spent in the local emergency room where I was poked and prodded by staff concerned about my balance, reasoning, and memory. They were well-intentioned and professional with me. I was surly and under-appreciative with them. I wanted out. I had an investigation to complete. They had a patient to treat. In the end, they won the battle to be kept indoors and under observation.

I think they cheated. I vaguely remember some drugs being administered.

Next, I went home, slept, woke, and slept some more.

On the second of November, I went to *Jimmie's*. Renee greeted me.

"You look like crap," she quipped.

"I've been worse." I mustered a thin smile.

"*That* I do not want to see." She laughed and I joined her.

"I'm surprised to find you back at work so soon," I said.

"Why?" she countered. "There's nothing going on at home."

"No repercussions?"

"The place is a ghost town. The newsstand is closed, half the shops are closed, and a small fleet of moving vans arrived the next day and hustled stuff out of a number of condos. Jake, you scared them into another state, maybe out of the country. It's over, Jake."

After breakfast, I went to the office and found that Renee was wrong.

Captain Foister found me two steps inside the door. "Thompson."

"Yes, Captain?"

"You got any paper for me?"

"No, Captain Foister. The auditors still have—"

"I don't care about that crap," she shouted. "I want your weapon's discharge forms."

"What?"

"Don't play dumb with me," she wailed. "Just who the hell do you think you are? You can't shoot up the lobby of a condo and get away with it on my watch."

"Huh... Sure... Sure, Captain. I'll do it right away."

"Six forms. For six rounds. By five o'clock tomorrow. Got it?"

"Got it," I said with a shrug.

"You better." She turned, headed to her office, and muttered, "And *I* thought we had gotten off to a good start."

I turned and headed for the door. Just before leaving, Pinkie, the receptionist, asked, "Headed to *Jimmie's*?"

"Yeah," I answered. "I can finish paperwork better in my favorite booth. See ya tomorrow at four-fifty-nine."

On the way to *Jimmie's*, a west wind whipped through the canyons formed by the man-made mountains of the Loop.

I caught a whiff of the coming rain and made a mental note to call Neville.

Inside *Jimmie's*, I finished the forms in half an hour and attacked a particularly difficult crossword. I wasn't stumped, but I called Neville anyway. I wanted him to know that I knew he was right again.

DEPUTY JAKE

I DO NOT RECALL SEEING PINKIE away from her desk very often. To be truthful, nor seeing her below the waist more than once. I've only known her as 'the person behind the AIU reception desk'. That's why I did not recognize her standing next to my booth at *Jimmie's*.

When something or someone is encountered outside its usual context, the mind goes blank. Everyone's mind works that way. At least that's my excuse for the dumb look on my face.

"*Jake*," she said. "Why aren't you answering your phone?"

"Huh?" I replied, shaking my head side to side. The dumb look stayed put.

"Jake, are you sick?"

Gears meshed and I put the incongruous data together. "Pinkie. I didn't recognize you. Jeez, you got legs—nice ones."

"I'll take it as a compliment—not sexual harass-ment." She slid into the booth.

"What brings you to *Jimmie's*?"

"You." See looked straight at me with that laser-beam stare women have.

"Me?" I looked back with the extra blank-male look.

"Yeah. Captain Foister is having kittens over you not being in the office and also not answering your phone or even your voicemail."

"My voicemail doesn't work."

"You know that for certain?"

"Yeah—when my phone is off it doesn't work."

"You mean your phone is..."

"Turned off." I finished for her, dumped the blank look, and grinned.

"Off?" It was her turn to have that dumb look on her face.

"I do that sometimes—usually when I eat break-fast."

"Jake, I know the department's phones are cheap crap, but they give them to you to be used. If you turn it off, how can we reach you?"

"Just call me here at *Jimmie's*."

"I tried that. They said they didn't know you." I looked over to where Jimmie held court behind the cash register and waved. Jimmie waved back and smiled.

Pinkie frowned, then continued. "They treat you like royalty here."

"Better," I said. "I'm a regular customer." Pinkie's eyes rolled back into her head.

Earline approached the booth. As soon as she had eyed my female visitor, Earline had taken up a hovering position just outside earshot.

"Do you want some coffee," she asked Pinkie.

"No—we *have* to go," Pinkie said to both me and Earline. To me she said, "Foister sent me to get you. She said that if I don't bring you back right away, she's going to get a warrant."

Earline backed up, turned, and sauntered toward the wait station. Over her shoulder she said, "I'll get your check."

Pinkie did her best to drag me out of the booth. "You're coming with me."

"Can't I just phone in?" I joked.

Pinkie's stare was lethal. I got up.

Back at AIU we were immediately greeted by a flustered and excited Captain Foister. "Thompson. I'm glad we found you."

Pinkie was visibly upset at the slight.

Mildred Foister was hopeless and could not find her butt with both hands if she tried. Her assignment as Director of AIU was the final step in a spotted career, and without Pinkie, AIU would have grinded to a halt.

"We've been worried to death—we need to get you to the DA's office right away. You've been temporarily assigned there," Foister said, looking toward Pinkie for help.

"Don't ask me," pouted Pinkie. "I found him— you can babysit him from here on out." She strutted to her desk and disappeared below the waist again.

"I can get to the DA's office on my own," I said.

"Then get going." Foister wildly waved her hands and shooed me toward the door. "Don't keep the DA waiting, Thompson. This could be good for all of us. Call me as soon as you know what it's about. This could be big. No—no—don't call me. I'll call you."

I was headed out the door when she stopped me. "Thompson. Turn your phone on. And leave it that way."

"Yes, Captain Foister—I promise never to turn it off again."

I am a man of my word. On my way to the DA's office, I tossed my phone's battery in the trash.

* * *

"I'm Detective Thompson, AIU," I told the gatekeeper in the DA's office.

It wasn't really the DA's office. I had been routed down the bureaucratic food chain to an Assistant Deputy District Attorney's assistant. He was the flunky whom I addressed. He seemed to be as impressed with me as I was with him.

"Jake Thompson?" he asked me and the wall behind me.

"That's me." I answered. He rummaged about his desk in a show of importance and made an act out of finding a large brown envelope.

"Here—take these." He tossed me the envelope like it was radioactive and then did his best to ignore me.

"What's this?" I grew tired of the runaround and tweaked the question with my best 'who the hell are you?' tone.

"Your vacation papers." He tried the same back but missed my level.

"What vacation?" I gave him the same dumb look I tried on Pinkie.

"This stuff was sent down ages ago. Jeez! Didn't anybody brief you?"

"Briefings are above my paygrade. Where I work, we talk to each other." He caught on that I was pissed.

That was easy—a corpse could have sensed it.

"Okay, okay. Relax." He took the envelope, opened it, and pointed to the cover letter. "Look here. You're going to China. The Chief Prosecutor of Hong Kong has requested your presence."

I grabbed the papers and scanned the important parts. "Sonic Kwan's case is being tried. No plea deal."

"And you are needed as a witness—right?"

"No—it's an open and shut case. This trial is about maintaining *face*. There's never been any doubt about Kwan going to prison for life. But he called out and assaulted a Hong Kong police officer in a very public manner while that officer was a guest overseas. The embarrassment—loss of face—must be addressed. In China you *do not* assault the police."

"So... Why the request for you?"

"They are being polite."

"Huh?"

"We are being given the opportunity to apologize and also save face."

"Us? Save face? Why?"

"We allowed Kwan to escape from county lockup."

"Oh, my." He pointed at papers, "Then you'll not want to miss your flight—it leaves in four hours."

* * *

In no way am I a fan of the circus act they call airport security. Sorry, but uniforms and badges *do not* make slouches into officers of the law. Checking IDs, scanning bags, and feeling up passengers is *not* police work.

As much as I bitched about AIU as the department's dumpster, it was full of real cops. I'd stake the worst of my unit against anything the airport clowns could scrape together.

At O'Hare, I flashed my shield, skirted the lines, and boarded the Hong Kong flight carrying my piece in a shoulder holster and a trusty back up on my ankle. No one really examined my badge or challenged me.

I rest my case.

During the eighteen hours in the air, I slept little. I invested my time with Hong Kong news, boned up on Chinese customs, completed a book of crossword puzzles, and avoided alcohol. I wanted to be fresh and alert for my meeting with Jimmy McIlveen. I had a hunch my colleague would be at the gate upon my arrival.

I was right.

"Welcome to Hong Kong." Jimmy shook my hand. "Jake, old man. Ye are looking fit."

"You, too," I answered. "You look great, Jimmy."

Not only did I respect Jimmy as a genuine first-rate policeman, I treasured him as a friend.

Jimmy shuttled me through Hong Kong's version of VIP immigration and customs, and we headed into the city. Along the way, I saw firsthand why Hong Kong was consistently ranked as a top-ranked free-market economy. I hoped it lasts.

The bustling cargo container docks were a complete and stark one-eighty opposite from the depressed and abandoned area I knew along Chicago's southern lake shore.

In less than a half-hour, we entered Hong Kong by way of the Cross Harbor Tunnel, passing under the bay which separates the island portion of the old colony from Kowloon.

It was late, yet the city was still alight and vibrantly active.

Jimmy's driver pulled into the driveway of a luxury hotel within a chip shot of the city's magnificent waterfront convention center.

"I only have time to buy one nightcap. I'll have a guide here for ye first thing in the morning," Jimmy told me.

"You're putting me up here?"

"Appropriate lodgings for an honored guest," Jimmy said.

"Nice not to have budget problems. What's with the guide—aren't we hanging out?"

"I'm in court all day every day until this case is over. Luckily ye are just on call—so I'm assigning someone to show ye around during the day. When ye are needed to testify, ye'll be brought to the courthouse."

"Sounds like a plan, except for one minor point."

"Which is?"

"I buy the nightcap."

* * *

Lee Chen, Jimmy's Number Two in Kowloon, was my guide. He called at eight, at nine, and again at ten. I finally made it to the lobby at eleven. He apologized for not realizing I had jet lag. I let it stand.

Lee was superbly fluent in English, but there was no way I could explain my sleep and work habits.

After coffee and a bagel, we were out and about in Hong Kong. As a cop, I wanted to see the city from a familiar perspective—the streets. My guide was amused at my desire to hang out in places other than the usual tourist sites, and I think he enjoyed my curiosity of his hometown.

Our sightseeing was interrupted at three when Lee took the call asking for me to appear at the trial.

Lee arranged everything. We got to the courthouse in a jiffy, and my testimony was over in less than ten minutes. Kwan was subdued, bordering on comatose—much different than when I had seen him last. Hong Kong's criminal justice system had taken all the wind from his sails. They play hardball in China.

Before I knew it, I was back on the streets with Lee eyeballing some more locales.

"Jimmy told me you would be an atypical visitor," Lee commented. After spending the day exploring the streets of Hong Kong, we were on the Wan Chai footbridge on our way to meet Jimmy at Three-Six-Nine, Jimmy's favorite restaurant.

"Watching people is what I love about police work," I said.

I was looking down on a street vendor and the assembled crowd. I saw a pickpocket and pointed him out. Lee made a phone call and, in minutes, a plainclothes team nabbed the culprit in mid-attempt only a half block further down the street.

"Nice work," I commented. "I'm impressed."

"Good call—it was all yours." Lee bowed slightly. "Today's excursion was not meant to be work," he said with a hint of apology.

"I'd bet otherwise," I said.

Lee Chen smiled and tried his best to act as if he did not have a clue to my meaning.

"Lee, I'm just a cop—but a good enough one to know my testimony today was window dressing. Jimmy used Sonic Kwan's case as an excuse to get me to Hong Kong. And I bet you know why. I'll also bet you'll stay mum about it—right?"

"Jimmy warned me you can read a situation like it's a book." Before I could press him for details, he pointed up the street. "There's Jimmy—he'll explain everything while we eat."

In Chicago we'd call Three-Six-Nine a joint— good food, fair prices, minimal decor. In many ways it reminded me of *Jimmie's Diner*. The main differ- ence was the seating. Single diners and parties of two, three, or four sat at large tables shared by up to a dozen people. The odds of finding a tourist eating at one were very slim.

Jimmy led us to a semi-crowded table.

"Everything here is excellent," Jimmy told me when the server arrived. "If ye are game, I'll order."

"Suits me," I said. "I'm your prisoner." I winked at Lee Chen.

Jimmy caught on, grinned, and addressed my guide. "There was no fooling him, right?"

"Right," echoed Lee. "He saw through us quite quickly."

"It was easy—too easy," I said. "I'm flown here, put up in a nice hotel, hand carried around as if I'm an actual VIP. Jimmy, I know we are friends, but I'm not worth the red-carpet treatment. I also know that my appearance in court today was unnecessary."

"Was it that obvious?" Jimmy asked.

"One look at Sonic Kwan and I knew that you had rung him dry months ago. You, the press, the entire Hong Kong PD, and the judges—everybody in the system has taken a bite out of him. It was while I was testifying that it came very clear to me I had to be in Hong Kong for something other than saving face for the Chicago PD."

I looked at my friend and mentor and pushed. "It can't be just for dinner. So, what is it—tell me—why *am* I here?"

Jimmy grinned ear to ear. "Jake, ye powers of observation *are astounding*. But before we talk business, let's enjoy our dinner."

I cannot recall a better meal. The three of us ate heartily, drank Chinese beer, and talked general cop talk. When the crowd thinned, Lee begged off and departed.

Jimmy then moved us to a small quiet corner where he ordered spiced tea and mini white lotus seed-paste mooncakes with two duck egg yolks.

"These are seasonal specialties," he informed me. "I always order them when I'm about to ask a friend for a favor."

He was pulling my leg, so I deadpanned my reply. "Never touch 'em."

Jimmy cracked up at my lame joke.

Moments like that were the treasures of friendships. We knew it, and the knowing made the tea and cakes more than just a delicacy for our stomachs—they were trophies for a special event.

After dessert, Jimmy began his explanation for my presence. "Jake, as I said, ye observational skills are the best of any law enforcement officer I've ever encountered."

I was going to protest with some humility when he cut me off.

"Don't try to stop me."

I let him talk.

"Bringing ye here for the trial was a cover move. We—no, I have a problem and I need ye'r kind of help."

"You've got tremendous assets—right here in Hong Kong—as good or better than any city in the world. What could I bring that you don't have?"

"Outside-the-box thinking."

"Come on. You gotta be—"

He hushed me. "Listen, Jake. *Listen*. I'm on delicate ground here."

I saw that he was serious—very serious.

"Sure—sure." I shut my trap.

"Jake, there are only a few officers like me still in Hong Kong. I am a holdover from the past. The Chinese have their ways. Westerners—ye and me—we are the minority. It's their show and rightly so. They *must* preserve *face*. That is why ye are here—to save face for Hong Kong's police."

"I'm lost, Jimmy. I thought I was here to make up for allowing Kwan to escape and assault you. How do I fit into for saving face for Hong Kong's police?"

"We cannot catch a serial killer."

"We can't catch all of ours."

"But at least ye can admit they are possible."

"*What*?" I'm certain I gave him that dumb look.

"Jake, I'll explain."

"Please do—I'm *really* lost."

"The Chinese see serial killers as a western problem—a product of western culture. Therefore, they cannot and do not exist here."

"But... I take it that you believe one *does* exist."

"It's not only me. There are others who see it as the only option."

"But, they can't say so. If they did, it would be an admission that they are tainted—westernized. Right?"

"Aye."

"And, if I try and fail there is no rub on them—they win both ways."

"Right, again."

"Tell me about it. Who's dead?"

"Eight women—maybe more."

"Maybe?"

"We don't have much. Ye see—they are missing. We have no bodies."

"With no bodies, how can you be sure it's murder? Let alone—" I stopped myself. Jimmy was certain. That's all I needed to know. "Sorry, Jimmy."

He took no offense and continued. "Eight young women have vanished—three in my jurisdiction of West Kowloon, and the others in various parts of Kowloon and Hong Kong proper. As far as we can ascertain, the women do not have connections to each other. They are total strangers who go out to perform an errand, to meet friends, or are headed home... Then, they just disappear.

"Jake, if it was one or two—maybe even three—they might have stayed below the radar. But disappearances of four women with similar physical characteristics caught me eye. I opened a joint file and was soundly beaten down for the idea. When the number hit six, I had support from several of me Chinese colleagues. They saw what I saw."

Jimmy pulled out a pack of cigarettes and lit one. The pressure on him must have been tremendous, as I've never known him to smoke.

He deeply inhaled the smoke, slumped back in his chair, and spoke to the ceiling as much as to me.

"We have very little experience with this sort of thing. Hong Kong has over seven million residents. Ye've seen this city—we are packed cheek-by-jowl. Add in the cultural traits of multiple generations living together, family unity, and so on—and ye know why serial killers are a rarity. This is a tight society. Ye can't easily be anonymous here."

It was apparent Jimmy was mired in the place he called home. After thirty years in Hong Kong, he was as Chinese as any Westerner could be.

He looked at me and said, "When the count reached eight, we decided to get outside help."

My stomach knotted. Bringing me in was a huge leap for everyone associated with the decision. The Hong Kong police would admit to needing help as readily as the Chicago PD would—namely never.

I had quit smoking years ago but needed one bad. I wanted to grab Jimmy's pack and puff up a storm. I wanted to guzzle booze, smoke, swear, rant, and rave.

Instead, I quietly said, "I'm flattered." My friend was in need, and it was no time to dwell on me. "Tell me what you want."

"Catch the bloody bastard."

"That's a tall order for a fish out of his pond."

"There's nothing fishy about ye, Jake." He looked at me like a drowning man does a life raft. "Evil crap is the same wherever you find it. And ye, me friend, have the ability to sniff it out. The case files are in ye hotel room. Lee Chen and I are at ye disposal. Whatever ye need—just ask."

Even though I knew it was coming, Jimmy's words knotted my stomach even tighter. He lectured cops from around the world on how to be a cop. Jimmy was asking me to solve a series of crimes that until recently were not even recognized as being related. The size of the challenge before me was awesome.

All I could say was, "I need to see those files."

Back at my hotel, I ignored the fabulous view of Hong Kong's famous harbor and read the files. I did not sleep. The files were very thorough. Jimmy and his colleagues knew their stuff. Times, dates, places, photos, and interviews—I had a lot to absorb.

I reread all of them again, and again. I tried not to think about what I read and saw. Instead, I immersed myself in details—swimming in them.

I was a fish in a new pond, alright. And I slowly swam in water made murky by all those damned details. The pond was a blur to me. I could not see the shore, nor did I know how far the bottom was beneath me. I sucked in opaque water and blew it out through my gill-like brain.

Every so often another fishtail brushed up against me. It was the killer. He too, was in the pond, swimming in the same detail-laden liquid looking for another girl, while I searched for a vital piece of information. I filtered the water for *that one clue*, the single detail, or lone idea, that would allow the police to hook and land the killer.

Within the dank swirls, one thought finally lodged in my mind. I called Jimmy.

"I want to see the places," I told him.

"Places?"

"Yeah, the places—all the last places where each girl was seen."

"When?"

"Right now—sooner, if we can do it."

"Then ye have something?" I felt his anticipation.

"I don't know... I've got an idea. I'll tell you on the way to see the places."

"I'm on me way." He ended the call.

Jimmy was at my door in less than five minutes.

"That was fast," I said as I opened the door.

"I was downstairs in the lobby."

"Waiting?"

"Aye."

"Jesus—you *are* desperate."

"Does it show?" He grimaced.

"As obvious as a penguin in a church pew."

"I'm that obvious?"

"Ever see one? It would stand out."

"Ye're joking—right?"

"I wish." I pointed down the hall. "Come on. Let's get out where things happen. You drive, I'll talk." I grabbed some papers from the files—the ones I thought mattered most. Also, I grabbed a Hong Kong street map and a copy of a complimentary newspaper that had been in my room.

Jimmy looked at it with puzzlement.

"Practicing on ye Chinese?" he asked.

"No—been looking at the pictures. It'll make sense later."

In the lobby, we were joined by Lee. The three of us piled into Jimmy's police-issued Toyota and we departed. Jimmy negotiated the crowded streets of Hong Kong with unassuming ease. Without discussing the destination, I knew we were headed for the site where the first girl had disappeared.

After being on the way for a couple of minutes, I told Jimmy what I thought about the files. I did so in a roundabout manner.

"You drive like a local," I said.

"It's an acquired skill—takes years to master."

"I bet that after all these years you think like one, too."

"Perhaps."

"I'd say so."

Jimmy kept driving and I kept talking.

"Back home, we can appear to be pretty callous when it comes to tossing jibes and jabs at each other based on ethnicity. To my Dago partner, Gino, I was a Pollock—simple as that. Micks, Greasers, Shines, Krauts—nobody ever gets too upset if it's clear—and

I mean crystal clear—such language is used without malice. In fact, with the right inflection, words that could be insults can actually become terms of endearment in an odd sort of way."

"Jake, I am certain ye line of reasoning is headed somewhere."

"Yeah—I guess it is." I admit, I was playing with him—only to highlight the cultural point was about to make. "Loose slang like I mentioned helps us deal with uncomfortable subtleties."

"Jake, ye lost me," Jimmy confessed.

"Chinese all look the same—at least to me," I said. I immediately looked to Lee hoping he caught my drift. He gave me the slightest nod. I proceeded. "Without being considered a racist—let me continue."

"I think you should," Lee said. His smile was as delicate as my topic.

"Members of homogeneous racial groups are able to detect the slightest variations in appearance as their means of identifying individuals. It's not the same for someone outside their group. That explains why what I just said is not merely a racially insensitive comment. Outsiders really do have difficulty telling the difference."

"But ye started with me," Jimmy said. "I'm not Chinese."

"True—but you might as well be," I answered. "Thirty years of being immersed in the culture—the language—art. Jimmy, you are a cop. Our profession is one of the most closed and clannish. Add it up and you are as much Chinese as anyone not born here can be."

"Here we are." Jimmy pulled the car over and pointed. "Outside that movie house is where Girl Number One was last seen."

I looked where he pointed and smiled. "Perfect," I said. "Let's see the others."

"Is that all?" asked Jimmy. I could tell he was getting a little frustrated with me. "You do not want to get out and at least look?"

"Nope—just get me to the next site and I bet I'm right," I said.

"Right about what?" Jimmy snapped. "Jake, ye have been talking in circles. What is it that ye know?"

"I *know* nothing—but get me to the next place and I'll tell you what I *think*."

In less than five minutes we were there. The ride over was silent. I wanted it that way for effect. The atmosphere was a little icy when we pulled aside the curb of a retail complex containing a movie theater and some trendy shops.

I got out as soon as we stopped. Jimmy and Lee were slower in following me to my destination. In front of the theater, I unveiled my theory.

"Even though they are remarkably alike, the eight girls who disappeared are still individuals in your eyes. You, who are inside the culture, see the subtle differences that make them unique. You see them as single items. Then, you look for similarities—things that link them together. It's the logical approach.

"I am an outsider—remember what I said? I can't tell the difference. To me these Chinese, they are all—"

"—the same." Lee interrupted. "You see all of us as being the same." There was no delicate smile.

"No, Lee. In this case it goes further—so much further. In this situation they aren't the same—they are *identical*." I almost shouted.

"Identical—the same?" asked Jimmy. "Aren't ye just playing with words?"

"I don't think so," I answered. Pointing at the theater marquee and holding up an ad from the newspaper. "After what I've shared does the pirate movie's leading lady look interesting to you? Take a good long look at her. Think gamine—think western anime."

I allowed my companions ample time to examine the posters in front of the theater based on my clues. When it was obvious that my ideas had not sunk in fully, I said, "You don't see it? The elf-like waif?"

Jimmy answered for them both. "It's obvious that the killer is fixated on a type—we already know that."

"Look at the poster. The type is western. The girl is *western*. The killer is looking for individuals who fit a *western* model. He sees the specific traits in each of the *Chinese* girls in an effort to match them to the posters. A western viewer would tend not to see the local girls that way. A westerner would see like I do—all the Chinese tend to look the same. A westerner would not see any individual traits to make links with."

"But you saw them," Lee said.

"Yes—finally. But it took me hours to see what he sees in seconds. If I stood outside this theater and watched all the girls in the right age group as they exited, I bet I could not pick out a potential victim quick enough."

"Jake, are ye certain about this?" asked Jimmy. "Three of the sites have no theaters anywhere close by—that defeats ye theory."

"Maybe not. I'd say we look for videos stores and other businesses that display images of that particular woman close to the spots where the girls vanished. I'd bet my pension and yours that we'll find them."

We made two stops and at both of them, I was correct. Images of the actress were plastered on the store windows.

When we had one more to go, Jimmy said to Lee, "Ye know the city better than anyone. Is the final site similar in any manner to what we've seen?"

"Yes—I know the location well. A large video and media outlet is nearby." He looked at me, smiled, and said, "It appears you have discerned what we could not."

Pleased but not gloating, I said, "Thanks. I had a hunch and pursued it. The files showed me the way— and now that we've checked it out here on the streets my theory seems plausible. From various angles and lines of sight the missing girls resemble the actress in the movie—so what? Is that enough to excite some pervert? And if so—the big questions are: how does he nab them, what is he doing with them, and why are there no clues—namely, no bodies?"

They looked at me as if I were the menu's daily special. They nodded agreement.

Jimmy said, "Jake, we don't know. We assumed that someone not from here was behind the disappearances. We thought it would be a foreigner."

"Jimmy, this city is a fishbowl. How on earth does anyone from outside hide eight corpses when people are packed so tight that they share rooms and need to go outside their homes to find a bit of privacy?"

"Agreed. Now do ye see why ye are here? This situation is so outside our usual, we had to seek help." His gaze was that of wanting deliverance.

"I'll need time—more time," I replied.

I looked around. I saw a city very unlike the one I knew so well. It was so different. Even so, I knew I could figure things out. I told myself *It's the same wherever you go. People are people.*

"The answers are always right before us—we see them all the time. We take 'em for granted and move on. Are we so busy that we just don't recognize them?" I preached to Jimmy and Lee and asked them at the same time.

Eight girls are missing, the little voice in my head kept telling me. *Eight, Jake—count 'em.* It nagged at me because it could and that's what it did. *You might have uncovered an angle that justifies the faith Jimmy has in you, but maybe not. You're out of gas and you have no clue about what to do next.*

"I need to walk," I announced. "I need to walk and think."

And walk I did. I had told Jimmy and Lee I had to do it alone. They agreed and disappeared. With map and files in hand, I made my way about the city on foot. I am certain they had me followed. It was easy to spot the tail they'd put on me. All Chinese do not look the exactly the same when you suspected one of them was your police-appointed babysitter.

I was not offended. It was admission of how important I was to them and how hopelessly lost we were on that case. My theory had no value if I could not tie it in some manner to how the kidnapper was abducting the girls. Kidnapper? Maybe it was a lot more. But *kidnapper* was all we could call him without a body or some other as proof of something worse. And, was it a *him*? Even that basic fact was not a certainty.

As I walked and tried to absorb the city, the little voice played me like a barroom jukebox—loud and constant.

This is only your third day in Hong Kong. What do you think you are, some sort of magician? You can't solve this case with tricks and illusion. You need real stuff and you've got nothing but an idea. No—half an idea. Get to work. Find how he does it.

It was September and still very warm. Correction—it was hot. Ninety degrees of heat was matched by ninety percent humidity. I sweated through my clothes like a whore in church but paid no attention to the steamy wet rags my clothes had become. Instead, I looked and sniffed, and then sniffed and looked. It was simple, there was no plan.

I was on the prowl, a predator looking for another predator.

I know what he looks for. I reminded myself. Then I asked, *How does he hunt? How does he hide his prey once he has taken them down?*

I traveled the city by foot and cab. Each location was experienced again. I drew a blank. I felt as if I was looking for a black cat in a dark room that wasn't there.

The little voice told me I was trying too hard.

Relax, it told me. *Don't push. Let it come.*

But I did push. Or at least my ego pushed back. It was more than not wanting to fail. I wanted to win big. I wanted to be a hero. I wanted to meet and exceed all of Jimmy's expectations.

When in doubt, blame your ego.

Hot, soggy, and tired, I grabbed another of Hong Kong's ubiquitous red taxis and told the driver to—

"Wait. That's it." I said aloud. The little voice stayed silent.

I had it. When the phantom voice inside abandons me, I know I have found what I was looking for. I told the cabbie to get me to my hotel as fast as possible.

In my room, I called Jimmy, grabbed a beer from the mini-bar, and jumped into the shower. I figured I would have five minutes until he arrived—enough time to hose off the sweat, don clean clothes, and chug down some replacement moisture.

Jimmy was at my door a minute early.

"I didn't see you waiting when I came in," I commented.

"Hiding in the bar," he joked. "Ye said ye had something," he reminded me in a more serious tone.

I hit the mini-bar for two whiskeys and tossed one to him. "Taxis. Or rather—a taxi. He's using a taxi. They are everywhere and therefore overlooked. I'm a foreigner and even I was ignored when I got into a cab."

"We thought of that and—"

"I know," I interrupted. "It's in the files. You checked with all the companies. You scanned and crosschecked logs. You took all the usual steps."

"Then, why do ye think he's using a taxi?"

"You checked taxi drivers. But did you check mechanics, supervisors, dispatchers, owners who are not drivers—all the people who might have access to taxis?"

"That's a huge group when ye say 'might'."

"I know. But just match it against someone who has the means to hide or dispose of eight bodies, and you have your guy. And it is a guy—I haven't seen a female cabbie. One would stick out. So, it's a guy. Find one who has access to cabs, enough space to hide bodies, and is a loner. Someone like that should stick out. It's not such a daunting task when you add in the qualifiers. This guy has resources. He's either got the space to hide bodies, or the ability to get rid of them without being seen... And, he's on to you."

"What? How? Ye're joking."

"Never—not about this," I assured him. I opened two more minis and poured us each another drink. "He's probably taken calls from your team—given answers—all aimed at deflecting suspicion. Eighteen thousand taxis in how many organizations? You've touched him and never knew it. My bet is a full sweep of the city would take forever to spot him. He's good—eight girls without a trace. He knows how to hide, and he knows you are looking for him. We'll have to lure him into the open."

"How?"

"Limit his range—take away all the sites except one."

"Close down theaters and videos shops?"

"No... No—just get all but one to stop showing that woman's image. Then, we plaster it all over the remaining site. Hell, maybe we should advertise a pirate film festival in honor of her. *Yes*. We heighten his desire and decrease his hunting grounds. Then, we set out a decoy and nab him in the act."

"We simply dangle a decoy?" He sounded very skeptical.

"Yes. There has to be at least one female officer who fits the part."

"It's one of the oldest tricks in the book. If he's as smart as ye say, why do you think it will work?"

"He's smart, but he's driven. He can't help himself. He'll give in to his desire. Trust me. This guy will reveal himself if we set the right trap." I could see Jimmy was still not totally on board with my view of things.

Sometimes it is impossible to meet expectations because when you do deliver the goods, you surprise even your staunchest supporters.

I reminded my friend I was not a volunteer.

"Jimmy, you wouldn't have brought me here if you thought I was going to come up with some sort of flaky crap. I said, 'trust me' and I meant it. This is not my best guess—this is my best gut. He's fixated on that chick. The guy is a perv. He's ashamed. I bet he's done some weird acts on the bodies—both before and after they stopped breathing. Do like I laid it out and you'll nail him. I bet my badge on it."

"Really? Ye bet your badge?"

"Damn right."

I should have known I had been baited. His grin was slow to appear. It took forever to evolve into a smile.

When it did, he said, "Glad to know that it's ye best gut feeling. It's just what I wanted. We'll try it ye'r way at a theater. I agree with all ye've said except the taxi connection. We have worked on it our way and that line of thought has produced nothing."

"I think you're wrong, but it's your call. You may nab him at the point of abduction." I felt I could not push any more. My profile, unsophisticated as it was, was only what was wanted. "I hope you get him."

He raided the mini-bar and that time did the pouring. "Here's to success," he toasted.

We downed the drinks, and he quickly went to work by phone. I was amazed. In a few short calls he accomplished more in less time than I thought possible.

"My team can have it all set by tomorrow noon," he announced.

"That was fast." I tried to hide my awe.

"This is China, Jake. We don't fool around once we know the goal."

* * *

I crashed. My feet were beat and swollen and our three drinks almost put me to sleep. Jimmy graciously allowed me beg off on dinner, and I hugged the sheets for well more than a dozen hours.

When I woke, it was to Jimmy's voice urging me to join him.

"Jake—Jake. It's time to spring the trap," he told me. "It will be dark soon. The theater will be emptying within the hour, and we have a decoy in place." He handed me a of black coffee as soon as I sat up.

"Did you lay out my clothes?" I smart-alecked.

"No—ye slept in them."

"Good. Then, let's go." I sprang from the bed and headed out the door. Rumpled, needing a shave, and with sleep sand in my eyes, I stepped into the humid night air and immediately began to sweat.

"Are ye feeling fit enough to do this, Jake?" asked Jimmy.

"Never felt better," I replied, wiping my brow. "I take it we'll be in a command post?"

"Aye," Jimmy explained. "We have an operations van parked down the street and across from the theater."

"With AC?"

"Of course—only the best for the special equipment we have inside."

High tech would be a low description of the van's contents. My first impression was that the Hong Kong police spent their entire technology budget on that one vehicle. Disguised as a utility repair truck, the van appeared to me as a tightly packed mini-version of NASA's ground control.

Jimmy and I squeezed into a couple of seats positioned behind operators who were jacked into listening devices while viewing multiple video displays.

A dozen mini-cams had been positioned to watch the sidewalks and alleyways around the theater. One was mounted on the decoy's belt buckle and another on the reverse side of her collar.

She was wired for sound and under direct visual observation by three night-vision cameras mounted on the van and four mini-hand held units with foot police in hiding. All told, she was being watched by over a dozen plainclothes officers, in addition to the van's four-man crew, Jimmy, Lee, and me.

"The media has been very cooperative in hyping the theater's unique offering," Lee told me. "And, we have darkened all other outlets of the woman's image. All we need now is the suspect."

It was then that I had what you could call a mild anxiety attack. I was in a tight spot having shot my mouth off. It was put up or shut up time and I was really uncomfortable sitting in such close quarters.

I willingly gave up the air conditioning inside the van in order to breathe easier. It was hot outside, but I immediately felt relieved. All that high-tech equipment was not me. I was a street cop and even on foreign ground that was where I belonged.

After a while, I grew somewhat accustomed to the hot, humid air. I found a spot to sit, and I waited. For what? I didn't know.

Sometimes cop work is just a matter of being in the right spot at the right time. In that instance, I just wanted to be away from the gadgets. If something came down, I was certain I'd know about it. The entire neighborhood crawled with undercover officers and I was within eyesight of the van.

The game plan was to have the decoy hang around the lobby after the movie's credits ran, let her ogle the posters, wander about the entrance area a bit, and then stroll down the most visible sidewalk—leaving the area. Foot traffic was moderate in volume, and the decoy was always within a few steps from an undercover backup.

The wager was the suspect would be in the crowd and follow her. It sounded good, but it was a plan built on only half of my reasoning.

Like I said, cop work isn't always brilliant. It has a lot of right-time right-place in it. By stepping out of the van, I hit that place.

Finding the killer did not go down as imagined. From my spot, I watched the girl. She certainly looked the part. She was a good decoy. Maybe too good. No one came close to her. It made no difference the real action was up the street, and if I had been in the van focused on the views offered by all the technology, I would not have seen the young man hop into a parked vehicle—a taxi.

The cab came down the street at normal speed, passed where the decoy stood, and turned left at the corner. In and of itself, no big deal. But a second pass by the same cab tuned me in. I made a mental note of the vehicle's number as it passed through the area without taking on a fare.

Something did not add up. I swear the driver gave me 'the look'. I believe he recognized me as a potential threat. Instead of making another full circuit the driver nosed the cab forward at the top of the street. He checked me out and kept going rather than turning down the street for a third pass.

Right time, right place. While everyone was focused on the decoy, I was looking in the right direction.

When I shared what I had seen, Jimmy called a stand-down. "Jake, if ye still believe it's a taxi driver, I'm willing to follow up on ye gut feeling. We saw nothing else tonight to act on."

"Check it out. I bet it's our guy."

"Bet ye badge?"

"Yep."

Jimmy gave a nod to the nearest techie to search the database and make some calls. Since my Chinese was rusty, I assumed by the exchange which followed the search produced something that fit my overall theory.

Jimmy had a 'sorry I doubted you' look when he told me, "*Spring Bird Taxis* is owned by James Choi. The dispatcher confirmed the cab number ye gave us is for the owner's personal vehicle. He rarely takes fares." He pointed to the door. "Let's go."

"What else did your guys find." I had sensed his urgency was based on something he had held back.

As we drove to a location along Belcher Bay, Jimmy explained. "The taxi company is on Fung Mat Road west of the city's center. The Chois are an old business family and quite well off. They have a sizable residence attached to a compound that includes the taxi office, a parking area, maintenance facilities, and structures for several other enterprises. James Choi is known to his employees as a bit of a recluse—his parents are deceased, and he lives alone. Everything fits. He's got the resources—it's just as ye said."

"I take it he's there—right?"

"Aye. The dispatcher confirmed he just arrived. Patrol units are on the way to seal off the compound."

Jimmy drove with purpose and silently focused on the route and traffic. As we slowed down to approach our destination, he spoke. "Thanks, Jake, for not saying, 'I told ye so'."

I did not audibly reply. Instead, I simply nodded my head. Sometimes, that's the best response to a friend.

We passed the patrol units and entered the compound. Jimmy parked and we were soon inside. The taxi dispatcher told us Choi was on the property, but he had no idea exactly where. Jimmy and I both sensed the dispatcher had tipped off his boss.

The few words of Chinese uttered by Jimmy needed no translator. I knew a threat when I heard one. The dispatcher trembled for a moment and then picked up the phone.

A few words were exchanged, and the receiver was handed to Jimmy.

The conversation with Choi was brief. I heard a familiar pop. Jimmy called out. There was no reply.

Putting down the phone, Jimmy told me, "He knew. He said he knew we would catch him."

The private quarters portion of the compound was the location of two deadly scenes. The site of Choi's final act was routine by suicide standards, the resting place of the eight unfortunate girls was not.

Choi had the assets to hide the outcome of his obsession. The bodies of his victims were neatly wrapped in plastic and stored in two large walk-in freezers. His private living space was lined with photos of the actress. His personal journal was filled with wild speculations on how he could capture and enjoy her essence.

Everything in my theory had turned out to be true. But being right on the case did not make me feel special.

My status as a police genius left me very flat. I sleepwalked through the following days. There was the on-site wrap-up, the congratulatory get-to-gethers, and the formal thank-yous from the higher ups. Jimmy's faith in me was vindicated and he was praised for bringing me in on the case. Showing me off was his due.

On my last night in town, I asked that he and I have a quiet dinner and a couple of drinks to say goodbye. It was simple—I was homesick. Beautiful and exotic Hong Kong could not rub off the Southside in me.

"Ye have not been ye'self these past few days," Jimmy observed.

"I'm okay," I told him, "I'm just ready to go home."

"I understand," he said. "I brought ye here under a ruse and cannot help but feel that in some way I deceived ye."

"Don't get all soapy on me, Jimmy. I'm glad to have helped. In fact, I was thrilled to know you thought so much of me. I just miss Chicago."

"Soon ye'll be there... But first—" He reached into his pocket. "Before ye leave, I have a token of Hong Kong's thanks for such an invaluable contribution. This is for ye."

The item he produced and handed to me was a gold badge. My smile grew as I read the inscription, "Jake Thompson, aka Jan Tomaszewski, Deputy Sheriff, Kowloon."

"Lee thought of it," Jimmy explained. "Ye said ye would bet ye badge on what ye gut said to you. It's only fitting that we cover that bet. Welcome to our force, *deputy*."

My cop soul ignited. I beamed and a weak 'Thank You' was all I could squeak out. My eyes misted and I said, "Damn—now I'm the one getting soapy."

"No fear, Laddie. I'll soon be retiring to the sunny Mediterranean, and seein' ye cry over our wee gesture will be the fondest of me memories as The Sheriff of West Kowloon."

I drank a bit too much that night, but I had plenty of time to sleep it off on the long flight home.

Upon landing at O'Hare Airport, I pinned the Hong Kong badge on my jacket and strolled past the security guards as if they did not exist.

Nobody said a word.

RIMBO

Have you ever noticed how much a place changes when it is occupied by different people?

I love *Jimmie's Diner*, but it was just not the same on the days my favorite waitress, Earline, was off. At *Jimmie's*, the diner fare I'd learned to live on and the oily liquid passing as coffee were unvarying constants, and although everything else remains the same, *Jimmie's* without Earline was somehow not truly *Jimmie's*.

Earline indeed may be the undefined spice in my life. But don't attempt to make too much out of it. We are not an item. Our relationship is simultaneously more and less than what it appears to be. Earline and I are close in a peculiarly vague sort of way. We share a unique faraway closeness born out of the sporadic intimacy we share as customer and waitress, man and woman, at my favorite booth in *Jimmie's Diner*.

Those who observed our relationship knew it for what it was—a friendship bordering on familial love, without the strings, broken promises, and disappointments of over knowing.

Like I said, the diner was not the same without Earline. That was why Jimmie broke precedent and stepped away from his perch at the cash register to talk to me about Earline's absence.

"Jake, you gotta look into what's wrong with Earline," he pleaded.

For a moment I was stunned. The man I had come to regard as a statue had actually moved and was seated across from me.

"Wrong? What do you mean by wrong?" I finally asked.

"Two days. She's been gone two days from work. Counting the weekend, that's four days."

I had also never heard Jimmie say that much in such a short period of time. In fact, I could not recall hearing him say so much, ever. Usually, he communicated through grunts and groans in a monosyllabic shorthand form of speech known in the diner as 'Jimmie Jabber.'

"Jimmie, is she sick?"

"No... She didn't sound sick when she called."

"If she's not sick and she called in—why should I check up on her?"

"She's never taken this much time off without plenty of notice. You know that, Jake. We all joke about how she bends your ear for weeks and bugs you to death with the details of her trips before she goes."

"Yeah, how could I forget? The trip to *Disney World* was only three days long but I must have heard about it every day for the six months before she actually went to Florida."

"*See*!? It's just not like Earline. Something is wrong. She called in, but she sounded different. She's been acting different, too. I've noticed things changing over the past couple of weeks. Jake, you wouldn't know because you come in at noon for breakfast. Earline's always been regular—here at seven and leaves at three. On the dot. Lately, she's been all over the clock, arriving late and rushing out of here early, and—"

I had to interrupt. Jimmie had gone beyond sentences and was speaking in paragraphs. Hearing him freaked me out. I almost shouted, "Okay, just stop talking. I'll do it."

"Do what? Say it. Come on—say it." Jimmie was a man on a mission.

"Okay. I'll find out what's up with Earline. That's what you want, right?"

"*Yes*," he answered. "Then it's settled—you'll see about her?"

"Anything to stop you from talking so much. It gives me the creeps."

Jimmie looked satisfied and relieved. He sighed, got up, and headed back to his perch, uttering some unintelligible sounds along the way.

In less than a minute, he came back. Without saying a word, he handed me a food receipt scrawled with Earline's address.

I took it as my cue to depart and immediately left the diner. To buy time for gathering my thoughts, I walked toward the address Jimmie had given me. It wasn't far. As I walked, I slowly realized that until a few moments earlier, I had not known where Earline lived. There was a lot I didn't know about her.

I searched my memory as I walked.

My slice of life with Earline was built upon diner talk: details of her trips, beefs with co-workers, shared crossword answers, sports page opinions— things like that. Over the years, I learned she hated flying and like me, bled for the Cubs.

Through one of my cases, I knew with certainty her favorite movie star was Ashley Morant. From diner buzz, I heard she was a widow with a grown daughter. And I thought I heard Earline's husband, who was somehow associated with the diner as a vendor or supplier, left her with some bucks. Whatever the relationship, it led to Earline working at *Jimmie's.*

That was it. Beyond those items I knew little else.

As I walked, I asked myself: *What is her favorite color? When is her birthday? How old is Earline, really? Does she prefer chocolate, or vanilla? Is her daughter named Jen, Jan, or Janna?*

Even though I could read her moods like the front page of the *Trib*—what *did* I really know? For a certain amount of time each day, Earline and I related as if we were the only two people in the world. Yet, outside that time at that location we were almost strangers.

Verifying the address, I picked up my pace, and quickly covered the final block to her condo.

Earline's place was in a nice building on the edge of the loop—one of the few in the area with a full-time receptionist in the lobby.

I flashed my shield and told the cheery-faced youth manning the desk, "I'm here to see the lady in One-G."

"Official business?" he asked, rising from his seat.

I angled past his station and said, "May be."

"Let me direct you to that unit," he offered.

I kept walking and told him, "I know the alphabet."

At Earline's unit, I rang the bell and waited. I told myself, *Everything is okay. Jimmie worries too much—and I'll probably be embarrassed for showing up here nosing around.*

I was wrong.

The person who answered the door of unit 1-G was not who I expected. She had Earline's face and form. But, the woman before me was not the front page of the *Trib* I was accustomed to reading at *Jimmie's*.

"Jake?!" She said with a mix of shock, dismay, and vague embarrassment. "What are you... I didn't expect... I mean—what a surprise."

She seemed off center and out of focus. It was that 'deer in the headlights' quality displayed by someone not in control of the moment. And if I knew anything about Earline, it was that right, wrong, or indifferent, she was always in control of her side of any moment. The situation activated my cop radar.

"Yeah—eh, yeah. I guess me being here is a little strange," I said, leaning toward her in the hope of getting inside.

"I'd say so. You're one of the last persons I'd expect," she murmured. For an instant she hesitated to invite me in. Again, not an Earline move.

I eased back, hoping that a counter ploy would work. "I'm sorry. If this is a bad time I could—"

"No, no. Oh... No," she weakly replied.

My strategy seemed to have worked. I put my radar up a notch and moved forward.

"Come on in," she said. "I... ah... We... ah... Were just about to have a drink." She and said, "Come join... Us. It should be okay."

I stepped in and followed her toward the condo's living area. Along the way I tried to engage her in small talk.

"Jimmie was all over me—I'm here 'cause of him," I chattered. "He's got the crazy notion that you are—" My cop radar turned itself on.

I stopped talking when I saw *Him*.

Now, after all is said and done, I know his name—but he'll always be just plain Him to me. In my opinion a slime ball like Him doesn't rate a name.

Here was what I encountered: Earline's living room was spacious and well appointed. By the look of things, her hubby must have done quite well. The top-drawer furnishings perfectly fit the room. I wish I could have said the same for the slug stretched out across the sofa like he owned the place.

Try to imagine a young and sinister Elmer Fudd in a silk robe and slippers. I know, it sounds impossibly offbeat that someone resembling a cartoon character could bug me so much.

However, as comical as the man looked, there was something peculiarly menacing about him. Maybe it was the combination of beady snake eyes, smart-assed smirk, and oily skin contrasted with his pudgy pinkness that set me back. He was not appealing to say the least.

What the hell? I asked myself. *This piece of work cannot be the reason Earline is skipping out of work.*

My radar went into red-alert overdrive.

"Morris, dear?" Earline timidly asked Him, "I've invited Jake to join us. Is that okay?" She quivered ever so slightly as she reached for glasses and ice. "I'll just fix us something..."

Men have time-honored communication rituals, and the most universal is the *guy nod.*

While Earline played hostess, after asking for permission to have a guest in her own nest, I extended a courtesy nod to Him.

My gesture was ignored and the snub was reinforced with a snarky answer aimed at both her and me.

"No—not now. Really, you should know better. I'm not taking visitors," he said in both a whiny accusing tone and staring at me like I was a leftover pizza.

For some reason, that guy wanted a confrontation. He had a bad aura—lizard-green, with *Cheeto*-orange accents.

I could have glared back, but getting into a contest of who can piss higher up the wall was not my game. I paid no attention to him.

The greatest insult is not to respond in kind, but rather to ignore someone altogether. It says, "I just don't care—for you."

He quickly upped the ante, "Huh. So, you're the security guard that hangs out at the diner. She mentioned you were a successful cop or a detective once upon a time." In support of this outright verbal slam, he made no attempt to rise or shake my hand. It was stepping up the ante after refusing to return my nod.

In the male-alpha-dog world, instead of offering some form of friendly or even neutral acknowledgment, he peed on my leg.

My radar beeped itself into a wail. I got no, "Hi. I'm Morris." I got no, "Pleased to meet you." I just got attitude and a wet leg.

Nobody likes being dissed and I'm worse than most. So, I obliged him with a zing in return, and a different contest was on.

"I'm still a cop—and, I'd be derelict if I didn't check you out."

"What?" He sat up.

I had struck a nerve.

Earline quivered more and ice rattled in the glass she held.

"Yeah—maybe I take you in," I threatened.

Standing up, he defiantly asked, "Take me in? For what?"

"For pissing me off, that's what." I stepped forward, he sat down, and Earline dropped the tumbler. The sound of broken glass brought the woman I knew back to the gathering for a few moments.

"Both of you—stop it. Please." She stepped between us to defuse the situation. "You're acting like children, and I'll not have any of this." She turned to face Him and continued, "If you're not up to having company then perhaps you need to retire for now."

Before she got an answer she turned to me, grabbed my arm, and guided me back as I had come.

"Jake, I think it's best for you to have a drink with us at some other time."

It was Earline's home. I took the suggestion and went along without a fuss.

From behind, I heard Him getting up and shuffle about the living room, fussing about me. In a moment, I was at the door and Earline was ushering me out.

As I stepped into the hallway Earline said, "Jake, tell Jimmie I'm fine and that I'll call him when I'm ready to come back to the diner." The new Earline abruptly closed the door before I could respond.

My life could be described as an unbroken chain of awkward moments—so one more should not have been anything new for me. However, that situation lit my fire. I had agreed to check on Earline's condition thinking it would be a waste of time. I was wrong—very wrong. Everything I knew about people told me my friend was in danger.

Him—the sinister cartoonish Mr. Fudd—was bad news. I'd have bet my pension on it. And what to do about Earline's plight was my first thought. I made my way back to see the helpful kid in the lobby.

"Can I be of assistance, Detective Thompson?" he asked.

The kid remembered my name from when I zipped past him. Most of the youngsters I run across are too zoned out on the crap coming through *iPods* and PDAs to remember their own names, let alone one flashed at them by a cop. I was impressed.

"What's your name?"

"Ben—Ben Fields." He was alert, smiled, and looked me square in the eye. I remained impressed.

"Okay, Ben. Tell me what you know about the turd in One-G."

He rolled his eyes. "Oh yeah—the amazing Mister Willard."

"A favorite of yours?"

"Hardly."

"Fill me in." I pulled out my notepad and pen.

"So... This is becoming official, right?"

"The lady is a friend—I'm concerned. I'll make it official if need be."

"Sure. I understand." He produced a card file from the desk. While thumbing the contents he said,

"Our garage is a big plus for owners." He found one and read, "Morris Dean Willard—drives a beat-up BMW—registered as a guest for unit One-G's visitor parking spot. He's a major pain in the ass. Acts like he owns the whole building." He placed the card on the counter and slid it toward me. "Here's all his info."

I jotted down the license number and noted that the date of registration on the card corresponded to the time Jimmie first observed Earline's behavior change.

"Any more you care to add?"

"He goes by his middle name, Dean—sometimes even Dino—hates being called Morris, or even Mister Willard. No one likes him... Well, no one except your friend in One-G." He seemed tentative about saying more.

"What else do you know?"

Ben remained silent.

I prodded. "Spill it, Ben."

"Ms. Drummond? She's changed..."

"Go on."

"She doesn't seem the same as—you know—before he showed up."

"Are you saying that just because he's a pain?"

"No—no. I... I... Ah, well I kinda know her daughter... And..." His helpful nature faded. He was hiding the obvious.

"Look, Ben, I don't care if you've been tappin' into the good stuff."

"No, no. It's not like *that*. Me and Janna—we're serious."

"I'm not investigating your love life. I just want to know about Dino Willard."

"Like I said, no one can stand him. He makes Janna's skin crawl. She hates to even *talk* about him."

"Tell me how I can reach her right away." I shot Ben my most trustworthy look.

He reached into his pocket for his cell phone. "Janna's at work. I could text her."

"Do it. Find out where she is—exactly. I want to talk with her after I check out Willard's car. I'll be back in a minute."

I headed for the doorway that had to lead to the building's parking spaces. In the brightly lit and well-marked garage, Willard's red BMW convertible was easy to find. It was an older model, poorly maintained, and dirty.

I peered inside and saw a cluttered mess of papers, clothes, and miscellaneous junk tossed around as if a large squirrel had nested in the backseat.

"Looks like he's a step away from being homeless," I muttered.

Getting inside was no problem. The lock on the passenger side door was broken. I swung the door open and immediately held my breath. The interior reeked of stale sweat covered up by cheap aftershave. Reluctantly, I leaned inside.

In the glove box, I found a bundle of letters and bills—all had the same address of an apartment in an older residential area of the city. Also in the box were a couple dozen parking tickets.

The locations on the tickets matched the streets near the address of the apartment.

I took a few minutes to jot down the ticket numbers. I placed all the papers back in their original spot and then aimed myself back toward Ben's security-guard perch. I had more questions.

"When did he show up?" I asked.

"About a month ago."

"He here often?"

"A lot—too often for my taste. Janna's, also."

"Did you reach her?"

"Yeah. Janna's at work—wants to talk to you. She's worried big time."

"Where? And when is she ready?"

"Any time—sooner the better. She sells designer dresses on The Miracle Mile directly across from *The Drake*."

"I know the place. Pricey clientele."

"Yeah, she designs some of them, but mostly just sells for a cranky owner that won't let Janna answer her own phone. She can talk now—the owner is gone. I'll text that you're coming."

"Tell her I'll be there in fifteen minutes," I said and was gone.

When I hit the street, a slight rain urged me to hail a cab. From the backseat, I called my old pal, Vick Lubienicki.

We've been friends since high school when Vick was an 'A' student, played cello in the orchestra, and bass in our garage band.

Me and the Other Guys was a big dream with little talent, except for Vick and our lead guitar player, Babe Patterson. We broke up after a couple of gigs but remained friends.

Vick ran a bank of semi-legal computers and provided information to those who needed it. A lot of Chicago's investigators hated to admit their success was based on Vick and his crew massaging the grid.

"Lube!"

"Jake! It's been ages."

"Yeah. Next time I buy."

"When?"

"Soon."

"But not now, right?"

"I need a favor."

"Just ask."

"Copy this—Willard—Morris Dean Willard, late forties, maybe fifty, drives a ninety-three Beamer, Illinois temp plate L-K-L seven-four-three. Go deep—get all you can on him."

"Sure, Jake. This official?"

"Not yet. You know I hate to use department channels."

"I see. I'll personally handle this. Gimme a while."

"Call when you finish?"

"The very second."

The cab dropped me at *The Drake*, and I sprinted between raindrops to the west side of the street.

Although I'd never been there, I knew the shop. I'd dropped some cash in similar joints. You know, one of those places a working guy like me would never enter unless a lot of make-up sex was in the plan.

Dresses for an angry wife or girlfriend started at a week's pay and hit the stratosphere in a heartbeat. The ladies gushed at just being there, and all was forgiven when they exited with an armload of bags.

Janna met me at the door.

"You must be Jake Thompson," said a younger version of Earline.

"It's that obvious?"

"Mom talks about you."

"Good stuff, I hope."

"Mostly."

"Not always?"

"She gets irritated when you obsess about baseball."

"Die-hard fans are hopeless. I sleep in Cubs pajamas."

"Cute."

"Just kidding. But, I did think about buying them once."

"But you're from the Southside. Shouldn't you be a Sox guy?"

"Was. It all changed for me on April 6, 1973."

"The Designated Hitter Rule. What are you going to do now that it's gone universal?"

Painfully, I answered, "I'm thinking about following Curling. You a baseball fan?"

"No—Jeopardy."

We shared the laugh, and she guided me to a spot in the shop where we could talk about why I'd come. In the cramped office she offered me coffee. I declined and got serious.

"Janna, I need some help—information actually."

"About Mom's *friend*, right?" She frowned.

"Morris Willard—yes."

"Dean or Dino is what he prefers." That time she smirked.

"I've heard. Tell me more—everything you can think of."

"He popped into view about six weeks ago. He located Mom through the internet and sent her an e-mail. Dean worked with her somewhere years ago and confessed he had a crush on her. He laid it on thick. She shared it with me. I thought it was border-line stalker. She was all giggly."

"I take it she replied."

"Yeah, I warned her. I had a bad feeling. Looks like I was right."

"How so?"

"You're here. Isn't that enough?"

"Point taken. Keep going. What's next?"

"They traded e-mails and then talked on the phone."

"Where was he living at the time?"

"Somewhere in Arizona—around Phoenix, I think. Does it matter?"

"Maybe. Any idea what he was doing there?"

"None. He's vague about his most recent past. Most of the time he's spinning tales about his life-time of exploits."

"Exploits?"

"Yeah. That's the best name I can give for all his crappy stories. He paints himself as a sort of mod-ern-day *Soldier of Fortune*."

My mind was filled with the incongruity of the man's image and Janna's terminology.

"Are you talking about the little bald pudge I saw earlier?" I asked in obvious disbelief.

"Oh, yeah. I know it's quite a leap for the mind to take, but to hear him tell it he's the thinking man's Rambo. To you and me, it's impossible for such a wimpy guy to be any kind of real-life hero. But Mom bought it hook, line, and sinker. He has her mesmerized with all the bunk he's tossed out.

"Get this: Among his claims are that he's ghost-written a half-dozen best sellers, served in the war on terror as a corporate mercenary, and created a new form of modern painting. All that is from a guy who couldn't scrape up airfare to Chicago last month when he came to see Mom. She paid for their initial meetup."

"I've seen his car. Looks to me like he was living in it."

"I think he was, too. He never told Mom exactly where he lived in Arizona. And all his communication with her was electronic—no letters or cards."

"You said Earline paid for him to come to Chicago."

"Yes. Wowed her and wooed her with his line of bull. And made plans to permanently come here—all in a weekend."

"So, he drove here when?"

"About four weeks ago."

"It all fits. You said your mother is mesmerized. How so?"

"She has started to parrot his views—on everything. And it's getting worse day by day. I hear less her and more him—or at least I did."

"Did? Meaning what?"

"I don't see much of her now that he's moved in."

"When did that happen?"

"Two or three days ago."

"Tell me about it." I could see that she was very upset.

"We argued some, but really I just gave up."

"Argued—about *Him*, right?"

"Right. As soon as he came to town he got a cheap weekly rental—a flop-house really. He wasn't there much, always hovering near Mom. He worked on her good. He talked his way into her place fast. Mom isn't Mom around him."

"I know. I saw her that way earlier today. Do you believe he has harmed her—physically?"

"Maybe? I can't say for certain. All I can say is he's not good for her, and..."

"And what?"

She hesitated. "I'm afraid. He's... He's..."

"Come on, Janna. Now's the time and I'm the one you can talk to."

"He's creepy in a... "

I waited.

I knew she was deeply troubled. I just had to wait.

"He's got a real oily kinky aura—like he's a world-class pervert lurking in the shadows."

"That's some response."

"The guy really gives me the creeps."

"Has he said, or done anything specific that you can hang your reaction on?"

"No. No. It's just a feeling I can't shake. He's a sicko, I just *know* it. Mom and I were close until he showed up. Progressively, she disappeared and now she's a different person. I tried to tell her what I was seeing. She turned me off. It's weird—like I'm the parent and she's the rebellious child. I'm scared something bad is going to happen. Isn't there anything you can do?"

"I don't know. That's why I asked about specifics. I don't like him any more than you do."

"Please, Jake. Mom adores you. As a true friend. You just *have* to do something."

Before I could answer, Janna's boss showed up. It was obvious I was not a customer, and her sour-puss expression told me that flashing my badge and spinning some tale about "official business" would've been a waste of time. Sometimes some people are not to be messed with.

I told Janna I'd be in touch and was out the door.

Call me old fashioned. Women in distress are my weakness. Toss in saving a friend from a creep and I'm your man. Janna's feelings reinforced my instincts about Earline's new beau. Vick's call removed all doubt that I had to act—fast.

"Jake, I've got what you asked for. You ready for an earful?" Vick's voice spilled over with that school-boy urgent excitement, telling me he had hit something juicy and just had to share the secret.

"All set."

"Morris Dean Willard—I love 'em. The man is a real turd with arms and legs. I haven't run across one like him in ages. He'd be a perfect *Sixty Minutes* exposé on bottom feeders. Here's the word."

"I am all ears."

"Dino, as he sometimes refers to himself, lies and cheats like a scoundrel in order to live like a gentleman. Fancies himself to be a renaissance man—you know, a combination scientist, writer, painter, a man of broad interests, multiple skills, and great ability."

"Sounds a bit much."

"Too much. It's all extrapolated whimsy or outright lies. He's actually a parasite—first-class bottom feeder. In truth, because he cannot believe anyone else would like him for what he really is, he constantly presents himself as something else. It's all based on an ingrained feeling of inferiority and is the major cause for him to prey on the gullible, especially women. I'll share more specifics later, but he has deep sexual hang ups—probably all displayed in erectile dysfunction, premature ejaculation, intimacy issues, etcetera. I bet he just can't get laid."

"I'll pass on his weirdness—what have you got that is more in my area of crimes?"

"I'll go in reverse. He left his last residence, Scottsdale, Arizona, in a hurry."

"Any warrants?"

"None—yet. From the look of things, he bailed on an apartment lease and skipped town one step ahead of the local gendarmes."

"Details?"

"Yeah—juicy ones. Like it or not we have to go weird. He's a person of interest in a nifty religious sex scam."

"Religion and sex? He can't be a defrocked priest—his interest is in the wrong gender. So, what have you got?"

"How does the *God's Sacred Temple of Love Energy* grab you?"

"By the horn. Tell me more."

He laughed at my lame humor and shared what he had found.

Morris Dean Willard had a long history of involvement in scams and cons. Vick started with the most recent.

"A couple of months ago, the good citizens of Phoenix were a-buzz over an exposé in the Sunday paper. A handful of enterprising hookers and a shake-and-bake evangelist weaseled their way through the freedom of religion laws to establish the aforementioned temple."

"Let me guess—they have liberal views about sex."

"Liberal would be conservative to this crowd. At the temple, hookers miraculously became 'Healing Princesses of Yoni'."

"Yoni? What's that?"

"Sanskrit for vagina." He laughed. I could tell he was also snickering.

"Vick, you must be loving this."

"I am—I am. This scam is brilliant. At the temple, all sex is referred to as the sacred union of energy and the life force. Everything having anything remotely to do with sex has been re-named. For example, orgasms are releases of sacred energy."

"And encouraged no doubt."

"Encouraged *and* assisted."

"I guess princesses have to do something."

"Like healing through tantric touch."

"Let me guess. Hand jobs. Right?"

"Oh, yes—and get this: Penises... Are... Are..." His laughter became uncontrollable. I waited for him to catch his breath. "Penises ...penises ...are *wands of light energy.*"

"Is this where I joke about your light saber?"

Vick began to hyperventilate.

"Ah... Ah... Ah... Oooh!" There was a thump.

"Vick—you okay?" I heard shuffling.

"Yeah, yeah. I'm good. Just fell off my chair."

"When you get stable, tell me about my boy's place in the scam."

"He was recruiting 'seekers'."

"Males only?"

"Of course."

"So, he was pimping."

"Appears so. Looks as if it was his pathway to the priesthood."

"Let me guess again—the priests get to rub genitals with the few women dumb enough to join the temple?"

Vick sneezed and wheezed his response. "*Someone* has to release the sacred energy."

"Relax, Vick. You'll pop a vein."

"Sorry. This is just *too* good."

I heard him take a deep breath to calm down. Then I asked, "I take it that the local cops could not pin anything on him, right?"

"They had nothing. There was no case unless one of the 'seekers' owned up to the fact their donations were actually payments for sex. Before they could crack one of the Johns—"

"Our boy skipped town."

"Yep—and landed right in your lap."

"Lucky me."

"So... *Why* is he in your sights?"

"He's moved in with a friend."

"I hope it's not a female."

"Why?"

"He's worked a con on the ladies before."

"Fill me in."

"He uses the usual bullshit approach—makes himself out to be some sort of expert—and then weasels money for some lame-assed project. What makes Willard interesting is that he switches the con between being an artist, photographer, writer, and get this—a Rambo-esque hero fighting terrorism."

"I just don't see it. That's the second time I've heard 'Rambo' used in connection with this guy. Vick, if you saw him, you'd laugh. Rambo? Never."

"Maybe he's a diminutive version? Like... Rimbo?"

"Yeah, Rimbo. Now, *that* fits." Somehow, I felt better. My adversary had the right name. "Any felony convictions?"

"No—nothing very big has stuck. But he's left quite a trail of bad checks and dropped complaints. I've sent an e-packet—it has all I've found... And some good photos, too."

"I appreciate it. But there are no current wants or warrants, right?"

"Sorry. All the confidence-scam related charges were dropped. Look as if his marks recanted... or conveniently forgot some details. This guy must be a real charmer."

"Just the sort of intellectual-warrior-artist that women go all goopy over—it's an attractive lie. A con man tells them what they want to hear. Romance novels are full of them. And there's a sucker born every minute who will believe the lie, especially, if it's big enough."

"Like your friend?"

"I'm afraid so."

"Sorry." He sighed and then added, "What are you going to do, Jake? You said this wasn't official."

"I'll figure something out."

"Well, if you need any more help, give a call."

"Sure, Vick. What do I owe you?"

"Nothing for this case."

"This case? You have another?"

"Yeah, Jake. When I'm ready to share it, I'll call in the favor."

"Fair enough."

"Jake?"

"Yeah."

"I know you can handle yourself but watch your back—this guy is a snake."

"Thanks for the warning, Vick."

* * *

The rain stopped and I decided to hike back to my office. I had no firm idea on how to proceed, but I knew that along the way my mind would stumble upon an answer to my dilemma.

Wandering through the city does that for me.

As I strolled, my instinct said, *Rush in and save your friend.* In opposition, my experience told me that any abrupt or direct move would spook Earline and prompt Rimbo into overdrive. The last thing I wanted was for him to spirit her away on some romantic jaunt. If he took her out of town, I would be powerless.

The thought of Earline in Rimbo's squalid Beamer made me wince.

Then it hit me. All I had to do was restrict his mobility.

"That's it." I exclaimed to no one in particular. "That's exactly what I'll do."

I abruptly halted my progress in the middle of the sidewalk, causing a startled couple to scamper for safety. The male assumed a defensive posture. The woman eased behind her man.

"Sorry," I said. "Brain fart—happens all the time."

I stepped backward, waved at a cab, and the couple moved on. In seconds, I was on my way to the office, not the booth at *Jimmie's*, but my real office— the one at AIU.

* * *

When I entered AIU, Pinkie, the ever-sharp receptionist, reminded me I'd not been in the office much.

"I don't believe it," she quipped. "You look exactly like Jake Thompson. They say he died a while back. Amazing how much you resemble him."

"Good to know I've been missed, Pinkie."

"I wouldn't go that far." She extended her middle finger, blew a kiss, and shot me a wink.

"Nice nails—I mean nail."

"You like?"

"Purple?"

"It's the new black."

"I'd have stayed with the old shade."

"Great advice coming from someone who hasn't upgraded his wardrobe in over a decade."

"What's a wardrobe?"

"From the look of things, it's what you sleep in."

I raised both hands in a sign of defeat. "You win. Purple it is." I nodded toward the offices behind her and asked, "Is Bender around?"

"Parked at his desk," she joked. "Where else would the Parking Guru be? Want me to buzz him?"

"No, Pinkie. I think I'll surprise him."

Rolling her eyes she said, "I'm sure that will make his day. You know, Jake, he's still upset with you."

"*Naw*," I answered. "It's only an act." I headed down the hallway to where I knew I'd find Maximilian Bender, Chicago's most notorious nitpicker.

Within the city's police force Maximilian Artemus Bender was known as "No Bend Bender" because he had never deviated from Standard Operating Procedure. More rigid than Patton's spine, it was a verified fact Bender had ticketed guests parked at the restaurant for his parent's fiftieth wedding anniversary celebration.

I entered his office without announcement. "Hey, Max," I shouted and plopped down in the chair before his desk.

"You have a lot of nerve showing your face here, Thompson," he shot at me. "I hate practical jokes as much as—"

I cut him off.

"Sure, sure, I know. Having your car ticketed and towed wasn't very nice of me. I'm here, my friend, to apologize... And to make it up to you."

"Scary. Very scary—you acting like my friend."

"Come on. It's not hard to imagine. We're so alike, right?" I looked about his office and held back my laughter.

Bender was so anal. Everything in the room was neat, squared, and tucked. Each item on his desk was meticulously placed in a specific spot.

My gaze was enough for Bender to primp and preen the top of his desk. He arranged the paperclips on the blotter and replied, "As alike as a bird and a snake, Thompson."

"Ouch! I'm wounded—truly wounded."

"Now, I am scared," he said. "You want something, Thompson—that's obvious."

I knew the fun and kidding had to stop.

"Okay," I told him, "I have a peace offering—with no strings."

He cautiously said, "Tell me about it."

"Better than telling—here," I tossed the list of ticket numbers I had taken from Willard's car on his desk. "How about a serial offender? Check the tickets and I bet you'll find none have been paid."

"Oh, my," he whispered. "What do we have here?"

Bender ignored the mess I made of his sanctum. I had not seen such avarice since Gollum eyed the ring.

I followed up with, "Here's the sweetener," and tossed him Earline's address and the number at her front desk. "Give Ben, the doorman, a call. He'll play spotter for when you deliver the warrant."

"And make the arrest?"

"Knock yourself out. Matter of fact, rumor sez the guy is potentially violent. Take some help."

"Thanks Jake, this makes my day. It *really* makes my day."

"Consider this my amends."

* * *

Cook County Jail was a big nasty place that rivaled any lockup in the country. I would not have wished it on anyone—except scumbags like Willard. It was a world unto itself, with nine thousand inmates.

I'm glad I only visit in the line of duty. Definitely not *Club Med*.

I dropped in to see Willard to explain the facts of life. I wanted him to know I was playing for keeps. He was not happy to see me.

"*You*," he spit out when I entered the interrogation room. "I thought so."

Willard was decked out in an orange jumpsuit, flip flops, and was restrained with cuffs linked to a chain belt attached to his chair. It also looked as if he had some bumps and bruises.

"Like the accommodations?"

"Screw you." He started to get up.

"Careful," I warned. "My friend Max Bender has gone to a lot of trouble arranging for your stay."

"Which won't be long," he stressed. "Parking violations? Ha! You must be kidding me."

"No, I'm not. Chicago PD does not fool around with the likes of you."

"What do you mean—the likes of me?"

"Habitual criminals."

"You're crazy."

"Maybe so. But I'm not your problem. No Bend Bender is on your case."

"Huh?" He was truly confused.

"The Public Defender will explain it more thoroughly, but here's my short version." I pointed my finger an inch from his nose. "You might be here for ninety days."

"Ninety days?!" he yowled.

"Shish," I warned. "It'll be longer if you make a scene—a lot longer."

"Ninety days," he whimpered. "Ninety days..."

"And that's just the start."

"What?!" He attempted to rise, but his chain held him down. The reality of his short tether quickly sobered him.

"Your car is at the impound. At a hundred a day, you'll never see it again—unless you are plush with cash. And we both know you are busted, living off women. Your mooching from my friend is done. I've filled her in on your past—all of it. It's over. This place is where you now live. If you survive, you will eventually leave. But when you do, you'll hit the streets as a vagrant—and in five minutes you'll be on a roller coaster that brings you right back here, over and over and over.''

"You're serious."

"Like death," I said. "When I am finished with you, you may walk, but you *will* limp."

"Oh, my God," he almost prayed. "Oh, my God."

"He can't help you. But I can."

"You? How?"

"I have my ways—leave it at that."

He eyed me looking for some leverage or an advantage and saw none.

"Okay, tell me what you have in mind."

"I'll have you out of here in two hours. Your car will be available—with a tank of gas."

"And?"

"No ands," I said. "You leave."

"I'd like to tell Earline—"

"I *said* that was over. You so much as think about her and I'll see that you live here forever." I restated the goal. "You leave."

"That's it? I just leave?"

"Yes."

"I just go?"

"And live like there is no Cook County, no Chicago." I gave him the meanest cop stare I ever mustered. "In two hours, you disappear from Earline's universe. Deal?" I offered.

I saw no *Soldier of Fortune*, no con man, no writer, no slick Casanova. I only saw a man with no options. And whatever Morris Dean Willard really was, it saw its only move, too.

"Deal."

"Good."

* * *

A couple of days later Earline showed up for work. She said nothing about her absence or what had kept her away. Jimmie and I also did not speak about why or how long she was gone.

In a few days, things were almost back to normal. I say almost because there was an underlying taut-ness in the air between Earline and me. It belied that peculiar kind of tension which haunts married cou-ples when one of the pair has broken an agreed-upon rule and needs to purge some guilt.

For the one time in my life, I kept quiet.

One morning, when it was noon for the rest of the world, my silence was rewarded when I slipped into my booth. Earline sloshed a cup of *Jimmie's* coffee before me and said, "Thanks, Jake. I don't know what came over me."

"What are you talking about?" I asked.

"Shut up and order," she said, "Breakfast is on me."

I did as I was told. Nothing more was said. There was no need.

THE COBBLER

They say, "Some days are diamonds, others are crap." They may be right, whoever "they" are.

Guess which kind of day that one was turning out to be? If you needed a hint, it had the newly evicted me schlepping boxes out of my office on day ninety of my retirement. I warned you about the crap. And it doesn't end there. That morning, my most recent girlfriend, Charlotte, tossed me out.

Maybe I should explain how I got into such a fix.

For years, I wanted to retire more than Romeo wanted what's her name. But I did not leap into it—I was pushed. Sure, I had ideas about what I would do to fill my days once I pulled the ripcord, but I was not ready for the actual event. Who could have imagined the Chicago PD being so efficient?

Some genius in HR paid an overeducated nerd to do a review of pension liabilities and it was determined I was in the enviable position of being one. They pulled the cord, letting me go more than a year before I expected.

Money was an issue—always was. However, Charlotte was an accountant and she had a plan. I foolishly went with it. She persuaded me to open a private investigative firm in the John Hancock building where she lived, and she asked me to move in with her.

You know how that went.

My office was on the twenty-first floor—a waiting area and two rooms. "Unparalleled Sophistication" was how the marketers billed it. Well furnished, very nice, and pricier than my cases could have supported. I was in over my head from the start, and that was the least of my problems.

I hated being a PI. Correction—I hated my clients. Second correction—I hated what they asked me to do.

Snooping on cheating spouses was not my idea of a meaningful second career. Neither was chasing down pampered juvenile delinquents. I did that once for free to help a friend. Doing it for money did not make the experience any more palatable.

And the money was not enough to pay for the unparalleled sophistication, nor could it sophisticate me enough to suit Charlotte. Hence my invitation to depart.

Like they say, some days are indeed crap—pure unadulterated crap.

At street level, I jammed office boxes and my clothes into my car. I was evicted from my parking space, too. My intent was to transport everything to Dewey Eisenhauer's apartment in Blue Island where I aimed to crash and then drink myself to sleep.

That's when she called.

"Mr. Thompson?"

"Yes," I answered.

"My name is Miriam Poteet. I need to meet with you." Promise coated her voice.

"Me? Meet with me—why?" I had to ask.

"You were highly recommended."

I forgot about Dewey's. "Recommended? By whom?"

We are all imbued with the love of praise.

"Jeremy Westlawn."

I kept silent. I stayed that way for longer than normal.

"Mr. Thompson?"

I remained silent.

"Mr. Thompson—please meet with me. I need your help."

That did it. Only heartless bastards and sociopaths are immune to those four words, "I need your help." A straight-forward appeal for assistance works ninety-nine percent of the time for fundraisers, street hustlers, and damsels in distress.

I bit—No, I nibbled.

"Okay, Ms. Poteet. Tell me about it."

"That means you'll help?" Authentic relief filled her voice and saturated the coat of promise with a sense of ease.

I looked at my car filled with the boxes representing my disheveled life. I wanted that promise I
heard in her voice. I wanted to help because I wanted
to meet her. I bit more.

"Yes, I'll help," I told her.

"That's wonderful."

Five pounds of promise hit me. I was hooked. I
really had to meet her.

Jimmie's was out of the question. Earline would
never leave me alone if she caught wind that her
favorite street-person-artist was involved in one of
my cases. We arranged to meet in an hour in the lobby
bar of the *Marriott* on the Miracle Mile.

I got there early. When she entered the lobby, I
immediately knew it was her. The description she had
given was accurate enough—just not exact. I assume
she had been modest with the self-description.

She was in her late thirties, maybe forty, well
maintained. A Kate Hepburn type, but taller, a little
fleshier, with a touch of raw-boned outdoorsy in her
stride. Pulled back auburn hair, green eyes, small
freckles under light makeup, and a business suit completed the package.

She obviously knew my mug and headed for me
before I could wave her over.

"Mr. Thompson—thank you for meeting with
me."

I played it cool and answered. "No problem, Ms.
Poteet. Just tell me what you want. But keep Westlawn
out of it."

"I think you have Jeremy all wrong. He's your *biggest* fan."

"A fan? Blind One-Legged Johnny?" I had to get in my dig.

She laughed. "I know he'd love to hear you call him that."

"Really?"

"Oh, yes. He's often told me that he considers it lucky. He believes he owes his success in the art world to it—and you, of course."

"I thought he'd be holding a grudge."

"A grudge? Why in heaven's name would he hold a grudge?"

"The IRS, maybe?"

"Oh, that? It's not as bad as one might think. He's working it out with them."

My mind tried to wrap itself around the sight of Westlawn, AKA Blind One-Legged Johnny negotiating with the government's tax goons. It made me smile.

"And he told you to call me?"

"Yes. He was most emphatic that I call you... And only you. He said you are an exceptional detective because only you could find him. And, he said, you are very honest."

I motioned for us to grab a seat. "Okay, I'm intrigued. What is this about?"

She eased onto the sofa and said, "Art."

"Art?" I said, not trying to be obvious in my pleasure with being so close to her.

"Yes, it's about art—a particular painting to be exact. Do you know anything about Vermeer?"

I gave her my best serious art student look. "He's Dutch. Known for his interesting use of light—cornflower blue, and yellow. Has only thirty-six paintings attributed to him—three are suspect, the thirty-seventh, entitled, *The Cobbler at His Workbench*, is due to be revealed at the Art Institute next week."

"I'm impressed."

"Don't be. I read all about it in the *Trib*."

"I am still impressed. Frankly, I took you for the sports page type."

"Only for baseball." I fessed up. "Since the World Series is over and we're a long way from pitchers and catchers reporting for spring training, I scanned the arts section. The Vermeer story caught my eye."

So did she. She knew it... And liked it.

Shifting the subject, she commented, "I noticed that you have more than a bit of a Southside accent—Sox fan?"

"Not since they started using the designated hitter."

"Interesting—so, you're sort of a purist. What now? Now that the DH is universal?"

"I'm considering my options."

"Options?"

"Seppuku... A monastery... Even thought about switching to curling, or cricket."

"You indeed *are* a purist."

"Only when it comes to baseball. You ought to try my blend of bourbons."

She laughed. "You *are* quick witted. Just how Jeremy described you."

My face soured.

She quickly recovered. "Oops! I'm so sorry. I promised not to mention Jeremy."

I un-soured.

"Go on—get it out," I told her.

"Are you sure?"

"Yeah, I'm just a bit sensitive. For all my sleuthing brilliance, I got exiled and he got a boatload of recognition. Plus, you said he's flush."

"He's well aware of the inequity of treatment you two received."

"That's nice." Even I cringed at the whine in my voice. "Sorry—I'm not having a good day." I wanted to change the slant of the encounter, so I asked, "Mind if we start over?" Before she could reply, I added, "Let's have a drink."

"Only if I order and buy," she answered.

"Have at it," I said.

She waved the server over and ordered. "I'll have a *Campari* and soda with lime... And my companion will have three shots of bourbon—one each of Old Grand Dad, Jim Beam, and Jack Daniels in a tall glass with one large cube."

"Now it's time for me to be impressed." I told her. "Who's the detective here?"

"Jeremy shared everything he knows about you. He thinks the world of you. Really, he does."

"I may have misjudged him. The past couple of years have been difficult. No—almost impossible. After the news coverage broke and I was still sidelined in AIU, it was worse than usual. It's my fault. I mistakenly expected some kind of reprieve was due me for breaking his case."

"As I said, he was emphatic about me contacting only you."

"Go on—explain how do you know Westlawn and why are we meeting?"

"I'm an art broker and appraiser. Chicago is now my home and I mostly work with artists based in the city. After you identified Jeremy, I followed up on his art and we established a business relationship. Basically, I handle the sale of his work. Like I said, he's negotiating with the IRS and is looking forward to being able to travel in the US again."

"What's he got to do with Vermeer?"

"Nothing directly." She reached for the drink being delivered and took a sip. I grabbed mine, swigged half of it in one gulp, and she went back to her story.

"I was asked to be one of the appraisers to look over the Vermeer. I've done work for the Art Institute over the years. When I found what I found, I called Jeremy. He told me to call you."

"What did you find?"

"That Winslow Holbrook, the exhibit's curator, has a fake Vermeer."

"That should piss off some folks—especially Holbrook."

"Not if he commissioned it."

"Why would he do that?"

"To sell the real one."

"What?"

"I believe that the Art Institute has a genuine Vermeer."

"I'm getting lost. I thought you said Holbrook had a fake."

"He does."

I took a second gulp and waved the server to bring another.

"Go on," I said. "This is getting good."

"There is a fake—a copy of *The Cobbler.* I saw it this morning."

"You sure?"

"I'd bet my career on it." She squeezed the lime in her *Campari.* "Holbrook has two Vermeers. I saw the fake being switched for the real one."

"Did anyone see you?"

"No. Holbrook and his assistant were preoccupied with making the switch. I was well hidden. After they were finished, I checked the remaining Vermeer. It's a fake—a good one—but a fake nonetheless."

"Are you sure?"

"Positive."

"How does he benefit from the switch?" I asked aloud, then answered my own question. "If the exhibit goes on, I am certain the fake will be exposed. The Art Institute will be embarrassed. There will be a lot of publicity and the market—the black market—will go zonkers for the real one when he lets it be known he has it. With a fake already having been exposed any and all speculation about *The Cobbler's* authenticity will go out the window. His painting, the real one, will be priceless, right?"

"You've got it. Jeremy had you pegged—you really *are* good."

"Why don't you spill what you know to the higher ups at the Institute?"

"I can't—remember I okayed the Vermeer as being real. How would it look if I pointed out the fake and was not able to produce the real one?"

"Your career and reputation really are on the line."

"Yes. I called Jeremy because he has—I mean had—real life experience with... With..."

"I think *fraud* is the word you are searching for." I grinned and she laughed.

"*And* you have a sense of humor."

"So—where's the real Vermeer?"

"Still in the Art Institute."

"How do you know?"

As I said, "I saw the switch take place just hours ago."

"You didn't waste any time getting to me."

"Would you?"

"How are you certain it's still in the building?"

"The place is locked down like Fort Knox. Unless they are magicians—it's still there. Nothing goes in or out except at designated times and under the closest scrutiny. Supplies and the like are inspected going in, and everything going out—even the trash— is thoroughly searched. Holbrook has to disguise the real Vermeer to it get out. That will take some time."

"How much?"

"Not much—a few more hours at best. I say he'll place it inside another slightly larger painting's frame and take it out of the building later today. There's a three P.M. equipment and trash run each afternoon. That's when I'd shuffle a low-grade painting past security. Art students and staff take their own work out all the time."

"You seem to have this figured out. Why do you need me?"

"I'm not certain that Holbrook will have the painting. Maybe Kyle, his assistant, is the one who will have the real Vermeer. I need help watching and trailing the two of them. But most of all I need help in what to do if believe one of them has the real painting."

"Let me handle that."

"What do you have in mind?"

"I have no idea, yet. But I'll think of something—soon. We better hustle. Three is not far off."

* * *

We sped to the Institute and on the way shared cell numbers. Then, we split up. I camped outside the staff exit and waited for Miriam to give me a call when either of our two suspects came through security. I figured that me hanging around with her would draw suspicion.

Holbrook came out first. That time of year, it got dark early and the light misty rain hampered my vision, but her description of my target was spot on.

Okay," I told her when I eyed him. "I've got a good ID." I added, "Jesus—he's even dweebier than you described."

I was surprised how unimpressive the mastermind art thief was in real life—small and frail, with thin wispy yellow-gray hair and a stooped gait.

He exited the building with what appeared to be a medium-sized frame wrapped in brown shipping paper.

I was following him at a safe distance when Miriam called again.

"What Holbrook took out must be it—Kyle just left with nothing."

"I'll take it from here," I said.

"Jake, I can't tell you how grateful I am for your help."

I did not miss her use of my first name and replied, "Think nothing of it, Miriam. Just buy me another round when all this is over."

"Sure—sure." She hesitated then added, "I'll cook you a dinner, too. Goodbye, Jake—and good luck."

"I'll call when I have something solid," I replied and quickly hung up. I did not want to give her a chance to re-think the dinner offer. I was hooked on more than just a good case. My mouth was watering, and it was not for a meal.

Taking stock of my day I told myself, *Jake, either you are on to something good, or you have been suckered. A few hours ago, you were headed to Dewey's and a couple of lost days drowning your sorrows inside a bottle. Now you are on a case—a real one. All it took was a sweet smile, some freckles, a good figure, and a story of woe to get you to tail an artsy nerd. Am I getting soft?*

Before I could answer myself, Holbrook hailed a cab. I jumped into the next one and followed him north on Michigan Avenue.

He headed east on Grand and stopped at one of the condos tall enough to overlook Navy Pier. He exited the cab and entered the building—with me discreetly keeping after him.

"Nice place to hang your hat," I mumbled to myself as I watched him enter the elevator. His name was on the register for a 12th floor address, so I knew he was home.

I would have flashed my PI badge at the guard on duty hoping that he'd mistake it for the real deal, but there was no need. Mr. Alert Security had nodded off.

I took the next ride up and gave Holbrook some time to get settled, then I knocked on his door.

"Yes?" the voice on the intercom asked. "Can I help you?"

"Open up, Winslow. We need to chat."

"Chat? What do you mean? Who are you?"

"I flipped my badge quick at the peep hole and said, "We can do this here or downtown—you pick." My ruse worked. He opened the door a small bit, and I shoved my way in.

"Wait," he protested. "You just can't—"

"I can't—what?" I loudly countered.

He was alone and scared. Breaking him was easy.

"Filching art is a big no-no, Winslow." I pushed up close and let him feel my breath, laced with double bourbons and contempt.

I was on a roll. The corny dialogue poured out of me.

"Come clean and maybe the city's artsy crowd will go easy on you. Six months or a year instead of ten very long ones dancing in the shower with some big guy named Leon."

Holbrook froze. I'd never seen such fear. He assumed what I would describe as a vertical fetal position.

"Please," he begged. "Don't hurt me. Just don't—I-I-" He pointed to the wrapped frame resting along the wall. "Take it. Go ahead. *Take* it."

I eyed the wrapper and slapped him across the mouth. "It's dry. Where's the one you walked out of the Institute with?" For good measure I slapped him again.

"Okay. Okay," he whined. "It's over there. What you want is back there." He pointed at the wet bar dividing the room from the kitchen area.

I pushed him back and down onto the sofa and ordered, "Stay."

I made my way to where he pointed and found a frame wrapped in rain-spattered paper. Peeling back the wet outer wrap was easy. Soon, I held what appeared to be a copy of a well-known impressionist painting. "Mind if I inspect this, Winslow?"

"No... No. I mean. *Yes*. You have no right to—"

"Shut up," I yelled. "I was not really asking for permission, you idiot. I've explained... I've got a strong feeling that you've hid something behind this." I yanked at the corner of the impressionist piece. Beneath it was a second painting. "Looks like you are headed to the prison showers," I taunted.

They say pride goes before a fall. The "they guys" are often right.

They also say a smart mouth leads to trouble.

In my case, I was talking and not listening. If I'd kept my mouth shut and not baited that frightened pathetic nerd, I would have heard Kyle enter the room.

Maybe I would have avoided being zonked from behind.

Although Creep Number Two had snuck in and dropped me with a good lick on my thick skull, he failed to follow up. Kyle should have bound my feet and hands instead of leaving me unbound where I fell.

Experienced criminals would have made certain I was no longer a threat. Anyone but Kyle and Winslow would have searched me thoroughly and taken all my weapons.

I was not out long. I opened my eye closest to the floor and peeped at my captors. They looked confused. With my head reeling and gut wanting to spew out the remnants of my liquid lunch, I listened to Holbrook and his assistant arguing.

"We *can't* do that," whined Winslow.

"Killing him is our only option," insisted Kyle. From my position on the floor, I saw he had the gun I usually carried in my shoulder holster. I felt relief that I could feel the weight of my backup piece near my ankle.

"Your idea is *ludicrous*," Holbrook protested.

"No. It isn't. Listen to me—he reeks of alcohol as it is." He placed my gun on the kitchen counter.

Good move, I thought. I saw his feet head toward the glass door to the outside.

I also heard it slide partially open. *Not good,* I told myself. *I need to make something happen.*

"I say we toss him over the balcony rail and simply claim that our drunken guest had an accident."

It's getting worse, I thought. The drift of the conversation told me I had to make my move, and soon.

"Wait. There *has* to be another way," Holbrook pleaded.

"If you can think of one, I'll go with it. But I say we have no choice."

There was a knock at the door.

"Who the hell is that?" Kyle asked. Not waiting for a reply, he yelled to Holbrook, "Whoever it is—I'll get rid of them."

It was the distraction I needed.

Kyle headed for the door. I sprung from my prone position, went for his legs, and caught him mid-stride. He crashed into Holbrook and the two of them landed on the sofa where I had deposited Holbrook earlier. Before they could collect themselves, I was on my feet with my back-up piece in hand.

"Don't move," I shouted. Kyle's eyes focused on the gun he had placed on the counter. "Go for it and I'll drop you with one shot," I warned.

He threw his hands up and yelled, "Alright, alright."

I eased toward the counter and grabbed the gun. I told him, "Keep your hands up," and instructed Holbrook to do the same.

"Monkey see, monkey do, Winslow."

"Jesus—oh, Jesus," he whined and cried. "Oh, Jesus."

There was another knock at the door followed by a shout. "Jake. Jake? Are you in there?"

It was Miriam.

"I'm here," I answered. "I'll be there in a sec."

Pointing my gun downward, I told my captives, "Put your hands on top of your heads... Real slow. Move forward and drop to your knees. Then get flat on the floor, face down."

After they had complied, I made my way backward to the door and opened it.

"Are you okay?" Miriam asked. Her eyes almost popped out when she realized I was holding two men at gunpoint. "What's going on? What's happening?"

I answered, "Nothing much," and pointed to the painting. "Take a peek at that, and tell me for sure I've got these two for thieving."

Miriam rushed over to the frame, peeled the cover painting away from the underlying work of art, and placed the potential Vermeer on the counter to examine it. After a few moments she exclaimed, "*This* is the *real* Vermeer. It's definitely the one I originally examined."

"That's good enough for me," I said. "Can you aim a gun?"

"I think so," she answered.

"I mean, could you shoot if they move?"

"Yes."

"Good." I motioned for her to take my position and handed her my gun. "This is a *Seecamp*. It has no safety. Just point and shoot if one of these idiots tries something."

"Got it," she affirmed.

I yanked the cords off two lamps and proceeded to hog-tie the captured thieves.

"Wait," cried Holbrook, "Miriam. Make him stop."

"This is all a mistake," added Kyle. "Wait. We can explain."

"I think not." I said, "Grand theft, aggravated assault, kidnapping, and conspiracy to commit murder are not talking points the police take kindly to."

"What?" screamed Holbrook. "What do you mean? Kidnapping? Murder?"

"Shut up," Kyle screamed back. "Shut up. He's bluffing. He had no right to be here—no search warrant. It's our word against his."

"He's right," Holbrook chimed in, "You busted in here without a warrant."

"You let me in, remember?"

"Well— Well— Well," he stammered. "There was no kidnapping—no murder."

I reassured him. "Relax, Winslow. I only said it was conspiracy to commit murder."

I tightened their bonds and then told him and Kyle the bad news. "You are in deep. Look, I'm a retired Chicago police detective—now a private investigator. I'm not a slouch when it comes to bagging jerks like you.

"On the low side, I say you are facing fifteen solid years in maximum security. On the high end, twenty-five." I pulled out my cell phone and to Miriam said, "I'm cashing in some old chits with friends of mine in the fraud department. They'll keep a lid on this for a while, but I assume the media whores will sniff this out fairly soon. If there is anyone you want in on the management of how this is shared with the world, I'd call them quick."

Over the sound of Kyle vomiting and Holbrook sobbing, she said, "Both of you need to consider everything and stay quiet—for your own good. Got it?"

The two scared men stiffened. To me she said, "Thanks for the tremendous effort, Jake. Missus Manning Pierce, the Institute's board chair and largest patron brought me in on this. I'll call her first. She, the executive director, and their connected friends will know what to do."

"Missus Manning Pierce. My, oh my. You do have friends with clout," I said.

"And now, so will you." Pointing to the Vermeer and staring down my captives she said, "Jake, you have no idea how big this is."

Miriam was right. I had no idea how important saving *The Cobbler at His Workbench* would be.

* * *

They say overnight success often comes only after a lifetime of effort. The "they guys" were right again. The years of slogging away in AIU that hung around my neck like weights, slipped off and I immediately was Chicago's "Golden Boy" once again.

Here was what the *Trib* had to say about me:

HEROES GONE? NO. TAKE A LOOK AT THIS GUY

JUST WHEN YOU ARE CERTAIN ALL THE GOOD GUYS HAVE DISAPPEARED, SOMEONE LIKE RETIRED POLICE DETECTIVE JAKE THOMPSON, NOW A PRIVATE INVESTIGATOR, COMES ALONG. JAKE'S COOL AND DELIBERATE ACTIONS IN THE RETRIEVAL OF ONE OF *CHICAGO ART INSTITUTE*'S PRICELESS PAINTINGS CONVINCES EVEN THE MOST CYNICAL OF US HEROES STILL EXIST AMONG US.

The article had a great photo of me and went on, and on, and on, in praising my skills as a PI. I even crossed my long-held loyalty line and bought a copy of the *Sun Times*. Their article rivaled the *Trib*'s:

POLICE DEPARTMENT'S LOSS IS CITY'S GAIN

WHEN THE POLICE DEPARTMENT EASED ONE OF ITS DETECTIVES INTO AN EARLY RETIREMENT, THE GOAL WAS TO SAVE A FEW BUCKS. LITTLE DID THE POWERS-THAT-BE KNOW THEY WERE UNLEASHING UPON THE CITY AN ASSET OF IMMENSE VALUE IN THE FORM OF JAKE THOMPSON, PRIVATE EYE.

LIKE THE HEROES OF SO MANY MOVIES AND TELEVISION PROGRAMS, JAKE CALLED UPON HIS REAL-WORLD EXPERIENCE AND ABILITY TO DECISIVELY ACT AND SAVED THE DAY AT THE *CHICAGO ART INSTITUTE*. WHEN THE NEED AROSE, HE SURPASSED IT.

More praise and another photo rounded out their version of how I saved *The Cobbler*.

Miriam was dead-on right about a lot of things. And I liked them all. Some very important people were delighted with my performance, especially Mrs. Pierce. Not only did she present me with a sizable check, Mrs. Moneybags herself paved the way for my reinvigorated career as a PI.

Based on her recommendations, scads of meaningful work would be coming my way.

But as good as it was, two things made it even better. The first was Miriam's promised dinner and the prospect of more time spent with her. I saved her career. She fixed dinner. That could have been that. But, she kept calling, and I'd always been a sucker for smart, attractive women who grilled steaks and poured Old Jimmy Jack.

The second special thing was my favorite article. It appeared in the small hip newspaper *Chicago Insider:*

HOWEVER YOU FEEL ABOUT COPS, YOU GOTTA LOVE THIS ONE

HE MAY NOW BE A PRIVATE EYE, BUT AT HEART JAKE THOMPSON IS ALL COP THROUGH AND THROUGH, AND A GREAT ONE BY ALL STANDARDS—SMART, BRAVE, AND BOLD. WHAT MORE CAN THE PUBLIC ASK FOR? TOSS IN THE FACT THAT HE IS A SOUTHSIDER, AND YOU HAVE THE MAKINGS OF A LOCAL LEGEND. THE SIDE OF TOWN LONG ON DECLINE AND MUCH MALIGNED HAS A NEW HERO.

The picture they ran must have been snapped by Earline or Jimmie, and the story was a truthful account of my life's ups and downs. The article made me laugh, cry, and sing inside all at once.

For the rest of my life that ego booster will be pinned to my shaving mirror... Whose current location was a problem.

* * *

"Now I've seen it all," quipped Earline, as she poured a cup of *Jimmie's* oily brew for me.

"You mean me reading something other than the *Trib*?"

"No. I mean the world finally agreeing with me that you are one helluva cop."

"A homeless cop." I pointed to the papers I was reading. "I need to find an apartment. Me crashing at Dewey's can only go on so long. At heart, I'm not a commuter."

"You can stay at my place if you want."

I shook my head in disbelief. "Earline, are you hitting on me?"

"I was thinking of the *spare bedroom*, Jake." She swatted at me and missed on purpose.

"Whew," I sighed. "You had me scared."

"Scared?! You think I'm *that* bad off?" She swatted again. That time with intent and better aim.

"No—no. I just would hate losing what we have here." I waved my arms to include the entire diner. I seasoned my gesture with a big smile and rubbed the spot where she had landed her jab.

"Good recovery," she said.

"I guess I still have the touch."

"You still have to tip me."

I blew her a kiss and said, "Seriously, I am homeless. I gave up my bachelor haven to move in with Charlotte. How will I ever find place as good as that?"

"You'll need a site with office space. Would you consider Spook Central?"

"Renee's building?"

"I was thinking Renee's place itself."

"Is she moving?"

"Going to Florida."

"She hit the lotto?"

"Kinda."

"What have I missed?"

"A long-ago beau reappeared and swept her off her feet. The wedding is next month. He's got a nice little place in Sarasota."

"Wonderful news," I said. She looked at me and I stayed quiet.

After what seemed like forever, Earline walked over to the counter, grabbed a piece of my favorite pecan pie, and brought it to the table.

"It's on me," she said.

"What's it for?"

"For not making any wise–ass comments about a woman getting all moony-eyed over some guy."

"Well... Thank you."

"No. Thank you." She got a little misty-eyed. "I owe you so much. If it wasn't for you, I might be tied up and beaten by a psycho—or worse. Jake, you're not only a good cop, you're a good man."

"No, Earline. I'm not a good man. I'm just trying to be one."

I played with my pie and absorbed the moment. I continued with, "Besides—it was nothing. Friends do things to help friends. It's as simple as that."

I gave her another big smile and then changed the subject. "Tell me where Renee is right now, and how much you think she'll want for her place. I've got some money burning a hole in my pocket."

THE RETURN OF BLIND ONE-LEGGED JOHNNY

I DID NOT BUY RENEE'S PLACE. In fact, I never made an offer. I held off cashing Mrs. Pierce's check, too. At the time, I could not have explained why, but later on it made perfect sense.

You might say I got diverted. Miriam laid on some heavy-duty charm, and I found myself back in the Caribbean as part of her scheme. Like I told you, I was neck deep in something that really could redeem me.

Here I am—focused on that pile of cash I mentioned way back in the beginning of this tale of tales.

Remember the money?

Its temptation keeps hitting me in waves like the surf outside. They say money talks. There's that 'they' again. Screw *they*. *They* are not there. I am—and that pile of cash seduces me.

Forget the beautiful blue water, the sunshine, the expensive booze. A pile of money makes a guy think—and dream. I've been thinking a lot about Miriam.

I stare at the money and sigh, "Miriam, Miriam, Miriam."

"Yes, Jake, dear," a soft voice asks. "Is there a problem?"

Miriam is there.

"A hundred thousand, right?" I ask the pile. There is no answer.

Miriam provides it. "I told you—that," she nods at the cash, "and much more—later." She presses me. "Is there a problem?"

I again look to the cash for a statement. It remains mute.

"Look," she says. "I have to go, or I'll miss my flight." She draws close, allows me to smell her perfume, kisses my ear, and purrs, "Jake, trust me. It's all good. Just do as I say, and everything will be fine."

"I'll see you tomorrow in Chicago," she coos, and then leaves.

Miriam should have waited for my answer.

For a brief time in my life, I was marginally handsome. That was eons ago. My mirror confirmed I was no longer the man once attractive enough to interest a future starlet.

Face it. I'm no catch, so it's not rocket science— Miriam is playing me. Correction, she *was* playing me. I'm not as dumb as some people think.

Miriam's mistake was in relying upon my spotty track record with any and all organizations and authority.

I'm a contrarian, not a loser.

If she really knew me, she might have learned my deep-seated identity crisis is really my defining essence. If crosswords were people puzzles, I'd be a good one.

The letter "T" begins my two parts. Remember my name? Tomaszewski. It is the original me—the *real me*. Underneath my callous smart-mouth South-sider skin, it's the honestly honest me. Tomaszewski is the soft gooey center that seeps through my charred exterior. Tomaszewski is why I am a cop. I cannot be anything else. The Tomaszewski inside me leaks out all the time and Miriam should have understood that about me.

I scold the green paper pile everyone worships. "Some help you are."

It remains silent.

I fill a large envelope with it, sit back in the familiar rattan chair, and wait for Jeremy to return from his quick trip to deliver Miriam to the island's airport.

I figured it would take less than a half hour—ten minutes both ways with a quickie kiss and breathy exchange in the middle.

Miriam is playing him, too. Jeremy does not know it. But I do. It was part of her game that I was not playing.

Miriam didn't know that.

I wait for Jeremy.

* * *

"I thought you would be on the beach enjoying our last day here in paradise," Jeremy said, when he found me slumped in the rattan chair.

"*Our* last day?" I asked. "Are you one-hundred percent certain you want to leave?"

"Yes. It's all set. Miriam will meet us tomorrow at the lawyer's office."

"Are you *sure*?" My voice dripped sarcasm.

"Yes, of course. I'm certain I want you to be the one turning me in."

"I meant, are you sure she'll be there?" I laid it out straight.

"What? What do you mean?" He was stumped. You'd expect that from a guy who less than an hour before was told by his lover *everything* was good. You'd expect that from a mark who had no idea he was being conned.

I tossed him the envelope filled with cash and said, "Maybe we should talk about this."

Jeremy caught my toss, opened the envelope, and peered inside.

"What's this?" he asked.

"My initial cut—a pay off."

"Pay off? For what?"

"Taking you to Chicago and turning you in—as soon as we land at O'Hare."

"At O'Hare? What about the lawyer's office? Miriam said—"

"Miriam has said a lot of things." The tone of my voice was unmistakable. Now he *knew*. He tried to hand the envelope back to me.

"It's yours—keep it."

"Mine?" He looked at me.

I nod.

With a dumb look, he started, "You mean she— She—"

"Yes—it's your money." I tried not to, but I laughed. He was genuinely hurt.

"Sorry," I said, "but it *is* funny. To tempt me she used your cash—among other things."

The news of Miriam sharing her physical blessings with more than him was beyond what Jeremy could take.

He collapsed in the chair next to me and moaned, "I trusted her."

"Jeremy, there's no deal with the IRS. If you went with me tomorrow, you'd be in jail for so long that at your age it might as well be forever. That's where she wants you."

"Why?"

"For the money—what else?"

"But she already has my limited power of attorney—and it's not for much beyond the IRS deal."

"Now, I don't understand," I said. "How much money is there for her to take if she uses it for herself?"

"A couple hundred thousand—maybe."

"Is that all?"

"Most of my wealth is tied up here in businesses like this hotel—and in real estate." He wore a blank expression.

There was so much more happening with him, Miriam, and other things.

I asked, "Was she in on your original scam?"

"No."

I got up, found a bottle, poured us a couple of stiff drinks, and continued. I thought he should know as much as me.

"When I tracked you—back when you went missing as Johnny—she was living next door, going by the name of Miriam, right?"

"Yeah."

"If she knew anything then she didn't let on. She waited until after everyone knew who you were. Then she made her move—sidestepped your agent—got close to you. You really thought she wanted to sell your art. How long before she slept—"

"Stop!"

"I'm just trying to verify her angle. If it isn't money—"

I stopped because it all fell into place. The money was just window dressing. The woman we both knew as Miriam wanted his talent.

I looked at Jeremy Westlawn, AKA Blind One-Legged Johnny. The man I once tracked, exposed, and considered scamming because Miriam asked me to, was just a duped fool.

I asked, "How well do you know Vermeer?"

He sat in silence.

I had my answer.

* * *

My legs ached from being first crammed into the island puddle jumper and then the coach seat to Chicago. Jeremy wanted to fly me home first class, but I had declined.

I also did not take the money he offered in thanks for my honesty. I thought it was hilarious coming from a guy who disguised himself as a blind cripple for over thirty years, and I told him so.

We had a good laugh when I told him he had to stop offering me money every time I saw him.

I am glad to say I departed as his friend.

As soon as the plane landed, I made my way to Miriam's apartment. Even though I did not expect to find her there, I was surprised it had been totally cleaned out. The office of the lawyer she had been using was the same. They obviously had been working together and did not want to be found.

I wondered aloud, "Is she sleeping with him, too?"

I didn't need to answer myself. I knew the truth and I did not really care. Like a bad penny, I knew she'd turn up again somewhere in the muddled tale called 'My Life'. I felt it in my bones.

Besides, there were more important matters to conclude.

* * *

"Mister Thompson—Missus Pierce will see you now," her personal assistant finally announced.

We had been cooling our heels in the outer office of the Pierce Corporation's executive suite about twice as long as necessary. It was meant as intimidation. The rich and powerful tried it all the time. It did not work on me.

I told my companion to stay put as I entered the office of the wealthiest woman in the city to hand her money back—and to discuss the truth.

Audra Manning Pierce's age was a secret. She was past middle age and so well-maintained that it was impossible to discern how old she actually was. Her hair, clothes, and jewelry spoke power.

She sat behind an aircraft-carrier-sized desk, positioned directly in front of the Vermeer Miriam had presented to her after I had busted the two creeps from the Art Institute.

She ignored me. Queen Bees do that to drones like me.

I approached her desk, pulled up a chair, and broke the first rule of meeting with people like Mrs. Pierce—I spoke first.

"Nice painting," I commented.

She was not amused and her way of letting me know was to continue with the silent treatment.

It remained my move.

"I said—"

"I heard you," she interrupted.

She turned to face me. There was no smile. "Mister Thompson, you have been irritatingly persistent. A man with that quality could be very useful to me—and my friends."

I reached into my pocket and produced the check she had sent me. "I think not," I told her. "I'm not for sale."

I flipped the check toward her, and we both watched it land in the center of her massive desk.

"Persistent and arrogant," she said. "You are certainly not what I expected."

"What did you expect?"

"A man like the one Miriam described. But I believe that she erred in her appraisal of you—erred quite a bit it seems."

"I like being underestimated."

"Another quality that could be useful."

"Useful, Missus Pierce? Why would you need a useful man? You have just about everything anyone could want. In fact, you even have a Vermeer."

"You mentioned that before."

"Yes. The Vermeer is why I came."

"It's a copy—you came to discuss a copy of a painting?"

"No. I came to talk about the one behind you— the real one."

She smiled. "Mr. Thompson, you are something."

"Did Miriam come to you, or did you think up the scam to produce a copy and do a double switch?"

"You are something indeed." She continued to smile but I saw a small twinge in her cheek. "You have an imagination, also."

It was my turn to ignore her. Instead, I continued to share what I figured out.

"I guess it makes no difference who originated the scheme. It just took your money to pull it off. Miriam got Westlawn to paint the copy. She roped those two losers into the plot. Recruits me to nab them and does the switch—twice. Since she is the one to authenticate the painting, no one is the wiser when you get the so-called copy as a gift. How am I doing?"

She did not reply. I knew I was on target.

"The two dupes are no problem. They can be tucked away nicely in jail and haven't a clue how they were used. Westlawn is another matter. If he ever showed up—he could identify his fake, which is in the museum's collection.

"Was it Miriam's idea to use me to get Westlawn back into a jurisdiction where he could be locked up?"

"Yes."

"That figures. My luck with women is still consistent. You must have paid her well—she's disappeared."

"She no longer interests me. But you do." She smiled. "I said you were persistent—that trait brought you here, and I ask, 'Where does this leave us?'"

She was all business. Her position in life was based upon myriad deals where she used her position, power, and money, and I was just one more deal. The rich had leverage, and to beat them you needed to be very smart at using the systems they created to keep all the "little people" in their place.

I launched into my finale.

"I know you will claim Miriam duped you into accepting the original. People with your kind of money never do time for simple theft."

"Knowing that, you still came here. Why?"

"I don't want you to have the painting. Also, I hate being used."

"Oh, is that all?"

"No. I want you to have some regret for screwing with people's lives—mine in particular. I want you to lose something you want—and, trust me, you will."

"Do you really think you can threaten me?"

"Me? Threaten you? I'm not that dumb. And I'm really not very persistent, either. If you admire persistence as much as you say, wait until my colleague in the outer office hands you his warrant for the Vermeer."

"I am certain I can handle any attempt to take *my* painting."

"Then get ready for the ride of a lifetime. Max Bender is persistence in the flesh."

I knew she had no clue about the size of the bomb I had just landed on her. In her mind, little people like me were just bits and pieces—parts and labor. Her perfect life of buying and selling whatever she wanted would continue.

The proof of which came in her following act.

With a deliberateness that was meant to impress, she picked up the check from her desk, tore it in half, and pushed it aside. Then, she opened the desk drawer, extracted one of those over-sized business checkbooks, and began to write. When finished, she removed the new check from the book and slid it toward me.

"Here," she said. "The amount is twice what I paid you before."

"For *that*... I assume you want me, Bender, and the warrant to go away."

"Yes."

"I told you, I am not for sale."

"Is that a decision you can live with, Mr. Thompson?" she asked. My mind raced back to my father's similar question.

"It works for me."

"We'll see," she said as she smiled, retrieved the second check, and tore it like the first. After writing again, she slid a third check all the way across her desk and said loudly, "You certainly are persistent, Mister Thompson." Pointing she said, "That is ten times the original amount."

It *was* a lot of money. And although I was retired, near broke, and technically homeless, I wasn't tempted for even a micro-second to take it. I knew who I was and from where I came.

Without hesitation, I tore up the check and declared, "My name really isn't Thompson—it's Tomaszewski."

As a wise man once said, "Your essence is more important than form."

And Popeye often said, "I am what I am."

WHAT DO YOU CALL A DO-OVER?

I DON'T PLAY GOLF, BUT I get a kick out of its vocabulary—particularly the old stuff. How can you not bust a gut over names like *brassie*, *mashie*, and *cleek*?

You have to give it to 'em. The old-timer Scots who invented the game certainly had the knack for names. I wonder how many gallons of scotch were consumed during liar's sessions before those word-gems faded away. It's a shame such colorful labels for clubs have been driven into the rough by television, high-tech golf equipment, and the game's own popularity.

Yet, no matter how bland golf's language may have become, all is not lost. There's still great fun to be had in using the game's old terms. For kicks, watch the blank expression on the face of some weekend Tiger Woods wannabe when you ask about the condition and performance of his *niblick*.

The dumbass will probably look down at his crotch and smile like some lounge lizard with a bad comb-over.

You can't make this stuff up—at least that's what *they* say. And *they* are right at least as often as *they* are wrong. Aren't they? But, right, wrong, or indifferent, golf still has the mulligan—the friendly do-over that is allowed after an errant swing.

And right then, I was in need of one. In golf terms, my last tee shot in life had landed me in a water hazard.

Like I said, I am not a golfer. Remember, I was just an old-fashioned cop with a nose for trouble and a taste for Old Jimmy Jack—my personal blend of *Old Grand Dad*, *Jim Beam*, and *Jack Daniels*.

Not so long ago, while solving Chicago's biggest art heist, I made a serious enemy when I exposed the city's most powerful and influential businesswoman as a common sneak thief.

My reward for poking my nose in that hornet's nest is I call the backroom at *Jimmie's Diner* my home. Oh yeah, not to mention I cannot find any suitable work.

It's true, I could really use a mulligan.

* * *

It was noon at *Jimmie's*. While the normal customers were ordering lunch, it was my usual time for breakfast. I wasn't lazy, I was a late riser—especially after consuming a snoot-full of bourbon.

While I waited for my life's next do-over, and stared at a crossword puzzle, Earline, my favorite waitress, poured me a third cup of the oily brew Jimmie called coffee.

"Are you eating?" she asked.

"Yeah, sure—guess I should."

"There are a lot of things you should do," she quipped, "but it looks as if I'm only here to feed you." Her words stung me like a swarm of homicidal bees on meth.

"Still sore I'm not bunking at your place?" I replied in self-defense.

She laser-beamed her peeps on my wounded hide and said, "Jake, my offer was *for the spare room only*."

Space-time grinded to a halt, iced smoke hung in the air. I eyeballed the inside of my cup, and sipped *Jimmie's* fuel oil. Earline knew I knew she was lying about her invitation. She also knew I'd never say 'yes'. If I took her offer and even temporarily hung my hat at her address, it would have jeopardized our unique relationship.

For me, Earline's place in my life was a rare and wonderful experience. There was magic in the conversations we had at *Jimmie's*. Real truth was spawned within our exchanges. Earline served as my personal truth barometer. Cohabitation, with or without a physical component, would have screwed things up.

I continued to ignore her comment, sipped again from my cup, and faked interest in my crossword puzzle. Earline left without taking my order.

It was a draw. Breakfast could wait.

I eased back in my booth for a snooze, and as drifted off to sleep, I heard a familiar click-click-click of high heels. In a flash, I was completely alert in anticipation of a treat.

The clicks stopped next to me and I was happily staring at the nicest pair of legs in God's creation, attached to the receptionist from my previous place of regular employment—the Administrative Investigations Unit of the Chicago PD.

I smiled and asked, "Hey, Pinkie. What brings you to Café d'Jimmie's?"

"You, Jake," she answered. "The reason is *you*. And, I never thought I'd say it, but thank God you're here."

I looked over at Earline. She disagreed with Pinkie's gratitude for my location. To Earline, I was still the asshole who would rather bunk down in a storeroom instead of her place. She turned her back to us.

Pinkie missed the significance of Earline's gesture and plowed on.

"Jake, when your mail kept being returned to the office, I told them where to find you, but ohhhhh noooooo, they won't listen to me. The geniuses at AIU looked everyplace but where I told them." She waved at me to get up and said, "C'mon, we gotta go. I told them I'd come here and bring you back myself."

"Stop it—I don't work there anymore. They forced me out on an early retirement. Remember?"

"No, Jake. Bad dreams come true—you still work for AIU."

"That's not even remotely funny."

"I know it sounds crazy, but you are *not* retired. *Really*."

"Pinkie, I've got the papers and a pittance of a pension to prove it."

"No. Your paperwork got reviewed when the pension office found out about your real name—the one you had when you were born."

"No big deal. Everyone knows my father changed our name from Tomaszewski to Thompson when I was a kid."

"Not the pension office." She grabbed my arm and pulled. "C'mon."

"You're serious, aren't you?"

"Serious as a heart attack. I didn't come into this greasy spoon because I miss the smell of your stale bourbon aftershave. By the way, why don't you answer your phone?"

She tugged harder before I could tell her about the dead battery.

"Come on, move it," she ordered. "Captain Foister needs to see you."

Ten minutes later, I sat in the seedy offices of the Director of the Administrative Investigations Unit, the Elephant's Graveyard of the Chicago PD. Foister was not happy to see me. A scowl the size of Navy Pier adorned her face.

"Good to see you, Mildred. How you been?" I greeted her. My being familiar upset her more.

My old boss barked, "It's Captain Foister to you, Thompson. Or should I call you Tomaszewski?"

I shrugged and offered a faint smile. It nudged her into the pissed-off zone supervisors entered when a subordinate just didn't care.

"Thompson, this is not a situation to joke about."

"What exactly is the situation?" I asked.

"*This*," She said, tapping the huge folder on her desk. "This nightmare called *you*."

I reached for the folder and asked, "Can I see?"

"Take a peek." She picked up the folder with two hands, lunged forward, and dropped it in my lap.

"They are making a big deal out of you originally being named Tomaszewski. It seems that someone slipped up on the paperwork when your father filed the change. Legally, you may still be a Tomaszewski, not a Thompson."

I was not impressed. "This is over a clerical error? I'm here because some desk jockey made a boo-boo?"

"That boo-boo was all it took to turn the system against you. Read it and you'll see that everyone in the chain of command has lined up against you. Missus Manning Pierce made that a certainty."

I scanned the folder and looked up. "It looks like she wants to get even."

"You cost her millions."

"Just peanuts for her."

"It goes beyond the money. You challenged her. Remember, she's the power behind the power in this city."

"I did my job."

"And because you did, she had to eat crow, give up the painting, pay a boatload of legal fees, and work twice as hard to convince the city's elite that it was all a mistake." She pointed at the folder. "As you can see, she's leaning hard on everyone to bring you down."

"By taking my pension?"

"Worse. Jake, sometimes you are the dog, sometimes you are the hydrant. Right now, the entire kennel club is hosing you down."

"Could I borrow your raincoat?"

"This is not something to joke about. Just look at what she has arranged. Missus Pierce is too smart to attack you directly. Instead, she found a glitch with your name. It's a well-planned institutional hit."

"A lot of people have had their names changed— at least three Presidents—Clinton, Ford, Obama."

"I suspect their influence is a little more potent than yours."

"I won't argue with you on that. I know my clout in this town is zero, zilch, nada. But what about loyalty? Where's the Blue Wall? Doesn't me being a Chicago cop for most of my life mean anything?"

"The only reason you have not been brought up on a fraud charge is the union's hesitancy to cave-in to pressure too quickly... And this morning's unfortunate accident."

"What accident?"

"A drunk doing over ninety tee-boned Missus Pierce's limo. She's in a coma."

"Lucky me."

"Her being unconscious buys us time."

"Us?"

"Read the file. The minions made a mistake. Until this matter is resolved—which means they need time to barbeque your nuts—you are re-instated here in AIU. It's 'us' because I'm stuck with you."

"Wonderful," I deadpanned. "Does that mean you and me get to swap spit?"

She got up, walked around from her seat, stood before me, and leaned over me.

"Okay, Jake. I admit that we don't like each other. But, as a police officer, I have tremendous respect for the work you've accomplished, even while being exiled to this wasteland. You're the closest thing I've ever seen to being a natural-born cop and, despite being assigned here in this backwater of backwaters, you have solved some very complex cases."

I was as uncomfortable with her closeness as I was surprised by her words. Defensively, I handed her the folder and asked, "Do I get my shield back while I wait for the guillotine to drop?"

She took the folder, backed up a bit, and nervously said, "Technically, yes. I guess you do."

"What on earth does that mean?"

"It means you ride a desk. And I mean *ride* it. No casework. As a matter of fact, you do *no* work at all."

"I'm confused. I work here, but do no actual work?"

"Yes. Every day you come in at nine, watch TV, read—just hang out. Pinkie will assign you to a cubicle."

"You gotta be crazy. Me? Hang out in a cubicle?"

She stepped close, leaned in again, and said, "I'm sorry, but the answer is 'Yes.' Pierce's allies will be watching you like a hungry cat eyeing a mouse sandwich. I don't want you near anything that could get you into any type of trouble."

"Trouble? How could that happen?"

"I've been your boss long enough to know you're a magnet for misfortune. I take that back—*shit* magnet fits better. Jake, you're an inch away from being annihilated by the forces that run Chicago, Cook County, and half the country. They know how to pressure the system and they will screw you and screw you good without batting an eye."

Her words hit home. At times I may be dense, but I knew a friend when I saw one. With Mildred, I just didn't know why she was on my side. Lord knows, I had given her some gray hair.

"We've been two cats in a bag, so why are you now my pal?" I asked.

"Nobody deserves to be treated the way this folder lays out your end. Luckily you caught a break when the higher-ups reassigned you to this godfor-saken excuse for a law enforcement unit. Your total ruin is what dear old Missus Manning Pierce was aiming for, but her mishap is a Godsend. Just stay out of trouble and pray that the rich old bitch never wakes up. Maybe, just maybe, you'll survive. Hell, you might even get to spend some of your pension money one day."

"Damn, Mildred, I've never seen you like this. You're *Zorro, Captain America*, and *Wonder Woman* all rolled into one feisty female. Did you know that you really are disturbingly attractive when you get riled up? If you weren't my boss, I'd be tempted to kiss you, ply you with liquor, and kiss you some more."

She tossed the folder on her desk, pointed to the door, and shouted, "Get your ass out of here before I regain sanity and change my mind about helping you."

I blew Mildred a kiss and headed out of her office. As I turned for the door, I told her, "Staying away from real work is okay with me, Mildred, but I'm not coming in just to sit in a cubicle. On my way out I plan to tell Pinkie that if anyone needs me, they can find me at *Jimmie's Diner*."

She threw the folder at the wall and yelled, "It's *Captain Foister*. And don't *ever* call me *Mildred* again."

I turned and prepared to make another smart remark, but I saw she was about to pop a vein.

"And get a battery for your damned phone," she yelled.

I tossed up my hands and silently mouthed, "Okay, okay," and slunk out the door.

My mind jumped to an explanation of my predicament. I had heard about the opposite version of a mulligan but never believed in it. Its existence had been respectfully whispered about by old men sipping drinks, playing chess, and reminiscing about their successes and failures. I thought it was an urban legend, a myth. I found myself facing my own reverse mulligan.

Here's the deal: When whatever you call it, fate, life, or *the system*, gets a do-over and puts the screws to an individual it's called a *Reverse Mulligan*.

The difference between a mulligan and a reverse one is not related only to the direction, but also its size. Think of karma with a bad attitude, or cosmic payback on steroids. A reverse mulligan is about a million times larger than a regular one.

Trust me, I know.

* * *

Back at the diner, I explained to Jimmie what was going on. He had abandoned his perch next to the cash register and was seated across from me. His relocation caused quite a buzz among the employees and patrons. He rarely left his favorite spot and never sat in a booth. I was awed and honored.

Jimmie normally bantered with customers in a dialect known as 'Jimmie Jabber'. When he was serious, Jimmie could speak just like you and me.

Ignoring the commotion he caused, Jimmie said, "It's time we have a talk."

"Talk?" I reply. "I'm in an episode of *The Twilight Zone*. It's like living in a surreal bubble of some kind. Retired, not retired, Thompson, Tomaszewski, sleeping in your backroom, and finally, I'm at AIU *again*."

Jimmie calmly responded. "Jake, you must have told me a thousand times, 'Nobody gets out of AIU. Nobody'."

He ordered for us. Coffee and two slabs of pecan pie. The buzz exponentially increased. Jimmie had never been known to eat in public. Earline delivered the coffee and pie with reverence fit for a cathedral. The buzz turned to prayer-like murmurs.

In a hushed whisper, I continued. "In addition to being forced back to work, the creeps aren't going to pay me. My travel and reimbursements for over twenty years were audited and they claim I owe money. They own me, Jimmie. I'm a friggin' prisoner."

He nodded and replied with some classic Jimmie Jabber.

"Everything is normal until you experience it. Eat some pie. Pay attention to the pecans."

I dumbly smiled and ate the pie.

"Well?" he asked.

"Well—what?"

"How's the pie?"

"It tastes fine."

"Did you hear anything?"

"What do you mean? I'm supposed to hear something? From where?"

"The pie."

"Huh?"

He slid out of the booth, stood next to me, broadly smiled, and said, "Then, it's settled."

"Jimmie, are you feeling alright?"

"Sure, I'm good," Jimmie said. Then he pointed at his plate and told me, "My pie says, you sleep in back room, eat here on the cuff, and lie low. Wait for the message."

"What message?"

"The message of synchronicity."

I gave him a big, "Huh?"

"Synchronicity. You know—right time, right place—when all the gears of existence mesh. Jake, you got your badge back for a reason. Just wait. Pretty soon everything will make sense."

Like I said, I had entered *The Twilight Zone*.

THE MESSENGER ARRIVED

FOR THE THIRD TIME THAT day, I waved off a second cup of coffee. It prompted Earline to ask, "Are you okay, Jake? You never have just one."

I focused on my crossword and casually explained, "I'm thinking about giving up bourbon." Earline dropped the pot. It clanged along the floor, creating a squiggly oil spill.

"*Damn*, Jake," she screamed. "What the hell is going on? Yesterday, Jimmie sat in a booth and orders food... And... And..." She threw a dish towel on the floor and stooped over to mop up the spill. "And today, everything is falling apart." She pointed at the floor. "Look at this mess."

"According to Jimmie it's all part of a plan," I told her.

"Well, it's a plan the world can certainly live without." She moaned more as she cleaned.

I commented, "If this is synchronicity, I'll opt for something else."

I was about to console her when a familiar voice boomed, "But can it live without me?"

The remark came from my old pal, Dewey Eisenhauer. We grew up together on the Southside.

Dewey is an ex-jock. His football career took a left turn years ago. Since then, he tends bar across the city line in Blue Island's Old Western Avenue historic area.

For a guy who never slept alone, he looked like crap, and I told him so.

"Good to see you, Dewey. By the way, you look like crap."

"I agree," added Earline. "How many days since you've slept, dear?"

"Two—no, three." He flopped down into my booth.

Earline patted his shoulder and said, "I'll get you some coffee." She looked at me. "Great plan so far, Jake, really great." She patted Dewey a second time and stuck her tongue out.

"What's with her?" asked Dewey. "I thought you and her—"

I interrupted. "Don't go there."

"Sure, okay. I was just—"

"Going there, you dog. Earline is off limits to you *and me*. Just think of her as your sister, a librarian, one soon to be a nun."

My second interruption coincided with the arrival of fresh coffee.

Dewey ignored Earline and she left with a world-class pout on her face.

"Good job, Dewey," I said. "So, where's my five bucks?"

"Oh yeah, I'm off—I really need some sleep." He extracted his wallet, produced a ten, and handed it to me. "Here, now you owe me."

I took the bill. I smiled.

"Sure. I'm good for it," I replied, "I'll find you later."

Dewey's expression told me he was there for something other than one of our reunions.

"Tell me why you look like shit."

"Mikie is missing."

I rolled my eyes. "Another one of his lame pay-backs?"

"No, this time it's serious."

Since we were kids, Tom "Mikie" Burns had been attempting various stunts to pay Dewey and me back for the original event that labeled him a patsy and bestowed upon him the nickname of Mikie.

Years ago, there was a popular TV commercial featuring a couple of kids playing upon the gullibility of their younger friend. The set-up line was, "Let's give it to Mikie, he'll eat anything." After watching Mikie test a bowl of cereal, the punch line was, "Hey! Mikie likes it."

With our gullible friend, the item we tested was not from the breakfast menu. Instead of cereal, we gave him a rare variety of jalapeño pepper capable of removing paint from auto fenders. He gulped the entire pepper all at once, and forever after, Tommy Burns was simply known as Mikie.

Over the years, Mikie had frequently and fruit-lessly tried to get back at us. Most of the attempts had been involved with some sort of disappearance. My guess was that Tom wanted Mikie to vanish. A psychiatrist would have had a field day figuring it out.

I asked, "What's going on?"

"It all began on Friday."

"You've been up since then?"

"Yeah, yeah—pretty much. That's when Mikie and I went to the Boat. He had a lucky feeling and wanted to test it out. You know how he is when he's got the bug."

They called it the Boat, but there was nothing aquatic about it. It was a gambling joint just across the city line where Chicago, Lake Michigan, and Indiana met.

The State of Indiana originally mandated casinos be located on actual boats. Over time things changed. The state relaxed its rules and the operations moved ashore.

The Golden Palace was the Boat's real name and those days it was a full-blown casino with a five-story attached parking garage.

Knowing what a zoo the Boat could be on that day of the week, I said, "I'm surprised you went on a Friday."

"I had some date-specific tickets for the buffet, asked Teddy to work my shift, and took the night off. Mikie wanted to do some serious drinking, so I drove."

"From the look of you, someone either won, or lost big."

"Mikie hit the mother lode."

"How big?"

"Just beyond four hundred and twenty thousand."

"Whoa!"

"I know—it comes to more than a quarter million after taxes. Some turnabout, eh? Mikie, the guy who never won anything in his life, finally landed the big fish."

Dewey chugged his coffee and waved to Earline for more. She smiled and headed our way, no doubt thinking that Dewey wanted more than coffee.

I asked Dewey, "You believe he's in trouble?"

Dewey's condition accented his reply. "*Serious* trouble—I can't find a trace of him anywhere."

Like me, Dewey was past his prime. But he had kept his athletic frame in decent shape, and was always neatly dressed, but I'd never seen him look that rough. That day he made me look good.

Earline was there with the coffee.

I reached into my jacket and produced a flask of my homemade mix of bourbon. She spotted it and scolded, "I thought you gave up the poison."

I emptied half the flask into Dewey's cup and replied seriously, "It's medicine—and it's not for me."

Earline nodded and backed off a mite. When Dewey continued to ignored her, she shot him the stink eye and strutted off.

I fibbed and said, "Good move, he's married."

Dewey gave me the 'thanks for nothing' glare. I reminded myself to ask Earline to thank me for keeping Dewey out of her personal life. It wouldn't have been good—for either of them. Dewey was a disaster for any woman after a week—no, a couple of days.

I looked over at Jimmie's perch. I mouthed to him, "I got the message."

Jimmie gazed back at me from within the combined aura of an ancient Shaolin monk, *Obie Wan Kenobi*, and the *Cheshire Cat*. He smiled.

Dewey took his medicine.

Earline made more coffee.

The cop in me awakened and said, "Go ahead, Dewey, tell me everything."

The universe was in sync. I had a case.

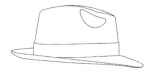

Your Lucky Number is "R"

"WE GOT THERE A LITTLE after nine," Dewey explained. "Mikie laid into the booze right off and had a good buzz going by nine-thirty. I drove, so I sipped beer—paced myself. Between the two of us, we frittered away a couple hundred bucks on table games before we hit the buffet line at eleven-thirty. It was a typical gambler's night—long on longing, short on results."

"When did it unravel?"

"After we ate." Dewey looked into his mug and then at me. I poured in the second half of the flask, and he downed it without the oily coffee as mixer. It made him cough. "Damn, that's rank," he said. "Why do you like this stuff?"

"It's an acquired taste. Besides, I seldom get asked to share it." I motioned for him to continue with his account of Mikie's good fortune and subsequent disappearance. He did.

"I hung around the dining area to chat up Tammy, our server," Dewey explained.

"That's a surprise," I quipped.

Dewey was a world-class ladies' man. He automatically gave me a run down. "Tall bubbly redhead, green eyes, great laugh, firm butt."

"I'm sure it was her laugh that interested you."

"Exactly."

"Get on with it, you liar."

"Since I wasn't drinking and the dining room was pretty slow, I hung around for at least an hour."

"That would mean it was a little after one?"

"Yeah—that's when the commotion started."

"Commotion?"

"Bells, whistles, lights flashing—it happens when someone hits a big one. The entire place gets saturated with noise and multi-colored lights. The casino figures if everyone in the place knows about a big win, they'll increase the size and frequency of their bets. Kinda like a feeding frenzy."

"It's the psychology of the business."

"It certainly works. I felt the buzz in the place shoot up right away."

"But you had no idea it was caused by Mikie, right?"

"Not a clue until Tammy's friend came over and told me the guy I was with was in the middle of the cheering crowd. I headed there fast, and sure enough, there was Mikie hugging the winning slot machine. It was a sight to behold. I've never seen a happier man."

"He was surrounded—did you get to him?"

"Yeah, I did. It took a bit of pushing and shoving. Winners acquire a lot of instant friends."

"I can imagine the type of people hanging on— quality folks for sure."

"The majority of them are back-slapping losers looking for free drinks or a handout. They seem to appear out of the woodwork like some form of mutant anti-cockroach attracted by the energy buzz. The worse ones are the bottom-feeding babes trolling for bucks. By the time I cut through the crowd, Anna Banana had latched her claws into Mikie pretty good."

"Anna Banana? That's a real *peach* of a name," Dewey groaned at my fruity pun. My humor, like my liquor, was an acquired taste. The main problem was few people have latched on to it.

Dewey said, "She earned her nickname the hard way." He made a back-and-forth hand motion, stuck his tongue against his cheek, and wiggled it for illustration. "It's in recognition of her special talent."

"A pro?" I asked.

"I'd say semi-pro, with major league ambition and minor league assets. She's past her prime. Never really was a looker. By the time I got to Mikie, she was all over him. Anna was attached to the poor guy like a barnacle to the dock. When the casino managers led us away, she tagged along."

"Paperwork, right?"

"Yeah, Mikie had lotsa papers to sign. The casino verifies the winner's ID, collects the taxes that go to the state and the feds, and issues a check. They also conduct a pitch session aimed at getting gullible chumps out to Vegas. Sun, fun, and sex are promised as perks for their newest Premium Elite Member."

"Premium Elite Member? Did he join the clan?" I joked.

It got Dewey to smile. "That's the top level for the casino's frequent gambler program," he explained. "Behavior modification based on perks as bait. Pure bullshit."

"Did Mikie fall for their lies?"

"Worse."

"How so?"

"You know how he hates flying? Mikie didn't want to get on a plane to Vegas. So, he opted for the cheapo version of their high-roller treatment."

"Which is..."

"Limo out to Joliet and stay next door to that casino in five-star digs on the river."

"Why Joliet?"

"The casino hacks spun a fairytale about Illinois having some sort of special legal arrangement where the casino's check can clear right away, even after hours. It's pure bullshit. The last thing they want is for a winner to call it a night and take the check home—and home is where most go since the Boat sits in a real suck-ass location. There's run down industrial crap and slum housing on one side and the lake on the other. A limo filled with champagne, a very friendly female, and a suite at the hotel was enough to lure Mikie."

"You couldn't talk him out of it?"

"No way. Anna Banana made it impossible for me to talk any sense into him. Mikie was buzzed, super happy, and set on crashing in that five-star room with her."

"He didn't dump you and leave with her, did he?"

"No, no, not even a *totally* drunk and wasted Mikie would do that. He wanted me to go with him. Mikie asked the casino hacks for a suite, got it, and then told me to meet him at the limo."

"You split up?"

"Yeah, I went after our jackets in the car."

"That's when he disappeared—right?"

"*Poof*! He vanished."

"Keep talkin'."

"I got the jackets, went to meet him, and he never showed. I waited and then backtracked to the casino offices. They told me he left for the limo with Anna. But when I went through the casino again on my way to the limo, I saw her without Mikie. She was at a Black Jack table placing good-sized bets. My first reaction was one of relief. I figured Mikie had wised up and told her to hit the road.

"I went back to the limo again. He wasn't there. His cell went straight to voicemail when I called it, so I waited. When he didn't show after another twenty minutes, the limo driver made a call to the casino reps and they told him to leave. They figured Mikie went home. I knew otherwise, so I searched the casino again. Mikie was nowhere to be found."

"Did you talk to Anna?"

"Yeah, sure did."

"How'd that go?"

"At first, when I asked her what happened to Mikie she played dumb. I didn't take it, so I asked again. I pressed her pretty hard. Under pressure, she told me Mikie gave her a couple of grand, said good-bye, and got in the limo. I guess the money he gave her came from some front cash that was part of the pitch.

"When I still tried to push her for even more details, she signaled the dealer and, in a flash, a goon shows up to escort me away from the table. He strongly advised me not to hassle any of the players."

Dewey showed me his left forearm with a couple distinct finger-sized bruises.

"The fool tried to muscle you?"

"Not for long."

Growing up on the Southside, we lived by a simple code: Do not lay a hand on another dude and do not let any dude lay one on you. Break the rule and you live with the consequences. Fail to enforce the rule and you suffer the consequence of being some-one's bitch.

Most people preferred to think otherwise, but like it or not, humans still live in a jungle. The trees and leaves are gone, but animals are there and dan-gerous.

"What happened?" I asked, knowing the answer.

"I returned the favor," he answered, with a slight grin. "He wimped-off to nurse his arm, but he had accomplished his mission. By the time I could get back to where Anna was playing cards she had evaporated."

"What more can you tell me about her?"

"Mid-forties... Boozer... Gambling addict... She lives in Alsip, no regular job. Once in a blue moon she waits tables and cocktails to look respectable. But mainly, she gets by hustling the old guys who hang out in the bars along the southern end of Western Avenue on the Chicago side. When she shows up in Blue Island, it's usually on weekends after an end-of-the-month payday."

"What kind of ride does she have?"

"A beat-up *Toyota Corolla*—powder-blue, dented right-rear fender, about fifteen years old."

"Dewey, you have a classic bartender's memory."

"Better. I saw her drive it off later."

"How'd that come about?"

"Since I couldn't find Mikie, I thought he might find me. I went back to the car and waited. That's where I saw Anna again."

"When was that?"

"About fifteen minutes after the goon with my fingerprint tattoo I made from his move on me. The same guy walked her to her car. It looked to me as if she knew him pretty well."

"He a customer of hers?"

"Maybe, but I don't think so. The talk and body language I saw was different. They were up to something other than sex."

"Did she ever hustle Mikie?"

"Nah, he was always too light on money for her."

"His hitting it big solved that."

"For sure."

"You had to be torn between following her and waiting."

"Sure was. Anna had latched on to Mikie so tight that I knew she had to know what happened to him. I wanted to chase her down and force her to talk, but instead I sat there holding out, hoping really, that Mikie was just playing one of his tricks. In the back of my mind, I saw him strolling up to the car with a big grin, a bottle of booze, and a couple of friendly girls."

"How long did you wait?"

"Another hour, and then some."

"Then what?"

"I searched the casino yet again, questioned the security guards, and wandered around hoping to find Mikie."

"But no Mikie."

"Total bust."

"Time?"

"Seven. That's when I found myself back in the dining area, famished from all the running around, so I decided to refuel. Tammy's friend, Lois, was still on duty. She was the one who told me about Mikie hitting it big. Lois got the chef to rustle up steak and eggs 'specially for me."

"Dewey, even when stressed, you know how to charm the ladies."

"Lois was just being nice. She asked about Mikie—seemed genuinely concerned."

"After that, did you leave the Boat?"

"Yeah—around eight. On the way home I hit every early-morning bar Mikie might visit, but there was no sign of him. Then, I did the breakfast joints."

"And his cell?"

"Still going straight to voicemail."

"Did you check his place?"

"Right after I scoped out the last diner—*Demars*—on Western in Blue Island, I went to his house. No sign of him there, either."

"He still has the place on Ann Street?"

"No, he moved out to Oak Forest, on one-fifty first near Bachelor Grove Woods."

"When did that happen?"

"Two, maybe three years ago."

"Jeez, have I been out of touch with him that long?"

"Longer."

Dewey's reply indicted me as a lousy friend. I felt like shit and wanted to avoid going on, but I needed to ask, "Is that why you didn't call me right away?"

"Yep." Dewey never lied to me. "You've been AWOL from his life for a while."

The silence between us roared.

Dewey increased my pain by adding, "I also didn't call because you aren't a cop anymore. I thought I could find him on my own."

"Retired cops still have resources," I told him.

"Enough to find Mikie?"

I reached into my pocket and pulled out my badge. "You're in luck. I've been reinstated."

"Makes a guy wanna believe in God."

"Or a reasonable facsimile."

* * *

Outside *Jimmie's*, I sucked in the city air and I told Dewey, "You better drive. My piece of crap will never get us to Alsip."

"Same old Jake," said Dewey. "People, not machines, are your world. I bet your wheels have never had an oil change."

"Oil?" I asked. "What's that?"

"Jake, auto maintenance is a guy thing."

I reminded my friend I was mechanically challenged. "Come on, Dewey, you know I've never been one for cars."

Unlike the typical American male, I do not gauge my manliness by horsepower, sticker price, or hood ornament.

We climb into his ride—a rebuilt muscle car from the 60s.

"For a guy, you can come across like such a wuss," he poked.

"I'll take the scent of perfume over the smell of gas and oil any day."

"What about sports?"

"I'm still following the Cubs."

"And not the Bears?"

"I'm not in love with football—of any sort. Truth be told, I only played it in high school as a dare. My Fantasy League is full of soft curvy women, the grown-up kind, not the stick figures with boobs that Hollywood and Madison Avenue throw at us."

"Yep—same old Jake." Dewey stared through the windshield.

My mind wandered up and down my fantasy line-up and stopped on Miriam, a fantastic redhead who played me for a fool. I was about to trade her for Michelle Williams when I was interrupted for directions.

"I take it that we are calling on Anna?" Dewey asked.

"Yeah, but it won't be for one of her specials." My joke fell flat. Dewey was bone tired.

I asked him, "You okay to drive?" I was still acutely aware of not having been a good friend. Asking did not ease my conscience and I was pleased. It proved I still had one.

"I'm good," he said. "Just worried about Mikie."

In minutes, he had us off the streets and headed south on the Dan Ryan. A couple minutes more and we took I-57. I tried to imagine Miriam but could not. All I could see was Mikie.

When we got to the exit at 119th, Dewey said, "Just to let you know, I tried her place a couple of times already."

"With no luck, right?"

"Yeah, I got nothing."

"I'll bet my jeopardized pension she's hiding."

"From what?"

"I don't know. You... Maybe."

"Me? Why me?"

"She knows that you know she was the last known person to be with Mikie. If she's involved with his disappearance, she's got to avoid you. And if Anna makes her living the way you said, she knows you've been asking about her. Trust me, she's got a grape-vine laced throughout the places she plies her trade.

"I say she's probably holed up with one of her regulars. Someone with an out-of-the-way place and is thrilled to be get freebies in exchange for her hanging out. I'd be real surprised if Anna surfaced anytime soon."

"Then why are we going to Alsip?"

"To search her place."

"Jake, you're a Chicago cop. How can you get a warrant for an address in Alsip?"

"I can't."

"Which means... What?"

"I'm searching the place without one."

"Won't you get in trouble doing that?"

"Not if no one tells."

"This, I gotta see."

Dewey pressed his foot to the floor. I thought, *This ride reminds him of our youthful road trips, only this time it's just the two of us.*

Dewey was always the wheel man, I rode shotgun, and Mikie handled the beer cooler in the back seat.

We headed west on 119th, zipped along the south edge of Blue Island, crossed Kedzie, and then quickly dodged left into a small and unimpressive condo community. We parked and got out of Dewey's car.

Where the hell is Mikie? I asked myself.

"That's Anna's place," Dewey said, pointing to the nearest door.

"Is there a way in around back?" I asked.

"Yep."

We headed there. At the back door, I knocked a couple of times. Nobody stirred. I told Dewey to stay put. He gave me the stink-eye. I blew him a kiss, and he flipped me off and reinforced the look.

I told him, "I need a lookout. If anything happens, like Anna showing up or a neighbor asking, 'what the hell is going on?' I might be able to fake my way out of trouble with my badge. But if someone really pushed it, as a civilian you could be in jeopardy. Besides, if you come in with me, how would we know if someone is coming?"

He dropped the stink eye.

My line of reasoning worked. Dewey hung back while I jimmied the door. As I opened it, he said, "I'll cough real loud as a warning sign. Don't want any interruptions while you're sniffing her panties."

Over my shoulder, I flipped my middle finger and gave him a pal warning, "Keep it up and I'm taking you off my Christmas list."

"Do it. Who needs another lame tie?"

"Was thinking socks for you." I replied, as I stepped inside the kitchen and closed the door behind me.

In an instant, I knew I was in a nasty place. Even in the shadows Anna's place looked like shit. It smelled like it, too.

The air was a rank mixture of rotten food, cigarettes, scented candles, weed, and cat piss. Images of Dorothy chanting, "There's no place like home, there's no place home," did not run through my mind as I pulled a mini flashlight from my pocket and scanned the room.

Dishes clogged the sink and lined the counter tops. The dinette and its four matching chairs were stacked with magazines, mail, half-filled bags of trash, pizza boxes, and more dirty dishes. A roach the size of my thumb scurried across the sticky floor and scuttled under the fridge.

I'd cased apartments and homes a couple thousand times, with and without warrants. It was the same technique as examining a crime scene. I reminded myself, *Don't touch any surfaces. The last thing you want is to leave evidence you have been here.* Also, I didn't want to contract any diseases.

Despite the toxic environment, I pressed on. The kitchen trash flowed into a great room. It was a tie for which sucked most. The large multi-purpose area was as filthy as the kitchen. Piles of clothes, handbags, and extraneous junk occupied every piece of furniture, with an assortment of fast-food boxes crowning each mound.

I told myself, *Anna's special talent must be some sort of compensation for her lack of cleaning skills.*

I kept looking. Leading off the large open space was a hallway to the master bedroom. It was as cluttered as the rest of the place, minus the food debris. The bed was almost made.

At least Anna has some minimal standards. I retracted the thought when I saw the john.

It was a porcelain version of the kitchen and great room with make-up containers, hairspray cans, and extraneous beauty items scattered about. The piles of junk emitted a mixed scent of stale perfume, cigarettes, and mold. In the middle of one pile, nearest the sink, sat Anna's purse and keys.

Like a spooked cat, I pounced backward landing in the bedroom.

Most women kept their purse and keys with them at all times. I jumped because I assumed she was hiding. I checked the closet.

No Anna.

In the great room, I searched the closet near the main entrance.

Again, I found nothing.

In the kitchen, I opened the pantry and found the same nothingness.

Maybe, she bolted—gone rabbit in a panic when she noticed we arrived.

I opened the back door, stepped out, and motioned for Dewey.

"What's up?" he asked.

"Her purse and keys are still here. Check around for her car."

"Done," he said and was gone.

I drew a blank. Then it hit me. I got overwhelmed with that self-accusing 'you're such a dumb-ass' feeling. It told me I missed something obvious.

I went back inside and slowly scanned the kitchen. That little voice said, "*It's* Sesame Street *Time, Jake. What fits and what does not belong?*"

I stared at the mess for a couple of minutes and found that what I had missed sat in plain sight. The refrigerator's shelves and racks were stacked on top. It could only mean one thing.

Dewey came in with his report. "I found her car behind the fence two units down the street," he said. He noticed my attention was fixed on the fridge.

"What's up?" he asked.

"Don't know yet," I said, reaching for the appliance's handle. "But I have a feeling Anna is chilling out." I opened the door and found my assumption correct. Leftover Anna was in the fridge.

"*Damn*," shouted Dewey. "Is she dead?"

"She ain't asleep," I quipped.

I got close and checked on Anna's real situation. She was facing forward and folded over in a quasi-fetal position. There was a small trail of blood originating from the side of her chest where a steak knife was buried to its hilt.

I told Dewey, "Looks like she was stabbed and immediately shoved inside. There's no blood on the floor or anywhere leading to the fridge."

"Shit," he exclaimed. "What'll we do now?"

I headed for the door and motioned for him to join me. Outside, I told him the bad news. "We have to call it in and wait for the local guys to arrive."

"You don't sound right," he observed.

My posture and demeanor had slumped.

"I've got plenty of reason not to be," I said. "This is going to seriously stall our search for Mikie... And based on what's inside... It doesn't look good for him."

"How so?"

"He's missing and the last person known to have seen him is dead."

"Holy shit."

"That about says it."

* * *

S. H. T. F.

Reporting Anna's date with the refrigerator was awkward. Alsip didn't see many homicides. They were not happy that a 'big city cop' found that one. The local boys were understandably miffed that a Chicago shield was outside his jurisdiction nosing around on their turf without so much as a courtesy call.

I told the lead guy, a mentally challenged boulder named Dillon, "I was in the heat of a chase, so to speak." I gave him that 'one cop to another' look and went on. "The case involves a close friend. The stiff in the icebox was the last one to see him. If time had allowed, I'd have called you guys for a date."

"Ooookaaaay," he said as slow as he thinks. "That's understandable." Pointing to Dewey, he asked, "Who's your sidekick?"

"A friend."

"He also on the Chicago payroll?"

"Civilian," I answered.

Dillon eyed Dewey with suspicion. He said, "I want to talk with him," and headed toward Dewey.

Before I could follow, I was blocked by an Alsip uni with a notepad and an attitude. He tapped the pad with his pen and said, "Detective Thompson, I'll take some notes for the preliminary report. You can submit a full one later."

I knew all about splitting up witnesses. I tried to step around him.

The uni was persistent. "It won't take but a minute," he said, leaning on the door.

I was out maneuvered. The small-town guys won that one.

I answered the questions, although I disliked being treated more like a run-of-the-mill witness than a fellow cop. The uni was slow and thorough. It took about ten minutes—long enough for Dillon to slow-grill Dewey.

When the uni was finished with me, I headed for Dewey. Dillon was still questioning him, and Dewey was looking like he did not like it one bit. I swore he was about to pop the dunce. Before I could intervene, my phone rang. I was surprised the battery had kept a charge.

"Thompson," I answered.

I heard an upset voice say, "Jake, it's me, Pinkie."

"What's shaking, honey?"

"Foister and half the known world."

"I take it she knows where I am?"

"I'll say. What the hell are you doing? She's beyond livid. A call came from up top after they got a call from the chief in Alsip. Captain Foister is so mad she wouldn't make this call to you. She screamed at me to get you back in the office—*immediately*. Jake, I'm not game for this. Tracking you down at the diner is one thing, but—"

I interrupted. "*Okay*, okay. Tell Mother Mildred I'm on my way. I'll be there as soon as I can."

The use of Foister's first name broke the tension. Pinkie relaxed some and added, "Jake, be careful. This is serious. She's talking about chaining you to a desk, and I think she actually means it."

I tried to ease her mind. "I'll be fine. Just tell her I'm on my way. Bye."

When I finished, Dewey was next to me. He wasn't pissed about playing twenty questions. Instead, he was excited about something else, grabbed my arm, and said, "Jake, we gotta get to Mikie's. Right *now*."

"What the hell?" I asked, as I jerked against his grasp. I told you about the Southside's code.

"Sorry, Jake. But he's there—Mikie's *there*."

"Mikie!? Where?"

"Home. He just called me. You were on your phone when that nosey cop finished with me, and *boom*! My phone rings and it's Mikie. He's home, but he sounds really messed up. Come on. We gotta go."

On the way to Mikie's, I called Pinkie. She was not thrilled when I told her what was up and asked, "Can you fend off Foister for a couple hours, maybe three?"

"Three hours? Are you nuts? Flames are coming out of her office and every couple of minutes she asks me about you. She's called your friend, Jimmie, at the diner and is planning to move your stuff from the diner into a cubicle. Jake, I'll do my best, but don't expect much. Get used to being on a very short leash." She hung up.

I told Dewey to step on it. "I'm in a bit of a jam with the Gestapo in the home office. Let's check on Mikie, and if need be, we can bring him along for the ride downtown."

"I thought you were re-instated."

"It's not that simple," I explained.

"Never is—it never is."

I Dunno

MIKIE'S PLACE WAS NICE; A 1960's rancher with a neat yard and a small attached garage. It was just what you'd expect from a solid citizen like Mikie. We parked in the drive and were immediately met by his neighbor, June. She looked like everyone's idea of the perfect grandmother. I'd bet a gallon of Old Jimmy Jack she knitted, baked, decoupaged, and had a cache of Lawrence Welk tapes for her decades-old VCR.

June fretted, "Thank God you're here." To Dewey she said, "I was so glad he could remember your number," and pointed inside. "He's on the sofa in the den."

Dewey nodded and headed for the door.

June looked over her shoulder up and down the street as if the paparazzi were about to pounce. She fretted some more.

"I had to help him get inside," she explained. "You know, I've never seen him this way. It's so not like him."

Before Dewey could respond, June waved and scurried across the walkway to her own back door. I was at the door to the den before she was safe inside her cubbyhole.

"Let's see what shape he's in," I told Dewey. "It better be one hell of a story."

After Anna's pigsty, Mikie's place was a delight. Mikie earned his bread by doing the books for about a dozen local businesses. He was not one of those anal neat freaks, but he was close. We found him laid back on the sofa with slobber and a half-dazed expression covering his face.

His expression changed to a smile when he recognized me.

"Hey, Jake, wassup ole pal?" he slurred slightly.

"You are, Mikie," I replied. "You are."

He saw Dewey and asked, "Where'd ya go lass nigh?"

"Same place as the two before—all over everywhere—looking for you." Dewey got up close and checked out Mikie's eyes. To me he said, "He's wasted on something. Doesn't smell like booze."

"Think we can get him to make sense?"

"Maybe. Let's flush him out."

"Sounds good to me," I said.

In five minutes, Dewey was pouring mega-strength coffee into Mikie after hydrating him with a gallon of water.

In five more minutes, Mikie was pissing like a racehorse on *Furosemide*.

Ten minutes after that, his mind was clear enough for us to ask questions and maybe get some un-slurred answers.

Then, we loaded a still half-dopey Mikie into the car and headed to my inevitable dressing down by Mildred Foister.

It was bizarrely like old times—Dewey drove, I rode the gun, and Mikie was in the back.

Dewey started out our interrogation with, "What the fuck happened?"

Mikie said, "I dunno. After the casino managers gave me the check, Anna led me to the elevator. I thought we were going to meet you and climb into the limo headed for Joliet. But in the elevator, a guy was waiting. He sprayed something into my face. After that it's all a hazy dream. I know I was not unconscious. Just can't remember what I did."

"Probably a mix including scopolamine. You have the right symptoms." I explained. "Zombie-like behavior and no memory." I shifted to right before he went bye-bye. "Tell me about the guy in the elevator."

"Tall, thin dude, real light hair. I think he's part of the casino's security staff."

Dewey asked, "What was he wearing?"

"Gray suit—shiny, like maybe sharkskin. No tie. He had one of those silky tee shirts on under the jacket."

"Your description fits one hundred percent with the joker I had to deal with when I was looking for you," Dewey said.

Mikie was alert enough to pick up that his thug was Dewey's thug. "So—you had a run in with him, too?"

"More like, he ran into me," Dewey said. He went on. "My burning question is this: What happened to your winnings?"

"I dunno. I just dunno. Can't remember much of anything."

I asked, "Did you go to Joliet?"

"Maybe... I think I was in the Joliet casino, but I can't be sure."

"And the money?" asked Dewey.

"I don't remember much. Everything is all swirls. Lights, sounds—they are mushed together. Nothing makes any sense. Maybe Anna was there—I dunno. I bet if we find her, she'll be able to tell what happened."

"That, I doubt," I told him.

He was optimistic. "Jake, you can make anyone crack."

Dewey informed him, "It's too late for that, Mikie. Anna's dead."

"Dead? How? When?"

"*How* is a knife stuck in her to the hilt," I said. "The *when* is a bit vague. She was folded neatly into the fridge in her condo. We found her a couple of hours ago. Dewey and I were making nice nice with the Alsip police when you called."

"Holy Moly. Do you think it's tied any way to what happened to me?"

I replied, "I'd say so, but it's hard to be certain since we really don't know exactly what *did* happen to you."

"Then let's get moving," Mikie said, "I'm out a whole bunch of money."

"Sure, sure," I said, "But it's not gonna happen right now."

"Not happen—why?"

I explained, "First, I have to tell my boss why I found a stiff in a refrigerator while investigating an out-of-my-jurisdiction non-reported missing-person case—all while I was restricted to twiddling my thumbs and supposed to be keeping a low profile."

Mikie bounced around the backseat, looked out the window, and said, "Makes sense to me. So, that's why we are headed downtown instead of going to the Boat?"

"Sit back and chill, Mikie, you're making me nervous," said Dewey.

"I gotta pee," Mikie whined.

Dewey reached over, grabbed a plastic milk jug, and tossed it back to Mikie. "Use this and quit movin' around. Also, try not to piss all over the car."

We finished the ride in dry silence.

Dewey drove, Mikie blankly gazed out the window, and I thought of ways to placate Godzilla in a Dress.

GROUNDED AND IN TIME-OUT

B ACK AT AIU, IT WAS not as bad as I thought. It was worse. Mildred's temper was in overdrive when she met me at the door. I knew I was in deep shit because she did not raise her voice to address me.

"Thompson, you are one sorry son of a bitch." Her voice was even and way too calm. "I placed my ass in jeopardy for you. And you repay me by leaving the safe spot *you picked out.* You must be crazy, and I must be even crazier for wasting my time on you right now."

I tried to apologize and did some world-class groveling, but she motioned for me to remain quiet.

"Don't utter a sound," she ordered. "I'm not buying any of your candy-coated swill. You absolutely have the lousiest judgment of any cop I know. You'd be brought up before a panel and at the mercy of the very people who want your head if it weren't for my special relationship with Alsip's Chief Buckner."

"Wait, wait," I joked. "Don't tell me—you're bangin' him?"

My humor failed. No, it spontaneously combusted and exploded. Mildred was not amused. She emitted a guttural growl and, I swore, she actually did pop a vein.

She pointed to her office. "There—now." was all she said.

I headed to the office and slunk into the chair in front of her desk as if I was visiting my junior high principal.

She came in a couple minutes later.

"I've sent your pals home," she told me. Before I could protest, she continued. "You can't be trusted. So, for the time being, *Jimmie's Diner* is off limits."

"But it's where I live."

"Not anymore."

"What exactly does that mean?"

"Your essential belongings, minus the bourbon, are here. During regular office hours your butt stays in the cubicle Pinkie assigns to you. The rest of the time you are restricted to the building."

"*This* building?"

"Yes."

"Where do I sleep?"

"In the basement."

"In *The Dungeon*? You're kidding."

"No, I am not."

"But—but—the place is beyond creepy. There are rumors that several janitors have entered there for routine purposes and have not been seen again."

She informed me, "There's a good-sized vacant storeroom down there set up with a bed, a radio, and a TV."

"What about meals, a shower—stuff normal people do?"

"Normal people don't have the city's power structure trying to nail their ass to a park bench. You eat take-out and shower across the street in the health club—under supervision."

I emitted a short laugh. "Me in a health club? Crosswords are my exercise."

She was not amused.

I couldn't help but laugh again. But that time it was longer and harder.

"This is not meant to be funny." She was pissed and it began to show as a slow burn.

"But it is funny," I protested. "Look—I'm a cop, you're a cop, and I'm being held against my will. I'm a prisoner—that's *got* to be funny."

"You're not a prisoner."

"That's how I see it. What else could it be?"

"Think of it as protective custody."

IN THE BELLY OF THE BEAST

IT APPEARED THAT MIKIE'S WINDFALL of a lifetime was totally kaput. Blown, spent, stolen, pissed away—who the hell knew what happened? The information was sketchy. No, it was less than sketchy.

The management types at the Joliet casino contended Mikie cashed his check and gambled it away. Mikie couldn't recall any details and had fallen into a deep depression.

How deep? Dewey described it as, "Lower than whale shit on the bottom of the Marianas Trench."

As the professional investigator in our trio, I felt rotten that I was powerless to help a friend. I was restricted to living within the four walls of AIU and my leash was an inch long. Right then, I was less than worthless in tracking where the money went. Dewey and Mikie had been nosing around without me. Last I heard, it was a stone-cold dead-on-arrival dead-end.

There was, however, some good news. Mildred had wrangled a concession out of the number-crunching gnomes in payroll. So, until I was charged, retired again, or dead, I was getting paid to be a squatter, and surprisingly, I had eased into a comfortable routine of delivered food, hanging out, and cleaning up at the health club.

Talk about seduction. It's easy to imagine how the welfare sops are ensnared by the system.

I believed that if I were permanently restricted to AIU's grimy offices, I might have easily succumbed to the temptation of being a handout-taking slave. I did nothing, received money and benefits, and my time was my own. Toss in a slick politician, some subtle race-baiting, and a pinch of class-fare, and you'd probably have had my vote.

In Cook County, you could even get it twice.

Depressingly weird? Sure was. But my days were better than the nights. Nine to five, Pinkie was on the reception desk and I was not ashamed to admit that I was addicted to admiring her legs. Wherever she moved, I found a reason to wander in her vicinity.

Don't worry. My viewing was just for sport, sort of a male *Audubon Society*, and was not at the pervert level. My peeking brought a new meaning to "birder," and was more in the category of 'it's great to still be interested at my age'.

My bitter-sweet pleasure in voyeurism definitely marked my official entrance into middle age. I'd fret over getting on in life, but I had a more immediate and bigger problem to address.

Routinely I told myself, "Jake, some of the most powerful people in Chicago want your ass on a sacrificial altar." So far, they had failed. *Contra mundum*—me against the world.

I would have liked to take credit for dodging a huge bullet, but I couldn't. Between periods of ogling Pinkie's sticks and going stir-crazy in my cubicle, I had figured out that I was safe at AIU only because Mildred Foister was my guardian angel. It led me to ask, "Why does she do it?" and, "How can I find out why?"

Pinkie was tight lipped about the subject. In fact, she was totally zipped up when it came to talking about the boss. The rest of the staff was just as mum. Captain Mildred Foister had led that unit longer than any of her predecessors, and the rats on the sinking tub known the S.S. *Loser* actually liked and admired their skipper.

I got nowhere with my investigation as to why she was protecting me.

The challenge spurred me on. If I had had some cheese, I would have baited a trap for a fellow AIU rat. But which one? Immediately I thought of the tightest sphincter in the up-tight bureaucratic world of anal retention.

Chicago's police lore was full of amusing stories about geeky cops meticulously following the rules. Some were devoted, but none were as fanatical as Maximilian Bender. The best tale was about him ticketing his own car.

Some people contended that AIU was originally created by the Chicago PD just to be a spot to place Max Bender. That was shortly after he towed the Mayor's limo and screwed up his inauguration ceremony. Bender was extreme, outside the box, and beyond the bell curve. His monkish devotion to parking statues was the stuff that inspired legends.

In an odd sort of way, I felt close to Max. On several occasions, he had been useful to me, and surprisingly, Max was easy to open up. You just needed the right bait. Besides, he owed me for bringing him in to help with a bust outside his usual territory.

I eased into his cubicle and said, "Max, we need to chat."

"Why?" His brief reply told me he was suspicious.

"You sound as if you think I'm up to something."

"That's because you usually are."

"Ouch!" I played the sympathy card. "I guess you could have a point," I added with a slight well-acted whimper. I invaded his space by repositioning the stapler on his desk. Max more than noticed. His desk was always just so and my move caught him off balance. It gave me space to make my move. While he was realigning the stapler, I asked, "What can you share about our fearless leader?"

He pretended to ignore me, finished his task, leaned back in his chair, and then whispered, "She likes you."

My mind came to a screeching halt. After a brief awkward silence I asked, "Could you expound a bit?"

Max let my request hang there for quite a while. Finally, he said, "It's not what you are imagining. It's professional."

"Whew," I exclaimed. "I'm not sure what I was thinking—only that I am not prepared for whatever it was." I squirmed in my seat. I thought Max was enjoying it, so I squirmed extra for effect. I asked, "Tell me why you think it's professional."

"I don't think—I know." Max sat back and smiled.

He really was enjoying it. He acted like it was the first time he had been on the inside and not the butt of a joke. I allowed him to enjoy the moment, because I knew how to work him. I continued the squirming, knowing it would push him over the edge.

Come on, Max. Do it—I know you can't wait to spill the beans.

Max was hooked. He told me, "Jake, you're her topic."

"Topic?"

"As in, *dissertation* topic." He grinned.

"Huh?" I played stupid—for real—and he really *really* enjoyed it.

"Let me explain," he said.

He was grinning like kid about to raid the cookie jar. I played it cool and commented, "That would be good."

"Captain Foister is enrolled in the Graduate Criminology program at the University of Chicago. She's writing her Ph.D. dissertation... On you."

"Funny, real funny."

"It may be funny alright... But, it's true."

"Keep talking." My interest was popping like a microwave full of *Orville's* best corn, but I acted as if I was half-asleep.

"Her dissertation is concerned with the criminal mind within the justice system... On the police side of the equation. You know, errant knights... Rogue cops... Vigilantes."

"Does she think I'm a criminal?" I was awake.

"Basically, yes—but in a good way." He sat up. "Mildred Foister has been studying you for some time, Jake. She knows everything about your career... And a lot more. Her theory is that you have all the traits of the classic criminal with the peculiar addition of a goodness barometer."

"What the hell is a goodness barometer?"

"It's her term for the unknown moral mechanism that makes you a positive deviant."

"Positive deviant? I think I need a drink."

"I thought you quit."

"I did. But as they say, this is driving me to drink."

"Sorry."

"Please, just tell me something that makes sense about the idiot female who was sentenced to this asylum and has now jailed me here."

"She's not as dumb as you think. Mildred actually requested her transfer to AIU."

"No one in their right mind would ask for AIU."

No Bend Bender sat back, laced his fingers behind his head, and delivered his best zinger. "Think about it, Jake. No one in their right mind would wrap you in a protective blanket like she did *unless there is a very good reason.* Mildred Foister is your guardian angel."

"Now, I *know* I need a drink."

MIRROR MIRROR

K NOWING THE TRUTH CAN BE unsettling. In that instance, it was way past unsettling and approached weird and scary territory. Here's my take on being under Mildred's microscope.

I could have lived with being just another one of the rats on the sinking ship known as the Administrative Investigations Unit of the Chicago Police Department. Although being relegated to the bottom of the ladder in The Elephant's Graveyard, The Dump, or, my least favorite name for the end of my career, The Final Stop for the Short Bus, was embarrassing, the situation was something I could have endured. Being brought back to that way-station-to-hell after I believed I had escaped through retirement was endurable, but learning I was a real-life lab rat was just too bizarre.

I looked at Max. He was beside himself with delight. I squirmed for real and asked, "How come you know so much about me being Mildred's secret project while I've been left in the dark?"

"I'm her dissertation mentor," he answered.

A wave of empathy hit me. I finally understood Earline's bewilderment on the day Dewey showed up in *Jimmie's* with the news about Mikie disappearing.

The world is indeed capable of turning itself upside down. And when it does, all you can do is sit and watch.

I was flabbergasted and my voice was full of disbelief. "Her mentor? You?"

"Yeah, I understand how it could shock you— me being such an OCD freak." No Bend Bender is as tough on himself as he is on anyone else.

His honesty concerning the source of his peculiar manner set me back as much as the news he was Mildred's mentor. Without thinking, I asked, "Wanna tell me about it?"

"No, not really... But I will."

I do not regret my impulsiveness. Every so often in life a knee-jerk reaction pays off. That time, I learned a lot about Max and his ride on the short bus of life.

"Jake, I haven't always been Chicago's Obsessive-Compulsive Parking Enforcement Weirdo," he said. His frankness concerning his status was a shock to me, but I said nothing.

Again, it was the right move. He opened up more.

"I admit that as a kid, I was a bit nerdy," he continued, "but it was nothing outside the usual stuff that separates my type from the cool guys. You know—the jocks and the pretty boys that cheerleaders get wet pants over."

I was an ex-jock, so I still kept my mouth shut. Max played like he didn't know why I was silent. I give him a guy nod. He nodded back OCD style and went on talking.

"Being zitty, rail-thin, and brainy is not the way to attract girls. I was way beyond invisible to them and pretty much everyone else. Becoming a cop was a way to break out of the nerd mold. I had fantasies of being the new *Sherlock Holmes*."

"An *elementary* plan."

"Good one," he said.

"Call me Watson."

Max's grin expanded and he went on with his tale. "In high school we had a traffic brigade—really just glorified crossing guards. Everyone thought we were losers and I can't tell you how much abuse we took. But, as the biggest cop wannabe in the group, I was totally determined to attain my dream of being a detective and I focused on it entirely. In college I ran cross country and toned up as best I could in order to pass the police academy physical test. I failed three times, but kept training and finally I got in. You could fill several football stadiums with surprised people."

"How'd you do at the academy?" I asked.

"Great in the classroom, okay on the shooting range, and marginal with the physical stuff. My performance averaged out with me being in the lowest quarter of the class." A memory mugged him and he frowned. "You know what kind of crappy assignment after graduation that meant."

"Definitely, Holmes, definitely."

He laughed.

"Where did they put you?" I asked.

The laughter stopped. Max half-mumbled, "Traffic and Parking Enforcement..." He looked down at the pile of papers in the middle of his desk as if they would finish the sentence for him.

There was a short awkward silence that I broke. "Because you were so... So—"

He read my mind and interrupted me. "No. My... eh... My fixation with the rules... That came later." He stopped. There was another silence. I waited.

You don't rush a man while he is showing you his insides.

Max removed the papers from his desk, placed them in a drawer, and sat back in his chair. "I hated that assignment," he began. "Every cell in my body wanted to solve crimes. Instead, I spent my days as a traffic mannequin, or a clerk with a badge and a book full of tickets."

"Sounds terrible."

"It was. Writing tickets was the worst. If we did not meet a quota on moving violations, we were delegated to foot patrols on crowded streets and told to ticket parked cars."

"Was the city into 'revenue enhancement' even back then?"

"Yeah—we were one of the earliest sources of easy money to shore up the budget."

"A real waste of police talent."

"Yes, and it grinds egos into mush."

"Is that why—"

He stopped me again. "No—it was my fault..." He paused.

I waited.

He restarted with, "I screwed up." He looked to me for understanding.

I nodded and reminded him, "My mouth out ran my brain. Everyone in AIU knows the story of my screw up. Hell, there was a time everyone in Chicago and a good part of the world knew. Jeez, how I hate the internet."

Max nodded back.

We are members of a brotherhood—prisoners in lives shaped by one significant hand that was badly played. My mistake was mouthing off in a rage after I failed to restrain a suspect and shot her as she attacked my partner. My words went viral and were shared with the world. In context, my wail was a protest filled with grief, angst and pain. It was understand-able—if someone took the time to understand it. But, in today's insta-world no one really takes time for anything. My remarks were seen as those of a racist cop rant and I became an overnight asshole—thanks to the web.

Remembering the event that caused my demise led me to ask, "What was it that tripped you up?"

He gulped and said, "I, ah... I, ahhhh... I missed a parked car."

"A parked car?"

"Yes, one parked car."

"Someone or something important had to be in it—right?"

Max went trance-like and told me, "Get-away driver for a bank heist. I missed him because I wanted to be a hero." His insides were oozing out. "Every day I read the fliers on suspects, wants, and warrants. I never missed a chance to know who and what was on the streets... My big chance came... And I blew it. If I had done my job—investigated the car—I'd have known that the guys inside the bank had backup. Instead, I went for *them*.

"The flier described *them* to a tee—a trio of punks—not more than kids. They were across the street and down about two blocks when I saw *them*. They went in the bank and I went after *them*. I did not see their backup."

"You were focused on suspects," I said in support.

"I was *too* focused on them. What I missed was the illegally parked car with the motor running. A fourth guy was right there at the wheel of the parked car. I walked right past him."

"So, he was behind you when—"

"—they came out." He finished my sentence and held up his hand. "I know, I know. It was a rookie move. I had no plan. I made no call for backup. My perimeter was not secured. I stood there waiting for *them* to walk out into my trap. It never happened. I was hit on the head from behind and dropped to the ground like so much dead meat."

"Anyone else hurt?"

"Not then."

"What do you mean?"

"The trio I let go was none other than the Miller Boys."

"Shit."

"Yep, that's an accurate description of my performance. The Millers killed four civilians and two cops during their next three heists alone. I could have prevented that... And a lot more."

"Every Chicago cop knows about the Millers, two brothers and some cousins dedicated to stealing and killing, but I've never heard about your involvement with them."

"Luckily, the media latched on to the Millers *after* I flubbed my chance at catching them. Unlike your situation, my failure stayed a departmental and personal matter."

"Personal?"

"My, eh... My condition..." Now it was his turn to squirm. "My condition... It first appeared only after the incident."

Max was troubled. I clammed up again and gave him room. After a moment, he continued.

"I spent a night in the hospital and I was then cleared for duty. When the Millers hit the next bank, everything fell apart for me. I felt terrible. I could not shake off the negative cloak that draped me. Weighted down by it, I walked about in a stupor of guilt. Eventually, I wandered back to the street where it happened... And... I..." He stopped talking, looked down, and slowly shook his head.

I told him, "You can stop if you want."

"I'm good. You know, getting it out, sharing it with you... It makes sense." He laughed and then finished. "I ticketed every car in the neighborhood—three days in a row."

"As therapy?"

"Guess so..."

"And?"

"It got me sent here."

"Was AIU around then? I thought—" Max read my mind and I was cut off.

"No, I am not the reason AIU exists. That's an urban myth." He used that to turn our talk's direction back on me. "If there's any cache today for AIU, it's tied to you, Jake."

"Me? You gotta be kidding. I'm—"

"The object of a great deal interest by not only our leader, but also academia, the press, and don't forget the powers that be running Chicago, just to name a few."

"Thanks for reminding me."

BOOZE NEVER HELPS A BAD SITUATION

I TRIED TALKING TO MILDRED ABOUT the info bomb Max dropped. It did not go well. Now, my head aches, my breath could melt metal, and I'm not absolutely certain what day it is.

In large quantities Old Jimmy Jack does that to me. Big mistake.

Here is what I remember of the encounter:

"Mildred," I called out as I barged into her office, "We need to talk."

I paid no attention to the other occupant in the room. Another big mistake. I'm not sure what pissed her off most, the unannounced interruption of her meeting, or the use of her first name.

She leapt from behind her desk. "What are you doing here? Get the hell out."

I ignored her command. The big mistakes continued.

"What? No time for me?" I asked. I was blank as to her having a guest and continued my assault. "Maybe you didn't expect a lab rat to discover his status, but I'm a deviant—and not a very positive one right now." My words had an effect. Unfortunately, it was all bad.

She pointed at the door, yelled, "THOMPSON! GET OUT!" She immediately apologized to her guest. "I'm sorry, Cindy. I'm so sorry. Especially since we—"

It was then that I realized we were not alone. I interrupted Mildred when I recognized the third person in the room.

"Ah shit," I exclaimed, "No, not *her*. Not her."

Cindy Vanderwahl, the reporter who did her best to ruin my life, calmly greeted me.

"Hello, Jake," she slurred out with a smile that would have made a vulture on a corpse proud. "Captain Foister was just trying to convince me that you're a new man. But I see you haven't changed a bit. You are just as rude, erratic, and *dangerous* as ever." She looked to Mildred and added, "Please tell me he's not armed. He has a disgusting habit of shooting women... And slandering them, too." She snarled to me, "I can see my next lead: Killer Cop Is Still Crazed—Could He Strike Again?"

I did my best to ignore Cindy, her comments, and the air she was fouling in the room, but her words wrapped around my spine and yanked me hard. For an instant, I was in that hellish part of space-time where and when my partner was maimed, a girl died, and I was forever crippled inside.

Facing Mildred, I simply told her, "You'll get nothing from me—nothing."

I walked out, retreated to the Dungeon, and uncovered my stash of bourbon.

That was yesterday... I think.

No... It was... It was... Three, maybe four, quarts ago.

Like I said, Old Jimmy Jack does that to me.

COME OUT, COME OUT, WHEREVER YOU ARE

N O GREAT THOUGHTS OCCUPY MY mind. I'm listening. Patiently, I wait for a crack in the plaster to release a message. I figure, if Jimmie can receive insight from a slice of pie, I can do the same with the ceiling of my prison cell.

The crack is mute.

So much for synchronicity. My Zen is zapped.

I am not drunk. Not anymore. Enough time has passed for me to run out of alcohol and sober up. Was getting wasted childish behavior? Yes. Was it understandable? Maybe. Max's information caught me off guard. Cindy's presence blindsided me. No excuses please. Change that 'maybe' to a 'yes' and I am still hung over. Mistakes have consequences.

I do not like hangovers.

Pinkie knocks on the door to my hiding place. "Jake, are you alright?" she asks.

I've been ignoring her and everyone else for days. My explosion in Mildred's office was known by all of the building's inhabitants thirty seconds after it occurred. AIU may not be much of a police unit, but it is a sort of family, and families know about such blow ups.

My police relatives gave me plenty of space. It's time to act my age and thank them.

"I'm good," I answer through the door.

"*Finally.* Jake, you've been in there way too long."

I open the door. "I've been distracted" I explain. "How long has it been?"

"Two days—three if you count the afternoon you pissed off Captain Foister and..."

"How's she doing?" I ask. I'm very aware that Pinkie is scoping out my condition. I know I'm a mess. I need a shave and a shower. No—I should be hosed down.

"She's pissed. Been gone. Right after you and her tussled, she—"

"Gone? Where to?" I interrupt.

"Alsip."

I laugh. "So, she's boinking Buckner after all."

"Not a chance. She's square with her old man," she says with that I have a woman-to-woman inside-information look.

"You sure?"

"Trust me. I know. Anyway, as I was saying when you butted in," She gives me that I'm-here-to-tell-you-something-important look. I nod that I understand. She continues. "She's due back in an hour and wants to see you."

"About what?"

"Can't say."

"Sounds more like '*won't say*'."

"Whatever *you say*." She turns her nose. "Better get started. From the smell down here you'll need the entire hour to get respectable."

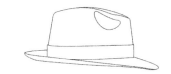

GOOD NEWS, BAD NEWS

MILDRED IS LATE. I'M IN her office waiting. To kill time, I'm sipping on a cup of coffee that is light years ahead of Jimmie's swill. Still, I miss it. Bad coffee poured by Earline is better than anything I can get at AIU.

Mildred arrives. There is no greeting. She makes no reference to our last meeting, and she jumps right in. "I've got good news and bad news, Thompson. Which do you want first?"

I tell her, "Unload the crap."

I'm a believer in taking a negative hit up front. If I'm still vertical after hearing whatever it is, then I want the soothing balm of the nice stuff later.

"I've been in Alsip. The Commissioner ordered me to patch up relations after you so royally screwed them up. Did I tell you Chief Buckner and I are close?"

Before I can respond she explains why. "*My cousin*, Dave, doesn't like Chicago cops poking around in his backyard."

To make amends I say, "Sorry about the 'banging him' joke."

"Shut up."

I do.

She continues. "His interest in the case is your bad news."

"How so?"

"I said, 'shut up'."

I do, again.

"The woman you found dead has been linked to your friend."

I un-shut up and say, "Of course. Mikie hooked up with her and—"

She gives me that shut-your-damn-pie-hole look and tells me, "It's your other friend—Eisenhauer."

I stay shut up. My mind is reeling. She eyeballs me to make certain I'm going to stay quiet.

She goes on. "I was in Alsip because the primary suspect in that murder, one Dwight Eisenhauer, just happened to be at the crime scene *with* a Chicago cop—you. The bad news is that he's been arrested, and you are going to be investigated for being linked to him."

"Dewey has been arrested? That's doesn't make sense. He just came to Anna's with me."

"It appears that he was there before. Early enough to stab the woman, put her in the fridge, and get you involved in the cover-up."

"Cover-up? What cover-up?"

"The one you are under investigation for."

"Oh, shit."

"It gets worse. Your friend is spinning an unbelievable tale about another friend being abducted."

"That's Mikie. It's why we—" This time I shut myself up.

"No help there," she says. "Thompson, it's your day for bad news. Mikie, the alibi, got sandwiched between two garbage trucks and is unconscious in the hospital. He may not make it. Naturally, he's not available to provide any plausible explanation why Eisenhauer's prints were found in the dead woman's condo *and* on the murder weapon. You were the means and reason he was at the crime scene. That is the reason for an investigation into your involvement in this massively screwed-up situation."

There is no need for her to tell me to be quiet. I am shaken by the news. *Dewey charged with murder? Mikie near death? Me under investigation?* My hangover disappears.

"You said something about good news," I mumble.

"Missus Manning Pierce died this morning."

"The evil queen is dead," I reply. "There is a God after all. This provides me a window of opportunity."

Mildred's look begs for an explanation.

I tell her, "While the-powers-that-be are distracted, busily filling the power vacuum created by her death, I'll have, maybe, the rest of today and tomorrow before Internal Affairs and the old lady's cronies link up to nail me. That's only thirty-six hours or so to figure things out."

"What do you mean by 'figure things out'?"

"Solve a murder, free my friend, save the day."

"How do you expect to accomplish that?"

"I'll find a way. All you have to do is cut me loose."

"You're crazy."

"What else did you expect from a positive deviant?"

Mildred's face goes blank.

Gotcha!

OLD DOG, OLD TRICKS

M ILDRED LET ME GO. I'D like to think it was because she is brilliant and really knows her subject. But even if she did let me go only to create some room between her and me, I'll take whatever I can get. Getting her okay tells me something. I think I can trust her.

Before my departure, Mildred tells me what she knows about the case against Dewey. As backup, I grill Pinkie for details of when I was out of it in the Dungeon. I stick everything in my cop brain and kick it into gear. There is nothing like the threat of total annihilation to get the juices flowing.

Right now, I'm back in the game. That's all that matters.

Maybe Mildred is right. I do think like a crook. Adding what she knows with Pinkie's information immediately gives me some angles to investigate. What happened to my friends is not a mystery to me. I need to confirm my view of what went down with Dewey and get to work clearing his name. Every minute counts.

Back on the job, I feel ten years younger and twenty pounds lighter. On my way to county lockup, I make some calls. The first is to long-time pal, Larry Wesselhoff in the Vice Department.

"Larboy," I call out over the phone, "I need some G-two quick."

"Just say what you need," he replies.

"You know anything about *The Golden Palace* Casino?"

"The Boat? That's Indiana."

"But it's right on the border—you must have some contacts."

"I do."

"Use 'em. Dewey Eisenhauer is facing a murder charge."

"Jesus. How'd I miss hearing about it?"

"It just went down, and it's over the line—in Alsip. I'm on my way to county jail. Dewey has been processed through the Markham facility, and he's headed to county now, or already in that scum pit."

I fill him in on what happened—Mikie's adventure, Anna's demise, and the subsequent events. There is silence. I know he's thinking.

I think, *Next, he'll play Q and A out loud.*

"So... What am I looking for?" Larry asks himself. He answers right away with, "Stolen winnings, murder, and mayhem. Who has the juice to frame a guy, steal piles of cash, and isn't shy of putting someone's lights out?"

I can hear his inner wheels turning.

He goes on. "It's not local predator stuff... And casinos are highly regulated... Rogue management, maybe? Could be the security guys have gone bad. How much time do I have?"

"None," I answer.

"Figures," he says.

"It might get worse—I could get yanked at any moment by IA. Some pretty powerful people have had me in their crosshairs."

"Gets better all the time. Where were you when all this went down?"

"Lame and lazy," I confess. "Nursing my fragile ego and laying low instead of beating the bushes to find Mikie's lost money. I can't help but think that Dewey and Mikie's current condition would be a lot better if I'd have stayed on the case."

"What case? From what you told me it was out of your jurisdiction. You're AWOL on this guilt trip. Get to county, talk to Dewey. I'll follow up on the ideas you gave me."

My next call is to Eddie Moocha, the best security hacker I know.

Eddie appeared on my radar when he mesmerized the city as its most popular vigilante ever. He's retired from the private vengeance scene and has a lucrative niche business, side-stepping computer passwords and the like.

I call and fill him in.

"So let me get this straight," he says. "All I have to do is sneak into the casino's security system and retrieve a few images?"

"Right."

"Piece o'cake. Give me the times and locations in the casino you want scoped... And anything you know about the principal players... You know, descriptions and so on. When I see 'em, and get an ID, I'll drop into the casino's HR files and do some additional mining."

"Eddie, you are the best," I tell him.

"Yeah, yeah. If I was, you wouldn't have caught me," he laughs. "I'm just glad you didn't turn me in. Now, I can pay you back."

"I'm glad, too," I reply.

A call to the diner lines up a couple of things I'll need. I plan to collect them after I see Dewey.

"Don't forget that we all care a great deal about you, Jake," Earline preaches with a tone of true concern.

I mumble my gratitude and tell her, "Thanks."

It's not much of a reply, but it's all I can muster. I'm focusing all my experience and energy on saving my friend.

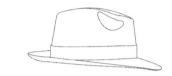

NOT MY FIRST CHOICE AS A VACATION SPOT

MAX GIVES ME A LIFT to South California Avenue where the world's largest single-site jail is located. He decides to wait in the car as I meet with Dewey. I cannot blame him.

On any given day, over eleven thousand inmates call Cook County's jail their home. Twenty-five per-cent of them are here for homicides or attempted homicides. Do the math. Give, or take, that's three thousand killers in one spot. It is not a nice place to be.

Inside, I register, stow my piece, and search out Johnny Peel, an old friend from years gone by.

Johnny and I joined the Army together back when dinosaurs roamed the earth. We shared Basic, AIT, and our first duty station. After Ft. Bragg, Johnny gravitated to stockade duty while I was tapped for the Criminal Investigations Command. When both of us came home to Cook County, we stayed in touch—often joking that only our locations changed.

"You catch 'em, and I'll cage 'em," Johnny likes to say. In his office he fills me in on Dewey's status.

"He made it through processing earlier today. Policy puts him in Division One."

"The oldest and toughest part of the facility," I comment.

"Yep. Capone, Nitty, Speck, Gacy—they all called it home at one time. Over a thousand are in that unit right now."

"Will he be okay?"

"I'd say so. Dewey is a big dude. He has a good chance of being left alone. It's funny. The worse the charge, the less prone an offender is to experience additional violence. I guess, if you are in for a murder rap you have nothing to prove about being violent, and the other guys around you are the same. Also, the place is abuzz with interest in Gary Auric."

"The animal who repeatedly raped that little girl?"

"Yes—he's on hold in special isolation. Details of the case leaked out and even the staff is under restrictions anywhere in his vicinity."

"Potential retribution?"

"Big time. The inmates read and log identities of the child molesters. Many of them are victims of abuse themselves and perverts like Auric make them see red. I've never seen anything like this level of interest before. There's a betting pool dedicated to when and how Auric has an accident."

"You know about the pool?"

"Oh, yeah—I put in fifty bucks."

"Johnny, don't you see that as a violation of your oath?"

"Not in this case, Jake. I told you the buzz was unprecedented. Auric raped that child for three years. And every time she cried out, he simply told her to stop because he had done it before, and she needed to get used to it. When he started, *she was only nine years old.*"

My blood pressure steams. "Is it too late to join the pool?" I ask.

"What pool?" he answers with a blank stare.

"'nuff said—I understand."

"Understand what?" He continues with the blank look.

"Okay, okay. Can I see Dewey?"

"Sure. I'll have him with you in five."

✳ ✳ ✳

Considering the location and circumstances, Dewey looks good in county garb. To lift his spirits, I tell him so.

"The jumpsuit makes you look years younger," I joke.

"F-you very much, sir," he counters with a grin. "Glad to see you, but—" he pats where pockets are on normal clothes. "I can't pay that five I owe you."

"There's a first time for everything," I say. "But you forgot. I owe you."

The situation collapses upon him. "What the hell is going on, Jake? What is happening?" A spirit of fear licks his neck and his face goes gray. "Yesterday I was tending bar. Now, I'm here."

"Not if I have anything to say about it," I tell him.

"What do you know, Jake? Did that asshole in Alsip tell you anything?"

"I haven't spoken to him—or anyone else in Alsip."

"Why not?"

"They have made their minds up."

"It's that bad?"

"It just *looks* terrible... I think I know their weak spot."

"Think?"

"Yeah. Go back to the morning after Mikie disappeared. What was the name of the waitress you hit on. The second one. The one that got you breakfast."

"Lois—her name is Lois."

"Any last name?"

"I didn't get that far."

"Not as far as you got with Anna—right?"

Dewey's face freezes with embarrassment.

"Cat got your tongue?" I ask. Before he can reply, I jab. "Better still, did Anna get your banana?"

Dewey blushes. "Come on, Jake. It was just once. I was loaded, she took me to her place, and... Things... Well, ah... Ah... Things... They... They just got out of hand."

"More like out of your pants." I cannot hold back my laughter. He turns red. After my last giggle I ask, "You wanna tell me about it?"

Still red, he asks, "Do I have to?"

"Wanna get out of here?"

"Okay—okay, but don't ever bring this up. I get sick whenever I think about it."

"I thought you said she was a pro."

"Semi-pro—I said semi-pro." He looks serious.

"That makes a *huge difference*." I point at his fly.

"Come on, Jake. I told you it only happened one time—"

"In the kitchen, up against the fridge."

"How'd you know?" His face is crimson again.

"Your inverted hand prints were found on the refrigerator door. I know you didn't touch anything in the place while there with me. Your prints had to have been placed there previously. Their position and location are easily explained by your red face."

My mind will forever be etched with contrasting visions of Anna—one slumped over in the fridge and the other kneeling before it in sordid prayer.

"I guess I should have told you," Dewey apologizes. "But..."

"I know—it's an awkward situation," I say with a grin. "Paying for what you normally get for free could ruin your reputation."

The red in Dewey's face lessens. It aims for gray when he looks about at his surroundings. "Where does it leave us?"

"Same as before—I still owe you five bucks." I smile. "Your secret is safe with me. The legend of Don Juan of the Southside will live on unblemished."

He smiles back and simply says, "Thanks."

I get us back to why I came to the jail. "Tell me what you know about Lois."

"Not much. That morning—right after Mikie vanished, she waited on me. Like I said, I didn't get anywhere with her. Why you so interested in her?"

"Fingerprints."

"The ones on the fridge?"

"No. The ones on the knife. Yours."

"Huh?"

"The knife stuck in Anna has your prints on it."

"No way."

"'fraid so. I thought you knew—it's why you're in here."

"When they arrested me, they didn't say much. And when I clammed up, they told me even less. I've been waiting on my lawyer... And you, Jake."

Doubt and uncertainty join the fear in his voice. Dewey is hanging tough, but Cook County Jail's Division One could rock anyone off their center point.

What I tell him provides some hope.

"Dewey, it didn't take much for me to figure out what happened. Lois palmed the knife from your steak and eggs breakfast. It was used to off Anna and frame you."

"Jake, I've always said you were the best detective in Chicago. You'll have me outta here in no time. For you, it's no problem, a piece of cake. Right?"

Dewey's confidence in my skills does not make me go all warm and fuzzy. My reply explains the difficulty of my challenge.

"Some piece of cake. All I have to do is get Lois to admit to supplying the knife... *And* get her to implicate whoever it was that shoved it in Anna... *And* come up with a motive... *And* get the Alsip police to buy it... *And* do it all before Internal Affairs is pressured to place me in here with you. Yeah. No problem. Piece of cake."

GROUND ZERO

Outside the jail, Max volunteers to stay on as my driver. He is excited about being away from his desk and working on a real case with me again. He had done some detail work for me when I caught Mrs. Manning Pierce trying to abscond with a priceless painting.

In his own peculiar way, Max now sees himself as my sidekick. Maybe he feels guilty that I caught all the heat in the aftermath of that case. Maybe he just knows friendship trumps organizations, their rules, and everything else.

My life is full of less-than-perfect people and I'm glad Max is on my side. On the way to the Boat, my new best friend critiques my plan of action.

"It sucks," he tells me honestly, "It absolutely sucks."

"Got anything better?" I ask.

"Given the amount of time we have, no—not really."

I look out the window at the gray rundown neighborhoods of the Southside, think about what my other friend, Larry, told me and I agree.

"You're right, it sucks. But I have no option. From what Larry says, the casino's management is rock solid. It's a unit of a big corporation that provides gobs of tax revenue to the State of Indiana. The place is squeaky clean. Audits upon audits, surveillance cameras, everything on the up-and-up—all under a microscope. Isolating and leaning on the woman is all I've got."

"It's all *we've* got," he corrects me.

I test the level of his friendship. "Are you sure you want in on this?"

He gives the right answer. "It's a two-man job."

I give him a thumbs up.

He nods and informs me with, "We'll be there soon."

I look out again at the terrain. The declining neighborhoods give way to an industrial area in even worse shape. We bank left around a corner. We pass an old plant that sits in its own decay like a dead tree amid its rotted leaves, then we bank right and head for a crossroads that would make any third world country proud.

The four corners of gas station, liquor store, quickie mart, and burnt-out laundromat are decorated with trash, debris, and broken glass and serves as the gateway for the road to the casino.

We enter and proceed.

Two large sandstone lumps on the lake shore come into view at the end of the road. They are as ugly as they were meant to be attractive. The Boat and its parking facility would offend the eye of a blind man.

"Real garden spot," I say.

"The Indiana and Illinois border. You are looking at the closest location to the target population for one state to invade the economy of the other," says Max with some authority.

"I read one of the early studies done by an anti-gambling nonprofit. They have it all figured out," he continues. "Welfare, Social Security payments, unemployment checks, and pensions paid in a primary catchment area are public record. The area's estimated payroll figures are almost as precise. With so little industry left, that amount has become less and less. Long and short of it is this—the casino owners know within a tenth of a percentage point how much they can drain out of the local economy."

"Gambling is for suckers," I comment.

Max does not hear me. The talkative part of his OCD has kicked in and he rambles on oblivious of what is around him. "It's like an unofficial sin tax. But it's really official—the state government okays everything and gets its share. Makes you wonder which side of the activity is the sinful part. Illinois is soon to copy it and allow gambling in Chicago. This place will have to compete. I bet it will only get worse."

I test his awareness again. "Guys like Mikie, they dream of the big score and..."

Max pays no attention and keeps going. "People will gamble wherever the nearest venue is located. People just want to gamble. It's as simple as that. It's an addiction—based upon a desire to escape. All they do is think about hitting it big. And they discard every bit of the common sense they use each day to live.

"Take your friend for example. He's an accountant—right? Accountants know how gambling is rigged for the house, yet he gambled anyway. He ought to know better, but—"

Dr. OCD, adjunct at one of the world's greatest universities, nerd extraordinaire, will go on forever, but I need to interrupt with driving instructions. "Hey, we're gonna miss the parking garage."

Max snaps back into this dimension and abruptly aims for the entrance to the parking facility. We fishtail into the driveway. To compensate for the dramatic move, Max transforms his driving style into that of a senior citizen. We creep through the garage looking for a place to park and find one on the second level.

We are not there more than two seconds and Max is chomping to go.

"I'm ready," he spouts. "I'll play good cop and, naturally, you be the mean one. Let's do this. Let's stir up the pot. Let's make it happen." OCD with a dab of vengeance is something to behold.

"Hold on, Max." I reach for my phone. "Larry Wesselhoff can get us in with a good cover story. But being phony investigators for the Joint Illinois-Indiana Gaming Task Force won't do us any good unless we know more than the first names of two waitresses.

I know it will be hard for you but relax. We need to wait for a call."

A little agitated, he asks, "From whom?"

"My hacker. He's poking into the casino's data system and its personnel records. I told you we need something more."

"I take it back."

"What?"

"Your plan. It doesn't suck all that much." He adjusts his seat and reclines. In a minute he is napping and all the tenseness from his driving, parking, and talking disappears.

I fiddle with the controls, my seat dips, and in a few more I join Max. We wait for Eddie Moocha's call.

TWO BLIND MICE

A CALL ENDS NAP TIME.

"The one you want is Fennell. F-E-N-N-E-L-L. Lois Fennell," Eddie tells me. "Her pal, the one that led her to Dewey and served Mikie and Dewey earlier, her name is Coles. C-O-L-E-S. Tammy Coles."

"Good work," I say.

"Thanks. I identified them by linking face recognition software, the security video disks, and the HR files. The date and time you gave me for the start of the evening's events were accurate. Dewey and Mikie's arrival, early gambling, and the meal were still there in the records."

"What do you mean, 'still there'?" I ask.

"A good deal of the security data has been scrubbed, Jake. All the images from the time Mikie won and going forward have been doctored, blacked out, dumped—you name it. I'd say that someone keyed on him and messed up the security files."

"Slick move."

"Not as slick as they should have been. Whoever did it went forward and not back. That's how I found Tammy and Lois. AND... That's how I found Roland Hefner."

"Roland Hefner?"

"The muscle that didn't muscle Dewey. Their little dance you shared is on the video. Like I said, they keyed in on Mikie's image—not Dewey's. Roland Hefner is the one who tangled with Dewey alright."

"Are you one hundred percent sure?" I had to ask.

"Yeah—yeah, I'm certain of it. He's the guy alright. I also have him going into the parking garage with Anna at the time Dewey says he saw the two of them. It's him—Roland Hefner, Assistant Shift Supervisor for Security—that's his name and title."

"That's fantastic, Eddie. Thanks." I end the call and immediately place another to Larry Wesselhoff. Larry answers after one ring.

"We good?" I ask.

"Yes. The Task Force called to set up your visit. Ralph Henneman, the shift manager in charge of the casino, has been told to expect Thompson and Bender. They asked him to extend 'every courtesy' to you."

"What's he know?"

"Not much beyond that. Henneman thinks you want to talk to some employees about background checks. Routine crap—yada yada yada—you know."

"The intro is all I need."

"Good—cause that's about all I can do. Unless you want me in on this."

I sense doubt in his voice and ask, "What's up?"

"Nothing." His voice has a tweak in it.

"Liar. Tell me what's bugging you."

"Bender."

"What about him?"

He almost laughs. "'No Bend' Bender has your back?"

"You'd be surprised," I say, nodding in my new sidekick's direction. "He's tougher and better than you think."

"Really?"

"Yeah. He had my back on that art heist case."

"No way."

"I couldn't have pulled it off without him."

"Jesus."

"He wasn't there," I joke. "But if Jesus was, he'd have okayed Bender."

"You're not making this up, are you?"

I pad the joke. "Trust me... And Jesus. It's gospel. Be a disciple and spread the word. Down deep, Bender is a cop's cop."

Max sits quietly listening. He is surprisingly subdued. I had thought that listening in would re-energize his peculiar behavior, but I am pleased that he has taken on a calm demeanor.

The last time we worked together it was okay that he was all 'No Bend' Bender. Then, I needed a rock-walled stickler for details.

But now it is different. Now, I need a cool head and I am thrilled to find how adaptive Max can be.

I end the call and Max immediately speaks to me. "Thanks, Jake. Nobody has ever stuck up for me like that."

I tell him straight out. "It's no big deal."

"Yes, it is. Jake, you know as well as I do. Once the cop brotherhood goes sour on you, it's over—you never get back their respect."

"Max, you're a good cop. And on this gig, you are my partner. If the brotherhood doesn't like it, they can all kiss my ass." Before Max can get all soupy, I move to get out of the car and add, "Now get your behind in gear. We've got work to do."

* * *

Inside we meet and greet Henneman. He is about what I expected and a perfect match for the backroom operations of the casino—all business. The working side of the casino is a complete one-eighty from the glitz and shine of all the bait out front. The offices are stripped and streamlined, very functional, without frills. Think of a medical clinic without the antiseptic smell.

We commandeer a conference room, request to see the three people Eddie identified, and Henneman informs us Roland Hefner has called in sick.

"Does he do that often?" Max asks.

"More than most," Henneman says with a distinct tint of displeasure.

I'm not asleep and sense from his tone that there is more to learn. I pry, "Sounds as if he's not on your favorites list."

"He has an air of entitlement about him," Henneman confides.

I pry more. "Usually that sort of stance is based on something, like a high perception of the value of past service, a special relationship with the higher ups—you know—an *in*."

He opens up. "His *in* is with Dennison—the chief of security. Roland Hefner is his pet. You'd think they were sleeping together if it weren't for Hefner believing that he is *Hugh* Hefner."

"Considers himself a ladies' man?" I ask.

"*That* I could take. The man is a walking sexual harassment lawsuit. HR is perpetually getting complaints about him. And Dennison is perpetually bailing him out."

"Bailing him out—how?" asks Max. "Harassment is no joke."

"Dennison has his ways. Let's leave it at that." Henneman realizes that he has said too much and swerves the topic away from his organization's lothario.

"Look, my food staff is stretched thin right now—which of the servers do you want to see first?"

I tell him, "Tammy Coles."

He agrees and heads out.

"Why her—if we want to pressure the other one?" Max asks.

I explain my way of cracking one member of a pair. "We want Lois Fennell to admit that she helped set up Dewey. So, we have Tammy go first. You do the talking. Go easy on her, make it fun, and cut her loose with a pat on the ass. If she and her pal are like any of the women I've known, Lois shows up here thinking she's in for the same nice-nice treatment. Not so. Mister Nice—you—disappears. And Mister Asshole—me—leans so hard she breaks like an egg tossed forty floors to the street."

"Jake, I really take back everything negative I said about your plan. It's brilliant."

"I hope so, 'cause it's all I've got."

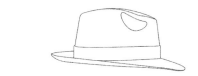

My Name is "Trouble" and You are in Me

THE CHAT WITH TAMMY IS going well. Max was born with good guy energy, and he perfectly plays the role of the 'nice' cop.

Tammy is a thirty-something on the make and Max is expertly manipulating the situation and playing her like a well-tuned instrument.

If I don't stop him, they'll soon be swapping spit.

I butt in. "Officer Bender, I think we've taken up enough of Miss Coles' time."

They both look disappointed that the interview, with its inane questions, has to end.

When Max hands Tammy a card with just his name and cell number on it, she melts. Getting her out the door takes several tries.

After Tammy is gone, Max gloats. "I think that went well. I bet she's really going to set Lois up for what comes next."

He is happier than he has been in years and is all teeth.

I agree that his performance is worthy of an Academy Award. It had me and I tell him so.

"Great job, Max. You nailed it."

"Really? You think so, Jake?"

"Yeah, but don't ease up." I begin to give him instructions for the next move. "It will take five minutes or so for Tammy to gush about you to Lois, tell her how easy the interview was, and another five for Lois to arrive. She ought to be prepped for Mister Nice Guy and be here in ten minutes—less if she wants to check you out."

"Jake, if this works—it will prove you're a genius."

"If I were such a genius, I'd be safely drawing my pension. Right now, I need you to wait outside for Lois. When she shows up, bring her in, and dump her in my lap, *fast*. Then I want you gone, pronto."

* * *

Tammy had delivered. Lois hits our bait hard. In what seems like an eye blink, she meets and greets Max and is chatting away at the conference room's door. In an inspired move, Max sets the hook by offering his card to her straight out. Lois does not melt, she evaporates.

Max ushers the bedazzled woman into the room and immediately to an uncomfortable straight-backed

chair. Before she can react, he says, "I'd like to introduce you to my partner, Detective Jake Thompson.
He'll be handling your interrogation."

In a blink, Max disappears.

Lois is totally confused. The guy her friend
touted as a white knight has abruptly abandoned her
with a stranger. Something approaching sinister.

"Hello, Miss Fennell," I say in a low threatening
monotone. "We need to talk."

"Talk?" she almost whispers. "About what?"

I slowly open a manila folder with her name
emblazoned on it for her to readily see. Lois fidgets.
I have her just as I want her. I slowly scan the contents of the folder and then silently stare at her for a
solid minute.

She stops fidgeting.

I stare again at the folder, stare at her, and
murmur, "Murder, murder, murder."

She freezes.

Lois Fennell is an attractive and not too bright
woman in her early thirties. She could pass as Tammy
Coles' sister, and I bet they operate as a pair in and
out of work. I also bet Tammy gets Lois in to and out
of a lot of situations.

And, after meeting them both, I'd bet a month's
pay that the casino's self-appointed stud, Roland
Hefner, is banging the two of them. All three are
somehow involved in stealing Mikie's money, killing
Anna, and framing Dewey.

How do I know these things? It comes from years on the streets watching, countless nights in bars wanting, and added time in my booth at *Jimmie's* absorbing a work in progress called, *My Life*. That is the answer.

In another time and place, Lois might be okay for a couple drinks and a laugh, maybe more if the Old Jimmy Jack flows in the right quantity. But right now, this less-than-bright woman is just an enemy.

My friend is facing a lifetime of misery because she served him steak and eggs. I figure Tammy and/or Roland put her up to palming the knife. Even though she's too dumb to have thought of it herself, I consider Lois Fennell as vile as a Gestapo thug stomping baby rabbits at a preschool pajama party. I want to break her—fast.

I continue staring at her, get close, invade her space. I breathe slow and loud. My monotone threatens.

"You are in trouble, Lois. I know all about *the knife*."

A tiny voice whimpers, "Knife?"

"Yes. Tell me about *Tammy*, *Roland*, and *the knife*."

She gasps. Her right hand covers her breastbone, the left one drops into her lap. She gasps again.

"Oh—oh," she moans and groans. "Oh, my, oh." Piss streams from between her legs. "Pleeeeeze," she begs and tries to rise. "I... I... Must... I—"

My monotone interrupts. "Forget it, Lois."

I push her back down into her mess. I inform her there will be no escape.

"Go ahead—shit yourself, too. You aren't getting up until you talk. I want to know it *all.*"

My right hand keeps her down. With my left, I phone Max.

"Get in here with some paper towels."

I Had No Idea

AT HEART MAX IS A nice guy, a really nice guy. He arrives with the towels and cringes at my callousness. But he supports the team and the plan by deferring to Mr. Bad Cop. Lois catches the drift. There is no white knight. She mops up her pee and begins to sing like a horny canary at mating time.

Yep. I have it right. Her best friend, Tammy, introduced her to the over-sexed over-muscled Roland. It was he who got Lois to take Dewey's steak knife from the table. Lois claims to know nothing more but slips up and acknowledges some details of Anna's date with a kitchen appliance—the sort of details the Alsip police have not made public.

Manipulated by her pseudo pal, Tammy, and screwed by Roland, in more ways than one, Lois is about as bright as any cow led up the chute and into the slaughterhouse. If I cared, I could feel sorry for her. But without Lois, Dewey would have never been implicated in Anna's murder. I need her to cooperate with the next step in my plan. I will use her any way I can.

By the way, I am right about the boinking situation. Lois confirms Roland is unfaithful to her with Tammy, and a chorus of other employees at the casino.

"I had no idea what a liar he is," she says quietly, looking about the room as if Hefner is going to pop into view at any moment. "He's mean, you know... And... And... I had no idea... No idea..." Her voice drifts off. She comes back with a world-class whine. "I haaaaaad noooooooo ideeeeeeah."

"It won't work." My Mr. Bad Cop monotone informs her. I stare at her with all the compassion of a lion eyeballing a baby antelope at lunchtime. "Listen, Lois. You face one of two outcomes... A long time in jail as an accomplice to murder... Or... You... Help... Us. Which will it be?"

She shoots a pleading look to Max.

He plays it perfect and deadpans a face that says, 'He's right.'

She looks back to me with that 'I had no idea' whine painted all over her face.

I guess she thinks I will go all soft and gooey out of compassion.

Wrong.

Instead, I think about Dewey sitting in Cook County's crappiest location and I give her a look that you can imagine.

When people are ripped off, murdered, and framed, I don't believe in coincidences. And I damn sure don't believe in mercy for the perps involved— duped or otherwise.

Mikie is lying in a hospital with tubes going in and out, and I doubt that his accident was accidental in any way.

I give Lois the stink eye of all stink eyes. She moans and pees herself again.

Max is Mr. Handy with more paper towels.

"Our talk is over," I announce to a semi-dry Lois. "While my partner hunts up some dry duds for you—" I look to Max and say, "There's got to be a lost and found here in the casino. Find her something unattractive and ill-fitting to wear." Then back at Lois, "Look, you have to decide. Start helping us, or I read you your rights and give you a gift of stainless-steel jewelry." I slip out a pair of cuffs. "What's it gonna be?"

"I... I... I'll help," she says. "I'll do *whatever* you want."

I have spent a good part of my life waiting for a woman, any woman, to say that.

Right words, wrong situation. I can't help but smile. Lois doesn't catch on. No wonder. It's *My Life* and a private joke.

"Where's your phone?" I ask.

"Here," she says, pointing to her one dry pocket.

While I scratch out a message, I ask her if she has a car and where she lives. I'm not surprised to learn that she lives four doors down from Anna's. When finished, I show her the message and ask, "Can you memorize it?"

She looks at it and says, "Maybe."

I tell her, "No good. Here." I hand her the paper. "Read it aloud, over and over."

She begins. "Tammy, this is Lois..." I head for the door, and she stops.

"Keep going," I tell her.

She starts again, and I step out into the hallway to find Henneman.

I find out from him that, as I suspect and hope for, casino employees cannot use their cell phones while on duty. Back in the conference room I find that Lois has stopped reading.

"Have you got it memorized?" I ask.

"I think so." Her voice waivers. The peeing, the pressure of my technique—it's almost too much for her. She is an inch from snapping in two. And just as I want her.

"Fine. Call Tammy. Leave the message on her voicemail."

"Wha-wha-what if she answers?"

"Start crying and hang up. Make sure she hears you cry."

"I-I-I—" She begins to well up. Lois is ripe. Time to pluck her.

"Make the damn call."

Head down, cowering, she punches the keys, sighs relief when Tammy does not answer, and waits through the four rings that dump her into voicemail.

Her rattled voice rivals a performance by Meryl Streep.

"Tammy, it's m-m-me, Lois. I'm g-g-going home. C-c-call me wa-wa-when you c-can. They know. They know... About *the knife*... And *you* and *R-r-roland*. They w-w-want to talk w-with me again t-t-tomorrow w-w-with a la—lawyer. C-c-call me."

Henneman told me Tammy's next break is an hour away. When she listens to her voicemail, things will begin to pop. Her impulse will be to call Lois. It will produce *nada*. I'll make certain of that.

The news in the call from Lois and then being blocked out from additional information will drive her to bring Roland into the mix.

Why should I search for him when Tammy can do the job? His reaction is what I am banking on.

With the call meeting my expectations and my plan progressing, I let Mr. Bad Cop ease up a bit and I tell Lois, "Good job."

"Really?" she asks with that 'kid needing approval' look plastered on her face.

It's my turn to melt some more and I say, "Yeah, you did good—real good."

Before things get mushy, Max returns from the casino's Lost and Found. He hands dry clothing to Lois, I take her phone, and we step outside allowing the lady to change.

In the hallway I do a Sam Spade and tell him what his next move will be. "You take her here." I hand him a slip with Earline's address. "Explain that

Lois is a star witness. Both of you sit on her. Do not let her have contact with anyone."

"What are you—"

I finish for him. "I'm taking her car. I'll park it in front of her place and wait inside for lover-boy Hefner."

"What happens when he shows up?"

"If I'm lucky, I get him to implicate himself."

"How?"

"Don't know."

Max grimaces. "I take back some of what I took back before. The plan is—"

"I know—I know the plan has slim odds. Maybe it's too lame to succeed. But it's all I can come up with on the fly. As AIU's finest, we are on our own, partner."

"Hey, I don't want the plan to suck again. It's just—"

"We haven't got any evidence. Hell, the only prints in this case are Dewey's." I point to the conference room door. "All we *do* have is my rock-solid knowledge that Dewey was framed, a hunch about who did it, and my ability to coerce Little Miss Airhead inside that room to set up a confrontation."

"Don't forget kidnapping," he says with a smirk. "We have no witness protection credentials. Holding her could be described as kidnapping."

"*Only* if we force her to go with us. Sure, we've misled her, but we haven't outright lied. Remember, we are not compelling her to do anything against her will. If I had more time and didn't have Internal Affairs to contend with, I'd do this in a more conventional manner."

Emphatically he says, "No you wouldn't."

"Huh?"

"Time or no time, IA or no IA, you'd do it your way no matter what." He looks at me with a wide grin and adds, "I'd expect no less from a positive deviant of your caliber."

ALL IN THE FAMILY

IT DOESN'T TAKE MUCH TO get Lois to go along with Max. She's scared to death of Roland and infatuated with Mr. Good Cop. I see them off and commandeer Lois' ride. On the way to her place, I call the office.

"Pinkie, how's the weather?" I ask.

"Damn, Jake," she yells. "Right now, the captain is a one-woman tornado. You know, her ears are close to the ground and she hears things. Things like you being off the reservation again. Indiana, Jake? Couldn't you just cross over into a suburb like before? I think when she gave you the all-clear to leave the building, she believed that you'd just hunker down for a while in that greasy spoon you call home before you started stirring up crap."

"Let me talk to her."

"Are you nuts?"

"Probably, but she knows all about me. Hook me up."

"Sure... Sure. It's your funeral."

In a couple of moments my phone goes radioactive.

"Thompson, I cut you loose, but I did *not* say you could take Bender with you. What the hell do you mean by—"

"MILDRED! PLEASE!" There is silence. I have her attention. "All I can say is that I am following my gut on something very important to me. If you know me as well as you think you do, you have to listen to me. I need your help."

More silence—from both of us. Those four words can be the most powerful four words ever spoken... if used in the right time and place. I know where and when. I also know how to wait.

Finally, she speaks. "Okay. Talk."

"My memory kicked in. And, like I said, it's a gut thing. To me and my gut, it's obvious that Dewey is being framed." I pause.

She says, "Go on."

"No offense to the wonderful folks in Alsip, but they have been led down a path to the easy solution. I don't blame them. They have the murder weapon, some prints, and information Dewey may have been harassing the victim earlier. And I understand that in their eyes Dewey taking me to the crime scene completes the picture of guilt. But they do not have all the bits and pieces. I do. When Dewey recounted the events around Mikie's disappearance, I just filed them away in my head and—pop—out they came. Murder is always a story—an intricate story—displayed in a jigsaw puzzle. And I have all the pieces." I pause again.

"You know, Jake, to most people listening this sounds simplistic—too simplistic."

"Murder usually is. It's just displayed in a lot of pieces. When you put them all together the puzzle is just a picture. And the picture tells a story. I know the story."

"The Alsip Police already have a story. To them, it's a good one."

"The wrong one. It's fiction."

"How do you convince them of that?"

"That's where you come in."

"Me?"

"Yes."

"How?"

"Call the Alsip PD and tell them I am about to poop in their nest again."

"Jake, please. Don't. If IA catches wind of this, you are toast—*burnt* toast."

"Give me an hour. Tell your kissin' cousin I am four doors south of the murder scene staking out the real deal. Tell him if I am wrong, he can spit barbeque me with your blessing."

"If you fail to make good on such a challenge, you'll get cooked—for real."

"Make the call." I pause, then add, "And, Mildred... Thanks."

QUACK! QUACK!

A SITTING DUCK IS SOMEONE EASY to target, and a decoy is a fake sitting duck. My hope is that Roland goes for my decoy. The weak link on their team is Lois. I'm betting on him wanting to silence her for good.

Lois' phone hums. I let it die, then check the number against her most recent call. It's Tammy. I wait. She calls again. I wait some more. In minutes, there is a call from a new number. I jot it down and call Eddie Moocha.

When he answers I tell him, "Find out who has this number. And if there's GPS on it, tell me where it's coming from."

"No problem."

"Fine." From my tone he knows it's high priority. There's no chit chat.

Eddie is soon gone, and I find myself in front of a condo that is the duplicate of Anna's.

"I bet Roland has a key," I say aloud to myself. I park the car sloppy to make it look like scared rabbit Lois was in a hurry to get inside to hide in her burrow.

Lois' phone hums. "Get moving, Tomaszewski. He'll be here soon," I tell myself. The phone hums again and I ignore it. It hums again, and again, and again.

Inside I find that Lois is a first-class maid compared to Anna. The kitchen is clean, and the great room is immaculate. I enter the bedroom, find a made bed and re-make it with an extra blanket and three pillows from the closet. I crunch a light bulb in a bath towel and sprinkle the broken pieces on the carpet outside the bedroom door.

Eddie calls with a one-word message. "Dennison," he says.

"What?"

"A guy named Dennison owns the phone."

"That's a surprise."

"A good one?"

"I don't think so." My mind races to fit this new piece into the puzzle. "Can you tell me where the phone is right now?" I ask.

"Yeah—it's in Alsip."

"Can you be a bit more specific?"

"Gimme a sec."

I hear a car outside, move to the nearest window and peek out. Two men get out and walk over to inspect Lois' car.

"Forget it," I say.

"Won't take long."

"Anything is too long."

"Wha—"

"Damn." I cut him off.

One guy points to the condo and the two of them start walking my way.

"Are you okay?" Eddie asks.

"We'll know soon," I tell him.

"Need some help?" he asks.

I watch the men coming closer.

"It's too late, Eddie. I gotta go."

ENTER WITHOUT KNOCKING

I RECOGNIZE THE GUY WITH THE muscles is Hefner. His companion acts as if he's in charge. That is likely to be Dennison. It didn't take them long to get here. I'm ready. But I did not expect two callers. I mute the phones, check my piece, and take a position behind the slightly open door.

It's pretty dark in the bedroom, but my eyes are accustomed to the poor light. Advantage mine. It's two against one. Advantage them.

I am right. Hefner has a key. They do not jimmy the door. I hear them entering. They make their way through the kitchen.

I hear one of them call out, "Lois?"

It must be Hefner.

The voice continues. "Baby? We need to talk."

Of course, there is no answer from the dummy lying in the bed.

The voice says, "Maybe she popped some pills— she does that."

I wonder if three pillows is fake enough. I hear them search the place. In about ten seconds, I hear a gruff and lower-pitched second voice say, "Find her. Do it. Just end this."

My mouth is as dry as a Baptist prayer meeting full of street walkers and I am certain my heart is thumping loud enough to hear in the next room. Sweat soaks my pits. My gut is flip-flopping. I hear the carpet crunch. He's so close I can smell his cologne—some cheap shit I can't put my finger on. A shadow sneaks into the room through the cracked door. He's within spitting distance.

The figure on the bed is perfectly positioned for the intruder to see through the partially open door. An extended gun barrel and hand moves past the door jam and into the room. It is aimed at the bed. There is the unmistakable hissing *poof, poof* of two silenced shots being fired.

It's now or never, Jake.

Before Hefner can switch on the light, or fully enter the room, I lunge against the door with all my might. The door slams into Hefner's extended arm with bone-breaking force. The sound is a combination crunch-and-snap. Hefner screams in pain, his gun drops to the floor, and the lead half of his mangled arm points that way also.

"Take *that* you lousy bastard," I yell.

Take it, he does. Hurt, and pissed, Hefner counter-lunges against the door. In a millisecond, I'm eating wood and my respect for Dewey reaches the stars.

How did he best this guy?

My piece flies out of my hand as I am propelled backward. I bounce off the wall and find myself in the middle of the room facing my wounded opponent.

I am no match for him. Broken arm, or no broken arm, this guy can beat the crap out of me left-handed. Twenty less years and forty more well-conditioned pounds has an edge. Toss in rage for being ambushed during a bushwhacking and—well, you get the picture.

With his good arm, Hefner lands a punch to my solar plexus that ping pongs both lungs against my spine. Air rushes out and nausea invades every cell in me. My legs fold like a cheap card table, and I am involuntarily in prayer position.

Mildred was right. I am cooked. Only it's a different chef than she predicted.

Time can slow down during such situations. My brain uses it to dump a dozen regrets, hopes, and reminders from the sub-conscious bin into the now-time hopper. The overload warps my perception.

Am I thinking about Max, or do I hear him?

There is a, "What the fuck?" said somewhere off in the condo. It's followed by a thump. No blow comes my way. I fold all the way over and vomit.

Nothing so bad has ever tasted so good.

I am still alive.

RIGHT TIME, RIGHT PLACE

DENNISON, UNARMED AND EXPECTING HEFNER to do the dirty work, was not prepared for Max arriving like the U.S. Cavalry. He was caught off guard and surprised to receive the business end of a pistol whipping.

Dennison fell to the floor unconscious and Max dropped with him.

With Dennison's body serving as a shield and aiming post, Max attends to his next opponent.

Hefner didn't have a chance. The big man fetches his weapon, whirls about, and is hit by two perfectly aimed rounds before he can shoot.

It is over before I can spit my puke out and hear the wonderful words, "Jake, are you okay?"

"Sure, Max, sure. Never been better," I tell him through puke spittle.

"Great—that's great. I'm glad. I was worried that I might get here too late."

He steps into the room and checks Hefner for a pulse. Finding none, he moves back to where Dennison lay, rolls him over on his front, and cuffs him.

"There," Max says firmly. "The job's over." He helps me stand up. I am wobbly, but mobile.

Max says, "Let's get you some fresh air."

We step outside.

"Thanks for the rescue," I tell him. "I didn't expect it, but you saved the day. Weren't you supposed to be guarding Lois?"

He smiles ear to ear and reminds me, "Like I said, this was a two-man job."

I laugh but stop because it hurts. "I take it she's alright."

"Sure—sure. She and Earline really hit it off. They were so happy gabbing about women stuff that I was as useless as a white crayon. A quarter hour into being there was enough for me, so I asked Lois for her address and decided to back you up."

"It's a good thing you did... Partner."

He is all teeth. "I told you the plan sucked."

This time I laugh and don't care how much it hurts.

* * *

Calling this in is a pleasure.

I informed Mildred's favorite relative of what I was doing. The Chief has been chomping at the bit to fry my derriere. Telling him I solved the case for him is real sweet. On the phone I explain how wrong he is about Dewey.

"Chief Buckner, I'm only on your turf again because your team got it wrong. If you want my butt, it's right here in Alsip."

"Captain Foister told me you went renegade again."

"Not so. *Your cousin*, Mildred, bet on me. She won."

"I don't believe you, Thompson. I've got a unit just minutes away with orders to apprehend you for—"

I butt in and wise ass. "Great move, Sherlock. When they arrive, they can also arrest one of the real killers and bag the other one for an autopsy."

"WHAT DID YOU SAY?" I feel it over the phone—his blood pressure is turning his eyeballs red.

"I SAID YOU GOOFED AND I AM COVERING FOR YOU!"

Have you ever remained silent on the phone? Try it sometime. When you want to make a point, twenty seconds of silence can seem like an eternity.

Buckner folds in fifteen.

"Talk to me," he says.

I fill him in, trying not to gloat too much. Happily, I fail.

"I said I have the real killers. The first one won't talk—because he's dead. But that's not a problem, since I have a witness on ice and ready to explain how she obtained and delivered the knife that framed my friend, Dewey.

"The second killer is the chief of security at the casino where all this began. He'll probably talk a lot—when he wakes up. I'll help with the interrogation if you want me to. Oh yeah, and I've got a bunch of additional evidence, too." I pause to allow what I've just said to sink in.

He does a complete one-eighty and announces, "I'm coming down there, Thompson. If what you say is true, I'll personally complete the paperwork and escort your friend out of jail."

"Chief Buckner, get your pen ready... And, grab a fork, too."

"Fork?"

"You're gonna need it for eating crow."

"UPON RECEIPT OF NEW EVIDENCE..."

T HE CHIEF PERSONALLY TOOK OVER both crime scenes, supervising the investigation into the trap that resulted in Roland Hefner's death and Dennison's arrest, as well as re-opening the forensic examination where Anna was put on ice.

Surprise, surprise. Strands of hair belonging to both Dennison and Hefner were found in the refrigerator, and their prints were on some of her personal items.

How did such evidence get overlooked? A rush to judgment? A quick fix?

The reality is that cops and prosecutors are loath to admit a mistake. And a vast majority of inmates protest that, "I'm innocent, I didn't do it."

The truth is somewhere in the mix—the innocent do upon occasion land in jail.

Rubbing my colleagues' noses in a mistake is not my style and I will keep my mouth shut. In fact, I take a back seat to Max and let him have his moment in the sun.

When a guy saves your bacon, you let him take the bows. All I wanted to do is clear Dewey's name and get him out of Cook County Jail.

It's late the next day when my mission is accomplished. Buckner is a man of his word and personally arranged Dewey's freedom. Paperwork takes time. But Dewey is cleared entirely.

* * *

Dewey comes out of the inmate release area with a smile that would make any orthodontist proud. He lays on a powerful guy-hug and almost cries while telling me, "Thanks, Jake. Thanks."

Before I can answer he reaches for his wallet and pulls a twenty from its secret compartment. "I'm surprised they missed this," he says, handing it to me. "Here, it's the five I owe you, five you'll owe me like always, and ten extra for a couple of beers as soon as we can get to a bar to sit in and hear the story. Jake, I believed you could clear me, and I just have to know how you did it."

"Sure, Dewey. But we need to make a stop first, to check on Mikie."

Concerned, he asks, "How's he doing?"

"He's in rough shape. We need to see him. On the way, I'll tell you all about what happened—how you got in jail, how we sprung you, and what took Mikie down."

Outside, we climb into my beast of car. It's a 1992 very-faded emerald green *Achieva*. When I say 'faded' I mean that for every feature of the car. Paint, interior—everything about my wheels is a statement of lost potential.

I hang on to it out of loyalty to the defunct brand. Like me, it's something from the past. The name, *Olds*, says a lot.

I talk while I drive south to the hospital in Blue Island. "Your dance partner, Hefner, was the spotter and up-front muscle. Dennison, the security chief, was the guy running the day-to-day operation. That's how the security records were erased."

"An inside job alright."

"Totally, in operation. But this went big. When Dennison woke up from the nap Max gave him, he realized that there was absolutely no way out and he did the safest thing. He lawyered up, cut a deal to enter witness protection, and squealed on the network that had systematically preyed on vulnerable winners at the casino."

"I take it that Mikie wasn't the first."

"Oh yeah—there were at least a dozen."

"What happened to the others?"

"Disposed of. Dennison admitted that the plan was to zero in on winners who were loners. They screwed up with Mikie. He slipped away and got lost, just as he did when he joked all those times with us."

"So, they got sloppy? That's it?"

"Yep Mikie walked off and they panicked. That's why Anna was killed, and you were framed. You were linked to the one mark who slipped away."

We are not too far from the spot where they caught up with him. I can tell that Dewey wants answers. I know the purpose of our drive weighs on him.

"Mikie's accident—"

"Was no accident. They saw him as a loose end—a very dangerous one."

"How'd they get two garbage trucks?"

"The people above Dennison are not your run-of-the-mill crooks with average resources."

"You have any idea who they are?"

"Some. But I'm cut out of that loop. Dennison started talking and a horde of Feds arrived. They politely thanked me for what I accomplished and then ushered me to the exit. Two minutes later they tossed Max out, too. Think about it. The Boat is scrutinized, audited, checked, and re-checked. Whoever planned and carried out a way to steal from the winners operates from a high level—hence the Feds being involved."

"Damn, Jake. You brought 'em down—don't you get *any* credit?"

"No—and I don't care."

I ease my faded green beast into the parking lot across the street from Metro South Medical Center. Years ago, it was St. Francis Hospital when the good Sisters of St. Mary ran the place. A lot of Southsiders like Dewey, Mikie, and me were born there. Even some well-known types like Curtis Granderson, the Yankee's center fielder, and superstar actor Gary Sinese started life in Blue Island.

We get out and head inside to check on Mikie.

It's not much of a visit. Mikie is heavily sedated and still hooked up to a web of tubes and monitors. I doubt if he knows we are there with him.

Mikie's condition has a visible effect on Dewey and after a couple of awkward minutes he simply says, "Let's go."

Outside, I suggest that we spend my extra ten dollars toasting our friend and we head for a popular waterhole.

At the bar, Dewey is still shaken, and in seeing it, I realize how much I missed by not staying in closer touch.

Life does not give mulligans for friendship. You just need to be there.

ROAD TRIP

We SPEND A LOT MORE than ten dollars. The toasting and reminiscing goes on and on and eventually I wake up on Dewey's couch with a terrible taste in my mouth, an Old Jimmy Jack hangover, and an extreme dislike for the incessant ringing in my head.

I mutter at my phone, "Life was better before you and your kind took over."

"Huh?" Dewey moans from somewhere on the floor. "It's not my fault you drank so much of that God-awful crap you mix."

"I was talking to my phone, not you," I moan back. I pick up the phone and scan the list of missed calls. I see that I have a dozen. Ten are from AIU, and two are from a local number I do not recognize. The current time and date on the display explains why I feel so rotten.

Dewey gets up and wanders into the kitchen. In a couple of minutes, I hear the clanking and banging of him making one of his hangover cures.

As a bartender, Dewey has tried them all. None of his concoctions have succeeded. Most have side effects worse to bear than what they aim to heal. The last one he pushed on me induced vomiting before producing near-crippling diarrhea.

When the blender stops, Dewey appears with two tall glasses of a lethal looking reddish-brown goop.

"I know what you are thinking, Jake. But you've got to trust me on this one. It works. It really works. Here, watch this." He upends the glass and consumes the entire contents with two huge gulps. "See? It goes down smooth," he accents it with a grin.

"I'll pass. Aspirin and extra water work fine for me."

"You don't know what—" he covers his mouth and sprints to the john. Soon, the sound of retching tells me his latest effort is like all the rest.

I turn my attention to the phone list, mutter, "I guess I'll have to check in," and call the office.

"Jake?" answers Pinkie. "Are you alright?"

"Sure, sure, kid. I've just got a touch of bottle flu."

"That's typical."

"I had to celebrate getting my pal clear of a murder charge."

"For which you are *almost* famous. Did you know everyone is looking for you?"

"It slipped my attention. When you say 'everyone' who do you mean?"

"You're a popular guy. Captain Foister, Captain Buckner from Alsip, Max Bender, the press, and two guys from Internal Affairs have all been asking me to get you in *asap*. Jake, I'll hold them off for a while longer, but you have to get in here."

"Okay, I'm on my way."

"Meaning—what?"

"Three, maybe four hours."

"Jake, I said they all want you in here—like yesterday—not in three or four hours."

I end the call by assuring her, "I'm on my way. I promise."

I pop some aspirins, down a quart of water, and call the number for the two other calls. It's the hospital.

My trip to AIU is off. Mikie is coming home.

* * *

The next few days are a blur. Buckner made good with me, too, and because he did, the IA boys only wanted to make it official that I was off the hook. Buckner was all smiles because Alsip was allowed to take the bow for solving a brutal murder without a mention of Dewey being targeted by mistake.

Max tried to share the glory with me, but I avoided the press, allowing them to run with him as the Chicago PD hero that helped the city's small neighbor nab the bad guys.

Of course, the real story will never be told. The state's gambling powers and the Feds buried any and all mention of Lois and Dennison. They were whisked into witness protection and I suspect that the need to keep the tax revenue flowing put the damper on any scandal.

Mildred was happy that her cuz, the Alsip Chief, was happy. She didn't say a word when I cleared all my gear out of the Dungeon and moved it back to *Jimmie's* storage room.

The lab rat escaped.

* * *

It is like old times. I am riding shotgun, Dewey is at the wheel, and Mikie is in the back seat next to the cooler. We are on our way to the Indiana Dunes State Park—the site of many of the best memories of our youth.

Our Scout Leader, Lou Arnold, had started our late-September tradition by taking us there to camp and hike the dunes. As we grew older and away from scouting, we kept coming back on our own. We had been the 'bad boys' of the group, first sneaking cigarettes, and then beer into the camp.

Today, we've quit smoking, but are still sneaking beers into the restricted park. We are also sneaking Mikie in.

At the campsite we dump our gear, grab the cooler, get Mikie from the back seat, and head for the dunes.

We climb up the dunes and on the highest point overlooking Lake Michigan. It is a solemn occasion.

Dewey and I each say a few words, we open the canister, and Mikie gets mixed in the sand. We agreed that making him part of the dunes that he loved so much is the best send-off we could give him.

This time our reminiscing is subdued. We sip a couple of beers and recall the best things about our friend. We will miss him. We know that.

And the knowing makes us appreciate each other more.

I LIKED YOU BETTER WHEN YOU WERE DEAD

THE DRIVE BACK TO CHICAGO is quiet. Both of us are lost in thoughts about the goodbye and its meaning. We respect each other's need for reflection until Dewey breaks the silence by asking me about my life being centered at the diner.

"Of all places, how on earth did you land there?"

"*Jimmie's* was the site of my first high profile collar. That arrest was how I got into plainclothes and later made detective."

"It must have been some case."

"Not really. Actually, it was my easiest. And in a weird sort of way, it revolves around what we just did—friendship."

"No kidding? *This* I have to hear. Tell me all about it."

I laugh. "Dewey, you *are* going soft—asking me to talk about me."

He laughs, too. "After the events of the past couple of weeks, I'm open for anything. Fire away."

Dewey eases into a comfortable slouchy position and I let my mind travel back to when I was a much younger man.

* * *

It was my first time in *Jimmie's*. I stopped in for a well-deserved meal after a long night shift that ended with me in an unfamiliar part of the city. Looking back, it was fate that led me there.

I liked the place as soon as I stepped inside. The only thing that has changed since then is that Jimmie's hair is a little grayer and, of course, he's hired Earline.

For some reason, I passed the empty seats near the door and landed in the booth behind the one I always sit in now. *My* booth was occupied, but at the time I paid little attention to the two men seated there.

It was after I sat behind them that I became aware of them and their conversation. They paid no attention to me.

I could not help but overhear them and I was fascinated by the intensity of the content of their conversation. The men were college educated, in their early sixties, and meeting for the first time after a very long hiatus in their friendship.

I think it was somewhere in the neighborhood of thirty years since they had met face to face.

There had been some banter and then my ears perked when Vic, the one seated with his back to me, said to Dale, "I liked you better when you were dead."

"That's sort of cruel, don't you think?"

"Not really. After years of looking and not knowing what happened to you, I choose to believe that you had died in some noble way. Instead, I've now come to learn that you're an aged wastrel."

"Coming from a friend, that's strong stuff," Dale replied.

"Correction—former friend. You and me were a long time ago."

"Where did all the negativity come from?"

"Don't even try to suggest that you don't know." Vic's sarcasm was thick.

An indignant Dale said, "Go ahead—inform me."

"You can't be serious."

"I'm dead serious. Why the big-time chip on your shoulder?"

"Get real, Dale. You disappeared for over three decades without a word—to anyone. Then you drop in from the alumni website and act as if nothing happened."

"I explained all that."

"No, you didn't. You blew off any real explanation. All you've ever said is, 'I fucked up.' That's an okay excuse for missing a hook up, forgetting to pay for the beer, or having a hangover. It's not enough for giving everyone you know the finger."

"The finger?"

"You heard me."

"I don't get you, man. I explained about living in Panama. The climate, the people, the easy-going culture. It's La La Land down there."

"It doesn't matter. You went there and turned your back on everyone you knew. No one—friends, family—nobody knew where you were. For God's sake, even your mother. She never knew what happened to you. She died not knowing."

"I told you, she and I had issues."

"What issues did you have with me?"

"Ah... Ah... Ah... None. But I just fucked up. Okay?"

"No. I told you *that* doesn't work."

As they say, the silence was deafening. And it was long. I can only imagine the eyeballing going on in that booth.

During the gap in their conversation, I ordered my meal and rustled about in the booth to let them know I was there. For some reason, I felt like a snoop.

The tension finally eased and they continued without paying me heed. For them, the nature of their talk made me invisible.

Dale said, "I don't understand what's got you so uptight."

"You're right, you don't understand. How could you? You missed everything."

"For instance, like what?"

"They call it *Life*. You know—the lives of the people you abandoned—our successes, failures, illnesses, births, and *deaths*."

"Please do not bring up my mother again."

"I wasn't. I was referring to Jim."

"Jim Magee?"

"Yeah—he's dead."

"I didn't know."

"You just made my point."

Dale dismissed it. "He and I weren't really that close."

"What about Jane? At one time, she, you, and I were as close as close could be."

"That won't hold, Vic. You are the one who let her down. After all the promises you made. And, you divorced her."

Another silence. That one was longer, and the tension was strong enough to change the atmosphere of the entire diner.

Finally, Vic responded.

"The illness I mentioned was hers."

"What illness?"

"Do you think I divorced her for the shear fun of it? She has mental problems—deep ones. I hung in with her for years—still do. Even though we are divorced, I take care of her financially. So, don't tell me about breaking promises, because I haven't broken any."

"You're so full of bullshit."

"Coming from you, that means nothing. No—it's less than nothing."

"Whatever."

More silence that deafens.

"Dale, you're a drunk and a fool. The frat boy antics that once were charming don't cut it thirty years later. Especially when you tack them on to being gone without a word for all that time. Why you popped up now is a mystery to all of us who once thought we knew you."

"I have my reasons."

"Based on your past they must be petty and self-centered."

"You just won't give in, will you?"

"I only call 'em the way I see 'em, Dale. You're a sixty-two-year-old man with a teenage girlfriend— if that's what you call her."

"Jealous?"

"Jesus, Dale, you really are a piece of work. Haven't you learned anything about life?"

"I'll tell you what I know. I now know Jim is dead and I'm not. It's as simple as that."

"If life is that simple for you, explain your dis- appearing."

"I told you, Panama is La La Land. Easy place to fuck up in."

"No, you just didn't care. *It's as simple as that.*"

"That's your call. Here's mine. Not so long ago I was sitting in Panama with some locals slugging down a few drinks and one of them asks me if I like my girlfriends to speak English. I told him it wasn't important and that the 'little negrita' I was with only knew the two expressions in English that I taught her. 'What are they?' he asked. I told him that one is 'Fuck you' and the other is 'Fuck me' and we get along just fine."

I heard Dale get up to leave, and he added a final comment.

"Adios por siempre. And *Fuck you.*"

I did not see Dale's departure from the booth, but from what I could gather later, he made a gesture.

Did he flip off Vic? I don't know.

But I do know there was a very brief scuffle, with Dale ending up on the floor dead, and Vic standing over him with a ketchup bottle in his hand.

It was red inside and out.

* * *

"Tough end for a friendship," Dewey says, as we park across the street from *Jimmie's*. We get out, cross the street, and enter the site of my tale.

Inside, Dewey gives the diner a good long look. "What happened to Vic?" he asks.

I head for my booth, and he follows. Slipping into the seat that Vic had occupied, I tell Dewey, "He was charged with second degree homicide, pled out to manslaughter, and got a light sentence—five to seven. Actually, he served less than three."

"A sentence like that for killing his friend? How did that happen?"

"When all the details came out, the sentencing judge was very understanding."

"Details? What sort of details could cover whacking a guy dead?" Dewey looks down and points at the spot where he figures Dale must have fallen. Earline greets us and drops off two cups of *Jimmie's* oil-based brew. In a minute, I address Dewey's question.

"As the arresting officer, that was my thought. Remember, I was there—or actually, here. I properly secured the bottle from his hand and heard him admit that he'd lost his cool when Dale told him goodbye forever and to 'get fucked' along the way. What I learned later explained a lot."

"What happened later?"

"I bumped into Vic after he got out. It was pure chance that I ran across him, but I just had to ask about the details behind the incident. He told me about how the two of them had once been the closest of friends. At least that is how Vic saw it. Roommates in college, traveled together, partied—you know guy-pals."

"Until Dale just left."

"Yes, like I said, Dale simply disappeared. He went thirty-plus years without so much as a phone call to anyone—even to the guy he had shared the most important years of his youth.

"Vic was devastated by the loss. He was deeply affected by not knowing what happened to his friend and had spent years searching for answers. He hired detectives, called in favors, did everything he could think of. In the end he grieved, or tried to, but without knowing for certain what happened there could be no real closure for him."

"And all that time Dale was living it up in Panama?"

"Pretty much. From what I learned, he worked at a number of jobs without any plan and just partied his life away. Several times over the years he came come back to the United States, but he contacted no one when he was here."

"What changed? Why did he finally call on his old friends?"

"He had a health scare and had spent all his money."

"Then, he was looking for help."

"Probably, maybe—who knows? It was never confirmed. The people he contacted, mostly college friends, were initially glad to know he was alive. But they had all moved on with their lives. Thirty years is a long time."

"How many people did he contact?"

"About a dozen, but only Vic was willing to meet with him."

"I'd say it did not play out like he wanted. A sad case all around."

"That's how the judge saw it. Vic's lawyer did a good job in laying out the pain and anguish caused by the entire chain of events and, hence, the light sentence."

"You said it was your first case with high visibility."

"Yeah—it was not a run-of-the-mill arrest and it put me in the viewfinder of the folks who selected guys for plainclothes assignments. I was lucky. I was at the right place at the right time. And I was invisible."

"And you kept coming back here, right?"

"Yep—you got it. My booth at *Jimmie's* has a special call for me. Through good and bad, up and down, thick and thin, I belong in this spot. It's as simple as that."

PLEASE DEFINE NORMAL

I

T'S AMAZING HOW FAST ONE'S life can get back to normal. Well, considering my life, sort of normal. Jimmie has graciously allowed me to return to the storeroom while I search for a permanent place to lay my head. And then there is my retirement. Maybe I'll get that sorted out soon.

Mildred and the attorney assigned to me from the police brotherhood have been banging away at the bureaucracy and it looks as if the gnomes guarding the pension vault might agree that my being born Jan Tomaszewski is not a punishable offense. Their change in attitude is in some part due to a threatening phone call they received from the Polish-American Anti-Defamation and Cultural Relations Improvement Council.

The council's three members, Dewey, me, and a stray boozer at *The Hide Out*, voted unanimously to express our outrage one afternoon just to stir things up. It appears our strategy worked. My case has been taken off the back burner, and while I wait for the final word from the gnomes, I am on 'light' duty.

"More coffee?" Earline asks.

"No—I'm good," I tell her. "I gotta go. This is Max's last day and I want to get into the office before he leaves."

"Forget it," she chirps.

"Say what?"

She places another cup on the table, fills it, points behind me, and says, "He's come to see you."

Max slides into my booth, sniffs *Jimmie's* oil-brew, pushes it away, and greets me with a grin. "Jake."

The sight of him confirms that miracles are real. Since the Shoot Out in Alsip, as I like to call it, he's been a new Max. No OCD, no tics, no manic behavior.

I greet him with, "Hey, professor, I was about to head over to the office to wish you well in your new endeavor."

"I bailed early while my rep is restored," he says.

"Good idea. Outside of retirement I've never known of someone to get away from AIU. I bet you're excited to put that place in your rear-view mirror."

"Most definitely. And, I owe it all to you, Jake."

"Me? You're wrong on that. It was your University of Chicago mentoring and brain creds that got you the teaching gig."

"Maybe. But without renewed self-respect, I'd never have had the guts to take the offer. You did that for me, Jake."

"No way, Max. You did it yourself. You made all the right decisions. And you met the test when nerves were called for. I'd have been toast without you backing me up. You proved that you really are an exceptional cop."

"Thanks, Jake. Coming from you means a lot." He blushes.

The transformation is complete. No Bend Bender is no more.

"I Don't Care"

I T HAS BEEN SAID THAT sometimes doing nothing is the best course of action. That may be true. But the opposite can be just as true. It's the circumstance that matters.

My crossword has me in such a fix, so I push it away and decide to let it be. My decision is to do nothing. I await the Universe in silence.

In just a moment, I sense a presence near me, and wrongly assume it is Earline with my umpteenth fill-up.

Then I hear a familiar voice from the past say, "Hey, Jake."

In response, I quip, "I was hoping *not* to be disturbed."

"You've *always* been disturbed," is the counter quip.

I look up at a long-ago face. It belongs to Dave Patten, one of the original members of our garage band, *Me and the Other Guys*.

He gently slaps my shoulder and eases into the seat across.

Dave looks the same. Older, but the same. He still has his signature mid-back ponytail, but with some gray. The youngest of our band, we simply called him The Kid.

"It's been a while, Kid."

"It has," he replies in the soft voice that made all the girls swoon. He killed 'em with it on ballads. Everything about Dave is soft and relaxed—always has been.

In our early teens, devoted to music, he was the one with talent—true talent—the type rooted in genius. Dave's gift was simply being an exemplar musician. His skill with instruments, first the cello in our school's music program, and then the guitar in our band, was like Paganini and the violin. Musical genius oozed from his every pore. Dave's gift was a wonder to behold, but my enjoyment of his gift was brief. Our pitiful little band failed, his family moved away, and our lives went separate ways.

Over the years stories and rumors reached me in spits and spurts. Here is what I learned: After joining and leaving numerous start-up groups, his talent was too great to contain. Dave's reputation grew as he continued to develop his gift. A few months before his sixteenth birthday, lightning struck when older, more established, and soon-to-be-famous musicians heard of "The Kid" and approached him for an audition.

Their band, still in formation, had a core of talented members from some semi-known groups. They had everything in place, but they lacked a stand-out lead guitarist. When they heard Dave play, they were wowed and immediately asked him to join them on the band's debut tour—in Europe. That's when Dave's life went sideways.

Being still fifteen, Dave had to get his parents' approval to obtain a passport. And out of concern over their son's touring with much older guys, they denied his request. Initially, Dave was devastated.

Then it got worse.

The band was a success. No—the band became a phenomenon.

Chances at fame and fortune are rare in life and in the music biz they are even rarer.

Young Dave did not merely miss his chance at reaching for the mythical brass ring—he had it in his hand and it was plucked out of his grip. Sadly, his musical genius, ever there, was perpetually a step behind the memory he chased. And try as he might, Dave knew such an opportunity would probably never come again.

Several of the bands he later joined had promise. But the promises never amounted to anything lasting. Dave's life became one long slow downward spiral. His unique underlying ability was there, but the fact that his "big chance" was behind him caused him to become cynical and dark. In the end, The Kid became "Dave Apathy."

He just did not care—about anything—even music. Dave all but gave up performing.

It was during that time when we lost touch.

Any knowledge we had of each other came through a friend of a friend, or some bit of rumor such as, "I heard that..."

Once in a blue moon, someone would pass on a snippet of information—a tale that went like, "I heard this dude play some licks at the XYZ Club—he was *phenomenal*.

They still used to call him The Kid.

The word came, "Some guys were jammin' and they said this super guitar player once known as The Kid showed up—he was *really* great."

The legend of a phantom master guitarist floated around, and just like all good legends it had no solid evidence, just whispers and word-of-mouth hints and nudges.

* * *

So, years later, here we are sitting in a booth at *Jimmie's*—me and one of the Other Guys.

"I'm certain you didn't drop in just for the coffee," I say.

"True that." He fidgets for a couple seconds, then directly jumps in to explain his appearance, "I need your *professional* help, Jake."

"What kind of trouble are you in? Is it serious?"

"No—it's not me. I'm good." He fidgets some more. "It's... It's... I heard something... Something about a crime—a murder. In fact, it's a famous murder."

He looks straight at me and goes silent. It is obvious Dave is profoundly shook.

When people jump right in to a story and then go blank, like a train hit them, my cop instincts kick in. I needed to be firm, but soft.

In almost a whisper, I tell him, "Take it slow, Kid. Tell me what you know—tell me everything."

Then, I wait.

He takes a couple deep breaths. "You know about the Donnelly case, right?"

I nod.

Every cop in three states knew the story: A four-year-old girl, Cassie Donnelly, got nabbed from her bed, and was found strangled a day later next to a dumpster. Her father was caught, tried, and convicted, only to be released on a technicality.

Dave grows intense and says, "Everybody thinks the guy who killed her is walking around free—and they're right. But it's *not* her father. It's some other guy. And I know who it is—*who it really is*."

"You're in the know to something special?"

Sheepishly he says, "I'm a cook now. Had a brief stint in jail and picked up the trade—gets me by." He pauses for my reaction.

"No big deal. Just get it all out."

"Sure... Yeah. Okay... There's this guy—Wade Matthews. He's a good mechanic. Does backyard work—cash—off the books. He's been a good friend—keeps me mobile. Every so often, Wade, and some of us hangout—drink beer and cook out at his place. I do the grilling. Sometimes, I'll play some licks as we gab and sip beers.

"Well, about a month ago, this little squirrelly dude, Ray Dubecky, is there. Up 'til then, I'd never seen him before. But I heard some guys say, 'He's crazy as a shit-house rat.' I was told his nickname around the area is either Jitterbug, or BeeBop—depends who you talk to. I just call him Dubecky.

"He looks and acts like Barney Fife on meth. Always making nervous herky-jerky motions—you know—creepy. He's a drunk, too. People say he drinks himself into a stupor and is found passed out all over town."

I ask, "How's he make ends meet?"

"He's the janitor and all-around flunky at the Alsip Flea Market—makes decent money but drinks it up before his next payday. Also, he gets high on other stuff. Word is that he's a part-time runner for Buddy Ames, who pushes any and all types of junk in the area."

"How'd he get into Wade's circle?"

"Tagged along with one of the non-regulars. He's good at weaseling his way into places he's not invited. But Wade didn't make a fuss—especially since Dubecky kept out of the way and just slurped free beer. In fact, we forgot he was there—until things broke up. Janitor-like, he made himself useful cleaning up.

"As I was headed out, Dubecky whined to Wade that he was stranded, and Wade asked me, as a favor, to give Dubecky a lift. I wasn't keen on Dubecky mooching a ride, but Wade's been good to me and my car, so I agreed."

Dave's face goes sour, and I interject, "I guess this is where it gets interesting—right?"

"It's why I'm here."

"I'm all ears."

I wave to Earline for some more oily brew and Dave goes on with his tale.

"Dubecky lives in a dumpy make-shift apartment attached to the flea market—and if it's anything like its resident, I bet it reeks. It took two cans of spray to get ten minutes of Dubecky's stink out of my ride. Thank God it was a short trip."

Dave's body lets out an involuntary shutter, but he keeps talking.

"On the ride, there was no small talk—he sensed I was put out at playing chauffeur. So, to impress me—I guess, as we pull into the parking area, we pass a dumpster, and he sez, 'That's where they found the Donnelly kid—didja know that?'

"I tell him, 'no' and he goes right to yakkin' non-stop. Like I said, just like a methed-out Barney Fife. So, he goes on all about how the cops were so stupid that they got the wrong guy. He really creeped me out. And to shut him up I yelled, 'How the fuck do you know anything?'

"And he whispers back, 'I know because I did it. I'm the one who snuffed the little bitch.' Then he just smiles—cool as a cucumber—no twitching—eyes all black—cold as death in January, he repeats, 'I did it. *I got away with murder.*'

"Jake, for that moment, he was absolutely weirdly truthful. I was totally shook-up, and could not get away from him fast enough."

"Dave, come on—a lot of people say crazy things. You just described this creep as a total waste product. Why should *anyone* believe him?"

"I've seen a lot of crap in my life, Jake—more than enough to know when someone is telling the truth."

"What you've told me is pure hearsay—based on mouthy garbage from a *very* dubious source."

"I figured you'd say that. But there's more—a lot more."

"Like I said, 'I'm all ears.'"

"I sniffed around for anything I could pick up on Dubecky, Jeff Donnelly, the father, and Linda, his wife—the mother of the little girl."

"What'd you find?"

"A lot. Jeff and Linda worked for Ames, too. But not part-time runners and gofers like Dubecky. They did regular runs, south to the border, transporting large amounts."

"Mules."

"Yeah. That was how they lived. But they screwed up. On their last trip, they dipped into the product— snorted and partied on the way home—and came up light enough for Ames to know it at weigh-in time."

"Not a smart move—bet Ames was pissed."

"Yes and no. The missing amount was small—just enough to party on, about a grand-worth, but enough to notice. Ames had to make a point of it, but he valued them as a delivery system. Surprisingly, he gave them a pass—sorta."

"A beating?"

"No, but that threat was there. Ames just demanded they pay him double for the junk—two grand within twenty-four hours or get a first-class beat down."

I quip, "That was generous of him."

Dave takes a sip of brew, winces, and says, "They got a pass, but screwed that up, too. Jeff thought he could double down, and convinced his wife that if they faked a kidnapping of their daughter, her parents would come up with five in cash—to save their grandchild."

"Five? I thought you said Ames wanted two."

"Jeff wanted more—enough to leave town for a while. Ya know—get off Ames' radar—patch things up. The extra was for that."

"That's a lot of backstory. You didn't get this off the street, did you? I bet you pumped Dubecky. That's why you really believe him and that's why you are here with me. Right?"

"Yes. Yes. And, yes. I took a case of cold brews to the flea market, strummed my guitar, and eased him into retelling what he brag-blurted the night I drove him home. And, this time I was prepared—got it all on a mini-recorder I hid in my pocket. He filled in the gaps and confessed again.

"The plan was to move the girl from home, keeping her at Dubecky's, while they show a phony kidnap scene to the grandparents, and milk them for the cash. The scene was a pathetic failure—just a broken window and a mussed-up bed. The idiots thought they'd just fess up to their mule work and convince the grands that all would be forgiven if they paid for the recreational dope."

"Tell me. What went wrong?"

"The grandparents freaked."

"Not surprising."

"Yeah. They rushed out and called the cops. That's when everything went south. The window had been broken from the *inside* and the cops knew instantly there was no *real* kidnapping. The girl's parents were suspected from the get-go."

"So, there's a missing girl, and it looks bad for the parents... How'd the girl die and how on earth did Dubecky skate out?"

"The mother clammed up right away and played dumb—really dumb. The dad thought the girl was okay—with Dubecky where he had taken her. I guess he believed Dubecky would just drop her somewhere, on a street corner. Maybe he thought it would just blow over—ya know, be seen as a toddler wandering off, something like that. He had no idea that Dubecky—drunk, wasted on dope, whatever—would get pissed at the kid and strangle her. With the mom tight as a drum, the cops aimed at the dad. He clammed up, too.

"Next morning—they find the girl. Right where Dubecky pointed out to me."

"Basically, on his doorstep."

"Exactly. And of course, the cops dragged him in. Now get *this*. Dubecky, cool as imaginable, sez to the cops, 'Do you think I'd be so stupid as to kidnap a kid, strangle her, and dump the body in plain sight fifty feet from my front door?' Then he rats, in an oblique way, on the dad. He hints to the cops that Jeff mused out loud that the kid's insurance might be able to help him out with a sticky financial problem.

"In a weird and believable way, what Dubecky laid out made sense. Nobody would be stupid enough to just dump a body so close to where they lived and worked. The cops investigating the murder bought it hook, line, and sinker and lost interest in Dubecky—even as an accomplice. Their response was to slam-dunk Jeff Donnelly—for kidnapping, murder, and a string of lesser charges. He was indicted, tried, and convicted in record time.

"But the speed of their actions was their mistake. Donnelly filed an appeal, also in record time. The conviction, riddled with rookie-like mistakes, was quickly overturned. In the end, he walked. And as far as the Midlothian cops are concerned, they got the guilty perp, but the system let him go. For them the case is closed. They got their man."

"So, Dave, what do you expect me to do about it? In this sort of case, the Blue Wall is bluer than blue—and it's more than solid as any rock you can find. Plus, your recording, no matter what it says, is worthless. Illinois is a two-party consent state. As far as the legal system is concerned, your evidence is meaningless. And it probably puts you at a greater risk than Dubecky."

"I know that. When I approached a guy I know on the force, he told me the same—read me the riot act. As a friend, he told me he had already forgot that he heard me out. And would even deny he knows me if I ever mention it to anyone, *ever*."

I stare at Dave and say, "I'd say he gave you good advice."

Dave looks off with the thousand-yard stare, reaches into his pocket, and produces a mini-tape recorder. He slides it across to me.

"Listen to it. Please. It's all that I'm asking."

All I can I say is, "Okay."

That's it. No further talk. No chit-chat. Dave rises, pats my shoulder, and hands me a slip of paper with his number, and is gone.

The situation put me in a bind. Dave had confessed to orchestrating an illegal recording, and I had it. Listening to it would clearly place me in the picture. But my role as a friend was to listen to it. My role as a cop was to report Dave's breach of the law. I made my choice and listened to the recording. It was everything Dave had described.

Dubecky, mad as a hatter, and creepy to boot, laid on in detail all the points that Dave had shared with me—and much more. The rambling account was full of bragging self-importance *and* tons of details about Ames' drug dealing. He even laid out details of the killing that he claimed were never released to the public.

It's a common ploy for investigators to hold back a detail or two to weed out fake confessors—the wannabe celebrity seekers. Dubecky claimed he mutilated the girl in a lame attempt to point towards a ritualistic murder—objects placed in all the body's orifices. Sick, creepy, and cruel—the perv wanted to confess all.

I believed him when I listened. Too bad the tape was illegal. When I finished listening, I called a friend for advice—and a favor.

* * *

Sara Lopez is one of the straightest, tough, and competent cops I know. Out of the State Police Academy, Sara hit the streets in some of the nastiest spots in Cook County under state jurisdiction. Chicagoland is more than just what is inside the city's limits.

Street savvy and way beyond smart, Sara found her professional home in solving cold cases. Her ability to find and track down missed or forgotten bits of information was uncanny and has become somewhat legendary. I knew her opinion of the situation would be gospel-like. It was a no-brainer for me to seek her advice. That would be easy. But the favor—asking her to hear the recording and pretending she hadn't—that would be pushing the limit.

Sara did the favor and listened to the recording. Her reaction set me back.

"Jake, don't even waste a second on the girl's murder."

"That was blunt—why so?"

"The father was tried and convicted. The over-turning of the case means he can't be tried again. Call the case a 'Double Jeopardy' married to the bluest of blue walls. As far as the system is concerned, he did it. The locals who caught him are convinced they got their perp. Nothing will sway them from that thought and there's no way anyone can pry the case open. Plus, there is not a prosecutor in the world who could or *would* go against what is considered to be 'a done deal' as far as the system is concerned. Add in the not-so-minor sticky-point that recording is illegal—your friend has nothing."

"So, it's a *complete* waste of time?"

"Yes... And no. I took some notes as I listened. I can sanitize some of the drug information and pass it on as anonymous tips to the narc squad. If you want, I'll tell your friend that his involvement has some potential to reduce the drug trade... But as far as the Donnelly thing is concerned—it's a nonstarter. That case is dead as a doornail."

Without a thought, I murmur, "No—it's dead as that little girl."

"Sad," she replies, "Oh, so sad." She hesitates, and then asks again, "Do you want me to break the news to your friend?"

Her posing the question a second time pricked my conscience. Would I be weaseling out if I let her deliver the bad news?

I was about to tell her not to call Dave when she says, "When I call him, I'll soften the blow by asking for some additional information to clarify what I'll pass on anonymously. At least he'll know all was not for naught."

I simply reply, "Okay."

And that was the end of it, or so I thought.

A week or so passed. The matter slid into one of the storage bins in the back of my mind, and I returned to the routine I call *My Life*, which was mildly interrupted by one of those bone-chilling freezes that usually arrive in January to remind us that the Windy City's winter air flow is from the Artic, not the Tropics.

During such times, you'll find me deeply huddled in my booth at *Jimmie's*.

On the fourth day of our deep freeze, I warm myself with a second cup of oily hot brew when Dave slides into my booth.

I put my copy of the *Trib* aside, and greet him with, "Hey pal—have some coffee and thaw out."

I wave to Earline for another cup and a refill for me. Earline's waitress-enhanced ESP senses that Dave's visit is business, and she is here and gone in a flash.

Dave sips in silence. His face is painted with a troubled look.

I probe him, "I take it Lopez filled you in, and you want to know if there's anything more to be done—right?"

"No—it's over. There's nothing more I can do. I made sure of that—that's what I'm here for." His troubled look goes deeper. "Sergeant Lopez was very thorough in explaining everything, and I want to thank you for bringing her in on this. But, like I said, I ended it."

I am confused by him describing the end as personal. For me, the system had ended it.

"*You* ended it? What do you mean? How?"

"Well, that's what I need to talk about. I gotta do what's right—tell you about it." Dave's face goes from troubled to serious and back to troubled. Something weighs on him—heavy.

"Okay. I'm here to listen. It has to be serious to bring you out on a day like this."

In an extremely serious tone, he says, "I took the news hard—real hard. A guy like that, doing what he said—the little girl—the lack of interest by people—the system..." He trails off, gulps some coffee, takes a deep breath and continues. "Well, I did something. I want—I have to..." He trails off again.

I stay silent.

Dave reaches for my copy of the *Trib*, pulls out the south county section, holds it up, and points to small article entitled:

LOCAL MAN FOUND FROZEN

"They found him early this morning." He absentmindedly sips. Within a dazed state of being, he says, "I did it. I did it alright—I made him pay for killing her."

I wait.

He continues.

"I took a case of beer and a quart of Jack to his place last night—got him wasted. It was easy. When he passed out, I carried him outside and left him at the dumpster... Let him freeze to death. Tossed him away just like he did to her—at the same spot." His face changes. He had confessed and the troubling deed's effect on his face disappeared.

I remain silent.

A new look creeps across Dave's face—one of bewilderment. My silence heightens his discomfort and makes him, ever so slightly, twitch.

He wheezes, "I had to tell you—confess. You see, it was I who brought you into this. I-I-I..."

I break my silence as I point to the *Trib*.

"It's sad some drunk froze himself to death. But as to how or why the jerk did it—I'm at a loss." I slip out of the booth, walk over to the trash bin, and place the *Trib* inside.

Back at the booth, I say to the former, never-to-be-seen-again Dave Apathy, "It's good to see you, Kid. How 'bout you buying me breakfast and us reminiscing about the days of *Me and the Other Guys*?"

HAVE YOU EVER SEEN A DREAM WALKING?

S PIRITS ARE HIGH. MY USUAL noon-time breakfast is on its way, *Jimmie's* coffee actually tastes something like coffee, and the sun is shining on this, my favorite day—the one *after* Halloween.

A while back I had a run-in with some genuine creeps on Devil's Night and getting through it to the next day just makes me feel so good. After my meal, I plan to settle down with the *Trib*'s sports page, the crossword, and maybe some more coffee.

A familiar voice calls out, "Jake, somebody said you were retired." It comes from my old partner, Gino Cavellini.

"Premature announcement," I reply. We shake hands and he takes a seat across from me. "Good to see you, Gino. How you been?"

"Good, good," he says with the best smile I've seen on him in years. The best since I fucked up, he got maimed, and our lives went separate ways.

"If it got any better, I'd be getting blow jobs *twice* a day." Gino always had a crude side.

I take his ready display of it is a sign that he has moved on past the event that ended our partnership with his injury and my exile to AIU.

"Slumming?" I ask.

"Need a favor—thought I'd lean on you."

"It's about time," I say, surprised. After all we've been through—his injury, my exile to AIU—Gino has never asked for anything from me. "I'm all ears," I tell him.

"I want you to do a job for me."

"An investigation?" Gino's medical retirement allows him to consult on security matters, and he works for some high-end types. "Sure, but your clients don't strike me as the types that would need a slug cop like me nosing around."

"Jake, this is made for you—a simple Go-Find."

"Who's missing?"

He laughs. "You're gonna love this." He laughs more, and finally says, "Resurrection Mary."

"What?" I am stunned. "Resurrection Mary is a ghost," I remind him.

"Yeah—yeah. That's just what my client said." He laughs some more.

I blankly look at him and ask, "What am I missing?"

He stops chuckling when he sees I am taking this seriously. "Okay, I'll fill you in."

"Like I said, 'I'm all ears'."

He tells me about the case. "My client is a young rich guy—the dude has more money than God. Last week he was at a party—a sort of 'Get Ready for Halloween' bash at *Edgewood Valley Country Club* in La Grange."

"Nice place."

"Yeah—real nice—and the perfect setting for a costume party."

"Where someone dressed up as Resurrection Mary?" I guess.

"*Bingo*! I told you this case was made for you, Jake. All you have to do is find the babe that came to the party dressed up like Resurrection Mary—*boom*! We're done. There's five grand in it. I'll give you half."

I am not impressed with my guess, his enthusiasm, or the split. It sounds too simple. "What's the catch?"

"Catch—what catch?"

"There has to be one, Gino. I'll bet all the money I have on me, that if you need me, there is a catch."

One of the good things about the time when Gino was my partner was the total honesty we threw at each other.

He tosses back the truth. "There is a catch, but it's a small one—I've already done some looking and

have come up with zilch. Also, my client has provided minimal information. He knows her first name
and can only blubber on about how good looking she
was."

"So—it's not a slam dunk."

"That's why I came to you."

I owe him, so I respond again, "Tell me more."

"The party was a swanky affair with everyone
dressed up for Halloween. For entertainment they
had scheduled re-enactments of various well-known
spooky and grisly Chicago deaths and murders. John
Wayne Gacy, Speck—"

"Jesus. *That's sick.*"

"I agree. Not a good theme."

"It certainly proves money has nothing to do
with good taste."

After my mini-outrage, Gino gets back to his
story.

"Somewhere in the mix there was a spot for Resurrection Mary to appear. She does, and *voila*! My
client gets a boner."

"And you couldn't find the actress?"

"Right. The talent agency who hired her said she
was a last-minute replacement and the info they had
proved bogus. I checked all the actors' organizations
and the girl, Marissa DeByrd, does not exist. It's a
dead end, and I'm out of time."

"What do you mean by 'out of time'?"

"I promised Jeannie, my new girl, that we'd go to Vegas. If I'm not on a plane with her tonight, I'm in for a ton of misery."

I am really stunned. "You? Pussy whipped?"

He shrugs. "First time for everything."

"You get no sympathy here, dude."

"I'm not asking for sympathy. I'm asking for a favor. Take the job. Do the look-see. Find the actress. One, two, three."

"Sure. But it will cost you four grand."

"Four?"

"If you can take Jeannie to Vegas, you can afford the four grand for me to putz around looking for some lost waif of an actress."

"Okay—find her and the four grand is yours."

I give him my best poor-kid-needing-food look. "Two now, for my time. Two later, when I find her. Fork over some dough and I'm all yours. I need to get my *Olds* out of hock at the garage."

He shrugs again and says, "Okay, it's a deal."

We shake hands and Gino lays out twenty Benjamins on the table. "I'd probably just lose it in Vegas anyway," he admits.

"You'll thank me later," I tell him as I pick up the cash.

"Sure—sure," he grins. "Just find that ghost of a woman."

RESURRECTION MARY

EVERY CITY HAS ITS FAVORITE ghost, and Chicago's is Resurrection Mary. Mary, the spirit of a beautiful young girl who was tragically killed in the 1930s by a hit-and-run driver on the road near Resurrection Cemetery, haunts the area by hitchhiking rides with strangers and then instantly disappearing from closed and/or moving vehicles.

Legend has it she was buried by her grieving parents in the same white dress and shoes she wore the night of the accident, and like all good legends, there is plenty of talk, but no real proof.

Growing up on the Southside, I heard all the stories about Mary. And like a lot of teenage adventurers, I drove down Archer Avenue at night beered up with my pals on spoof ghost hunts. Nothing came of it, just as nothing ever came of similar jaunts into Bachelor's Woods, another Southside ghost venue. Kid's Stuff, pure fun, plus alcohol.

Over the years there have been a lot of Mary sightings, or to be exact, claims of sightings. But no actual evidence. How do you verify the supernatural?

You can't. I think people just like to have something spooky to talk about. My call on the subject is that ghosts do not exist. Period.

With Gino's money, I have freed my *Achieva* from the garage and I head for *White's Talent Bookings* in Justice, Illinois to chat with Kyle White, the owner.

At the office, I find Kyle to be evasive, vague, confused, and eager to get me to leave.

What follows is undoubtedly the most peculiar interview that I have ever experienced.

"I already told your friend that she was a last-minute replacement," Kyle says. He is not thrilled with a second stranger asking about his business. "She did the gig, I paid her cash, end of story."

"Wrong answer, Kyle," I tell him.

"What?" He goes 'tough guy' on me. "You heard me."

Wrong move.

"No tax records?" I ask with a tinge of 'the IRS might want to know about it' in my voice. "That's got to violate a bunch of codes and guidelines. You know—the law."

He buys into my threat. "Ah-ah-ah— No— No— It's standard to pay cash, you know. Really, it's the way we do business."

"Not really," I deadpan. "I need something, Kyle." I show him my badge.

"Is this official?" he asks.

"Only if you want to go there."

He reaches for a notepad. "Here—let me see. Yes, I have an address for Marissa." He hands me the pad and points. "See? It's here—seventy-four-hundred Archer Avenue, Justice, Illinois."

The name, Marissa DuBerg, is scribbled in pencil. Behind it, crossed over once and smudged, is an address.

"DuBerg?" I read. "I thought her name was *DeByrd*."

"It's DuBerg—definitely... I think. I must have pronounced it wrong for your friend."

"And the address? Did you find that later?" I give him my most threatening look. On a scale of one to a hundred it approaches one-fifty.

He melts.

"I m-m-must have," he whines. "I-I-I d-don't know. I-I-I..." he trails off into almost a whimper.

"Look, Kyle, I just want to know, 'What's the deal with Miss DuBerg?'"

"I n-n-never r-r-really saw her," he whispers.

"Yet you hired her? How'd that come about?"

Faintly, "She c-c-came here and—"

"Wait. Just wait," I call out. "She was here, you hired her, yet you didn't see her?"

"Yes," he says just loud enough for me to hear. "She was beautiful... So beautiful... That's all I remember. I met her, but I didn't. I'm not really sure."

Exasperated, I ask, "Is that it? You cop to having a brain freeze?"

He gives me a weak smile and nods.

I know I'll get nowhere with him, so I tuck the address in my pocket and leave.

Outside, I assess my progress.

Gino passed this one off on me for good reason. His client can provide no details, and Kyle is in La La Land. At least I now have a real name and address. It's an obvious and easy next step. If she's there, this wild-goose chase is over and I'm another two grand to the good.

It was not that simple.

The address is for a business—a tavern. *Chet's Melody Lounge* is a well-known spot for reports of Resurrection Mary, as it is conveniently located across from her namesake, Resurrection Cemetery. I arrive and all I can do is chuckle.

"Marissa has a sense of humor," I mutter aloud. Resigned at getting the bum steer, I add, "At least I can have a drink."

Into the tavern I go.

* * *

Chet's is a nice place, a neighborhood bar, and the home of the best gag-named drinks ever. And yes, you can order a Bloody Mary. I slide onto a barstool and order a beer. Herb, the observant day-time barkeep, spots me for a cop or gumshoe. In this case he is right both ways.

He delivers the beer and asks, "You want to talk?"

"Is it that obvious?"

He grins, "No, I'm just that good." He sticks a huge hand at me and says, "I'm Herb."

"Jake," I counter, as I grab his paw and shake. "What gave me away."

"Day time, not a regular, scanning the joint, seat selection—should I go on?"

I grin. "Enough."

"What do you want to talk about?"

I gesture about the bar. "Stuff that will embarrass me."

He grins again. "What about Mary do you want to know?"

I smile back. "Was she in on October thirty-first with a guy in a *Zorro* costume?"

Herb explodes in laughter. "How'd you know about that?"

"Zorro misses her."

"He ought to."

"You remember her?"

"How could I not? She's a doll. Is Zorro paying you to find her?"

"Yep."

"Figures."

"You were here then?"

"Yeah—big night for us. I was helping the night guy."

"What can you share?"

"Zorro was smitten. She wasn't. She bailed when he went to the john."

"Neat move."

"He made a big deal out of it. Stormed out the door looking for her."

"You know who she is?"

"Yeah—name's Marissa. She's been in a few times."

I laugh. "So, she's not a ghost."

"She's real alright."

"Could you tell me where I can find her."

"Only if you agree to a couple of things."

"Name 'em."

"If she says she's not interested in Zorro—you forget you found her."

"Fair enough. Even if it costs me, Herb, I promise to let the lady decide."

He tells me, "Check the local flea market, or one of the kiosks at the mall. From the couple of times she has been in here, I gather she imports knick-knack stuff and sells direct to people in those type places."

"Thanks, Herb. What's the second thing I need to do?"

"Come back and tell me what you think."

"About what?"

"If she's as hot as Zorro thinks... And how I remember."

"Deal."

This time, I extend my paw. And drop an extra twenty on the bar.

Outside, I look across to Resurrection Cemetery, the site of where Mary the ghost is supposed to reside, and again ponder the situation.

I've got a decent lead. If I find Marissa, I'll fill her in on why I did the search and give her the option of getting in touch with Zorro.

A LITTLE THIS AND THAT

FLEA MARKETS ARE THE LAST great refuge for true capitalism. Goods on display, willing buyers, willing sellers, and all advertising is verbal. Commerce does not get any purer.

In flea market circles, it does not take long for me to get a line on Marissa. People immediately know who I am referring to when I ask about the attractive blonde lady who sells imported goods. She is easy to locate. When I actually find her, I agree with Zorro and Herb. Marissa DuBerg is extremely attractive. But in a different way than I expected.

"Are you Marissa DuBerg?" I ask.

She beams, "Yes. And you must be the man who has been asking about me."

It does not happen often, but I am caught off guard. All I can do is stare and then, after an embarrassing amount of time, nod. I guess that is what happens when you are face to face with perfection.

Marissa is not beauty queen gorgeous. Nor is she the *PlayBoy* centerfold type. If pressed, I cannot tell you what is the source of her beauty. In fact, I cannot tell you much if anything about any specific quality she may possess. But I can tell you about her aura. Yes, she has one. It is all-consuming. Wonderful.

"Cat got your tongue," she kids.

I recover. "Just thinking."

"Good recovery." She winks.

I melt some. No. I melt a lot. There is not much left to say. I can understand how Zorro lost it over this one.

Getting back to business, I ask, "Do you have a few minutes to talk?"

"Sure—Mister..."

"Thompson—Jake Thompson." I extend my right hand. She grabs it with her left.

"Come on," she says. I obey. She leads me a few steps to a vacant picnic table. "Take a seat and ask away."

"What should I 'ask away' about?"

"Mary—that's why you are here. Right?"

"How'd you know I—"

She winks again and my melt is past complete. I'm a puddle.

I take a deep breath and reset my gauges. "Is acting a hobby?"

She emits a small giggle. "Who said I was acting?"

I can tell when I am being spoofed, but in this instance, I had that chill-thing zing up my spine. "Zorro," I explain.

"Ugh!" She frowns. "Is he why you are here?"

"He was smitten. I take it you weren't?"

"Definitely not."

"But you *did* leave with him."

"I needed a ride to *Chet's*. He insisted."

"And you disappeared... Just like Mary."

"You *could* say I was staying in character."

Remembering my pledge to Herb, I say, "I could also say that I failed to find you."

"I doubt that. You're too good of a cop."

"I don't recall saying I was a cop."

"No need to."

"How did you—"

"The buzz."

"The buzz?"

"The people here—the regulars—they can sense it. Cops come and go around here—usually causing grief over piddle-and-drip regulations. I just caught their buzz. In this world, it's difficult to hide what you are. They, and I, had you pegged in a heartbeat."

"I'm harmless—and I tend to disobey regulations, too. Some would say I've ruined a career that way." I grin.

She laughs and says, "I'll be sure to tell them."

"And I'll be sure *not* to tell Zorro where you are." I was tossing away two grand and never felt so good—until she says my name and I feel even better.

"Thank you, Jake. Thank you," she says. "I find disappearing to be so tiresome." She stands and flashes a smile that gives me that spine zing again.

I know it's time to go, but I want to stay. I dawdle in following her lead. I nod toward her stand and ask, "Ah... Ah... Does your stuff sell?"

"Yes, when it's the right stuff."

"How's that happen?" I give her my best 'Gee, I just gotta know' look and I wait.

Tick tock, tick tock.

She drags it out. She knows I've crossed the line. I'm almost twice her age and I'm obviously hitting on her.

"It depends," she finally answers. "Price, selection, quality and age, or should I say vintage, of the buyer."

The next wink sends me to La La Land.

* * *

The next few days are a blur. After bailing the *Acheiva* out of the grasp of Bill "The Hold-up Man" at the garage, I had almost fourteen hundred in cash. It went fast. Best money I ever spent.

What can I say? The call for my presence at
AIU was minimal and I fell for Marissa in a big way.
Spending time and money with her came easy, and
like I said, it was a blur.

After that first chat, I hung around the market
acting like I was seriously interested in the vast array
of offered goods. Marissa kept an eye on me, and I
knew she knew that I was angling for more than a fol-
low-up talk. About ten minutes before closing time, I
made my move, such as it was.

"Need any help closing up?" I ask in as casual a
tone as I can muster.

"No." With that, I think I am shut down, but her
sense of humor matches the mystery and allure that
got me to her. She adds, "But, I could use a drink.
How about taking me to *Chet's*?"

Marissa is half my age, but she can play me like
I'm a toddler begging for a treat. I try to answer without too much slobbering. "Yeah—yeah—sure. *Chet's*
is fine."

"I'll see you there in half an hour," she tells me.

I'm cooked.

* * *

Chet's was the start of a three-day whirlwind
that swept me through bars, restaurants, coffee shops,
movies, bookstores, and art galleries. I saw places
I have heard of but would not have visited without
Marissa goading me on. I enjoyed life as I have never
enjoyed it.

And, yes, we did *that*. But except to say that *The Drake* hotel has a great view of the Lake Shore Drive, it's none of your business. Enough said.

So, what happened? Why did it end? Why only three days? The answer is simple: Marissa vanished. She was there one minute and gone the next. Well, not exactly that fast, but she did quickly disappear from my life.

Here is what I can tell you.

Just after dark, at the end of our third day together, we were driving north along Archer Avenue when she asked me to pull the car over about twenty-five yards from the cemetery's entrance. I did.

"Jake, I need to get some air," she said.

"Air? It's cold, pitch black, and it's supposed to rain. Are you nuts?"

"No, I'm not. But I do want to walk a bit." She pointed. "Look. You can see *Chet's* from here. Just let me out to walk and I'll be there in a minute or two— probably by the time you park."

The tone of her voice told me she would take no answer but 'yes'.

I stopped, pulled over, let her jump out, and scooted down and across the road to a parking spot at *Chet's*. I was out, on foot in less than a minute, and headed back to meet her. But she was not to be found.

"Okay, Marissa," I shouted. "You can end the joke."

From behind, I heard a cute little giggle. It sounded like a munchkin or pixie hiding in the weeds.

"Had you going—didn't I?" She taunted me like a kid on the playground.

"Marissa, don't do that again. You scared the crap out of me," I complained. She giggled some more and skipped to the bar's entrance.

Inside, I was aware everyone in the place sensed I was upset. I ordered drinks from the bar and carried them to our table with every set of eyes in the place on me. When I sat, I did some whining and sulking.

"I'm serious, Marissa. Next time you want to take a hike—do it in the daylight. Promise?"

She crossed her heart, blew me a cute little kiss, and giggled again. "Will do," she promised. "Will do."

I should have been happy, but that zingy thing went up my backside again and all I wanted to do was drink it away.

Soon, I was a couple of drinks ahead of her and it was clear that the night would end with her driving me home in the *Achieva*.

"Come on," she ordered. "Give me your keys. You've never taken me to *Jimmie's*," she said. "It's about time we go there. And I suspect that the oily coffee you talk about is the best thing to sober you up."

I did not question how she knew about *Jimmie's* brew. I just did as I was told and handed over my keys. I don't remember getting there, but in my booth at *Jimmie's*, I sipped more booze, and we talked.

We talked and talked and talked.

How long? A couple of hours, I guess. I dunno exactly, because I nodded off in the booth.

DON'T WORRY, I'M OKAY

"JAKE! JAKE!" EARLINE SHOUTS, AS she shakes my shoulder to wake me from my booth nap. "Wake up. *Jake*!"

"Huh?" I answer from within a cloud.

She shoves a cup of coffee at me. "Here—drink this."

"Wha—what?" I am disoriented. "I dunno what's going on," I mumble.

"Three days of drinking will do that," she quips, and slides into the seat across from me. "Drink up," she orders. "We need to talk."

Earline seldom sits with me. Her action and the coffee jerk me into a state of semi-awareness.

"What do you mean—drinking for three days?"

"It's called counting," she says holding up one finger at a time. "One—two—three. You've been at it three days."

"At *it?* What, exactly, do you think I've been doing?"

"Mumbling, wandering about, talking to yourself, and generally scaring the bejeezuz out of anyone who gets near you."

"Even Marissa?"

"Who?"

With more than a touch of 'smart-ass' I say, "Marissa. You know—the woman I came in with."

Earline gives me her world-class 'don't be such a dumb-ass' stare, and says, "Didn't you hear me? You've been scaring the locals by talking to *yourself.*"

"I'm confused. Where's Marissa?"

She reaches over and grabs my shoulder. *"Listen to me, Jake.* I don't know about any Marissa. You came in *alone,* and you've been sitting here *alone.*"

"Gotta find her," I mumble. "I gotta find Marissa."

"Jake, you are alone—and probably will be alone forever, unless you grab hold of yourself and stop drinking that stupid concoction of yours. Admit it, Jake. Boozing like a college freshman isn't working for you."

Earline's words hit home.

"I bet Marissa had enough and left because I was over doing the drinking," I say. Before she can speak, I pull out my travel stash of Old Jimmy Jack and place it on the table. "Take it," I tell her. "You're right. I'm done."

She swipes it away and says, "Maybe yes, maybe no. Right now, you're too drunk to trust."

I down the cup before me in two gulps and slide the mug across to her. "Then I'll just have to sober up. Just keep the coffee coming until I puke or pee my pants."

"Both I can do without," she says, pouring me another cup. "Do you want something solid?"

"No—no food. Just keep the coffee coming. I got something really important to do."

SOMETIMES LIFE AIN'T WHAT YOU THINK IT IS

AFTER TWO HOURS AND TWO gallons, I'm wired on caffeine and sober enough to look for Marissa. Trial apologies spin about in my head. I want to say, "I'm sorry" and I'm anxious to explain that I'm off the juice for good. I need to tell Marissa that—and a lot more.

I head for *Chet's*. That's where I started, and I figure that Herb may have a lead on how I can find her again. When I get to *Chet's* I find that I figured wrong.

"Hey, Herb," I chirp with a smile and a friendly wave. "By any chance have you seen Marissa?"

Herb does not respond well to my presence. In fact, he is downright hostile.

"Get *out* of here," he barks.

A couple of close-by patrons give me a quick look and then ease away. I fill the vacuum with a cheery response in an attempt to lighten his mood.

"The day can't be that bad, Herb. Things will get better." My attempt at nice-nice flops.

"I said, 'get lost,' you freakin' nut job."

"But, Herb—"

He cuts me off with a rant.

"Look, pal. I said, 'Beat it.' I'm not puttin' up with your crap anymore. You been in and out of here the past couple of days annoying me and scaring the customers with this Resurrection Mary garbage. Okay, it's good for business—as a joke thing. But not when you take it as far as you do. If you want to drink and talk to yourself, go do it somewhere else. This is a bar, not a looney bin. Get your therapy somewhere else. Now, get out of here before I call the cops."

"*But I am the cops,*" I answer.

"Sure—sure," he mocks. "And Mary ain't just a ghost story." He points at the door and gives me what has to be the nastiest look he can muster. My sparring with Herb would make as much sense as arguing with Earline, so I do as I'm told, and make a fast retreat.

In the parking lot, I slump into the *Achieva*. Looking into the rear-view mirror, I see a soft bloated remnant of the Jake that solo-patrolled the Southside decades ago. I tell him, "Earline is right. You aren't a freshman, and life isn't a frat party."

The binge I've been on is about to take its toll. My caffeine overdose is wearing off and I feel a huge crash coming. Driving back to *Jimmie's* and the back-room I call home is not a possibility. And based on Herb's attitude, sleeping in *Chet's* parking lot is not a good idea.

"Where will she be in the morning?" I ask the messed-up Jake in the mirror.

"Flea market," he reminds me. "That's where she works."

"Sounds like a plan. Nap in the parking lot and apologize in the morning," I tell my two selves and aim the *Achieva* toward that destination.

There is nothing more forlorn than a vacant flea market. The color of the wares and the cheerfulness of the people are gone, replaced by silent empty stalls.

In the parking lot of the abandoned economic church, the *Acheiva* finds a spot on its own.

I grab a blanket from the trunk, roll my jacket into a pillow, and quickly fall asleep.

No, I pass out.

* * *

At daybreak, a security guard taps on the window and informs me breakfast is not part of this particular B&B's plan.

"Hey, Mister. You aren't supposed to be here. Wake up and move along," he says with the all the authority he can muster.

Hung over, I am not at my best. Plus, 'moving along' is not on my agenda. Rolling down the window lets in a rush of cold air. It's good for the hangover. My first thought is to tell him off, but I respect the situation. He's just doing his job.

I reach into my jacket/pillow, locate my shield, and hold it up for him to see. He's visibly impressed.

"I'm Gene Evans, chief of security here," he informs me with evident pride.

"Come back when the market opens, chief," I tell him with the hope that I could sleep some more.

In a perfect imitation of Barney Fife asking Sheriff Andy, he asks, "Gee, are you on a stakeout?"

I can't tell if he's joking or not, but I sense that more sleep is not in my immediate future, and I introduce myself.

"I'm Jake Thompson. Rustle up some coffee and I'll fill you in on why I'm here."

My new best friend says, "Sure thing, sure thing. I've got a half-gallon thermo jug in the office—and some sausage biscuits, too. You want to come up there? It's a whole lot warmer and more comfortable than your car."

A sucker for free food and with an urge to pee, I tell him, "Be there in a minute."

He scampers off, I unfold myself from the *Acheiva*, and in a couple of minutes I'm in a toasty warm office drinking real coffee and munching away.

Gene drops the Barney-Fife act and opens up with a line of jabber that is self-revealing and informative. The flea market biz is more than I thought it was.

"I'm usually not here this early," he tells me. "Been on vacation and to pay back my staff, I'm filling in this morning. Lucky for you. Usually, Old Ed is the early man. He'd have had you towed away while you slept." He laughs. "Now, tell me. What brings you here?"

"It's more personal that official."

"Really? Personal? I was hoping for some action," he says with disappointment. "All we get here are purse snatchers and shoplifters." He points to the impressive bank of video screens linked to cameras. We have state-of-the-art surveillance. Have to—with all the merchandise and cash. Every inch of this place is being watched."

"Impressive."

"Owners want a clean operation. They really know how to cultivate the customers. You know—give 'em the impression that this is a gypsy-like street fair full of real deals, while all the time it's a well-oiled and very safe machine aimed at making money for the owners."

"Even more impressive."

He shifts gears. "So, tell me about the personal business and I'll see what I can do to help."

I blush a little. "Well... There's a lady involved."

"Always is," he chuckles. "Always is."

"Her name is Marissa—Marissa DuBerg. She runs a stall here."

"DuBerg?" He looks stumped. "I think I know all the vendors. That one doesn't sound familiar. A lady... What type?"

"Blonde, attractive—very attractive," I gush.

He laughs. "Come on—quit kidding."

"Huh?"

"I mean—I know all the female vendors here and there's not a good looking blonde among them. Trust me."

"How could you not notice Marissa?"

"Are you sure she works here?"

"Yes, of course. I've been to her stall several times."

"Which one is it?"

"The one next to the guy with all the leather goods."

He gives me a look. "Are you sure?"

"Yes, I'm certain."

"But it can't be. That one has been vacant for quite a while."

"Impossible."

"Trust me, I know." He turns to face the video screens and reaches for the computer's mouse. In a second, he has focused one of cameras on an empty booth. "Look. Here's the booth. It's vacant. See?"

I ask, "You sure you have the right stall?"

"Yeah." He pans camera to the right. "Look here... This is the leather guy's spot right next door."

I stare at the screen. After a moment I say, "It can't be. I was there three days ago."

I look at him and almost plead in my asking, "Do you think she, maybe, packed up and moved?"

"That's not likely. But I can check."

"How?"

He fiddles with the controls. "The system is digital, and everything is stored. I'll scroll past in time and see when there was last activity in that spot."

"Go back to nine A.M. three days ago. You'll see. I was there—and she was, too."

"Easy enough," he says, fiddling some more with the controls. "Here we go. Three days ago at... Eight... Fifty... Nine. Nothing."

A still blank stall occupies the screen. I stare in disbelief.

"No, that's not right," I protest. "She was there... She was there... I know she was there. I was *there* with her."

Just then, the screen shows a lone figure appearing in the stall. It's nine A.M., just as I told him. The figure is me and I am alone. I am gesturing and obviously talking to myself.

Gene looks over at me with a perplexed face. I'm a cop, but I'm damaged goods. I know he's trying to figure out the right way to handle me and the situation.

He goes direct.

"You have a... Ah... A substance or drinking problem, Jake?"

"Did. I quit."

He eyes the screen, waits to think, and says, "Good enough for me." He looks back at me and asks, "You sure you're okay?"

There are approximately seven-and-a-half billion moments in the average person's life and if you put a gun to someone's head, they can only recall a few that are really important.

This was one of mine. You know those moments, the life-changers, the kind that people share when they call in to a late-night radio show. Everyone gets them—flashes of total clarity—like stepping out of a dense fog into a clear sunny day.

Hung over and facing the embarrassing truth, I had the clearest of thoughts. The past few days were real for me, but not for the rest of the world.

"Yeah, I'm good," I tell him. "I'm good."

"You sure?"

"All I needed was a wake-up call." I rise and shake his hand. "Time for me to go, I have a report to write. Thanks for breakfast and the show. I think I'll leave parts of it out of what I write."

"Sure, sure," he says. "Glad to help."

* * *

Back at *Jimmie's*, I gulp coffee and reflect on what happened.

"Some detective you are, Jake," I chide myself. "You missed the most obvious clue—her name."

Marissa is a derivation for Mary, as is Marie, May, Maura, and Molly. I had met the real Mary. It was her. I *knew* it. And just like, Zorro, I fell for her hook, line, and sinker.

Writing my report was the hardest and also the easiest thing I ever did.

When Gino got back from Vegas, he read what I penned and said, "Jake, you are crazy if you think I'm giving this to my client."

"He'll understand."

"Understand what? That he—and you—were taken in by a phantom?"

"That's what I wrote because that's what happened."

"You say." He gives me a serious I-can't-believe-it look.

"No—I know it. *It happened*. Just give it to him."

"I dunno."

"Trust me. When all else fails, try honesty."

He shrugs and says, "I guess I have to. I need to give him something and I've got nothing else."

He puts the report in his briefcase and heads for the door.

Over his shoulder Gino says, "If he wants his money returned, I'll be back."

* * *

Gino did not come back. But he did call to fill me in on Zorro's response.

"He agreed with you, man. I couldn't believe it. He just nodded and said, 'I thought so'."

"I just told the truth, Gino. I just told the truth."

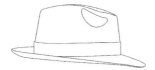

THE RETURN OF DUCT MAN

EDDIE MOOCHA'S LOOKS ARE DISTINCTLY unmemorable. I guess you could say he has a *Xerox* face. You know, that vague washed-out look attributed to making a copy of a copy of a copy of a copy. Eddie looks like everyone else and easily gets lost in the crowd. Put him in a line up and he will blend into the wallpaper.

If his appearance is forgettable, Eddie, however, is not. On two occasions he saved my life. First, as Duct Man, Chicago's most-admired vigilante, when he dramatically took out some creeps and gave me all the credit. And second, as the creator of a surveillance apparatus that luckily stopped a bullet meant for me.

I'd do anything for Eddie, and his showing up unannounced at *Jimmie's* is a welcomed surprise.

When he slips into my booth, Eddie looks worried and does not beat around the bush. "I need help, Jake. I'm in a fix," he tells me. His face says he's in trouble.

I say the only thing I can. "Anything for you, Eddie. Tell me what brings you here."

"Duct Man."

"Crap."

He holds up his hands in a defensive gesture. "I know, I know. I promised that he was a done deal and—"

I cut him off. "Eddie, Duct Man was not a good idea. Running around Chicago as a private crime fighter was dangerous. Remember?"

"No one forgets about shooting two people."

"So, why did you start up again?" My voice is overflowing with disappointment.

"I never intended to be him again. It just got out of hand."

"Out of hand? Explain it to me. What got out of hand?"

"His posse—Duct Man's posse. That's what got away from me."

"Double crap. A posse means accomplices. Just how many people know you were Duct Man?"

"None. Other than you, it's zero."

"Didn't you say it was *Duct Man's* posse?"

"Duct Man only inspired the posse. They never met him. They just know me as me."

"I'm confused."

"I'll explain."

"Good. Start at the beginning, take it slow and don't leave anything out."

"Jake, you gotta believe me," Eddie starts out with that desperate look one friend shares with another when being believed and trusted is all that matters.

I nod assurance as he continues, "I've kept my promise. Ever since the shooting I've not spent one second of my life as Duct Man," he explains. "I retired him—for good. You, of all people, know I found other ways to spend my free time. I'm a tech geek. The action-hero stuff is way in my past."

"Okay, I believe you. Are you still driving the school bus to pay the rent?"

"Yeah—and that's how the posse thing got started."

"With a school bus?"

"Sort of."

I say nothing. My look says it all. I'm still confused.

Eddie continues.

"Driving middle school kids to and fro you can't help getting to know them. Some of them are pains in the ass, some are just okay, but some are special—like family."

"Makes sense. But they aren't the makings for a posse."

"No—no, but they were the reason it came about."

"Go on."

"One of the kids, a real cutie named Zooey Perkins, got caught in a crossfire from a drug deal gone bad."

"Sad, but it happens all the time in Chicago."

"Yes, but not on *my* route. My route is all in good neighborhoods. You know the Southside is not all one big shooting gallery. Some really nice areas still exist."

"But you said there was a shooting."

"Yeah, it was mobile. In broad daylight, a couple of bangers went at each other out the windows of two speeding cars. Zooey caught one in the abdomen."

"Bad?"

"She almost didn't make it. Bled out to near death twenty feet from where I let her off." Eddie's *Xerox* face vanishes. He looks singularly grieved, totally unique. No other man could look like that.

"Obviously you took it hard, yet you did not return to being Duct Man, the vigilante."

"I thought about it."

"What stopped you?"

"I've seen enough violence and blood and thought I had a better idea."

"To form a posse?"

"No—that came about by itself."

I wave for Earline to bring more coffee. She senses that something is up between us, micro-nods to me, delivers the java, and gives us a lot of space to continue talking. Eddie goes on, not noticing our interaction.

"I didn't jump in like I did before—as Duct Man would. My plan was simply to find out the 'why' of what happened. I remember what you shared about Gino's Uncle Vinnie, how he assembled all the information on the gangs and that it helped bring a lot of them down. I hoped I could do the same with the drug pushers. So, I sat back and watched."

"Big job for one guy."

"A huge one—but I wasn't alone. I was being watched while I was watching."

"The posse?"

"Yes, but they were not that yet. They were just a bunch of pissed off people who had the same idea—find out what was happening in our previously safe neighborhood. One night they saw me staked out doing my thing. I guess the non-Duct-Man me was pretty obvious."

"What did they do?"

"They just approached me—direct—asked me what I was doing."

"They? Tell me about them. How many? Who?"

"A dozen or so of Zooey's family, friends, and neighbors. They saw me watching the same spots they were watching, and they confronted me. I was surprised and babbled on about wanting to make a difference like Duct Man. That struck a chord, and well..."

"As you said, things got out of hand."

"Oh boy, did they. Just mentioning Duct Man set them on fire," explains Eddie. With a pride-laced grin he says, "I had no idea how popular I—I mean *he* was."

I point over to the coffee station. "If you want to get an ear load about how wonderful Chicago's Robin Hood is, just ask Earline about Duct Man. She believes you, I mean him, are the sort of stuff people want to believe in—a modern messiah of the law."

"Really?" he says with a wider grin.

I frown and do a bad imitation of an old geezer in a B western. "Well, young feller, it seems that the town folk need a hero. Like in them *Batman*, or *Ironman* moving picture shows."

He grins more and says, "Life imitating art?"

"Only if you could call those crappy movies art."

"Ouch." The grin fades.

"Go on with your story. You said, they were watching you watch. What did you see?"

"That the drug business is a business—pure, simple. That's why it's so damned hard to suppress. It is capitalism boiled down to the bone. It's open twenty-four seven, all cash, with willing buyers and willing sellers exchanging money for products. Toss in zero regulation with all that money and you have a volatile mix."

"And you thought you could fight that?"

"Yes. I thought I could assemble enough information, share it with the police, and close down the local drug trade. When confronted by the neighbors,

I told them what I was going to do, mentioned that Duct Man as my example—you know someone doing something—and off we went.

"We blanketed the area night after night, photo'd deals going down, mapped each and every drug house, and ID'd every runner, pusher, and dealer in the area. We did it all—captured every nook and cranny of the business. But it wasn't enough."

"Let me guess. You turned the information over to one of the locals and got zero police response—right?"

"How'd you know?"

"Been there, done that."

"But—"

"But nothing—it's the money. Way too much money is involved. Cash corrupts when there's a lot of it floating around."

"You don't seem surprised at all."

"Nope—the only thing that would surprise me is that you are here. Tell me what got out of hand. What went wrong?"

Eddie looks like a kid caught skipping out of study hall. "The people I was with—"

"The posse."

"Yeah, the posse. That's what got out of control. At first, I was flattered when they called themselves Duct Man's Posse, even though I couldn't tell them who I was. Too bad they thought something would happen right away."

"And when it didn't, they took things into their own hands—right?"

"It's amazing. Jake, how come you know all this?"

"I just know people. Especially, the type who need a hero and are willing to join a vigilante group. They aren't patient when one of their own is hurt. How many jumped off the reservation and did something dumb?"

"Just one."

"That's enough. "Which is it? Father of the girl, brother, an uncle?"

"The father—he ran over one of the alleged shooters."

"How bad is it?"

"Maybe vehicular homicide."

"Gets better as we go."

"Damn, Jake. I had no idea things would go this way."

"Any charges been filed?"

"No, not yet. But it could get ugly. The local police contact may have flipped on us. I understand that the area's Assistant DA is sniffing around as if we are the bad guys."

"Is your contact on the take, or just playing it safe?"

"I don't know. All I can say for certain is that he knows who the driver was and also that Zooey's father was his only link to the group. If the ADA leans hard, gets him charged, and Zooey's dad is convinced it's best for him to give up the others, then we are all cooked. That's why I came to you for help, Jake."

"Revenge does have a way of back-biting everyone in sight," I tell him.

The mood in my booth gets really somber.

"You think Zooey's dad will give us up?" asks Eddie.

"Yes," I answer. "If he's charged and pressured, I think he will."

Eddie slumps like he was hit by a heavyweight's best punch.

"Let me think," I say. "It would be a one hell of a world if the good guys got nailed in a criminal conspiracy."

After a moment of thought, I pontificate a little before my young friend.

"People usually talk. No, they blab. They do it because they have to. They just can't help it. Everyone is connected to someone else and talking about the connections is part and parcel of the human condition. People can't help themselves. But, don't worry. All is not lost."

Eddie perks up a bit. "This is my last attempt to change the world—honest, Jake."

"Sure, but before you quit, I need all the information you can muster," I tell him. "Grab a pen and some paper. Write down the names of the ADA, your contact, and all the members of the posse—and get me a copy of the data the posse collected. *I'm going to need it all when it's my time to do the talking.*"

ONE MAN'S SODA IS ANOTHER MAN'S ROOT BEER

ALTHOUGH I AM DWELLING IN the professional back-water called the Administrative Investigations Unit, I do remember "the good times" when I was making quality busts on a regular basis. Back then, I was an up-and-coming star in law enforcement and made a lot of friends.

I take Eddie's list and head to the Cook County State's Attorney's office to share it with one of my favorite folks from those better days, and from even before.

When you look at Emily Potowski, you cannot image her growing up in the Southside's Polish enclave. She's way too exotic looking for that.

Em, as I fondly call her, was brought from Korea to Chicago by the Catholic Relief Society and has excelled at everything she has ever tried. Em is drop-dead gorgeous, as smart as they come, a rabid White Sox fan, and the adopted sister of one of my boyhood pals.

She grew up as a tomboy tagging after her brother, me, and a half dozen or so Polish-American toughs bent on making it as athletes rather than scholars. On her worst day, Emily could outsmart the lot of us. And she easily zipped through college and law school before any of us even caught sight of success.

I poke my head into an office marked, DEPUTY ASSISTANT CHIEF OF STAFF and say, "How's my favorite Asian-Pollock lawyer girl?"

"Jake, you racist, chauvinist pig," she squeals. "Where the hell have you been hiding?" She bolts from behind her desk and gives me a bear hug that leaves no doubt about her affection for me.

I squeeze her back and tell her, "Same place as ever—AIU."

She frowns, "Even after saving that priceless painting?"

I spout my mantra, "Once AIU, always AIU," and shrug. "You know, my PD brothers will never forgive me for letting Gino get stabbed. I'll die in exile."

She responds with, "Jake, they're nuts. Wasting a good cop's talents by not using you on the good stuff is criminal."

I try not to laugh at her lousy joke. "Em, that's sick."

She points to her desk.

"There are at least a dozen projects sitting right there that need someone like you. I'm serious. Transferring you to this office as an investigator would accomplish wonders."

"Never in a million years," I tell her. "As a matter of fact, I'm just existing there in a state of retirement limbo."

"Retirement limbo? What the hell is that?"

"It's a long story, not worth wasting our time on."

"Speaking of time. I'm curious. I haven't seen you in ages. I'm dying to know what brings you here. Business or pleasure? I'd like to think it's because you miss me, but Jake you're a cop through and through and I'll bet you want a favor."

"Em, I hate to break your heart, but I *am* here to help a friend."

She dons a great fake pout and says, "Who's in trouble?"

"Can't tell you."

"It's that serious, huh?"

"Let's say that it's best that identities remain vague for now."

"Identities? At first you said, 'a friend' and now it's multiples. Which is it?"

I answer, "Both," and squirm a bit. "It's complicated," I add.

"With you it always is." She gives me that 'I'm a lawyer' look and says, "Jake, when I was a kid looking up to you and my brother, you two played that 'you don't get the right answer unless you ask the right question' game with the adults all the time. It won't work on me. Spill the beans, or I'm not playing along."

"If I tell you, it's only because we go back to prehistoric times."

"Thanks for reminding me of my advanced age," she jokes.

I ease her age anxiety with, "You're way younger than me."

I change gears and get serious. "Em, I need to know what you think of an ADA named Randall Lipscomb. Any chance he's on the take?"

"Lipscomb? Naw, he's squeaky clean and way too ambitious—the little creep. Went to the Markham office hoping to make a name for himself. Why are you interested in him?"

I wave both hands around her office. "What I tell you has to be outside all this. If I spill any beans, you have to promise, no org-chart hierarchy, no lawyer bullshit, just Southside Pollock loyalty."

Her beautiful Korean eyes light up. "Jesus, Jake, that's so refreshing. Nobody in this politically correct rat maze would even think those words let alone say them." She hugs me again. "I miss the crap out of you—and the old days."

"I miss 'em, too," I tell her. "I really do." Her hug feels wonderful. It takes me back to better times.

"It was so much easier then. Where did this world go wrong?" she asks.

"SJWs, the designated hitter, social media, casual Fridays—take your pick—too much introspection, technology, and organization did it."

"Good cop—*and* a philosopher."

"Em, do we have a deal?"

"Yep. Start spilling, Jano."

Her use of my original Polish name warms my heart and preps me to start my tell-all.

I put the information Eddie gave me on her desk. I know her well enough not to hold anything back. Emily is sharp as a tack, and she'd sniff out any slacking on my part.

I tell her all I know about Eddie's group and their activities.

Emily listens with her eyes closed and when I'm finished, she says, "Is your pal, Eddie, really Duct Man?"

"Swear to it."

She stares at the ceiling. After a long silence she says, "Boy, Jake, you've handed me one tricky legal mess. Professionally, ethically, and morally I should probably ally myself with that sneaky weasel Lipscomb. If he chooses to nail your over-zealous father, he will eventually get the others, too. And then there is Duct Man. Bagging Duct Man is exactly the sort of thing he's after.

"Jeez, Duct Man was front page news for months. Going about the city apprehending lowlife's with duct tape, making the police look like fools—he was a piece of work. A Duct Man trophy could catapult Lipscomb to the spot he wants in the DA's office. I guess I have to help you—just to protect my future. Having that little prick around here would be terrible."

"So, can you fix it?"

She scoops up all the information I laid out and says, "Depends."

"On what?"

She points again to the cases piled on her desk. "On how many of these would you be willing to work on in exchange?"

"Is one for one okay with you?"

"Hah! I want two."

I give her a whiny weepy look, she blows me a kiss, and she flips me the bird.

I grin and ask, "Okay—two. How do we proceed?"

She quickly sorts through the stack on her desk and gives me a half dozen folders. "Pick from these."

"And?"

"I'll handle Lipscomb."

"It's that easy?"

"You were expecting paperwork? Maybe fill out some forms?" She laughs. "Jake, you know how it works in organizations with hierarchies—crap rolls downhill." She eyes the posse list. "I just inform Lipscomb that someone up here in the DA's office is running a citizen-based drug intel op and that this list of names are our assets on the Southside.

"Trust me—Lipscomb is so tuned into pleasing the higher ups that he will back off. He'll treat the people on the list as if they are Saints in training."

"What about the dealer getting run over?"

"I'll tell Lipscomb it was collateral damage."

"You sound like the Feds."

"Hardly—they'd just call it in. This I'll have to do face-to-face. I want to eyeball his reaction when I mention Duct Man. If he hasn't linked your pal, Eddie, to that potential media bonanza, Lipscomb will drop everything in a heartbeat."

"Are you sure?"

"As much as any Asian-Pollock lawyer girl could be."

THE OTHER SIDE OF A DIFFERENT COIN

EMILY PARKS ME IN A conference room where I can examine the case files while she attends to setting up a meeting with Lipscomb. Of the six cases, four are straight-up surveillance jobs, one for a less-than-honest cop, and the other three for politicians suspected of peddling influence.

It's ironic that I view these four suspects as selfish and dishonest professionals when Emily and I are skirting the rules ourselves. Since our intent is not based on self-benefit, I give us an ethics pass and toss their cases into a "no" pile.

My action leaves no choice other than taking on the remaining two and the first one is a real eye-opening experience for a Neanderthal like me.

To say that I am not into technology is a gross understatement. Born in the twentieth century, living in the twenty-first, I long for the simplicity of the nineteenth. I make Luddites look like Trekkies. It's not a joke. I willingly admit to being the poster boy for low tech.

Take for example, phones. For me, my cell phone is just a phone. Even the low-budget models issued by the department have loads of features, and I use none of them—no speed dialing, no surfing the net, no photos, and no social media.

By the way, this case is full of social media—and porn—and blackmail. It also has suicide.

Here's what I gleaned from the file:

Mae Baymore was a stay-at-home mom with two kids and a super stable accountant husband. Mae Bay, to her friends and all who knew her, was the epitome of her kind. An attractive home-crafter, den mother, homeroom helper, and shuttle driver supreme. With good friends, great kids, a wonderful house, and a solid marriage, Mae Bay had it all. No one suspected she was unhappy and looking for more.

As any attractive woman knows, sex is easy to find. Just step outside, go to the grocery store, the gym, anywhere. Good-looking women have little trouble finding playmates. But physical pleasure was not Mae Bay's goal. She truly wanted something beyond the usual.

Question: What does an unfulfilled fortyish Martha Stewart wannabe do in such a situation? Answer: Explore the internet for something *truly* different.

Second Question: How do you know it's real when you find it? Answer: You don't.

Mae Bay surfed right through the dating and relationship websites. She was not on the prowl. Mae Bay was not searching for love. It was relevance, enrichment, and fulfillment that she wanted.

What she landed on was a quirky chatroom. She believed she had found a doorway to her dreams. *The People Pen* was promoted as a "meeting place for soulful types wanting to find goodness in life". In reality, it was a device that was created to entrap trusting people.

Mae Bay had no idea part of the internet truly was a net to catch fish like her.

Under the code name, THOUGHTFULSEARCHER12 Mae Bay posted a sensible and restrained statement about her desire to find something "new and beautiful" as the central point of her growth and renewal.

She was immediately welcomed into the chatroom by a dozen responses—seven from actual people and five from electronic shills created solely to milk information from the unsuspecting inhabitants of *The People Pen*.

ZENGUY27 welcomed her, said hello, commented on her comment, and encouraged her to, "Stay with this group, they are super." The CHANTEUSEPHILOSOPHER chimed in with similar swill, and others, such as LIFEPROFESSOR14, ZABBA147, and THEYODELINGMISCREANT did the same. Mae Bay was soon immersed in a swirl of comments, discussions, and postings. Her life was transformed.

Over the next couple of weeks, whenever she could, she carved out of her busy schedule time to join her new friends. Art, literature, philosophy, politics, and current events were just the tip of the topical iceberg that floated Mae Bay out of the everyday world and transported her to a virtual paradise.

Too bad it was all a sham.

Mae Bay was certain she had found what had been sought. Safety was not a concern. She had no idea she had been scrutinized from the instant she entered the aptly named *people* pen. The intrusion into her privacy was as unnoticeable as it was complete.

The people behind *The People Pen* sprung their trap.

It came softly by way of an off-hand comment.

"Typical male response, and more typical of him," MISSLILLIAN04 posted, when THINKERDUDE set forth one of his views.

"How so?" was the question by Mae Bay, as THOUGHTFULSEARCHER12.

"Wanna step into a private chat to learn about him and more?" tempted MISSLILLIAN04.

"Sure. How?" Mae Bay asked. Until then, she had never left the site.

Lillian gave instructions and soon the two were exchanging thoughts in a separate room where Lillian gave Mae Bay "the scoop" on ThinkerDude and some additional People Pen regulars.

Mae Bay was further entrapped when, after several similar sessions, Lillian suggested an exchange of personal e-mail addresses. Mae Bay readily agreed. She had no idea ThinkerDude and MissLillian, and many others on the site, were the same person and the request was a step in a well-calculated plan to extort money from her.

Lillian's next step was to get Mae Bay's cell phone number.

It was easy. She just asked.

Lillian worked hard to become Mae Bay's best friend. She did a superb job. And just as it was online, Mae Bay opened up. Without realizing it, she shared everything about herself with Lillian, even her most closely held secrets.

And Lillian also shared secrets. The things she wanted. Things she did.

One admission was that she had posed nude at home and shared the results with a photographer to get his professional opinion.

Intrigued, Mae Bay asked, "Why on earth would you do that?"

"To feel empowered."

"Empowered—how?" Mae Bay pressed her friend.

"You know—sexy—as an in-charge female."

"How did you feel?"

"Wonderful... And desirable."

"Really?"

"*Yes*. You ought to try it."

"Me? *Never*."

"Trust me—it was *transformative*. Women our age should be appreciated."

"I just couldn't do something like that. I wouldn't feel safe."

"It's perfectly safe. There's absolutely no risk. Jeffery, my photographer friend, is totally discreet.

His interest and opinion are only professional—he's gay." Lillian laughed and moved the conversation on to another topic.

Lillian later brought up her photo session again and ended up getting Mae Bay to agree to, "snap a couple of shots, just for fun and send them to Jeffery. You might be surprised by his evaluation."

Mae Bay followed Lillian's instructions. She practiced a few poses, dolled up, took some photos, some very edgy, and e-mailed them to Jeffery. The initial embarrassment Mae Bay felt faded as she anxiously waited for his reply.

What came back rocked her world. The pictures were not as she sent them, and Jeffery was *not* a friend.

When Mae Bay saw the pictures, she went into shock. The e-mail message accompanying the photos simply said, "Like your pics? Wait for instructions."

For what seemed like an eternity she stared at the computer screen and mumbled, "No, no, no... Oh, *no*."

When she came out of her stupor, Mae Bay called her friend. Lillian was waiting for the call.

Breathless, Mae Bay declared in near panic, "The-the photos are all, *all wrong*. They— They— Have *things* in them. Things that are— Wrong— And dirty. No— No, *filthy*."

"What do you mean?" Lillian sounded vague and detached.

"There are hands groping m-my p-p-private areas... And... And—"

"And what?" It was almost a full taunt.

Mae Bay missed the tone of Lillian's comment entirely. "I-I-can't say. It's disgusting, just disgusting," she said again. "Just disgusting."

"Well, you should not have posed."

"But you— You— Said he was safe," Mae Bay whined.

"My advice is to wait for his instructions and follow them... To the letter."

"*What!?*"

"You heard me. Do as he says... And don't call me *again*." The line went dead.

Mae Bay trembled as she tried to redial Lillian's number. It took several attempts for her to complete the task.

When she did, she got a message telling her the number was already defunct. Stunned, she brought up her e-mail and waited. It did not take long for her instructions to arrive.

What also arrived was a detailed explanation of why she would follow them.

Lillian had done her job well. All the side chats, e-mails, and phone calls had provided her network of thieving colleagues with enough information to ferret out Mae Bay's passwords and gain access to her social media sites.

Her instructions were to "pay up" or have her family, friends, and everyone who knew her exposed to "her role in the vilest pornography imaginable".

I flipped through the file and have to admit the pics were as bad as anything I could imagine. Sex toys used as probes, semen shots to the face—you name it. The folks who photo-shopped Mae Bay's poses were masters of deception, not to mention devotees of hardcore raunchiness.

It turned my stomach.

What it did to Mae Bay was worse. She took the threat to her reputation seriously and assumed the threat of releasing the pictures would be continual. She had no intention of paying. In an act of equal parts desperation and defiance she took her own life.

"Nasty crap," comments Emily as she enters the room and sees my reading material. "Why'd you pick that one?"

Pointing to the rejects, I say, "I hate snooping, which leaves me this and the other one. And you're right. This one is straight out of the shitter."

"Yeah, it reeks."

"Any leads?"

"Loads—all digital, as you can imagine—and beyond my capacity. I'm without tech support on this. What's worse is that the perps are probably nowhere near my jurisdiction. Add in that it's not a homicide, the extortion is low level, and the vic is a nobody... You know how it goes."

"Then why is it still on your desk?"

"Her husband does my taxes."

"So, it's personal."

"Yep. You got any ideas?"

I lean back and stare at the ceiling.

"Well?"

I tell her, "Duct Man."

"Duct Man?"

"Yep."

"Jake, you're crazy. The last thing I need is a whack-job vigilante running around with a roll of duct tape. I'm not going to adopt him just because he's your pal and I'm bailing his butt out of a jam—"

I interrupt. "Listen to me." She pauses. I continue. "For real. He's your answer."

"The hell you say."

"Trust me on this. Eddie Moocha, AKA Duct Man, is a world-class techno-geek. He'll wind his way along the electronic trail these creeps left and—"

She interrupts me. "And what? If they are out of Cook County, which is a ninety-nine point ninety-nine percent certainty, then I've still got squat."

"It's simple—we lure them here."

A SIMPLE SLEIGHT OF HAND

I'M AN IN-YOUR-FACE KIND OF guy. I like to see my enemies. Over the next several weeks, I learn more about the digital world than I ever could have imagined and come to believe that it's a dangerous place, full of hiding places—a perfect criminal's playground.

I'm glad Eddie jumped in and let me stay on the sidelines to watch.

After chasing the virtual rabbit down the hole, Eddie explains to me what he found.

"They're zinging communications from server to server to server to hide, but I'd say this gang is just over the border from Detroit in Windsor, Canada."

That bit of news makes me smile ear to ear. "Connect with them in the same way Mae Bay did," I order. "We just got lucky."

Eddie knows what to do. He immediately creates a fictional person complete with social media accounts, e-mail addresses, and so on. "I'll hide behind a phony ID just like them."

"A game of cat and mouse—right?"

"Nope. Fake mouse, to lure a fake cat," laughs Eddie.

"Will it work?"

"If they really dig, we're in trouble," he tells me.

"Why?" I'm learning about data.

"The account histories are short. Let's hope they're greedy, just pick up our bait, and move forward without looking too far back in time."

Greed prevails, and our phony person's newest phony best friend, Lillian, has us in a side chatroom, and then swapping e-mails on a timeline similar to Mae Bay's.

"What do we do when she wants to talk on the phone?" asks Eddie. "I can't fake a woman's voice."

"Don't sweat it," I tell him, "I'll think of something."

Earline was not only willing to perform as our phony victim, she was really good at laying on the phone gab. As our front, Eva Perez, Earline was a non-stop chatterbox, and Lillian never suspected that *that* time the deception was also coming from the other side of the relationship.

It was an amazing performance, and when Lillian edged Eva into the photo shoot, I am certain Lillian thought she had another fish firmly hooked.

Earline prepped Lillian and her crooked colleagues by saying, "I was a looker in my day and I'm really anxious to get Jeffery's reaction."

Eddie took a modeling session from a local photographer, doctored the file to disguise the actual person, and photo-shopped it to look homemade.

The scammers are being scammed. The chum is in the water.

Now, all we have to do is wait.

HEY, IT'S CASH

EARLINE'S VOICE SAYS IT ALL.

Cranked up an octave, trembling with anxiety, and a little bit too loud, it has just the right amount of desperation. "Lillian— Lillian! The pictures— My pictures— They are just *terrible*," she wails. "I'm *so* embarrassed."

Lillian's response is as before, quickly laying down a path for the victim right where expected.

"Do as you are told in the e-mail or your life will be ruined," she says. "And don't call me anymore."

The e-mail arrives. The instructions are blackmail—pure and simple. To paraphrase: "Give us money or we send the pictures to your family, friends, employer—anyone who you care about." The unsaid message is, "You will be destroyed."

Eva/Earline responds, but not as expected. The content of the response is clear and simple. As I had told Emily, we have to get the crooks to come to us.

We played it perfectly.

"I'll pay to get the file destroyed," Eva e-mails back to Jeffery, in reply to her instructions. "But only if I pay the twenty-five-thousand dollars in cash. I want no more electronic trail of this sordid affair," she explains, "And I want some form of assurance that *this* is it. Plus, if you want the money, you'll have to meet with me in Chicago to get it."

Was it too defiant a statement for a victim to make? Not really.

Jeffery raises the ante and asks for more. The new amount is double the original.

Since there really is no cash, Eva naturally agrees, but only after some back-and-forth angst over assurances the pics would really disappear.

All is heading for closure, but we stall on setting the time and place for the meeting. We had to deal with one final problem.

"Who is going to meet the blackmailers?" I ask Eddie.

"Huh?" He goes blank.

"You created the photo file out of thin air. Earline was Eva over the phone, but now we need a real person. The exchange is face to face."

"Damn, I didn't think about that," he answers. "I wanted to protect the person in the original photos, so I fiddled with the details. I don't know of anybody who looks like the woman I created. I'm sorry, Jake."

I admit the error is mine, not his. "I should have thought of this."

"Got any ideas?" asks Eddie.

"How do you look in heavy makeup?" I say with a grin.

"No way."

"Just kidding," I assure him, then add, "You couldn't even pass as an unattractive woman."

"Funny."

"But true."

"So—what do we do?

"We get someone as close as possible in looks and pick a spot with bad lighting."

"Your crack about makeup wasn't far off," says Eddie. "We need someone with eighty to ninety percent of the photos' appearance and some Hollywood-level help. How do we do that?"

"I'll talk to Emily. We can't place a civilian in a spot like that. Let's see what kind of clout Emily has in getting us an undercover officer who fits the bill."

THE DECOY AND THE PLAN

"SO, LET ME GET THIS straight," Valerie (Val) Parks says as she looks at the pictures with a huge frown. "You think I look like this?"

She was a decent match for Eddie's creation. Raven hair, angular features, and black piercing eyes. In her day she must have been a world-class heart breaker. Now, she was showing some miles.

"Well, yes," I reply.

She shoots me an evil look and I backpedal fast.

"But only as the *basis* of the character," I add.

"You mean, it's me minus the cum shots—right, asshole?" Her evil-eye look gets more evil.

I bite my tongue and suppress the urge to smack her for the insult. But we need her. And, at times, I *am* an asshole. In the entire pool of available officers, she is the only one who fits the bill as our decoy. It's a good thing Val Parks has a rep for being crusty and very hard to work with.

I keep talking. "Okay—okay." I start the begging process in a pitch to win her over. "Please give it a look. I can see you're not happy about the assignment. But look at it this way. You'll be ridding the world of a group of creeps who have ruined lives and caused at least one suicide, and—"

"Shut up. I know the patter."

She's pissed, so I pipe down, and she gives me an earful of her favorite term. "Look—I'm all for nailing this bunch of assholes. But I'm not going to be happy when the assholes I work with get wind of me looking like some dumb asshole housewife who posed for these asshole blackmailers. What kind of asshole dupe do you take me for?"

"A foul-mouthed one."

"*What*!?" Her dark eyes laser me.

"Have you ever listened to yourself? *Asshole*." I just had to let her have it.

She blinks several times, stares at me, and mumbles, "I-I-I— Well— I—"

"Time out," Emily says. "This is an ongoing investigation from *my office*. As referee, I'm calling this fight a draw between *two* assholes. You children can play out the drama later. Right now, we've got some bad guys to catch—*remember*?" Emily stares at the two of us.

I give Val a 'let's drop this crap' look and she nods back.

"Good," says Emily. "Now that you've shared a kumbaya moment, can we get on with it?"

I nod and explain, "Jeffery, as he is known to us, has selected a wide-open spot for the meeting. I'd say that he thinks a bench on East Balbo Drive near Lake Shore Drive in Grant Park will provide a good spot to run from if anything goes wrong."

"And it certainly will go wrong for that ass—," Val cuts herself off. "Sorry, Jake. I'll try to clean it up."

"Thanks," I tell her. "It's much appreciated."

Emily gets us back on point again by asking, "Jake, are you and Eddie enough backup for this operation?"

"No. The wide-open spaces of Grant Park won't give us much cover and there are multiple directions for the pick-up person to run. We'll need at least three, maybe four backups on foot, two chase vehicles, plus a spotter," I answer.

"That's a lot of bodies. Can you do with less?"

"Only if I have to," I say as I nod toward Val. "She's got to be protected."

Val nods back with a real smile and says, "I apologize for calling you an asshole."

Em smiles, too. Now, we're a team.

"Is there any place you can tap for people, call in a favor?" asks Em.

I laugh. "Emily, I've been shit-canned to AIU and—" I freeze. Eddie, Val, and Emily look at me as if I'm having a stroke. My brain sputters and I belch out a brilliant idea. "AIU! We task AIU."

"How?" asks Emily. "As I told you this case is personal. There's no push from on high to get it done. I used all my clout in getting Detective Parks assigned to this."

"How? That's easy," I explain. "We lie."

More funny looks.

I go on. "Mildred Foister quivers like Barney Fife on meth whenever word comes down from above. Just call and order her to fork over some bodies for a very important undercover assignment. She'll assume it's high priority and totally sanctioned based on your title. AIU will be ours."

"You think it's that easy?" Emily asks with a look that tells me she thinks I'm nuts.

"Sure—just trust me."

"It's come to that?" Emily quips with a grin.

"'fraid so."

"Seriously, Jake. Can they cover it?"

"Yes. AIU can handle this bust," I reply with an unaccustomed sense of pride.

She shrugs and says, "This is a castoff case, so why not use the department's castoffs?"

"It's cool," I say. "What AIU doesn't have in competence it makes up in numbers. Call Mildred, lay it on heavy with vague references about the importance of what we are doing, and I'll select from the AIU staff those who are okay. Just trust me."

She grins and says, "I guess I will. Besides, I have no other choice."

GOTCHA!

T HE BAD GUYS PICKED A good place for an exchange. The spot in question is on Balbo near Lake Shore Drive, and good access for an escape. There is a bench with nothing around it but the open spaces of Grant Park.

Val is on that bench a half hour ahead of the meeting's designated time with a small leather satchel stuffed with fake money. She's wired for sound and under surveillance from almost all of AIU. I did not have the heart to exclude anyone who volunteered after word got around about *the big case*.

Some of my AIU pals are posing as gardening staff, others are joggers, and the rest are way back on the outer fringes of the park near trees and flower beds. They are as inconspicuous as any of the best undercover types, and I am proud of their efforts.

Me? I'm leaning on the front fender of a cab with its hood raised. Val and the bench are twenty-five yards away. We are all linked by radio. Depending upon the routes of the joggers, I may be the team member closest to Val.

Five minutes after the appointed meeting-time, the only people in the vicinity of the bench are a young couple with two toddlers. The team shows no signs of getting antsy. Radio discipline is good. All we can do is wait.

At ten minutes past meeting time, the male in the couple walks over to Val and appears to say something. There is a lot of static in my earpiece, and I take it that he is asking her a question. For a split-second I'm not concerned, but something just does not mesh.

"That's it," I announce to the team amid a rush of static. "He's there to make the pickup." I look about, and none of the team moves. They cannot hear me. The static is too much.

I wave to attract the attention of two *faux* gardeners.

They get my drift and immediately move toward Val who is now slumped over. The perp sees them, grabs the money bag, and waves to his female partner.

In a flash, and seemingly out of nowhere, an SUV swerves off Lake Shore Drive, jumps the curb, and speeds across the lawn to pick up the man, the woman, and the toddlers.

In a blink, the SUV is back in traffic and headed south.

Damn. We got suckered. They jammed our radios and fooled us with the kids, I tell myself, as I yell to my team members headed toward Val. "Is she hit?"

The static dies. My radio comes alive. Multiple voices overlap in the commotion, but I hear, "She's been doped, but looks okay. We'll stay with her."

I slam down the cab's hood and jump behind the wheel. In seconds, I'm pushing my luck and weaving through traffic to catch up to the fleeing SUV. My drive is short.

Up ahead, the lanes are blocked by three patrol units and a tactical vehicle emptying itself of what appears to be half of AIU.

"God Bless Mildred Foister," I mutter with equal parts of admiration and disbelief.

By the time I park the cab and sprint forward, Mildred is in the thick of things, supervising the detention of the SUV's driver and passengers. She waves at me and smiles as if I were Santa himself.

"I just couldn't sit back and let this opportunity pass," she tells me. "A call from the Chief of Staff in the State Attorney General's office asking for assistance with a high priority case is just what AIU needs." She smiles and slaps me on the shoulder. "*Damn*, Jake. Damn. This is *soooo* good," she shouts.

"Yeah. Yeah." I loudly blather back. "It's real good." I don't have the heart to tell her that Emily is merely the deputy assistant to the Chief of Staff and this is an orphaned assignment. Why ruin Mildred's buzz?

Traffic is backed up on Lake Shore Drive and news vans are already approaching the scene. I bet Mildred has a cousin hidden somewhere in the media. If she plays it right, something good for AIU might come out of this for Captain Foister's forlorn unit.

Obviously, the news hounds' scanners weren't overcome with the static that wiped out our communications and they are quickly on site. The chatter was vague, because no one beyond Em, Eddie, Val, and me really knows what the case is all about.

But jammed traffic on the lake front is "visual" and the TV hounds love it. And, I can't rule out Mildred's potential relative.

The news editors love it. Add the tactical vehicle, flashing lights, some confusion to the mix, and, *Voila*! You have the promo for tonight's lead-in piece for the news.

"Hold on, Chicago. Channel X, Y, or Z. The team you can trust has the news covered." Too bad they get most of it wrong. Correction, they just do not get much, due to believing the garbled tale shouted out by the SUV's driver—who, high when nabbed—confessed, denied, and confessed again to being "in on it all".

As expected, Mildred chattered on camera and told about the arrests of members of an extortion ring, touted her unit, and that's pretty much it as far as the news knew—AIU was full of great cops.

So, what really did go down?

The "bad guys", as Emily appropriately tagged them, were a strange combination of efficient high-tech thieves impregnated with a healthy amount of good old-fashioned stupidity.

Mildred owns the bust and, after her brief news interview, she makes certain the arrested couple and the kids are carted off to AIU's holding cell. I beat a trail there and find the place has fully embraced pandemonium.

The perps: Mom, Dad, driver, and the kids, are French-Canadians. At least that's the rumor. They carry Canadian passports and, with the aid of the best high school French, my AIU colleagues can muster communication is not that good.

The main perp, the dad, is the only one talking. He insists the arrests are all a horrible mistake. As an extra annoyance, he punctuates his broken English with threats that the group's detention will be the basis of an international brouhaha as well as a huge civil lawsuit.

Mildred is shaken at the prospect of her media coup tanking. She has a call out for a real translator and has put any interrogation on hold.

You can cut the air with a knife.

"Let me take a stab at easing the atmosphere," I offer.

"Do you speak French?" Mildred asks.

"*Oui*," I answer with a smile. I grab the thin file and look at the passport photos.

"Great," she exclaims. Pointing to the holding area she says, "Just get in there and calm him down." She does not press me for any more French, which is good. I flunked every language course I ever took.

In the holding area, my testy opponent smirks as I enter. He has buffaloed Mildred and the rest of AIU with his bombastic French-laced threats, and I'm just another dupe as far as he is concerned. I pay him no mind, continue looking at the file, and slide into the chair across the table from him.

After a long wait I look up and say, "Jean Pierre Levesque?"

He says nothing. His silence oozes contempt.

I smile and say, "Maybe I should just do this in English, Johnny."

He smirks some more and gives me a fuck-you shrug.

I ease back in my chair and say, "Aw, come on. That wasn't nice."

He gives me a second F-you look.

I grin and say, "I know... I know. You don't have to talk... And you've made it clear all this is terrible mistake... For which we will pay a dear price."

He shares a third nasty look.

"Time to go to a third language," I tell him.

He is confused gives me a 'say-what?' look.

"Let me explain in *Southside*. It's an American dialect spoken only in Chicago," I say loudly, getting out of my chair, grabbing the table's edge, and overturning it with a swift violent motion. The table slams to the floor, coffee cups break, and papers fly.

Levesque is startled and speechless.

"Do I have your fuckin' attention!?" I yell.

He stares at me without making a sound.

I lean in close.

"Listen up. I don't give a shit that you asked for a lawyer, I also don't give a rat's ass about international relations. Where I come from... On the Southside... We say French Canadians are like the French, but without the nice parts. Trouble is, we don't think the French have any nice parts."

I lean in closer. "Get your bi-lingual brain in gear and listen up real good, 'cause I ain't going over this twice." I jab two fingers into his chest really hard.

He coughs and gasps. I jab again with all my fingers.

"Here's how it's gonna work, Johnny Boy," I spit my words out at him. "You ain't going home... *Never.* We got you on the attempted homicide of a police officer, extortion, felony escape, and a dozen other counts. We'll ignore the speeding and jay walking to give you a break because you're guests in our country. But you got two kids involved, and that really *pisses us off.*"

I lean in so close I'm almost kissing him.

"In a few minutes, you and your driver pal are headed to Cook County Jail, the worst shit-hole in America. Believe me, you'll not like it." I back away so I can eye him. "But it won't be 'cause no one likes you. In that place, you'll be *real* popular. Trust me on this—the thugs in County think anyone who speaks French is queer. So, you'll have loads of friends. In fact, you'll have so many new friends drilling your ass, you'll think it's a Saudi oil field."

Levesque is sweating. His eyes are darting all over. I have him spooked.

"And I don't think it's going to be any better for the missus," I hiss. "She's headed to the ladies' side of county where decently-dressed white women not on meth are pretty much a rarity. I hope she speaks street lingo and enjoys licking."

Before he can absorb what I've thrown at him, I go for the jugular. "Oh... I almost forgot," I sneer. "The kids. I forgot about the little ones. Are they yours?"

He stiffens, and I go for the kill.

"Forget about them. The Canadian Consulate will have to fill out a boatload of paperwork to get those innocents out of the meat grinder we jokingly call child protective services. If I have anything to say about it, they'll be parked in an over-packed foster home counting roaches and fending off the brutal older kids that are going to be pissed at them just for being there."

With that verbal punch in the gut, Levesque folds. In perfect English he says, "Alright, alright. I get the picture."

I push back just to be certain I have him on the hook for good. "I hope so, because you have one chance to make a deal—and *I am it*."

"What's the deal?"

"There's no negotiating. You spill your guts. Tell me *everything I want to know*. If I like what I hear, we go light on Momma. She and the kids go home. You take the fall."

I jab him again to punctuate my position. "Do we have a deal?"

He tries to get more time by asking, "What about *my* lawyer?"

"Forget it. We'll appoint one," I tell him.

"Why?"

"'cause, I say so."

ROUND TWO

SOME GUYS ARE WHAT I call "smart-stupid". Jean Pierre was such a character. He was the showcase combination of the clever criminal who could devise and manage a lucrative scam only to get caught by doing something really dumb. Merging porn, social media, and blackmail showed some thought. Agreeing to pick up the money in Chicago was foolhardy. Bringing his family along was rock-like stupid.

Although brilliant, Jean Pierre left a trail in the digital world where Eddie just as brilliantly followed it. That was how we devised a simple trap—the one that Jean Pierre's greed and stupidity led him to. When our *faux*-Eva balked at delivering the money via the internet, Jean Pierre failed to evaluate the risk. Personally, picking up the money was really stupid, and making the trip to Chicago a family outing was worse.

After I explained Chicago's version of the facts of life, Jean Pierre talked up a storm. We couldn't shut him up. What else would you expect from a dolt who brings his family along to pick up blackmail money? He talked to save them.

Also, in the face of getting caught red-handed, he blabbed with the hope of getting a good deal and a light sentence.

Fat chance for that, Johnny. Here is the truth: Cops lie all the time during interrogations and any verbal agreement is only worth as much as the paper it is written on.

By the time Johnny finished spilling his guts, we had enough to put him away forever, and then some. I was bluffing when I told him he would never go home, but I wasn't that far off. In the end he was happy to agree to a deal for fifteen to twenty-five years.

* * *

"Thanks, Jake, you did it," Emily says, as I enter her office.

"Did what?" I ask with a phony sense of innocent wonder. "Solved the case?"

"Yes... That, too. What I meant to say was, 'you solved my tech support problem'."

"Huh?" I give her an 'I'm at a loss' look. "Tech support problem?"

"Eddie. I'm referring to Eddie. He was brilliant. I hired him as a consultant. And if I have any luck in the next budget cycle, I'm going to bring him on board permanently."

I draw in a deep breath and then laugh uncontrollably.

Emily is stumped until I explain. "That's ripe," I tell her, "God does have a sense of humor—Duct Man working for the DA's office."

She joins in. "Yeah, you're right. But in a weird way it makes sense. Misguided as he was, Eddie is a crime fighter at heart and belongs here... Besides, he's kinda cute."

I laugh more. "Me playing cupid—now, *that* is funny. Besides, he's too young for you."

Emily blushes and changes the subject by reminding me I owe her. "Cupid or not, Jake, you still have another assignment." She hands me the last folder and says, "You have to do this one alone and low key. No cavalry to the rescue, no Captain Foister, and no AIU."

"How come?"

"First, my boss is not crazy about media attention and he's fuming over Mildred trying to use the positive buzz from this case as a means to get promoted out of AIU. Catching the bad guys is good, but playing with the media is risky. You know as well as anyone they will turn on you in a millisecond."

Her reference to the low spot of my life erases all my gaiety. She notices and plows on to get me past the past. "Second, this one is out of your jurisdiction. It's in ours, but just over the city line on the Southside."

I perk up and attempt a joke. "I'm going rogue in Alsip again?"

"Next door," she answers.

"Blue Island?"

"Yes." She points to the file. "Murder. Six months ago. Eyewitness ID'd the obvious suspect doing the deed."

"What's the catch? And why do you have the case?"

"Airtight, iron-clad alibi."

I flop in a chair and open the file. "This, I gotta see."

* * *

Dewey is still in bed when I bust into his place. It's two P.M., he's groggy, slow to move, and not happy to see me.

The babe with him feels the same way.

"C'mon. Get up, Romeo," I shout while tossing clothes at him.

"Good to see you, too, Jake," he barks, throwing the clothes back at me. Pointing to his companion he says, "Jake, meet Mindy. Mindy, this is Jake Thompson, aka Jan Tomaszewski, Chicagoland's best cop and worst wake-up call."

Mindy, an ash blond with sleepy gray eyes, nice curves, and a crooked smile, half waves and half flips me off. She says, "It figures that you'd show up now. Dewey talks about you all the time. I suppose I should be glad to meet you?"

I simply say, "Hello, Mindy."

The fact that she's naked does not faze me. Or her. I've experienced this a thousand times with Dewey and expected nothing less. Dewey never sleeps alone.

I toss Dewey's duds his way again, head for the door, and say, "Mindy, you'll have to say 'bye bye' fast. Dewey and I need to talk."

A couple minutes later, the back door slams and Dewey meets me in the den. "She did not take it well. This is my day off. She made plans."

"You worried?"

"Nope."

"Good."

"What brings you south of the border?" he asks.

119th Street is the end of Chicago and the beginning of Blue Island. Dewey lives on the Blue Island side at the corner of 120th Place and Maple.

"What can you tell me about Karl Fetzer?"

Dewey whistles and rolls his eyes. "Karl 'Big Bo' Fetzer is arrogant, rich, and mean. Has his fingers in at least a dozen legal enterprises and an equal number of shady, if not totally illegal ones. He drinks a lot and gets nasty when he does—real nasty. Oh, I almost forgot... He killed Chubbie Barker. Is Chubbie's murder why you interrupted my pajama party?"

"I didn't see much in the way of PJs. But what I did see looked alright."

"Mindy is okay. A little hot tempered, but only when she's told to leave by intruders."

"I'll guess I'll just have to get over the fact that she doesn't like me." I focus back on why I came. "You said Big Bo killed Chubbie."

"Yeah, sure. Everyone says so. Rumor has it that he walked into the pizza place and aced his partner."

"Funny, that's what the eyewitness said."

"Yeah, the news hounds were all over her. Janice Karst, the cashier, is a nice lady. Great legs in her day and possessed other tremendous qualities, too."

I catch his drift and say, "So you know her in the biblical way?"

"I never kiss and tell." Which means Dewey slept with her.

"Duly noted." I say, "Any chance you could introduce me?"

"Not now. The grapevine says she lucked into a windfall and relocated somewhere near Ocala, Florida. She's into horses and that area is second only to Kentucky for saddle enthusiasts."

"Great timing," I say. "What sort of windfall?"

"Wasn't the lottery."

"Fetzer?"

"Maybe."

"And you say the street says he did it."

"Most definitely."

"No other buzz?"

"None," he quietly says. Dewey looks agitated.

I press. "You're not mad about me running Mindy off, are you?"

"No. She'll be back."

"Then, what's eating you?"

He stares at my hands. "Where's my fiver?"

"Oh, crap," I exclaim, realizing that I forgot our ritual. I reach for my wallet and apologize. "I'm not thinking straight," I tell him while handing over a crisp ten.

He takes it and sighs with relief. "Can't end the streak, man. Now I owe you five."

"Sorry, Dewey. I'm really fixed on this case."

He sighs again.

"Chubbie was shot in the original *Beggar Man's* at one-twenty-seventh and Western, which is way outside of Chicago. Remember all the heat you got for working a case in Alsip? The-powers-that-be barbequed you for leaving your jurisdiction. Jake, you're on thin ice again."

"Relax. I'm official... Well, semi-official. I'm doing a favor for a friend in the Cook County DA's office. The case hit a wall. Fetzer produced a video from a sports bar in Lemont clearly placing him there seventeen minutes after the shooting took place," I explain.

"Lockport? That's at least forty minutes away," Dewey says.

"Even more in rush hour," I add.

"Let me get this," he says. "The shooting went down at five-fifteen and Fetzer's proof puts him in the Lemont bar at five-thirty-two?"

"Right," I say.

"So, his lawyers argued that it's impossible to be in two places at once."

"Right again. The video is hard evidence, and it trumps an eyewitness. Fetzer walked on the murder rap."

"Unless he sprouted wings, he could not have done it."

"But, like you told me, the street says he did it."

"The street is just repeating what Big Bo has been saying. He's proud he got away with murder and has been overheard bragging about it."

WHAT'S YOURS IS MINE

CHUBBIE BARKER STARTED WITH ONE small take-out pizzeria and transformed it into a small chain of profitable restaurants by offering good food at fair prices in popular locations. His only mistake was to take on Big Bo Fetzer as a partner. Chubbie wrongly believed that financing with Fetzer would be easier than with the banks.

There are a dozen *Beggar Man's* on the Southside, and now a self-proclaimed murderer owns them all.

I want to see the crime scene, so Dewey and I visit the site of the shooting—the first *Beggar Man's* at the corner of Burr Oak Avenue (127th St.) and Western Avenue. We are met at the counter by a slack-jawed youth sporting a nose ring and ear gauges. Multi-colored tats creep out of his collar and sleeves, hinting that he is into ink as much as face and head metal.

"Wha' kinda p'za ya wan'?" he half mumbles and slurs when we enter.

I look at him and say nothing.

"Wha' kinda p'za, man?" he slurs again.

I pull out my badge.

I'm counting Doofus couldn't tell the difference between a Chicago shield and a hall pass.

I'm right. With glazed eyes he stares at my credentials as if they are from the planet Zenon.

"Five-Oh?" he mumbles.

"Yeah," I say. "Five-Oh, the Man, the Heat."

"So... Wha' kinda p'za ya wan'?"

"None, Speedy. As a courtesy I want to let the manager know I'm reviewing a crime scene."

"There been a crime?" His eyes glaze more. "Did sombuddy call?"

A customer comes in and stands behind us.

I step aside and tell him, "Sir, go ahead and order."

Doofus looks at me and says, "Then, ya really don't wanna p'za?"

Dewey and I walk about the small restaurant. The floor plan of the small original takeout place has been extended to add some dining, but it is still a small establishment. An eyewitness would have to be blind to misidentify Chubbie's assailant.

"Any chance your friend, Janice ID'd the wrong guy?" I ask.

"None."

"She said Fetzer walked in, shot Chubbie, and went straight out the rear of the restaurant."

We walk through the kitchen and out the back door. No one says a thing to challenge us.

"Brain dead," I say. "The staff is almost comatose."

"Minimum-wage America," Dewey comments, as we head close the door behind us.

Outside is an alley.

"Nice place to be picked up by an accomplice. This case is eating at me something fierce," I tell Dewey. "The solution is clear and simple. And my gut tells me the answer is hiding right out in the open."

"Fetzer is not the kind of guy to pull this off by himself. Has there been any work done at finding his accomplice or accomplices?" Like me, Dewey knows even the most despicable people have friends.

"No. After the video popped on the scene, this case was dropped. It's alive only because Emily won't let it go."

"Emily? As in Emily Potowski? Joey's kid sister?"

"Yes. She's the friend in the DA's office I am helping."

"*Damn*! She was beautiful when we were young. Please tell me she held up well over the years. Maybe I should look her up." Dewey's pastime is women. But this time I deflate his testosterone balloon.

"She's still very attractive," I say. "But you can forget about romancing her with a walk down our old neighborhood's memory lane. She's securely involved with *another* friend of mine." I'm stretching the Eddie/Emily thing.

"Who is it? One of your pals at AIU?"

"None of your business."

"Don't tell me she's gay." Dewey loves women and sees each lesbian as one more not available for him.

"You know, you're disgusting."

"Ah, come on. Tell me the truth," he whines, and gives me a sad look that is supposed to open me up.

"Stop."

"Who is it?"

"Dewey, give it a break. She's practically family."

"Okay, but it's her loss." He pouts, then asks, "Would you promise me one thing?"

"What?"

"Just mention to her that I—"

"NO!"

"Okay—okay, you win."

I know I'll hear about this topic again. To get back on track I ask, "Want to see how fast you can drive to Lemont?"

"Can I use a light and siren?" He beams like a kid.

I disappoint him again. "Sorry."

Dewey pouts again.

I check my watch. "We need to simulate an escape. It's almost the same time that Chubbie was killed. Let's get moving."

We travel using the most direct route; West on 127th taking the jog north to 123rd and then into Lemont. Traffic is congested and the going is slow.

After forty-seven minutes, we arrive at our destination—a trendy watering hole with a name that tickles my gag reflex.

Looking at an over-sized blinking sign, Dewey asks, "Does a fancy name like *The Burnt Embers Micro Brew Sports Emporium* make the beer tastes better?"

"It's all marketing," I reply. "Names like that come from the wonderful world of modern schmoozing. I bet some whiz kid with an MBA and a predilection for snooty beers commissioned a survey with leading questions like, 'Do you prefer quality hops from Austria, or the standard domestic variety from Nebraska?'

"And then had a brain-storming session with a dozen hustlers just like himself to arrive at 'a descriptive, market-sensitive appellation representative of socio-economic demographics and customer preference trends'. It's amazing what four years of college and a couple extra more in grad school can do to common sense."

"If you can buy a draught beer in this joint for less than eight bucks, I'll kiss your butt in broad daylight," Dewey says shaking his old-school bartender's head in amazement and disgust.

"I pass on both the beer and the butt kiss," I reply. "People would talk if I paid that much for a beer." I head for the entrance and Dewey follows.

"I thought you agreed that the beer was too pricey in here," Dewey says, catching up to me.

"I want to see the camera set up. It won't take long,"

Inside, we are greeted by an attractive young lady named Jennifer. I show my badge, Dewey goes into gear, Jennifer motions to Brent, the shift manager, and I'm getting a briefing on the restaurant's state-of-the-art security system while Dewey playfully hits on a babe half his age.

Ten minutes later we trade notes in the parking lot.

"What do you think," asks Dewey.

"Fetzer chose this place well. The video system is the latest. Perfect for his alibi. No chance of an error in establishing his being here at a particular time."

"No. I meant Jennifer. What do you think of—"

I cut him off. "Put your dick away, Dewey. I'm on the clock."

He apologizes, "Sorry, Jake. As you were saying..."

I smile, nod, and continue. "*As I was saying*, this is a perfect set up for an alibi. Lots of security cameras, loads of witnesses. *It's too perfect.* His alibi is way too solid. I smell bad fish."

Dewey is back on point. "And, *as I said*, the only way to bust his alibi is to prove he can fly."

"That's it," I tell him.

"Yes," he gloats a tiny bit.

"He flew, Dewey. He flew."

"But how?"

"I don't know, but get me to Midway Airport and I'll find out."

* * *

An hour later we are in the supervisor's office for the air traffic controllers working at Chicago's Midway Airport. Ed Lickter, the shift manager, tells us the bad news.

"There's absolutely no way for your suspect to have traveled by air at the time you gave me on the date in question," he says with certainty.

"How can you be so sure?" I ask.

"It's easy. Every time Air Force One comes to Chicago, all our butts are on the hot seat. Nothing flies in or out when the President's plane is taking off or landing, and your incident is dead center in the middle of one of those periods. I can attest that no plane or helicopter was in the airspace between Blue Island and Lemont at the time in question."

My theory crumbles. Big Bo is not Big Bird.

KNOW YOUR FOE

THE RIDE AWAY FROM MIDWAY is quiet. Dewey knows when to clam up.

My mind races across the details stamped in my memory. I'm drawing a blank.

I keep telling myself, *He did it—he even says he did.* I bang my head a couple times. *So, what am I missing? What am I missing?*

I break the silence and ask, "Dewey, where can I find Big Bo Fetzer?"

"You want to meet him?"

"I just want to eyeball the opposition in real life. His photos in the file are terrible."

Dewey glances at his watch. "This time of day he's probably holding court in some bar. Give me a couple of minutes to call around and I'll get a line on his whereabouts."

I lay back and close my eyes. I need to relax and let the case tell me what to do. I'm not into meditation.

It takes more discipline than I can muster. But on a regular basis, I flirt with my own Polish-American version of Zen. I call it Tomaszenskin'.

I focus on being unfocused. An inner voice tells me I am obsessing on the case. I answer, *I know.* It tells me to, "chill, relax, smell the roses, slow down, cool it."

I do, and I drift.

Sometime later, Dewey jabs me in the side. "Wake up, Sunshine," he says.

"I'm not a sleep," I warn him. Tomaszenskin' has not taught me how to fully suppress the surly side of my aura. "I was just doing my thinking thing."

"Coulda fooled me," he says. "You haven't stirred in a while. And you did not respond when I mentioned Fetzer's location."

"You got a line on him?"

"Yeah." The tone of his voice sinks. "He's at *The Hideout*."

"Ugh! That's not good." I express Dewey's feelings for him.

Dewey bartends at *The Hideout* and has a long-standing policy of not showing up where he works on his day off.

We ride in silence until I say, "I got a plan."

More riding. More silence.

Dewey finally asks, "You go in alone?"

"Just to peek. I order one drink, eyeball Big Bo, and leave."

"What do I do while you're playing Inspector Clouseau?"

"A slider run. You drop me, do the run, swing back to get me, and we crash at your place."

Dewey grins. "Okay," he agrees, "sounds like a plan."

"Just like the old days."

Dewey drops me off and I walk to the bar. I figure Dewey's trip to and from *White Castle* for burgers and onion rings will take twenty minutes—plenty of time for me to evaluate Big Bo Fetzer.

I enter the bar and in a couple of minutes I get what I am after.

The Hideout is almost empty. A couple of secretary types are at a high-top table nursing margaritas, gossiping, and flirting with two salesmen slurping beer and whoofing down wings. Just as Dewey predicted, Big Bo is present.

Holding court with the only other occupants of the bar, Fetzer is mountainous pile of pinkish flesh decorated with flashy clothes and jewelry. He is large, but not as imposing as I expected. Loud, boisterous, wildly gesturing, Big Bo is a big deal—especially to Big Bo.

Walking toward a vacant barstool, I experience a slight panic attack. Since giving up Old Jimmy Jack, I've been totally off alcohol. If I order a club soda in *The Hideout*, I would stick out like a turd in the punch bowl, so I take up residence down the bar from Fetzer and friends and order a draught beer. I melt into the barstool, sip my beer, and watch the show.

As I said, I get what I need. Since first examining the case file, I wondered what type of man, one with money and power, would ace his partner himself. Why take the risk in doing it yourself?

Big Bo gives me such insight and as he recounts his afternoon on the links for his audience.

"We were on the fifth fairway jawing about my ball's lie when this piece o' shit behind us calls out *again* for us to speed up our play. That's three holes in a row."

"Must have pissed you off good. Right, Bo?" one of the adoring listeners, a world-class toady, says as if on cue.

"Yeah, you could say that and more," he answers with the sort of swagger that suggests more will follow. Fetzer sips his drink and motions for the crowd to wait for his next statement. "So, I wave for this asshole to come up and talk. He does... The dumb shit." Big Bo sips again. The crowd patiently waits.

"When he gets close, just when he's about to talk, I ping a ball off his head and tell him to shut the fuck up," Big Bo finishes. "Guess what? I get no more requests to speed up play."

The crowd roars. Big Bo roars with them.

Then they all laugh, slap backs, and wait for him to reward them with another round. After another story and another round, the toady eases close and whispers something to Fetzer.

I watch them both and sense they spend a lot of time together as master and man.

Dewey was right about an accomplice, my inner voice says. It also reminds me, *it's time to go.* I down my beer, leave a tip, and slink out unnoticed—just a guy in for a quick brew on the way home.

As I leave, I look down and see something that dope-slaps me.

Boat shoes? My inner voice asks. *How often do you see boat shoes on the Southside?* Unlike other parts of the country, Chicagoland's driveways and garages are not blocked by bass boats, ski boats, personal watercraft and the like because there are not many lakes to speak of. Other than a few rivers, streams, and canals. *Wait... I think I know how he did it.*

At the pickup spot, my wait is brief.

Dewey arrives and I jump into his car to be enveloped by the all-encompassing and totally hypnotic smell of warm *White Castles*. Sliders, AKA *White Castle* hamburgers, are an acquired taste. If you liked them as a kid, you are addicted for life. There's no treatment or rehab. For a moment I forget the case.

Dewey brings me back to reality. "Did you get anything at *The Hideout*?"

"Yeah, I think so." I dig into the glove box. "You got any maps in here?"

"No. Why would I need a map? I know where I am."

"How 'bout at home?"

"Yeah, I have some there."

"Great. Sliders and sleuthing. It can't get any better."

* * *

Two If by Sea

A T Dewey's, we pile sliders and onion rings on a table next to a Triple-A map of Illinois and get to work. I point to a thin blue line representing the Cal-Sag canal that runs roughly east to west from Blue Island to Lemont and explain my idea.

Dewey chews and nods.

Between bites I ask, "What do you think? Could it work?"

Dewey disappears a slider in one gulp. "It's easy to see how the water route was overlooked. Other than an occasional barge, practically no one uses the canal anymore."

"Yeah, yeah, but could it be done?" I ask myself aloud. I use a piece of paper from the *White Castle* bag to measure the route against the scale info on the map. "Fourteen miles, give or take."

"The timeline is tight," Dewey says. "But, it could work."

"They'd have to do seventy or eighty miles an hour to cover the distance," I estimate.

"That would be one hell of a ride, especially if a barge or another boat is on the water."

"It would take at least two accomplices to pull it off. Fetzer does the shooting, he's picked up in the alley, driven to the canal by the fastest route, and is met by a second accomplice in a boat—"

"—a fast boat, a *very* fast boat." Dewey is a believer.

"One that could get to Lemont in about twelve minutes."

"Twelve?" Dewey asks.

"Yeah, if I give them a total of five minutes front and back, to get to the boat in Blue Island and from it in Lemont, they have only twelve minutes on the waterway."

"Boats are hard to come by around here and one that fast should really stick out. If we want to look, there's only one place to start."

"Where?" I ask

"*Skipper's Dockside*," he answers. "The one and only boat facility near the route."

"A marina?" My curiosity is roused. I had no idea that such a place existed on the Southside.

Dewey explains. "I wouldn't go so far as calling it a marina. *Skipper's* is more like a dock with gas pumps, a ramp, and a dump of a place masquerading as a bar and store. To get to it, you have to wind down a narrow street on the backside of Calumet Park's least desirable area."

"Behind the projects?"

"Almost. You skirt them on the way to where the Calumet River dumps into the canal. The place is surrounded by chain-link fences topped with barbed wire. *Skipper's* is definitely not a tourist destination. Its claim to fame is that it's the sole source of Down Scope."

"Down Scope? What's Down Scope?"

"Homemade poison. It's made by mixing all the white liquors together."

"Like Long Island Tea?"

"No, it's better."

"How so?"

"Skipper flavors it with some super-secret special limeade that he buys from an unknown source and then spikes with additional ingredients. The final concoction is a mystery sort of like *Coca Cola* or Colonel Sanders. No one has been able to crack the formula. People swear that it's the perfect party punch."

"They take it home, or party at *Skipper's*?"

"It's mostly for takeout."

"So, at the time, and on the date in question, someone could launch a boat from there without a lot of people noticing?"

"Yeah, I suppose so. But Skipper is pretty much there all the time."

"Let's go."

He looks at the rest of the sliders. "Like now?"

"Yeah. I'll spring for a fresh batch on the way back."

* * *

Dewey was not kidding. If you were at *Skipper's*, it was because you really wanted to be there. Along with the negatives Dewey had mentioned, was the water of the Cal-Sag Canal. Let's just say that it was not the shade of bright blue that was on the map.

It's not even remotely blue.

"Pretty nasty water," I comment, as Dewey swings us into a parking spot next to *The Lodge*.

"You should have seen it before the EPA did their thing," he jokes. "Before then it was really polluted. It's been rumored that it was so thick, Jesus learned to walk on it."

"Brown with gray foam. How nice," I say.

We get out and head for the main dilapidated building. A voice from the doorway greets us. It belongs to a withered wisp of a man somewhere between seventy and a hundred.

He says to Dewey, "Hey, General. Haven't seen you in ages." His snow-white hair hangs down to his waist in ponytails that would make Willie Nelson jealous.

"Yo, Skipper," Dewey replies.

"What chased you out here?" the old man asks.

Dewey points my way and explains, "My friend, Jake, has never tasted your stuff."

Skipper waves. "Welcome to paradise, Jake."

"Thanks, Skipper," I reply. "Glad to meet you."

Skipper addresses us. "If you boys want to buy Down Scope, you're too late. My gear is all tied up. I'm in the middle of experimenting with my hang-over medicine. Gonna call it 'Up Scope'." He starts to giggle and says, "I tell the ladies, I'm not going Down until I get it Up."

With the delivery of his joke, Skipper laughs until he starts coughing. "Fuckin' cigars," he says. "Doctor cut me down to five a day. Wants me to give up drinkin', too." He waves us toward the door. "C'mon in. I still have a little Down Scope hidden. I'll share a taste for your pal."

The inside of the building is a wonder to behold. Time stopped for it decades ago. The neon signs, mir-rors, tables, chairs, and pinball machines all look to be vintage 1950s. There is no TV anywhere.

"It true you've never tried Down Scope?" Skip-per asks me.

"Never."

"You a drinkin' man?" He has tall glasses and a large pitcher filled with green liquid, presumably Down Scope.

"Was... pretty heavy. Recently I've been on the wagon." I can smell the limeade.

Skipper eases back a step. He puts a glass on a shelf and grabs a much smaller one. He says, "I think just a little is all I'll share if you're on the wagon." He pours a couple of ounces.

I drink. "Mmmmm," I say, tasting the-not-too sweet fruity lime liquid. "This is wonderful. Tastes like a *Nehi* soda from the old days—when I was just a kid."

"The kick comes later," Dewey explains.

It does, but not as I expect.

"Smooth," I say.

"It sneaks up on you," Skipper says.

It does.

After two, maybe three ounces, I'm feeling light. I want more but know better. "It's amazing, Skipper. Tasting Down Scope is a bonus for this visit."

Skipper shares a knowing smile. "I figured you were here for something more than my juice." Pointing at Dewey, he chuckles and says, "You're not his date—not this poon-hound's type. I figure you gotta be a bartender like him, or a cop. I'd bet cop. Not Cal Park. Not Blue Island either. Odds are on something else, so I bet Chicago PD."

I tell him, "You're good."

"Thanks. It comes from bootlegging juice to everyone and anyone, including cops. Hell, I'd be broke if I didn't sell Down Scope to cops." He pours some more in a regular size glass for Dewey. "Here—you can have a real wallop."

Dewey says, "Thanks," and hands me the keys to his car. "If I down this, I'm not driving."

Skipper gets back to why we are visiting. "Tell me, Jake. You aren't here for the juice, so you dropping in must be boat related."

"Yes," I say. "I'm interested in a particular date's activity."

Skipper asks, "When that pizza guy was shot, right?"

Dewey and I are caught off guard by Skipper's frontal approach.

"Well... Yeah... Ah... Ah... Chubbie Barker's murder," I finally get out of my mouth.

"'bout time someone figured it out," he says. "That loud-mouth jerk, Fetzer, and his pals did it real slick-like... Used the canal as a superhighway."

"You knew?" Dewey asks.

"Sure," replies Skipper. "I don't miss much of anything that happens around here."

"Why didn't you say something?" I asked.

"I'm no rat," Skipper bluntly explains.

"You haven't spoken to *anyone* about it?" I ask.

"No one. I'd have answered questions... If asked properly. That's not being a rat."

"Care to talk now?" I ask.

"Sure."

"What do you know?" I ask.

"Big Bo's pals hauled a bass boat in here the day the guy was shot."

"A fishing boat?" Dewey asks.

"Yep—a fast-as-hell bass boat," Skipper explains. "Bass fishermen are crazy for speed. During tournaments they have to outrun the next guy to get to their favorite spot. A good bass boat can do over a hundred—easy. I knew those guys were up to no good when I saw their boat. It was an *Allison*."

He stops and almost runs to and from the small office behind the bar. "Here," he says, shoving a brochure at me. "Look at the cover."

I do and see an action shot of an *Allison XB-21 Pro Sport* touted with a headline as being able to 'SCREAM TO YOUR FAVORITE SPOT AT 110 MILE PER HOUR'.

"Are you certain this was the type of boat," I ask.

"One hundred percent." He points at the brochure. "They left this right here in *The Lodge*."

"And *they* are who?" I ask.

"Billy Withers and Cal Mollohan. I know them as well as any of the other folks that come here to buy Down Scope. They're a couple of losers—Fetzer's gophers." Skipper points at the boat ramp. "They put that boat in the water right there. Took it out the next day—laughing and joking about how fast they went."

"Would you swear to that?"

"Do I look like a fool?" he asks me back. Before I can reply he says, "I just fessed up to you, a Chicago cop, that I saw them. I'd be a real dumb ass to lie now about what I told you. I'll talk. It's okay this way. I'm not ratting on them. I'm just answering questions from the only cop smart enough to figure out what happened."

* * *

After that, it was still uphill. Skipper made a formal statement and with it I made my case to Emily. In light of his much dramatic previous release, she wanted an airtight case before going after Fetzer.

"Jake, your theory is sound. Your witness is excellent, and I'm on board with you all the way. But I need more to get the mud off everyone's face. Fetzer's lawyers made fools out of us. I need more than a theory and the testimony of an old bootlegger to issue an arrest warrant."

I tell her, "I signed on for two successful cases and I can deliver this one if you do two things."

"Name them," says Emily.

"I need you to come to Blue Island with me and Dewey, And, I need Eddie to go to Lemont," I tell her.

"Done, and done."

* * *

PROVE IT

DEWEY LOCATED A BOAT SIMILAR to the one Skipper said Fetzer used. Without a budget to support my investigation, I had to be creative on getting the boat dealer to allow us to abuse, I mean use, his boat. I spun a great tale about the "increased after-event market value for a watercraft used in a high-profile homicide investigation".

I am going to hell for lying, among other things.

The clincher to getting the boat at low cost was me swearing-in the dealer to secrecy about the intended use of his boat. He was impressed to be an insider.

With permission granted to use the boat and my new team members, we put into action my plan to nail Big Bo Fetzer for the murder of Chubbie Barker.

My plan was simple. As they say, "It ain't rocket science."

Here is how it plays out: I walk into *Beggar Man's* and out the back door. In the alley, Emily is waiting to drive me to the canal. We take the shortest quickest route—out the alley, left on 127th, and right on Western Avenue to Vermont Street.

So far, the trip has taken less than a minute.

At Vermont Avenue, we catch the light perfectly, turn left, and proceed to Chatham. After a right on Chatham, we travel three blocks to the blocked bridge across the canal.

At the bridge, I leave Emily's car and scurry down the bank underneath the bridge to meet Dewey in the awaiting borrowed boat.

It is there that the choice of a bass boat is made clear to me. Along with great speed, the boat has a long flat forward deck made for standing upon while fishing. This feature is perfect for getting on board when the boat is nosed up to a bank.

My jump onto the deck is quick and easy. In seconds, I am strapped into the seat next to Dewey and ready for the trip to Lemont. I do not remember what I was expecting. What I got was the most terrifying ride of my life.

I think Dewey loves speed almost as much as women. In an instant, I am slammed back into the seat with my stomach wrapped around my spine as we hit eighty miles an hour.

"Here," Dewey yells. He hands me a set of ear-phones with an attached mike. I slap them on so we can communicate. "What's our time look like?" he asks.

I extract a stopwatch from my pocket, look at it, and report. "We have ten-and-a-half minutes to remain on schedule."

"No problem," he says, as he pushes throttle to
its maximum. With another, albeit lesser, surge we
accelerate to the craft's top speed of one hundred
plus.

"Thank God there's no traffic," I yell. My appreciation to God is well placed. The banks of the canal
are made of ten- to fifteen-foot-high concrete walls.
At our speed, flying inches above the water, should
we encounter any other boats, a barge, or debris, we
are toast.

I remember playing the role of spotter and
attempting to chat with Dewey as we flew across the
canal's surface, but to be honest, the remainder of
the ride is a blur. In just under ten minutes Dewey
calmly proclaims, "We're here," when he slows for
our approach to Canal Street in Lemont.

I check the stopwatch and smile. "We can do
this," I tell him.

Dewey points at the open spot of quasi-shoreline
and says, "There's Eddie."

I wave to Eddie, my pickup man, as Dewey nuz-
zles the boat up to the tiny bank.

It is clear again to me why Fetzer picked this
type of craft. The flat deck indeed proves to be a perfect platform for jumping on *and off*. I step off the
Allison and scamper up the slanted concrete bank.

Eddie's car is my ride for the three blocks to the
bar. All I need is light traffic in Lemont if I am going
to beat the clock.

"How's the time?" Eddie asks.

"Close," I say, "real close."

He revs the engine, gets us moving, and we cover the three blocks in less than a minute.

At the bar, I get out, walk as normal as possible into the entryway camera's field of vision, and extract the stopwatch from my pocket.

"Yes." I almost shout when I see the time. "Sixteen minutes, forty-two seconds."

Jennifer, the hostess Dewey flirted with during our earlier visit, sees me at the entrance and gives me a wave. *Maybe Dewey made a good impression on her.* She bounds over to me and says, "Hi. Where's your friend?"

He *did* impress her. Whatever is in Dewey's genes, it's magical.

I respond with, "Hi, Jennifer. I'd love to talk and would even get a charge out of sharing with you all the tales I could about Dewey." I flash my badge. "He's a great guy for a recently released sex offender with a manageable drug problem. A young girlfriend is just what he needs. I'll bet—" She instantly disappears.

I need Dewey and justify my actions by knowing he'll never sleep alone. Besides, Jennifer is way too young for him. She seems like a nice girl.

Back at the curb, I climb into Eddie's car. "Did you have a chance to scope out the location of any camera that might help us," I ask him.

"I saw six along our route," he reports.

"Good. Get the names of the businesses who own them and I'll have Emily prepare warrants. If what I think is on them, Big Bo will be doing big time."

* * *

Two days later, I'm with Eddie, Dewey, and Emily in a conference room down the hall from her office. Eddie is set up to show us the videos he pulled from the Lemont businesses.

"Two of the cameras produced nothing we can use. Two more had images of Fetzer, but the time-and-date stamps were corrupted. One had a rear shot of him, no face, but it can be used if we match his shoes and clothing," Eddie explains. He flashes a slight grin.

"Match it to what?" I ask, knowing that this is his moment. He is going to deliver the goods.

Eddie's grin expands as he reveals the evidence. "This," he says as he brings up an image. "We have a camera that got it all. An ATM aimed at the exact spot where Fetzer comes up and over the canal's bank. We've got a clear picture of him following the water route you and Dewey proved is possible—at the time you predicted. The photo's time and date stamp is verified and indisputable."

"You got him, Jake," Emily says. "Congratulations."

"Thanks, but it was a team effort. I'm still woozy from the thrill ride Dewey piloted. And, without Eddie's keen eye, we'd never have found the photo."

Emily smiles and stands a bit closer to Eddie. The connection between the two is evident and for a split second, I am filled with an immensely good feeling for bringing them together, even if their ages are off a bit. In the midst of wallowing in the negative backwash of Fetzer's greed and brutality, some good was accomplished.

Flowers from compost and mushrooms from decay, is the thought that bounces inside my cranium in Marissa's voice. For a moment I am in another time and space. *It must be the after effects of Down Scope,* I tell myself and smile.

"Jake, are you alright?" asks Emily.

I come back from Neverland and say, "Yeah, yeah. I heard a ghost and saw the synchronicity of the universe in play—that's all."

THE 19TH HOLE

THE CROSSWORD HAS ME STUMPED, but I don't care. The Cubs hold fourth place in a five-team divisional race, and I'm not concerned. The life I so often fretted over, the one of lost opportunities, and unmet potential, does not weigh upon me. After a couple of sub-par rounds, I am in my clubhouse, content and subdued.

Earline slides into the booth. This time she is next to me, not across.

I am okay with that, too. Her closeness is not a threat. I am at peace for the first time in recent memory.

"I understand that Jimmie wants his storeroom back," she says.

I chuckle. "He mentioned it at six this morning when he woke me up."

"Subtle move," she says. "How did you take it?"

"It's time for me to move out."

She presses my hand in a simple thoughtful gesture. "My offer still stands."

"Thanks." I press back. "I may take you up on it... For a short stay... In the spare room only." I look directly at her to check her reaction.

"Jake, that's okay." She is calm. "I'm not going to push you on our relationship."

"I prefer *friendship* over *relationship*," I say.

"Whatever." She slides out of the booth, does a quick to and fro from the coffee stand, and returns with what appears to be a scrapbook.

"What is that?" I ask.

"My Jake Book," she says opening it. "First, I *am* your friend. And second, I am your greatest fan. Anything else that may or may not develop between us will be a bonus."

I point to the scrapbook. "*That* is your *Jake Book*?"

"Yes. My collection of news articles recounting your exploits... Accompanied by additional information and my personal reflections."

"I am dumbfounded," I reply.

"Why?"

It takes me a long moment to collect my thoughts. "Why? My exploits? You must be joking. I'm a professional failure. AIU is the end of the end of the road. I—"

She cuts me off.

"Jake, everyone knows AIU isn't much to speak of. But you've solved some amazing cases." She flips to the end of the scrapbook and says, "Look right here." She points at articles for my last cases, the ones I did for Emily. "Two front pagers in the *Trib*."

I am aware of them.

I comment, "Thanks, Earline. But they barely mention my role in either of them. Eddie and Emily got the print, and rightly so. They were her cases and Eddie was a key player in making them stick."

She strongly disagrees. "Bull Hockey! I know you put him in those two cases, and I know why." She smiles and waves a finger at me. "Jake, I know more about you, these cases, and Eddie than you can imagine."

"Eddie? What do you know about Eddie?"

"He's a nice kid. Eddie's a lot deeper than those bland good looks belie, and he's a little young for Emily. But I'm good with that because she's a little young for you. She and Eddie make an interesting pair."

"How so?"

She smiles. "Their positions in life, before and after. You know. One day, cat and mouse, fox and hound. Then the next, they are the city's crime fighting dynamic duo. Two peas in a pod."

"What are you driving at?"

"Jake, I read lips. Also, I eavesdrop on conversations and read letters upside down."

"That is called *snooping*."

She shrugs. "I call it an occupational asset. I use it to anticipate people's needs. It sure helps with the tips. And, if I was in your line of work no one would care."

"Point taken."

"If that's an apology, I accept."

"Good. Now, let's get back to where we were. Care to share something *specific*?" I'm not letting it go. "What do you think you know about Eddie?"

"He is... Or, more correctly, was Duct Man."

"Damn, Earline. You're fantastic."

"No, Jake. You're the one to admire."

"Me? What did I do?"

She taps the scrapbook. "Jake, you solved two blockbuster cases and let others take the credit."

"And, I did this for what reason?"

"Payback. You wanted Emily to protect Eddie and his friends."

"His friends? What friends?"

"Duct Man's Posse."

She knows a lot more than I ever gave her credit for, I tell myself. "Why would I do that?"

"Justice."

"Justice?"

"Yes. You are one half-soiled white knight in dented armor crossed with a modern-day Don Quixote. And you are as much a vigilante as Duct Man."

"Really?"

"Don't play dumb, Jake." I have eight *Trib* articles that pertain to the eradication of the drug business in a section of the Southside within a one-mile radius of where Eddie lives."

"And?"

"*And I connected the dots.* Eddie and his friends provided exact and specific information that was used to wipe out the local drug trade. Their meticulously gathered information put the gangs out of business and disclosed the identities of crooked cops. However, there was one loose string—an overzealous father.

"The distraught dad decided that a car's fender made a good weapon and brought the heat down on them all. Eddie felt responsible for the whole mess and came to you for help. You, the friend that you are, got Emily to cover for all of them—Eddie, the misguided locals who were inspired by Duct Man's legend, and even the dad. You were sympathetic to their cause and bailed them out."

"Earline, your skills as a detective are phenomenal. You are indeed unbelievable."

"Thank you, Jake. But, if I am so unbelievable, why are you forever stalling on moving into my place? I can handle an arrangement... Even if you are in the spare room... For starters."

"Earline, it's exactly because you are so unbelievable that I am declining your offer."

"That's your reason?"

"Yes. No man can live with a woman possessing your observational skills. It's an oil and water sort of thing. Earline, we are tremendous friends here at *Jimmie's*, but I'd be as nervous as a squirrel sitting under the watchful eye of an eagle living in the same space as you."

"Sounds more like you're a coward."

"That, too."

1728 North Sedgwick

So here is what happened. I moved, Jimmie got his storeroom back, and Earline was disappointed. Everyone who knows me was surprised at where I landed. For the first time in my life, beyond college and a stint in the Army, I am not living on the Southside.

Perhaps I am a coward, and I was just running away from having a relationship with Earline outside of the safety of *Jimmie's Diner*. Or it could be that the location of my new digs is a desperate and complex statement about my failed career.

Maybe it is simple rebellion. In any event, right when everything in the universe was pointing me in one direction, I went the other way.

Again, my choice of location did take everyone by surprise, including me.

Where did I go?

I moved to Old Town and rented the apartment that Jeremy Westlawn, the artist-turned-criminal turned-artist, used as his studio for so many years at 1728 North Sedgewick.

Now the center of my universe is north of the loop, and I am experiencing a wave of small behavior changes that are liberating, even for an anti-establishment type like me.

I live simply. I do not own a television or a tie. For entertainment, I read or listen to WGN 720 AM— mostly the Rollye James Show.

On Monday nights, Dewey and I leave our phones on speaker and play trivia along with Rollye and her guests. For fun, we nickel-and-dime bet against each other to make it more meaningful.

I only wear socks in cold weather and my phone is in the fridge when I am not betting on trivia or on the clock.

Speaking of which, I am still on the force and in the same status. The police union is using me as a negotiating piece in some weird strategy that boggles the mind.

So, yes, I remain in limbo.

However, I have not been abandoned.

For her stellar support of the blackmailing bust, the higher-ups rewarded Mildred with just a letter of commendation. She is as much a prisoner of the professional wasteland known as AIU as I am.

The one good element in Mildred's plight is that she has abandoned any idea of holding me down. She has cut me loose and I am able to freelance on the cases my friends bring me, or I am able to uncover on my own.

Hopefully, there will be more about that later. Wherever you go, there you are.

* * *

HIDING IN PLAIN SIGHT

O PTIMISM COATS ME LIKE FRESH powder on a baby's butt. And as I finish my third month of abstinence, I gotta admit sobriety has its benefits. For instance, I start my days with a clear head. Without the day-after head-slamming pain brought on by Old Jimmy Jack, I can appreciate the atmosphere of *Jimmie's Diner* with a peaceful clarity that even the Dali Lama would envy.

Right now, all of God's Children who are fortunate enough to live in Chicago would agree that I, Jake Thompson, once a lowly booze-soaked public servant, am now the much-improved 2.0 version of my previously scorned and ridiculed self.

Without the tri-blend of *Old Grand Dad*, *Jim Beam*, and *Jack Daniels* coursing through my veins I am able to get past—no, get way beyond being a guilt-ridden, middle-aged, going-nowhere grump.

Today, I can and do proclaim that, "Life is good."

And to prove the point, Earline, my personal choice for the Best Waitress in the Universe Award, speaks for the all the happy people of the Windy City when she smiles and lovingly asks, "More coffee, Jake?"

In sync with my mood, I kindly reply. Instead of countering with a customary dig about the brew's unique oily nature, I near-whisper in my best Dali Lama voice, "No, thank you."

Earline smiles again and pats my head lightly as if it actually is an infant's bottom. I smile like Buddha himself and break off a piece of the day's positive energy and project it toward her. It is an effort in my subtle scheme to end her quest—a chess move in our mind game to maintain versus alter the status quo.

Earline is focused on getting me to move in with her. I've been resisting.

I like things the way they are—she living in her condo and me at my new digs in Old Town. I don't think it's working.

You decide.

She says, "Jake Thompson, I swear. *You really are something.*" Her tone fails to mask the underlying intent, which is to ensnare my ass in more than conversation. I know what she wants. It involves me, her, the future, and a ring.

Domestication is not for me. I play dumb. "Me?" I reply. "I'm something? How so?"

"You know—polite, alert, clear-eyed, and *still sober.*"

"Yeah—well, it's all in the vegetation."

"Vegetation?"

"I've turned over a new leaf."

"Cute," says she, "...very cute." Which means it definitely is not.

"Aw shucks, ma'am," I weakly joke. "I've never actually been called *cute* before."

"No, no, Jake. It's more than you just *being cute.* It's sincerely *nice.* Please, keep it up."

"Will do, ma'am, will do." I try to play the fool some more.

She remains serious. "You've been so good as of late... I just might re-instate my offer." Her look is full of longing, promises, and desire.

If not cooked, I am feeling the heat.

"Huh—what do you mean?" I keep playing the fool with the hope to aim her away from bringing up her offer again and again. I stare at my coffee cup for dramatic emphasis, and as an escape say, "I'm okay on the coffee."

Earline slaps the back of my head and says loud enough for the residents of Milwaukee to hear, "Just when I thought you were capable of changing—there you go again—being difficult."

I know the slap was more than in fun. In yet another attempt to sidestep her offer, I say, "I suppose I will have some more of *Jimmie's* gourmet coffee."

I am slapped again. This time for real.

She hisses, "Damn it, Jake. You aren't the least bit funny."

I'm in trouble. I know it. I try to head off an incident. "Sorry... Really."

She is not buying my excuse, and soon I hear an elongated sigh woven within a message that is meant as much for everyone in earshot as it is for me. In a plain serious voice she says, "Jake, I've had an offer—"

I cut her off. "Chicago real estate is way up—by all means, sell your condo."

"I was talking about something much more serious... A matter that... That.... Means so much." She sniffles. "And all you want to do is... Is... Is... *whaaaaaaaaaaaa*!" She bolts for the waitress cubby.

Regular customers, as well as total strangers, give me the stink eye. For within the cubby's confines, her sobs and moans travel out to where all can hear. I get eye-screwed some more. Then, I am ignored. Except by Jimmie, the diner's owner.

From his elevated perch behind the register. Jimmie normally sits like the guru on a mountain. From there he dispenses his views on life amongst us mere mortals. His banter, known as Jimmie Jabber, is the diner's unassailable gold standard of truth.

I look to him for my judgment and he immediately lets me know how bad I blew it. Jimmie places a finger next to his temple and mimes sending an invisible slug through his brain.

His act cracks me up.

I emit a laugh-snort and piss everyone off more. The result is that I get another dose of stink eye, as the positive vibe I was just boasting about moments before is expelled from the diner like spent air from a punctured balloon.

A kid's balloon and I'm the Grinch adult with the needle.

If I have learned anything in life, I know when I've "screwed the pooch." I exit the diner and head to AIU, a place where I can be ignored and hide.

* * *

I was premature in my wish.

Mildred greets me as soon as I open the door. I immediately know something is up.

"Hey, Sunshine," says my lying-in-wait boss. She has a smile on her face.

It puts me on my guard. No—on my Super Guard.

"Hey, yourself," I counter. "What's up with the reception? You being here waiting can only mean one of two things. Either, I'm in the doghouse, or I'm in the doghouse's outhouse."

"The trouble with you, Jake, is that you have no faith," She replies, while fingering an envelope with way too much care.

I go into Ultimate Super Guard and eye the envelope as if it is Kryptonite.

Her eyes watch mine, and she says, "This is our ticket out of here, Jake. I think we need to have a chat."

I eyeball the envelope, hoping to see its return address. No luck. Mildred is clutching it like Gollum does the ring. I'm boxed in.

"Okay," I say. "I'm up for a talk."

* * *

When Mildred said, "chat", I envisioned her sitting behind her desk with me camped out in the hot seat in front. I was miles off on what she meant. A half-hour later she, I, and a bunch of Chicago PD Higher Ups, were in a posh conference room at the Department HQ. I'd heard rumors about the place, but never paid them much mind.

Now, I am in that mythical room's seat of honor being chummed-up by more police brass and police union leaders than I ever thought existed.

The gist of it all becomes clear when I shake off all the glad-handling BS and go into my South-side inner-self. In short, I ask myself, *What do these phony assholes want?*

I draw a blank.

No—I am overwhelmed.

The amount and level of two-faced schmoozing—all aimed at me—prevent me thinking. Toothy-grinned faces come and go. My back is slapped. My hand is pumped. No one actually speaks directly to me—as in having a real conversation. All I hear is snippets floating about the room.

"Special situations", "public relations initiative", "media awareness", "narrative control", "that unfortunate snafu", "union demands" drift in and out of conversations near me. Mildred cruises about, smiling, soaking it all in, clutching the envelope as if it is priceless.

No one is in charge—everyone is in charge. It is surreal.

Then, a moment of silence. The mayor's head pops through the doorway.

"I see it it's all going nicely. Great job, all." The mayor disappears in an instant—the seal of approval given. The buzz resumes. More snippets. Then, suddenly the sounds fade and the room clears. The final occupants left in the room are Mildred, Gary Winder, the union head, and me.

"What the hell happened?" I ask them.

Mildred, flashes the envelope. "*This* she said. *This* is what happened."

"Care to *share it?*" I ask, mustering as much indignation as my befuddled mind can produce.

"Here—read it."

I grab and open the envelope. Inside is the briefest of letters—appointing Mildred as the OIC of Chicago PD's newly created Special Investigations Unit. It is signed by the mayor, the department's chief, and the union CEO.

"It's the ticket out of AIU," Mildred says with a huge smile. She motions both arms about the empty room. "And all this—is 'what the hell it was about.' SIU is just what the name implics. A team set up to

handle *special cases*—the ones too hot to handle—
the PR nightmares, the political bombshells. Jake,
after the Smollett shitstorm, the decision was made
to create a *special* unit to handle the really tough
important cases—and it is *mine*." She looks at me as
if she were a kid with a new puppy. "I'm out, Jake,
I'm out of AIU. And—with a promotion."

"Mildred, I'm glad for you—really am. But I'm
still in the dark," I state. "What is this new unit to
me?"

Gary steps in. "It's your new home, too."

"*What*!?"

Gary produces a second letter. "Here, Jake. This
is for you. It's a post-dated guarantee for your retirement—no strings. All you have to do is be part of the
new unit... for a year."

"A *year*?" I feel as if I have been cut off at my
knees. "You guys—the union—you're supposed to be
on my side."

I *was* retired. They hauled me back in. It's all
payback, set up by Chicago's most powerful woman—
who is now dead as can be, but obviously still pulling
strings from the grave. And still—with all that crap
over me—I did my job. No—I performed a miracle. I
wiped the stink off of AIU."

There is a pause. I end it with a near whimper,
"And you guys promised to sort out my retirement."

"And, Jake—we *did*," Gary finally said. "But
the union had other demands, issues, needs—clearing
your retirement mess was just one of them. The city's
powers-that-be were stonewalling us on everything.

They needed a way out of the constant media scrutiny that was killing their image. The new unit was their idea. And your recent success was, in the city's thinking, a way for all of us to get something."

"That's all well and good," I say, "but *exactly* how do I figure in this?"

"You were our bargaining chip. The city negotiators said they'd give into our requests—including your pension—if you'd just be part of the new unit. It's only for a year, Jake."

"Great. Just *great*," I mutter in disgust, as I threw up my hands. "They didn't really want me for the unit. They have no intention of honoring their deal. They just want a place I can't escape handling their next fiasco, ala-Smollett. They'll toss it on me, I'll take the heat, they'll dig up my reputation, and everyone—the media, outraged citizens, advocacy groups, the whole shebang—will be crying for my head." I look at Mildred, and add, "You think this new unit is a good thing, but it isn't. It's just AIU on steroids."

Mildred immediately counters, "Jake, you're paranoid... And your ego is in overdrive." She waves her appointment letter at me. "This *will* work. Trust me, Jake. You just have to *trust me*."

I blankly stare at the two of them as a wave of helplessness washes over me.

The last time I was so demoralized, Gino was crippled, a girl died, and I was publicly pegged a racist-knuckle-dragging monster. The post-dated letter said it all.

I am painted into a corner—trapped in a maze with no exit.

I am going to be eaten alive.

Or maybe not.

I'll just have to survive *one* year.

* * *

My first inclination is to leap off the wagon and drown my sorrows in a liberal bath of Old Jimmy Jack. But, I resist. Somehow, I know in my bones the real demons I am fighting will rely on my past behavior.

I am smarter than before. I do not take the bait of booze.

Immediately, every lever and gear is pulled to meet the goal of completing the establishment of the Special Investigations Unit. The mayor, the Chief of Police, union brass, and Mildred preen and pose for the media.

The official announcement is TV fodder of the first order. It is so big and self-absorbed no one notices my passive-aggressive participation. In every photo-op, I am in the rear—a shadow, an unfocused inhabitant of the back row.

Once we, Chicago's latest Dream Team, were physically ensconced in our new digs, at a slightly better decorated and equally obscure location, I dig in and assume a psychological demeanor for my approach to my new, and potentially dangerous, position. I become a modern Bartleby.

If you are not familiar with Melville's tale of Bartleby the Scrivener, I suggest it as the ultimate guide to noncompliance through passive resistance. Briefly, whenever asked to perform a task, Bartleby simply responded with, "I prefer not to." He did so without rancor or indication of a threat, violence, or even disagreeableness. Basically, he stonewalled everything associated with his job.

Taking Bartleby as my example, and adding in some of my own spices, I pull in my extremities, become a human-turtle, and retreat into my shell. Malingering is an art, and the key to its success is to become the benign victim of everything while remaining non-confrontational, amiable, and pleasant.

It works even better when you are invisible.

In decades of service, I never used such benefits as ploys to avoid the work I loved. When chasing down the bad guys, I always was Johnny on the spot. As a workaholic, I cannot count the number of stake-outs I endured with colds, flu, and the like. Fortified with bureaucratic tools—my considerable cache of sick leave, personal days, comp-time, and holidays—I became a myth, a wisp of a spirit, a rumor.

Having a boss like Mildred made it easy for me to coast through more than eight months of professional hide-and-seek. With the zealous faith of a True Believer, she embraced every opportunity to take the lead on a case, no matter how trivial, to demonstrate her support for our group's mission. Fortunately, nothing serious popped up on the city's radar.

Imagine, the Land of Oz really existed—Chicago was scandal free, and with slightly more than three months to go, I could see the light at the end of the tunnel. But I soberly knew it could not—would not—last.

When I ran out of days the system allotted me, I evoke the spirit of Bartleby even more diligently. I become the poster child for cordial passive resistance—and I do it with a sense of humor.

As the Great Lao-Tsu said: "It is only when you see a mosquito landing on your testicles that you come to realize that there can be value in solving problems without using violence."

I know such a statement is frivolous and jokey. But sometimes a joke, no matter how bad or good, holds the sort of wisdom ordinary guys like me will absorb, maybe think about, maybe do something about. Without booze to clog my mind, I've been pondering the notion of violence—that form of action which lurks in the shadows of my past.

When you take someone's life, two people die. The person you just killed and the human being you used to be. You're never the same after that—it changes you forever and not in a good way. No matter how hard you try, you can't go back to the innocence you had—never.

Avoiding the game being played on me by the "powers that be" is one thing—dealing with killing that girl is another—and maybe the first is the Justice of the Universe paying me back for the second. I am at an all-important point in life and I tell myself, "Jake, it's time to grow up, face the music. Be a *real* asset in the game of life—stop fooling around on the sidelines."

So, what did I do?

Nothing.

But I did it on purpose.

I went all Zen-like, assuming the role of the ready pupil, calmly waiting for my teacher to appear. I continued my routines, avoiding work, hanging out at *Jimmie's*, listening to Rollye on WGN radio, scanning the *Trib*, and pokey-joking with Earline to kept her at a safe distance. Basically, I actively tried to *not* change myself, my surroundings, and most importantly the world. I became a Non-Participating Character in the video game called *My Life*. Without plan or purpose, I waited. And waited. And waited some more.

So, what happened?

For a while—just like me—the world did nothing. It and I were in perfect synchronicity. I was simultaneously trapped and yet free. Not so much as held within, as not minding that I was there. In peacefulness, I did not proceed or retreat—I simply was.

Then it happened. It came out of nowhere.

Actually, it wasn't from nowhere. It was in the *Trib*—which, if you know anything about declining newspaper readership, is almost as good as nowhere. But regardless, the sad situation, me, the *Trib,* and *Jimmie's* brew are still the Second Holy Trinity. Let me tell you about it.

When it comes to newspapers, I agree with the insight once stated in *The Nation* magazine:

THE *WALL STREET JOURNAL* IS READ BY THE PEOPLE WHO RUN THE COUNTRY. THE *NEW YORK TIMES* IS READ BY PEOPLE WHO THINK THEY RUN THE COUNTRY. THE *WASHINGTON POST* IS READ

BY PEOPLE WHO THINK THEY OUGHT TO RUN THE
COUNTRY. *USA TODAY* IS READ BY PEOPLE WHO
THINK THEY OUGHT TO RUN THE COUNTRY BUT
DON'T UNDERSTAND THE *WASHINGTON POST*.
THE *LOS ANGELES TIMES* IS READ BY PEOPLE
WHO WOULDN'T MIND RUNNING THE COUNTRY
IF THEY COULD SPARE THE TIME. THE *BOSTON
GLOBE* IS READ BY PEOPLE WHOSE PARENTS USED
TO RUN THE COUNTRY.

Then there are people who read the *Trib*. They
know that whatever the residents of flyover country
care about doesn't count to the staffs of those papers.
So, *Trib* readers tend to fixate on sports. They whine
about the Cubs, talk all the time about the Bears, root
for The Blackhawks, and dream about Michael Jor-
dan's glory days with the Bulls.

It's no big leap to figure that I read the *Trib*.
Well, most of it—sometimes.

After the sports page, my interest tends to wear
thin. And I admit that I seldom get to the arts section.
But one day I lazy-eyed that section's front page and
my Zen time was over. Up to then, I knew nothing
about Caravaggio, the Italian master. After eyeballing
the lead story's photo, I learned a lot, and everything
changed.

In a nutshell, Caravaggio was—no, *is*—one of
painting's most important figures. Loved and hated by
his peers, doomed to almost two centuries of obscu-
rity, he is now considered one of the most important
painters ever. Best known for being "the master of
light". Renowned for using real models in contempo-
rary dress, prone to depict Biblical stories as visceral
and bloody dramas taking place in the present day
(the late 1500s and early 1600s).

Caravaggio is known for his works of genius such as *Sick Bacchus, The Musicians, Head of the Medusa, The Conversion of St. Paul, The Entombment of Christ,* and *The Beheading of St. John.*

He is also known for having to flee Rome in 1606, after killing a man during a brawl sparked by a dispute over a game of tennis. And that is the reason *The Betrayal of Christ* will perhaps become his best-known work—all due to the earth-shattering news of the discovery that that masterpiece has a second version—one in which Caravaggio used his own guilty murderous face as that of Judas. Smaller than his usual works, deeply personal, intense, rumored to have been kept for himself, never seen during his lifetime, sequestered, and lost. It's the stuff of legends.

By chance, the clone painting was found at a villa near Naples, mounted behind a peer's lesser-known work, *Saint Agatha,* by Massimo Stanzione. It was being prepared for auction when an inspecting curator noticed what appeared to be an irregularity with *Saint Agatha's* frame. Upon closer examination, the Caravaggio was discovered.

Interesting, I know, but all that I've just shared is the backstory I learned later.

What got my attention was the photo, taken from behind. It showed an audience observing the painting—no, the two works—pointing at the newly discovered Caravaggio.

The hand, its position, its angle, its use of *two* fingers to point—it was so familiar to me. It was *her* hand—Miriam's. It was the hand of that beautiful redheaded crook. The one who got away.

If she is there, it's some sort of scam and I'd bet anything the Caravaggio is a fake.

"Damn, damn, damn," I mutter, as I bounced between giddy elation and a peculiar apprehension. I know Round Two of my time in the world of art fraud is about to begin. Zen-time is over. I need to get off my butt.

"I want in on this—I want in."

* * *

Nobody appreciates uninvited strangers stepping onto their turf. That goes double for cops. And what I have in mind was an enormous international butt-in. But all I can hear is Miriam's voice telling me her creed, "I live in a world where nothing has value, but everything has a price."

That confession taught me, one-hundred percent certain, that she is up to no good.

I tell myself, *Personal feelings aside, if they like it or not, it's my duty to help my Italian colleagues. There is a dangerous woman in their midst, and I have had first-hand experience with her involvement in art scams. I'm a cop and she must be stopped.*

Looking back, it was so natural. And in my mind—oh, so right. All I had to do was alert the Italians and get an invite to the party.

Once pointed toward my goal, I am a whirlwind of activity. My first move is to inform my boss I am no longer on the sidelines. Mildred is not impressed. Definitely hesitant, I'd say—like turning blue mad.

"You're crazy, Jake. Absolutely crazy. After months of laying out—lolly gagging, dilly dallying, stone walling—you think you can just waltz in here and *simply announce* you are about to 'solve an international crime of *huge* importance' and you want my okay? You are *wrong*. No. Beyond wrong—way beyond. Plus, you want me to pay your travel costs? For a vacation, is what it really is. Crazy, arrogant, self-serving." She stops to breathe.

"Now, listen—" I attempt to interject.

She shuts me up. "No. No! NO!!"

"But—"

"No." She holds tough.

"Just—"

"NO! When I needed you, you were a ghost. Now, *get out*." She points to the door. "And I mean *all* the way out."

I hate to admit it, but I did as I was told.

Previously, in times like this, I would have surrendered to the quick fix—a bout with Old Jimmy Jack. However, the new me rebounds without the aid of alcohol. I lick my wounds and justly chastise myself.

A slinky has more backbone, observes my inner-self. Ashamed, I put on my thinking cap and examine my assets. *Where there is a will—there is a way,* I tell myself. *What you need is a little help from a friend—a crusty Scot.*

* * *

The phone is answered on twelfth ring. "Ye are a persistent bastard. Ye better have a bonnie reason to disturb me," is the greeting.

"Sorry, Jimmy, forgot about the time change." I am sincerely embarrassed. My skewed sense of urgency had seriously muddled my brain.

I totally forgot Jimmy had retired to Italy, and I called him thinking on Hong Kong time, twelve hours—totally opposite. I should have been thinking seven hours for Rome.

"I'm *really* sorry."

"Jake, me lad. No bother—just got home. In fact, I was just about to open that fine bottle of *Jura* that ye gifted me upon retirement."

"How is retirement? Is life on the sunny hills of Italy all you dreamt it would be?"

"Nay, Jake, nay. I've had nary a week's peace this past year. In fact, I'm off early tomorrow for a lecture stint in Berlin where somehow me kidnap reputation has impressed someone."

"Before you go, do you have time for a favor?" I say with the tiniest hint of a beg.

"Jake, ye should know better. Anything for ye—ask away," is his sincere reply.

A wave of embarrassment sweeps over me and is immediately replaced by the warm glow of love based on friendship. It is a good feeling.

"Know anyone involved with protecting the Caravaggio just found near Naples?" I ask.

"Nay, but Ciro Motta will know."

"Who's he?"

"The finest member of our profession in all of Italy. And, Naples is his patch. I'll connect him with ye." After the shortest of pauses, "Nay, I'll have him call ye as soon as possible. Knowing ye, this is an emergency."

"Jimmy, you are a saint."

Following a laugh, I hear, "Ye must tell that to Saint Peter as a diversion when I sneak in the gate. But for now, I want a nightcap before bed. I have an early fight in the morn'."

"Understood."

"G'night, Jake—I'm certain one of ye will share the details."

"It'll be me—*and in person.*"

* * *

Jimmy makes good on his word. Naples' Chief of Detectives, Ciro Motta, calls me within hours. Something more than the speed of the call hits me. It is his accent, or rather the lack of one that surprises me.

Later, after spending time with Ciro, I learned that his being truly bi-lingual was due to living in the USA for more than a decade early in his life. His parents gave it a try, but their love for the ways and customs of their homeland wooed the family back to Naples and Ciro's Mid-Atlantic pronunciation of English never left him.

The call went like this:

"Detective Thompson?"

"Yes."

"This is Chief of Detectives Ciro Motta calling from Naples. Our mutual friend, James McIlveen strongly suggested that I contact you immediately."

"Thank you for calling. Jimmy said you would be my best source for information concerning the recently discovered Caravaggio painting. Is he correct?"

"Perhaps. I *am* aware of the painting, but to my knowledge there—" I cut him off.

"Detective Motta—that painting is a fraud. I am certain of it. And, I have direct experience with a key player whom I believe is involved."

"Based on James' opinion of your ability, I would be most interested in hearing your—"

I immediately jumped in, "Good. Miriam Poteet was photographed examining the Caravaggio—and if she is in any way involved, there is a fraud at hand." Almost frantic, I added, "I'll be there as soon as possible."

"But—"

Again, I cut him off, "I'm on the next available flight. I'll get the details to you very soon."

That was it.

Soon, I was headed to O'Hare immersed in my quest to thwart the *they* who were out to get me. In a fog of naïve optimism, all in my head was focused upon the belief that I would run out the clock, throw a Hail Mary, toss up the game winning three-pointer, and slide home beating their tag. I was certain I would win.

So much for dreams.

Just before boarding, I check my phone for messages—three missed—all from my favorite waitress.

She'll have to wait, I think.

* * *

In Rome, I ooze impatience toward the customs and immigration staff, dash to a connecting puddle-jumper flight, and arrive in Naples still hyped for combat, never thinking that I was anything but totally fulfilling a righteous quest.

At the Naples airport, I am greeted by Ciro Motta himself.

"Jake, our mutual friend described you to a tee," he says in perfect English.

I am still set back a bit by his American accent when speaking English.

I pump his offered hand, and say, "Greetings, Ciro. Thank you for meeting me here upon arrival. I caught a bit of New Jersey in your speech—maybe the Shore?" I offer.

"Remarkable—I was raised in Ocean City. Jimmy told me you had exceptional observational skills. But I admit, I was not ready for them to be that good. I envy your gift."

It is at this point in our meeting that I push ahead my thesis. "My entire reason for being here is based upon experience and what I have observed. I am one-hundred percent certain that the Caravaggio painting is the key to a tremendous art fraud."

Looking back on that meeting, I am startled at my then inability to read any clue. My self-righteous energy allowed no other thought into my mind. I was so full of myself. Embarrassing.

"Detective Thompson. I think you'll find that—" Ciro attempts his best to enlighten me with important information. I have none of it.

"Miriam Poteet is a bad customer—the worst double-dealing fraudster you can imagine."

"I think—"

I blow him off again. "If she's around, we need to find her, and arrest her conniving ass." I am on a quest, and Ciro steps aside.

He is much smarter than I am willing to accept. Strike one for fate.

My second swing and miss comes quite soon.

Ciro, to my delight, says, "Then, let's get to the heart of your theory right away."

"What are you suggesting?" I ask.

"We go immediately to Count di'Nola."

"Who is he?"

"A *nobiluomo*—a minor member of the Pignatelli family. He and his wife, the Contessa, are the owners of the paintings in question."

"Any chance that he may be involved in the scam?"

"Perhaps—perhaps not." Ciro flashes a slight ironic smile.

"Then—let's find out."

"Most certainly we will—we will *indeed*."

As I add, "Drive on," Ciro's smile increases.

* * *

The drive is short and fast. We speed Italian grand-prix style into the country and I cannot recall how many idyllic estates we pass. After I lose count of the vineyards, olive groves, and fields we turn onto a narrow drive aimed at a villa so old that it could have been owned by a retired centurion.

"Nice digs," I observe aloud. "If this is how the minor nobles live, I'd like to see where the major ones bunk."

Ciro laughs and informs me that, "The Count lives well. He has mainly business interests."

"So, he's known to you?"

"Oh, yes."

And again, there is that smile.

As we approach the main building, it is apparent that some sort of festivities are being planned. Service vehicles and several media vans encircle a large tent.

"Any idea what's up?" I ask.

"Tonight is the pre-auction revealing of both paintings. I admit it is a contributing reason for my decision to come immediately here upon your arrival. You can 'see the goods' as they say, and you can meet the paintings' owners."

"Smart," I comment.

We park the car and walk to the front door of the villa, where we are greeted by a stout middle-aged woman who gives the distinct impression that she runs the estate. Her air is kind and warm, but it is certain that she is the person in control of all activities of importance. She does not introduce herself, nor does Ciro make any pleasantries as we are directed into what appears to be a study and are told, "Chief Detective... The master shares his regrets he cannot greet you now, as he is immersed in details for tonight's event. However, the Contessa will be with you soon."

Ciro is unaffected and I quietly follow his lead. It gives me an opportunity to survey our surroundings, which drips of the sort of wealth that tells you not only do the owners know and appreciate art—they live their lives within it.

Modern, old, *avant-garde*, it makes no difference. There is a lot of it and it all fits. The space is warm and alive. The art is part of the space—no, it *is* the space. It all is so *real*—and so *right*.

Behind me, I hear steps. I think, *That must be the Contessa approaching.* I am right. I turn and am shocked beyond belief. It is Miriam Poteet who had entered the room.

* * *

"Ciro," she boldly says without a hint of surprise at my presence, "It is always such a pleasure to see you. And doubly so, when you have brought a visitor, who is such an old friend." Miriam immediately reaches out to me with polite open arms and the briefest kiss of welcome, adding, "Jake, it is so wonderful to see you again."

At that moment, my reality goes cartoon.

Let me explain.

Wile E. Coyote screeches to a halt, feet ablaze. He looks down just before realizing he is yards past the cliff's edge. His fall is long, almost endless, as we hear a whimpered scream, he hits the ground with a "*poof!*" coming from a small cloud of dust.

At that moment it is me, not the coyote, who hits the ground.

As I climb out of my cartoon hole, Ciro and Miriam exchange knowing glances. Ciro speaks first. "My apology for the surprise, Detective Thompson."

He looks honest and sincere enough for me to let him go on. "With, in your—shall I say—somewhat emphatic and hurried entrance into the current situation, you focused upon the Contessa's maiden name in such a negative manner, I found no other path than to be direct in my approach to the matter. So, I immediately contacted the Contessa and bowed to her wishes after hearing her side of your mutual involvement some years ago in an art-based legal case."

"Not very subtle," I smirk.

"No," he replies. "As said in America, 'I meant to hit the nail on the head'."

"I'll say." I look straight at Miriam and say, "And you told him what?"

She looks straight back and says, "The truth."

"Such as?"

"The old lady had me in a corner. Of course, I knew she was scamming a lot of people. But she was an immensely powerful person who had me trapped."

"How so?"

"I had been 'liberal' in stating my qualifications as an art advisor. She found out and threatened to ruin me. She pressed me into a role I wished not to play."

"And in doing so, you played me."

"I'm sorry, Jake, but I had no choice. And besides... You *outplayed her* in the end."

"Yeah. But it never did end. The Powers That Be have endlessly made me pay for being your chump." After that, my voice cracks and goes soft, "Miriam, I really cared for you."

Upon hearing that whiny closing remark, Ciro makes for the door. His expression is that of one who has sniffed something foul.

On the way, he excuses his abandoning me by stating, "I believe the Count and I need to go over the final details for tonight."

I am glad he left quick and does not see my knees warp. Frenzied focus, jet lag, shock, and the abrupt arrival into a reality I had no ability to predict catches up with me as I grab a chair back to steady myself.

What is going on? What am I doing? How did I get here? Why? runs through my head, as I slump onto the chair.

"Are you okay?" Miriam asks.

I hear myself mutter, "Sure, sure." Then, after a couple deep breaths, I say, "So, the painting—no the paintings—may be legit?"

"Yes," Miriam replies. "My husband's family owned the Stanzione painting for generations. It hung in the villa's morning room. Recently, we decided to place it for auction, and it was during the preparations—cleaning and such—that the false back and the *potential* Caravaggio was found."

"Potential? What do you mean by potential? I thought it was proclaimed as a new original—miraculously found—authentic and all that goes with an uncovered masterpiece.

"Don't trust what you read in the news, Jake." She quips. "It makes a good story, but tonight's event will make an even better one."

"Please fill me in."

"How does intrigue, speculation, and a scandalous backstory sound?"

"Sounds like money."

"Nothing bad about that," she laughs, and then continues, "but, as I said, the goal was just to prep a modestly important artwork for sale." She waves her hands slightly to her surroundings and says, "All this—my husband's family legacy—requires a signif-icant amount of money to operate and maintain."

"Looks plush," I agree.

"You cannot imagine how the discovery of a mas-terpiece hidden behind the Stanzione is beneficial to our household's financial situation."

"Yeah—a *real* streak of luck," I say with a dis-believing grin.

"Jake, there's no way this discovery could be faked. Come to tonight's event—you'll see that the world's elite judges of art will agree with this amaz-ing find."

She looks so confident and assured in her truth.

"So, the Caravaggio *is* legit."

"No, it's a fake—but not a fake like you imagine. You jumped into this thinking I was part of a scam—like in Chicago—one where an Old Master's work is reproduced by meticulously finding and using materi-als that are true to an era hundreds of years before our time. Today's fake is from the Master's own time."

"Huh?" is all I could muster.

"Jake, you must get past *me* being in this." She looks to me for acknowledgment that her request is possible.

"Okay, go ahead—give it a whirl. Tell me what's really going down."

"Behind his painting, in Stanzione's own hand, with the 'supposed' Caravaggio, a letter—more of a note—was found. The note was a sort of confessional explanation for the hidden painting. Stanzione, a member of the school of painting that came a generation following Caravaggio, copied his style as an act of devotion. At the time of his effort Stanzione was embarrassed by his *panache* and over-extended ego. He was proud of his effort but ashamed of his brashness. He hid the painting and enclosed his note as a sort of artistic time capsule."

"So, you didn't create a fake?"

"Sorry—but I'm clean of this one."

I sigh and slump downward, deep into the cushions. There is silence. How long? I do not know.

Eventually, and with care and respect for a tired almost-broken man, Miriam says, "Jake, you need rest. Please, stay—be our guest. After some rest, come to tonight's event."

I nod in agreement.

She calls for the head staff lady to rustle up a valet. And in a jiff, I am shaved, showered, and napping in luxury.

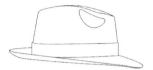

WRONG PLACE–WRONG TIME

H AVE YOU EVER BEEN JOLTED awake by a thought that is so clear, bright, and true that sleep is impossible? I have. In Naples.

It is dark when I am jerked aware by this thought: *Jake, you've been duped—the fake is a FAKE.* My following thought process is, *No one will seriously scrutinize the phony Caravaggio if it is openly claimed to be one. Yep, the Caravaggio is a fake, as part of an elaborate back story—of artistic intrigue—all aimed at catapulting the value of the coupled paintings.* It is the perfect scam. Create a one-of-a-kind collection—then blame a long-dead forger for its existence.

I turn on the lights, find my clothes, and mutter, "I hope I haven't slept through the party." I dress and head toward the sounds of gaiety. My destination is the event tent and I am bent on confronting Miriam about my revelation.

As I enter the tent, Miriam sees me and waves me toward a spot near herself and Carlo, her husband. He looks exactly as I imagined—tall, elegant to the edges, at ease in the spotlight of the proceedings.

As I head toward them, he is cued by an underling to take a position nearer the paintings and is handed a microphone. It turns out I am right on time.

I make a beeline through the crowd, impervious to the fact I am dressed as the odd man out. Everyone is in black tie. I pay no heed to ladies sporting jewels, and men in patent leather slip-ons. And no one pays attention to me, the fast walker in travel attire.

As I near my spot, not far from the center of attention, and close to Miriam, I perceive something. My cop senses detects an out-of-place energy—violence is about to happen.

There is unusual movement to the right. A member of the wait staff lunges forward, gun in hand, just as my footing departs via a patch of spilled wine. Airborne, I see more waiters rush forward with Ciro and his aides close behind. All are armed.

My momentum takes me forward and to the left, directly headed toward Carlo and the paintings. I soundly slam into him and both easels, as multiple shots ring out. There are screams. Pain envelopes my head, and everything goes dark.

THE END AS A BEGINNING

L IGHTS PASS OVERHEAD, IN MY field of vision, they go in and out, one after another. A single-minded team of specialists speed me on a cart from their domain, the emergency room, to the OR. All I hear is, "Mo. Mo! *MO!*" (Italian for *Stat!*)

I suspect they think I'm dying. No—I know they think so.

Their speed picks up. We are dashing to a physical destination with, perhaps, a spiritual conclusion.

There is, however, no 'light at the end of the tunnel' experience for me. My near-death experience is me looking up at an open sky from the bottom of a well. While gazing at countless stars draped before infinity, all I can think about is that I should be doing something useful.

In my mind, I audibly keep asking, "WHAT?"

I hear no answer.

All I see is my career as a cop in an endless loop—all my cases—the cruising, the stakeouts, the warnings given, and the collars.

"Aren't these actions useful?" I ask.

No answer. Just the endless loop over and over and over—they come and go. The procession is endless. I suppose they are background, or a form of evidence, not the answer, for what I should do. Yet, no firm answer comes.

How long? While happening, I had zero sense of time. Comas do that. The loop kept looping... And then...

I woke up.

First, there is light. Movement is next. Then, I hear a nurse's voice, "Try not to move suddenly. I'm going to get the doctor."

For about a half hour, I am examined, questioned, and probed more than I wish. But the attention is well intended and I willingly, even enthusiastically, comply. Really, I am so grateful for the end of that nonstop show running in my head.

When things calm down, the docs share information on my medical situation and how I had come into their care.

I had a great deal to learn, as I had been in a coma for twenty-three days. Induced comas are normally two to three days, with six or seven not being out of the realm of concern. But when I failed to be revived, the docs caring for me got a bit manic. What puzzled them was the pattern of my brain waves—cyclical in nature and marked by a consistent spike at the same point in every cycle.

I assume, but do not tell them, it was at the spot in my dream where I screwed up and Gino was marred.

I learn some interesting facts.

The slug that bounced off my skull, by a hair's width, did not kill me. I had bled profusely, hence the induced coma. But, as noted, I was reluctant in coming out of it.

Now, everyone is elated I finally returned to the conscious world, and tell me about my "heroic act".

The guy who shot me, disguised as a waiter, was one of five Albanian gang members who had infiltrated the event's staff. Four waiters and an assistant chef aimed to heist the paintings. They wrongfully assumed security would be loose at the Villa, but Ciro was a step ahead. What no one could have planned for was me—the fly in the ointment.

My tumble, literally into the middle of the action, ended the attempted theft.

Police were also undercover. The shooter and a colleague were killed. The others were identified and captured as they made for an expertly timed helicopter landing. They—and maybe the paintings—could have made a clean departure. But, again, Ciro's efforts disrupted their escape.

The copter was grounded by a couple well-placed shots by one of his men, and a much sought-after criminal cell was totally eradicated. The Italian media went into overdrive, and I was again basking in fifteen minutes of fame.

The following day, Miriam visits me. "Too bad you pretty much slept through it all," she says from a chair beside my bed. "You're a hero, especially in the art world."

"How so?"

"You saved a priceless Caravaggio. Not to mention taking a bullet for the owner, my dear Carlo."

"But you admitted that it's a fake."

"No-no-no. That fact was *about* to be shared. But your heroics have placed the paintings on a different course. No one who cares about great art wants to hear that. They want to believe a different tale. Jake, your blood is splattered all over it." She becomes animated. "Jake, the Caravaggio is real—hidden in an act of devotion. And saved from evil thieves by *you,* To even suggest that it be examined is now a sacrilege." She beams when she says, "It's now *beyond priceless.*"

"Lucky break for you and Carlo," I smirk. "What if I spill the beans?"

"You won't."

"Why wouldn't I?"

"Carlo's generosity."

"What do you mean—Carlo's generosity?"

"Carlo is *very* influential. He's delved into your past and the troubles you've had... And he's placed significant pressure on select people in Chicago to lay off you."

Ciro's knowing grin and statements about *The Count* pops into my head. *So, Miriam's husband plays both sides of the game? Yes,* I thought. *If you are right about being duped—the painting is a fake fake—a leopard does not change spots. Miriam married well—to another con artist, no doubt.*

"You're saying what—you're bribing me?!"

"No, Jake. I'm telling you how the world works. Rest up. Go home. Retire quietly, and enjoy your life."

And with that, Miriam blows me a kiss and leaves.

I don't think I'll be seeing her again.

* * *

After three days of PT, I feel great. All I want to do was go home. The day before I am to depart, my cell phone is located, returned, and in use—by me.

"Dewey—this is me, Jake," I almost shout.

"Jake. I'm thrilled to know for sure that the news you awoke is true." He sincerely sounds like a kid getting his wish-gift at Christmas. "When are you coming home?"

"Tomorrow—as soon as I have travel details, I'll call."

* * *

The next day I give Dewey the details. He is still happy, but I sense there is something else going on when he says, "I'll be at O'Hare when your flight arrives... And I'll have a certain woman friend of yours with me."

"Great," I said. "I've been trying to reach Earline and all I get is a dumb message. Tell her to get her phone fixed."

"Uh, sure, Jake... Sure... Will do." That *something* is still there, but I blow it off.

* * *

Upon arriving home, I am happily smothered by Dewey's bear hug, and disappointed by my "certain woman friend" as he had described her. Peeling away from a second of Dewey's bone-crushing embraces, I say, "Hello Mildred—didn't expect you to be part of a homecoming."

She nods hello and says, "I didn't expect it either, Jake. Here—this is for you."

She hands forward a large brown envelope, adding, "I'm here on business. I got the call to make it official." She is cold, distant... You know—all professional avoidance mode.

Riding downtown in Dewey's car, I eye the envelope and ask Mildred, "Let me guess... Retirement papers?"

"Yes. Backdated two weeks."

"Days before I woke up."

"Seems that you have influential friends. It's over, Jake. All the bullshit is history."

"But there's a catch?"

"There always is."

Dewey breaks into our conversation with, "What's wrong with you getting help to retire, Jake? Heck, you been through a lot. Imagine if you never woke up. Y'know—friends are friends."

"Yeah, and help is help—but these *friends* wanted me to wake up in their pocket, which is as good as being dead—dead silent," I tell him.

Mildred tosses in her view based on some hard reality, "Jake, you've been out gunned your entire career. You've been 'the unappreciated good guy' for decades and put up a good fight. A way out has been given to you. Call it a truce and gracefully retire."

A late autumn heavy rain begins. The kind that easily turns into snow, reminding Chicago that winter is only a few degrees away. As we pull up to let her out, I ask Mildred, "You're saying that I should take the money and run?"

Getting out of the car into the cold wind-driven moisture, she warns me with her answer, "Yes, Jake, take the deal—but remember the RULE. If you take their retirement money, you remain silent. Do you think you can do that, Jake?"

"I dunno, Boss. What comes to mind is General MacArthur's advice, 'you are remembered for the rule you break'."

She leans back into the car and says, "Jake, you are one incorrigible tick in the world's hide."

I grin and pose to her, "Do you think there's a market for my memoir?"

Her laugh is mixed with emotions of joy, dread, and much more. She parts with, "Good luck with that Jake—Good luck with that." She waves goodbye and disappears into the crowd entering police headquarters. The "system" sucks her up.

The heavy raindrops are changing into those oversized flakes that become slush all too quick. As it often did, winter has arrived in minutes.

"All this has made me hungry," I tell Dewey. "What'd ya' say we go to *Jimmie's*? I've not been able to connect with Earline. Two birds—one stone."

"No can do," is Dewey's flat reply.

"*I'll buy*," I say in my best alluring come on.

"No good, Jake. We can't. *Jimmie's* is closed."

"Closed? What d'ya mean, *closed*?"

"Closed—as in not open."

"It isn't a holiday. Did they blow a water main, or something? Jimmie isn't sick—is he?"

"No—it's none of those. But like I told you, it's closed—as in *closed for good*."

"For good? *Never*. That's impossible. You must've heard wrong."

"Jake—it's closed."

"How do you know?"

"Gail—from the breakfast shift—she told me."

"Gail? With the-the-the— Don't tell me. She finally..." My mind can't picture Gail ever giving in to Dewey. Total oil and water. His desire to know what happened must have shaken the earth's foundation for her to open up to him.

"Drive over there pronto—tell me *everything* on the way."

Through showers of huge wet flakes, we make our way to *Jimmie's* and he tells me, "Two weeks ago, I was in Barney Callaghan's—ya know,the pub at one-hundred-sixth and Western? I dropped in and before I take my first sip of Guinness, Gail comes up for *a chat*. She never gave me the time of day, but out of the blue she wants to chat. She looked great by the way—all out-of-season tanned. I ask about it, and she tells me, 'It's compliments of Jimmie.' What she shared blew me away.

"A week or ten days before, Jimmie called all his employees in for a meeting and tells them the diner is closed as of then—right after the meeting. He explains a national chain has offered him an outrageous amount for the place, and he's accepted. Bim, bam, boom—it's a done deal. *Jimmie's* was on a fast track to become the twenty-first restaurant in the MILLENIALZ chain."

"MILLENIALZ? Never heard of them."

"Veggie bowls, sushi bar, trendy cocktails, and micro-vineyard wines—mostly whites."

"Yuck. What the fuck is wrong with this country? You can't smoke in a restaurant or bar and now you can't even *eat*. Raw fish is *not* food."

"That's not all, Jake. Before that fact could sink in, he hands everyone a grand in cash. That was it for the total crew—game over. But then... Jimmie asks the wait staff—all the gals—to stay for a few minutes. His next announcement is where the tan comes in.

"Jimmie tells them he's headed to Sarasota where he has rented a seaside B&B, and they all are invited to come to Florida. Round-trip airfare was included in the offer. Six of them took him up on the trip. And from what Gail said, they enjoyed a week of non-stop soaking up sun and partying. Gail and two other well-tanned and exhausted gals came home—leaving Lorraine, Karen, and Earline behind. That was about two weeks ago. Then, a week ago Lorraine and Karen returned."

"Earline stayed? My Earline?"

"Yes. And from what I hear, she's not coming back anytime soon. Rumor has it she and Jimmie are house hunting."

"Nah... Nah... That can't be."

Dewey puts on his serious 'I'm telling you the truth, Bro' face and says, "Jake, if there is anything I know about women, it's that they need some sort of plan or vision for their future—even if it's only a dream sort of thing."

"What's that got to do with me and Earline?"

"Jake, no woman was more patient than she was. Even when she strayed off one time with that squirrelly dude, she came back to her 'moon eyed' affection for you. But, in the end, she'd had it with you. Jake, if I were a woman, I'd have nothing to do with you. Your attention is always elsewhere. Your cop tales *are* your life."

My mind returns to the last day I saw her. I ignored her request to talk. She tried to tell me about an offer, and it wasn't about her condo. She knew something was up with the diner because Jimmie was pressing her.

Dewey continues. "You can't fault her for her actions, Jake. Think about it—she knows Jimmie. He's loaded now. He'll treat her right. She went for a soft landing in a knowable future."

"But—"

Dewey's cut off is lightning fast. "There's no *but*, Jake. Face the music—she's gone."

When we get to *Jimmie's*, I cannot believe what I see. Nothing. No cars are parked in the lot. Locked doors. Nobody inside. It is worse than nothing. It has that abandoned look and feel of a ghost town. The life of the place is gone.

All I can say as I looked to Dewey is, "It's true."

The best thing about a friend like Dewey is him *always* being the delivery man for the truth. As I stand there letting his message sink in, Dewey does the best thing possible. He reaches for his wallet and pulls out a ten.

Handing it over, he apologizes. "Oh—stupid of me. With all the doings going on, I forgot. Here's what I owe ya—plus an extra five."

"So, now I owe you," I reply.

I begin to tear up. "We better spend it quick. If we don't, I'll probably lose it."

"Okay, pal—what ya wanna do with it?"

"I'm thinking beer and sliders and we talk over old times... Of course, I'll take notes on everything worth putting in a memoir." Before Dewey can remind me I'm on the wagon, I add, "Beer is not really drinking, since it occupies one of the basic food groups when paired with sliders."

"Fine with me—sounds like a plan."

Looking at Mildred's envelope, I agree, "Yeah, it's a plan alright—an alternative retirement plan."

Dewey gives me a reflective look, saying, "Before becoming a cop—you dreamed of writing the sort of tales you ended up living. I say, go for it, Dude—write what you know."

My mind goes to an old saying, "Every journey begins with a single step. And, if you do not take it, you will stand on one foot forever."

Skin tingling, ears humming, with an overwhelming sense of purpose, I know exactly how and where to start—and of course, my first step smells slightly of beer and sliders.

* * *

EPILOGUE

WHEN ASKED ABOUT MY LATE-IN-LIFE success as a writer, I briefly answer, "I was inspired."

But upon occasion, if pressed nicely, I share, "The most important thing I have learned in life is that God created us as plain and simple beings. But we screw things up. And to repent for my role in this mess called Life, I simply wrote: "Greetings. I'm Jake Thompson, a worn-out has-been cop who is tired of chasing phantoms and hoping for miracles..."

So, I have shared with you these tales of Tomaszewski.

ABOUT THE AUTHOR

DEL STAECKER IS AN AWARD-WINNING American writer of novels, novellas, short stories, and non-fiction in a number of genres, including suspense, crime, philosophical fiction, satire, and memoir.

He is a Life Fellow of the Royal Society of Arts (London) and Knight of Honor, Order of St. John (Malta). He was educated at The Citadel, Wheaton College, and The University of Puget Sound.

Made in United States
North Haven, CT
16 July 2024

54842697R00378